Hello Gina---and friend...

# TOWER
# 18

A Novel by

## TONY BATHEY

I welcome comments and feedback. :)

Tony Bathey

Print Book ISBN 13: 9781945449079
eBook ISBN 13: 9781945449086
Library of Congress: 2016942596

Tower 18 is a work of fiction. The names, characters, places,
and incidents are the products of the author's imagination or are
used fictitiously. Any resemblance to actual persons, living or dead,
is entirely coincidental.

# PART 1

Improvise: To compose and perform without preparation; to make do with whatever is at hand.

Late Afternoon,
Wednesday, December 5, 2001
Tower 18, Mission Beach, San Diego, California

Ocean lifeguard Mike Johnson was the first backup to arrive on scene. Driving a city-issued, bright yellow Toyota 4x4, he had just sped *Code 3* across two miles of empty beach.

*Code 3.*

*Lights and sirens, haul ass, and get there safely.*

Johnson parked his truck high on the sandy beach, flipped his siren off, and placed the vehicle's transmission into park. He reached for a pair of binoculars and exited the truck with urgency. An unmanned truck similar to his was already there, its driver side door was still open, and its bright strobe lights were still flashing.

Johnson hustled to the rear of the vehicle, pulled the tailgate down, and vaulted himself up onto the truck bed. He focused his field glasses for a few moments before spotting two swimmers that he already knew were out there. The swimmers were approximately 75 yards offshore, and were caught in a powerful rip current that was pulling them out to sea. He recognized one of the swimmers as lifeguard Marisol Escobar. She stroked head up toward the other swimmer while a tethered, red rescue buoy trailed her on the surface.

Johnson mumbled softly, encouraging his colleague.

"Go Escobar. Get there!"

Johnson then turned away and placed his binoculars on the truck's tailgate. He reached up and released a black bungee strap that secured a long rescue board to the truck's rack then hopped down, his bare feet landing deftly in the soft, damp sand. He grabbed a handle mounted to the board's deck and slid it backward several feet until it cleared the rear rail of the overhead rack, gathered his binoculars with one hand, and snatched the falling board with the other. Securing the board beneath his armpit, Johnson turned and moved swiftly to the front of the vehicle. He tossed the board on the sand in front of him, stood tall, looked into the binoculars again, and spotted Escobar, who had made progress and was now nearly side by side with the head of the struggling swimmer.

Johnson muttered softly, "I've got you right where I want you. There is no way you'll get out of this mess without failing. You're done."

As he continued to observe the scene out in the ocean, he spoke out loud again, this time with a tone of indignant curiosity in his voice.

"But why are you letting Escobar get so close to you, Cynthia? She was not supposed to see that it's you."

Everything had been going precisely according to his plan—until now. He knew that the struggling swimmer was one of his colleagues, lifeguard Cynthia Harden, a woman whom he trusted and considered a friend.

"Dammit."

Suddenly, he noticed that Escobar was looking directly at Cynthia, and it appeared that the two women might be speaking to each other.

"What the hell are you doing, Cynthia? This was NOT part of the plan."

**2**

Wednesday, December 5, 2001
Tower 18, Mission Beach

E scobar looked frantic to Johnson, and, as he observed her, she seemed to be unsure of what to do next. He watched her turn her head toward him and look at the beach, then turn back to look at Harden. She began repeating the sequence of looking back and forth, but took no further action.

Johnson then heard a siren approaching from the south and muttered again, a little louder than before.

"Cynthia, what the hell are you doing? You were supposed to be long gone by now."

Johnson grinned, however, when he noticed Escobar turn south toward the Mission Beach main tower and begin frantically waving her right arm up and down. She was signaling that she needed immediate assistance and that a respiratory emergency was taking place in the water.

Johnson shouted, "Yes!" when he saw Marisol then cross both of her arms over her head to make an X.

He knew then that all available resources would be dispatched to her location to assist her, and that their ensuing rescue attempts would result in an exhausting search for a body that wasn't there. The search would waste the time and energy of several local emergency response agencies and would create a costly, and entirely unnecessary, expense for the city's taxpayers.

Appearing confused, Johnson muttered, "But why is she giving the *Code X* signal if Cynthia is still at the surface?"

*Code X.*

*There's a human body at the bottom of the ocean.*

*Drop what you're doing.*

*Get your team together.*

*Find that body now.*

Escobar's emergency signals were observed by two different main tower guards, one looking north from the Mission Beach main tower, and the other looking south from the main tower in Pacific Beach. Although each manned an observation deck that was located nearly a mile away from Escobar's location, they watched through powerful Zeiss binoculars. Both could clearly see the female lifeguard, the red buoy, and the nearby swimmer who just bobbed up and down, head turned away from the shore.

Upon seeing Escobar's signals, both men immediately radioed their chain of command. After completing their radio transmissions and receiving confirmation that assistance was on the way, the two main tower guards, Martin Arias from Pacific Beach and Mark Davis from Mission Beach, then used land lines to inform other rescue agencies in San Diego County that they were requesting immediate assistance to rescue and recover the body of a distressed swimmer who had disappeared in the ocean, 100 yards in front of Tower 18, at Mission Beach in San Diego, California.

Wednesday, December 5, 2001
Tower 18, Mission Beach

As he observed what was happening in the ocean, Johnson realized that something *was* wrong.

*Harden has something up her sleeve,* he thought. *I sure hope she knows what she's doing.*

Called into action by Escobar's signals, Johnson returned to his truck, pulled on a tight-fitting neoprene top, wrapped the strap of a diving mask and snorkel around his right forearm, quickly slid the ankle straps of his swimming fins around his heels, and, with an adjusted stride, headed down the sloped beach with his rescue board in tow. He quickly mounted the board and paddled through the incoming surf. He made rapid progress and arrived at the spot where he expected to find Escobar on the surface.

Johnson kneeled tall on the rescue board's deck, and extended his body as high as he could to gain a better view. Seeing nothing but choppy ocean water, he shrugged his shoulders and held his hands out to his sides, palms up. He twisted his trunk back and forth, and completed several 360-degree spins. Confused and concerned, he shouted, "Escobar! Where the hell are you?"

He looked toward the beach, noticed that another lifeguard was on his way out on a rescue board, and saw a third lifeguard driving a rescue vehicle at *Code 3* speed toward the scene. Without further pause, Johnson secured his diving mask, inhaled deeply, and dove to the bottom of the ocean.

Wednesday, December 5, 2001
Tower 18, Mission Beach

Several minutes later, Mike Johnson's head broke the surface of the cold December Pacific Ocean. He panted as choppy, undulating waves slapped against his diving mask. His respirations were elevated, and he was uncharacteristically panicked. Although there was poor visibility in the water, Johnson was sure that he had spotted the dark figure of a body on the bottom. Uncertain about who it might be, he thought, *I can't believe this is happening. What the hell am I supposed to do now?*

Before Johnson regained his breath, lifeguard Alan Henderson surfaced about 10 feet away. Henderson was also gasping for air. Lifeguard Randy Shields surfaced moments later, breathing a little easier than the other two. Each waterman was equipped with a long-sleeve neoprene top designed to conserve body heat, a pair of Duck Feet fins, and a diving mask with a snorkel attached. Johnson knew that one of the other two men would soon spot the body.

Between breaths, Henderson shouted, "Anything?"

"Negative," Johnson replied. "Let's catch our breath before we try again."

"Screw that!" Shields yelled. "We can catch our breath later. We're going to dive again right now, and we're not coming up without a body. It's been too long already."

The group dove in unison, and, on their way down, Johnson felt Henderson tapping him on the arm. He looked over and saw Henderson pointing at a dark figure that was resting on the ocean floor. The two men immediately moved to the body, reached under an armpit, and pushed off the sandy bottom. Shields dove beneath them, placed his hands on the limp body's hips, and assisted by kicking toward the surface as fast as he could.

The three rescuers surfaced moments later, and saw a Patrol rescue boat close by. The winded divers handed the body off to a warmly-dressed sergeant, and, with the help of his medically trained two-man crew, they quickly loaded the flaccid body onto the flat deck. As the boat sped away, their attempts to revive the unresponsive victim were in full force.

A fire rescue helicopter was on its way to meet the boat at lifeguard headquarters at Quivira Basin in Mission Bay, and would likely arrive just as the boat pulled into the docks. The handoff to the helicopter trauma team and the flight time to the hospital would take no more than five minutes. Once there, the emergency room medical staff would continue attempting to revive the victim.

Back at the scene, as the rescue boat sped toward the channel, Johnson glanced out at the kelp beds and spotted a small, low profile, inflatable skiff with a large outboard motor floating unmanned at the surface of the ocean.

Johnson thought, *How did this happen?*

The three men were finally relieved of duty just after sundown, once rescue divers in full scuba gear had arrived with underwater lighting equipment. By then Johnson, Henderson, and Shields had all begun to suffer from exhaustion and near-hypothermia. Pulsing headaches pounded at their temples. Their repeated descents to a depth of approximately 25 feet in 58-degree water had also caused an annoying and unrelenting condition of tinnitus. The three men were numb, each was concerned about the condition of the victim they had recovered, and each was confused about the unknown location of a second person they had all seen in the water.

Veteran lifeguard Randy Shields had a sense that, from the very beginning of the call, something wasn't right. The events that led up to the rescue had all been extremely odd, and each was way out of place on such a cold and miserable winter afternoon at the beach.

Adding to his intuition was the fact that, when he and his crewmates initiated their ascent with the body, Shields had noticed a metallic glimmer very close to where the body had lain. He could tell that the object was a small oxygen tank and thought, *What is that thing doing there? That cannot be a coincidence.*

During the subsequent search for the second body, Shields confirmed what he thought he had seen earlier, and he retrieved a small, cylindrical oxygen tank with a black mouthpiece attached to its top. He tucked the narrow bottle into the waistband of his trunks, concealed it beneath his wetsuit top, then continued searching for a second body.

When Shields returned to the beach long after sunset, he discreetly placed the small air tank behind the seat in his lifeguard truck. He then slid into the driver's seat and shivered violently while turning the ignition key. He immediately adjusted the heat to full, briskly rubbed his arms, and hoped for his body temperature to rise soon.

Minutes later, warmer, he drove back to the Pacific Beach main tower, and, as he unloaded his gear, Randy Shields considered the diving instrument that he had found during the rescue. *Who was using this thing, and where are they now? And, without it, why didn't they ever surface to take a breath? Everything about this is wrong. None of this should have ever happened…*

# PART 2

Resurrection:
Coming back into notice; revival.

PART 2

Five Years Earlier
Tuesday Morning, February 4, 1997
Lifeguard Headquarters, Quivira Basin
Mission Bay

The reception desk phone buzzed twice before it was answered. "Lifeguard Headquarters, this is Gabriella. How may I help you?"
Gabriella paused.
"Yes, sir, one moment please."
She pushed a button, then paused.
"Lt. Morgan, it's the mayor on line one."
Down the hall and around the corner, sitting in front of a glass wall that looked out across Mission Bay, Senior Lieutenant Richard Morgan was working at his desk. He wore a polished badge, gold lieutenant bars on his collar, and several small, colorful ribbons and shiny pins on the breast of his sharp Class A dress blues.

His first scheduled meeting with the new mayor would also find in attendance: the city manager, the police and fire chiefs, two city council representatives from the north and south beach districts, and a few other civilian delegates. Newly-elected San Diego mayor, Eddie Peete, had demanded that all of his public safety leaders dress impeccably for this occasion, as he believed it would enable his chief staff to think more clearly and to act more effectively. Mayor Peete had promised to run a tight ship, and Lt. Morgan was supportive of the new paradigm.

His city's former boss had never served in the military or in emergency response, and her leadership style was more familial and democratic . . . like a former educator's might be, which she was. Peete, a retired naval officer, would emphasize a stronger chain of command, and his style would be more autocratic.

Lt. Morgan was clean-shaven with a short, bristly haircut that revealed a sprinkling of grey. He sat at his desk reviewing résumés and applications, and held a clipboard with a long list of cadets' names that would be participating in his upcoming pre-hiring academy. The start date of the lifeguard tryout program was less than 30 days away, and preparations were now his primary task. He heard his phone buzz again and picked up the handset.

"Good morning, sir."

"Good morning, Richard. I realize, of course, that we convene in less than an hour, but I've just been given some information that is likely to affect the Patrol. I wanted to brief you now, so we can follow up after the session."

"*Affect* the Patrol, sir?"

"Well, yes . . . I believe so. Actually, I know so. It's a young woman who works for the city, Lieutenant, a woman whose parents are very important to me, and for whom I have no choice but to advocate for and support unconditionally."

"Unconditionally, sir? Who is she? Who are they?"

"Her name is Marisol Escobar. She's a supervisor in our department of aquatics and recreation. She coaches a very talented swim team at the new pool down in Lincoln Heights. That's quite a facility. Have you seen it?"

"Yes, sir, I was at the dedication with my daughter. We spent the entire afternoon playing on the slide and jumping off the diving board."

Morgan paused briefly, then said, "The city did a real nice job with the locker rooms. They're much nicer than the Cracker Jack boxes we have in our main towers . . . sir."

Mayor Peete laughed.

"Is that another plea for help?"

"I'm just saying, sir."

"Well played, Richard."

Both men paused briefly before the mayor continued.

"Anyhow, this young woman has developed some finely-skilled athletes and she's no slouch herself. Her family obviously provided her with strong genetic programming, to say the least. Her father played internationally as a soccer goalie, and I watched her mother drain a fifteen-foot birdie putt on the eighteenth green at Torrey Pines South. She finished the round one over par at a celebrity charity event a few years ago. Marisol Escobar is an outstanding coach and athlete. And she's a smart, ambitious woman with smart, ambitious, and powerful parents."

Morgan raised his eyebrows and made a note on his clipboard, but said nothing.

"She has also created a successful summer program that teaches hundreds of young children how to swim safely. The program is committed to teaching the children of as many low-income families as they possibly can all of the necessary skills required to avoid drowning."

"Yes, sir, I am familiar with that program. They teach those kids an extremely valuable life skill. It's our department's goal as well. If our beach patrons would all be trained by her first, our job might be easier."

"You may be right about that. I'm sure this young lady would appreciate hearing you say so."

Morgan remained silent.

"Her mother and father were instrumental in developing an endowment that provides the program's funding. The opportunities for qualifying low-income families to participate without fees are now abundant. Enrollment numbers are staggering, and subsequent data shows that the program is making a difference. Nine-one-one responses to water-related emergencies are down in numerous communities that are being serviced by our pools. Richard, under this young lady's direction, there has developed quite a long waiting list to participate in the program."

"Good for you. Good for her. Good for them. Win-win-win. Nice play yourself, sir."

"Thank you, but that's not all. She also hires and trains a large percentage of our summer and year-round pool staff . . . lifeguards, instructors, maintenance staff, and low-level administrators. She's recruited very well from within these communities, and has hired and trained an unprecedented number of qualified minorities, who are now receiving good pay and outstanding benefits. She's helping them build their communities by offering teenagers and young adults the opportunity to gain some independence. They're also paying taxes, accepting civic responsibility, and contributing."

Morgan said nothing, but listened closely.

"That's a previously under-represented minority group, a group that deserved that opportunity all along. But there was no one there to lead them, Richard. Not until Marisol appeared and changed all of that. She's become an overnight celebrity in several midtown and South Bay precincts. Most of the registered voters there are long-standing democrats that we failed to win votes from, Richard. Republicans rarely win points from those precincts. But, with her family's support, we did, and now . . . I'm your new mayor."

Morgan had been glancing at one of the résumés on his desk as he listened. He raised his head and listened more attentively after hearing the word "precincts" a second time, thinking, *Here come the terms and conditions.* He avoided the thought and replied calmly, "You know how pleased I am with the election results, Eddie. You supported us very well while you served on the city council. If that family had something to do with this outcome, well, I guess you could say that I may be indebted to them in some way."

"That's what I hoped you would say."

Morgan said nothing and listened closely, something Peete greatly appreciated.

"I have known Marisol and her family for a long time, Richard. Amanda Villareal, her mother, and Victor Trujillo-Escobar, her father, are people we need to support. They've been supporting me since the very beginning of my career in politics, and I will depend on their generosity in the next election as well."

"Understood, sir."

"This young lady's mother is an extremely outspoken liberal activist, but she is also a very, very talented fundraiser. Her father is one of the wealthiest men in the state, with business and political contacts that extend across this country and deep into Mexico. He has been a registered Republican for as long as I've known him."

Peete paused, appearing as if to choose his words cautiously.

"Richard . . . they have a long-term plan for Marisol's future that you will soon play a critical role in. She's requesting a transfer from her current pay grade of aquatics supervisor to the position of permanent ocean lifeguard, under your command. Amanda called me earlier this morning and gave me an outline of their plan."

The lieutenant scowled.

"Eddie, she can't just transfer into a permanent position. She has to do what everybody else does and has always done. She has to graduate from the academy first, and only then can she be offered a *seasonal* position on the Bay. After at least one full summer on the Bay, she'll have to earn an ocean qualification, and once she gets to the oceanfront, she'll have to show that she can spot and make rescues consistently and effectively, sir. Our academy is just the first step. She'll have to enroll, pass the course, and graduate first."

Morgan paused.

Peete listened closely.

"I know you're aware of how our program works, sir, but this swim coach and her mother might not be. Our guards have to earn the attention of a training officer before testing on a lengthy list of skills. She will need to receive advanced training and certifications for main tower observation, SCUBA, EMT, and personal watercraft operator."

Morgan's tone was stern.

"She's got a long way to go before becoming eligible to even submit an application for POL. Eddie, that process takes several summers of seasonal training."

Peete remained silent.

Morgan's tone softened.

"Eddie, it took me *four years* of seasonal work to promote to permanent. Some of our current POLs spent as many as ten years as seasonal employees before they get promoted. With all due respect, sir, it's not a simple transition."

Morgan took a deep breath.

"Transfer in as a POL? No, sir, that can't happen."

The mayor remained calm.

"I do understand, Richard. You've told me all of this before, and what I told the girl's mother was very similar to what you just said. After some discussion, she relented, but their vision moves along pretty swiftly, Richard. They are very intentional about this."

Lt. Morgan remained silent.

*Just as I thought. Here it comes.*

"You need to know more about their expectations. I'll brief you further after our session this morning. Whatever the case, each time this young lady passes some kind of test, you're going to move her along with velocity. Are we clear?"

"She has a lot of work to do first, sir."

"Velocity, Lieutenant. Are we clear?"

"Like a Santa Ana night, sir."

Morgan recognized an opportunity to gain a bargaining chip. In reviewing candidates' résumés, he had been strongly impressed with the potential of one particular incoming female candidate.

"As long as we're talking about outstanding and ambitious young women, I have a résumé and recommendation letters that I think you should see."

"Fair enough. Go ahead and fax them over now."

"Done, sir."

Lt. Morgan hung up the phone, stood, and bounded through his office doorway. As he approached the reception area, his secretary, Gabby, looked up.

"Gabby, I need you to pull Cynthia Harden's file and fax it to Mayor

Peete's office now."

Morgan smiled and bowed his head.

"Please."

Gabby smiled back.

"Yes, sir. I'm on it."

**6**

One Month Earlier
After Midnight, Saturday, January 11, 1997
Downtown San Diego, California

After delivering another round of drinks and turning to walk away from the rude but generous customer, Cynthia Harden was fairly certain that she had heard him say, ". . . and suck his . . ."

The club's sound system was very loud though, so his offensive comments did not carry to the front door where a massively built bouncer stood.

She abruptly turned back toward the table and glared at the man, who had become an ugly drunkard. Since the dancers were no longer willing to offer the rude man a private table dance, Cynthia had become his sole human interaction. She stepped toward a small, smoke-shrouded tabletop, on which sat a filthy ashtray that she had already emptied and replaced several times. A seventh bottle of MGD and a third shot of Jack sat alongside balled-up bottle labels, damp, torn, and shredded cocktail napkins, and a fairly large pile of assorted bills.

He sat adjacent to the main stage, staring at the night's featured headliner, an adult-film star named Karen Summer. His eyes were hidden behind a pair of thick, tinted lenses set in large, gold Elvis frames.

He wore a touristy Tommy Bahama shirt that was at least one size too small, and, as he reclined lazily in an upholstered chair, Cynthia noticed unsightly openings between the shirt's buttons that exposed his flesh. His protruding belly pressed against the parrots, tropical flowers, and palm fronds like an overstuffed pillow, his thinning, dirty black hair partially combed over his balding scalp.

Cynthia leaned in closer to speak over the driving beat of Diana King's "Shy Guy."

"Excuse me. Were you speaking to me?"

He took a long and deep drag from his 25th cigarette, exhaled upward, and continued staring at Ms. Summer, a tall brunette who proudly displayed a large, firm, and expensive pair of breasts. Summer writhed rhythmically across the stage, flinging a furry white boa from side to side, partially concealing herself, teasing the crowd. She briefly exposed her nipples as she pranced in front of several men seated along the stage. She arched her back and placed her palms on the stage floor then spread her legs, seductively gyrated her hips in a circular motion, and allowed her targeted sources of income to gain an unobstructed view of her scantily covered vagina.

While maintaining his view of the entertainer, the obese drunk loudly replied to his waitress.

"Hell yeah, I was talking to you. You heard me the first time . . . you know it's true. Look, honey, the only way you'll ever make it in here is to walk that big, round ass of yours up into the manager's office, drop to your knees, unzip his fly, finish the job right so he can see how committed you are, then beg for him to put you up on stage like the rest of these tramps did. It'll pay off for you right away."

He turned away from Summer and looked up at Cynthia. Once he was sure that he had her attention, he reached down to his crotch with both hands and unzipped his Dockers.

"Here, you can warm up on me."

Cynthia glanced at the Samoan doorman, made brief eye contact, and nodded that she was okay. As soon as the bouncer looked away, she dumped two martinis, three bottles of Bud, and two pints of draft beer right on top of the man's head. Before he could move his arms up to protect himself, his glasses were knocked off of his face and onto the floor beside his chair. Cynthia then shoved the wet cork surface of her empty tray against his face, pushed him backwards, and sent him sprawling. She stood over him for a moment, as if she was daring him to get up, then shouted, "Asshole! Go fuck yourself!"

The Samoan doorman appeared immediately, grabbed the pile of cash from the table, then picked up the wet drunk and twisted his wrist behind his back.

The soaked patron yelled, "That bitch attacked me! You should be throwing her outta here, not me! Do you know how much money I spend in here?"

Junior knew, but he didn't care. His customer extraction philosophy developed from his time as a Marine: Kill 'em all, let God sort 'em out.

The 86'd man's glasses remained behind on the club's floor, and without them, he had a very difficult time locating his greenbacks that were now strewn across the breezy parking lot. Cynthia laughed at the struggling drunk, now on his knees, blindly swiping the asphalt with his hands like a hasty game show contestant.

Disgusted by the pathetic man's behavior, she turned away and walked back into the club, but then stopped abruptly when she felt something snap. She looked down, and beneath the soles of her black Chuck Taylor high tops, she saw the man's Elvis glasses, shattered into pieces.

**7**

Saturday, January 11, 1997
Downtown San Diego

Cynthia's actions, perhaps socially justifiable to some of the club's nearby observers, were becoming much too familiar, and way too costly for others. This was the third such incident since she was hired the week before Halloween. The club manager and Cynthia did have a meeting in his office that night, just as the obese drunk had suggested, and although there was no fellatio, quite a tongue-lashing ensued.

Cynthia was being challenged by a male authority figure, and, once again, she disagreed with his assessment of her actions.

*He just doesn't get it. When will they understand?*

The club's manager continued admonishing Cynthia until she finally shouted back and stepped toward him.

"That guy's a jerk, everybody knows that! He had it coming!"

Stepping between the two was the much calmer, much wiser entrepreneur and club owner, Nico Cianfraco. He knew that his excitable, occasionally coked-up manager and the tall, powerful waitress with the type-A personality would continue to clash about what had really happened. Nico respectfully dismissed his manager by nodding toward the office doorway. As he exited the room, the prideful manager glared at Cynthia over his shoulder, while Cynthia scowled back at him, never losing eye contact until the tall man with a ponytail disappeared into the hallway.

Cianfraco, a well-dressed, middle-aged man, approached Cynthia calmly, tapping his chest firmly with his fingertips several times, forcing his dark, silk tie and neatly pressed Italian designer shirt against his sternum as he spoke.

"Cynthia, you do understand that this is *my* place of business, where I earn *my* living, right?"

He paused.

"That *jerk* has a name. It's Larry Pangino. He was successful in pharmaceutical sales since way before he started slinging Viagra to every limp-dick old man across this continent."

Cynthia snorted softly and offered a thin-lipped smile.

Nico shook his head.

"Do you have any idea how much money he drops in here? He's in my club at least every other month, sometimes three, four nights in a row. When he comes to town, he usually brings in a whole crew of salesmen with deep pockets, too."

Cynthia did not change her expression. She'd seen the guy before.

*He was an asshole during each and every visit. They're all assholes, and there's plenty more where they came from.*

Nico tilted his head to one side.

"You know, Cyn, everybody here really likes you . . . well, Larry, not so much . . . but most of the time you do a pretty good job of keeping those jerks from crossing the line. That requires a refined skill, Cynthia, don't get me wrong, it really does. It ain't easy being a cocktail waitress in a place like this."

Cynthia looked down and said nothing.

"You handle yourself well, but maybe you could've been a little bit more tolerant, or maybe not so punitive . . . It is a strip club, after all. You're not likely to see a lot of men with high character in here. You know?"

Nico waited for Cynthia to look up, then nodded toward the office door.

"But those dancers out there . . . that's how they earn their living. Over and over again, night after night, they just suck it up and pretend that they don't hear a word."

He shook his head.

"But you . . . that's obviously not your style."

Cynthia frowned as Nico continued.

"I can tell that my dancers admire you. I guarantee you, they all wish they had your courage and strength."

Again, he shook his head.

"They're going to miss you, Cynthia. I'm going to miss you."

**8**

Saturday, January 11, 1997
Downtown San Diego

The room was as silent as a strip club manager's office could be this close to midnight. Nico Cianfraco moved to the chair behind the office's only desk, sat down, and continued speaking in a relaxed, but curious tone.

"I just have one question, and maybe a couple of comments, if you don't mind."

He motioned toward a plush leather chair across from his desk.

"Have a seat."

Cynthia sighed and sat in the chair, thinking, *Why do these guys always feel the need to teach me something?*

Nico brought his hands together, interlocked his thick fingers, and rested his forearms on the desktop.

"Sweetheart, how do you expect to have any sort of a happy, fulfilling life with all of this . . . vengeance, or whatever it is that you keep dishing out on these men?"

Cynthia did not speak.

"Look . . . we all got something that we remained very angry at for far too long. Well . . . those of us who were smart enough to figure it out before somebody got killed."

He raised his eyebrows, shrugged, pointed his thumbs upward while keeping his fingers locked together, and said, "When I was a young man, it was the local cops in Chicago. Some had turned corrupt. They nearly put my father out of business. Forty years ago he packed up the entire family, sold everything for half of what it was once worth, and moved us all here."

Cynthia was already agitated and was becoming impatient. Her heart rate and blood pressure were elevated, and she was quickly losing interest.

*And your point is?*

"I hated all cops for a long time, Cynthia, and when I failed the attitude test, I paid dearly for it."

He leaned across the desk and pointed to a small, round scar above a slightly-raised bump on the bridge of his nose.

"See this?"

Cynthia focused her eyes and nodded.

"This is from a left jab a cop hit me with, right after I called him a, well, let's just say I called him the one thing I shouldn't have."

Cynthia stared at the injury that she hadn't noticed before.

*Yeah, well, that jerk did the one thing he shouldn't have . . . and all I did was push him off his chair . . . he got off easy.*

He looked squarely into Cynthia's eyes and continued in a softer tone.

"I came *this* close to losing everything more than that one time, Cynthia . . . I had to learn, or I was going to die . . . Really."

Nico paused, reclined into the chair, and shook his head several times.

"Maybe Larry will learn something, too. Who knows?"

His face showed empathy as he continued.

"Resentment held me back for a long time, Cynthia. I had to identify and change a lot of old habits. I had to completely reprogram my thinking. Am I making any sense to you?"

Cynthia nodded and blinked repeatedly before tipping her head down.

*I really don't want to get into this.*

"Cynthia, you got too much of that resentment inside of you. You gotta let that shit go. If this thing that you got going on in here, with these men, is what you got going on out there . . . then I gotta tell you, Cynthia, you're gonna have a real hard time."

Cynthia glared at the club owner with a scowl.

Nico smiled, then pointed at her.

"You're still a young woman, though, and I think you're smart enough to figure it out. You just can't see it yet. It seems to me like you haven't learned how to get outside of yourself so you can observe your own behaviors objectively. You lack that third-person ability still."

Cynthia said nothing.

"You'll have it someday, though. I can see that happening."

Nico shook his head, then leaned forward.

"I wish you the best, Cynthia, I really do, but you gotta go. I can't keep you. You're costing me too much money now."

Nico lightly slapped his palms on the desktop and pushed himself upward. He stood and reached into a front pocket of his dark Gabardine slacks and removed a shiny gold money clip that held a thick stack of neatly-folded bills. While slowly shaking his head, he peeled three crisp bills from the stack and extended his right hand toward Cynthia.

"It's a goddamn shame that I have to do this . . . It really is. We were just getting started. Here, take three hundred bucks. We'll call it severance pay. Fair enough?"

She wanted to tell Nico to keep the money.

*It's not about the money.*

Instead, she nodded and accepted the gift.

"Good luck, Cynthia. You're a good kid. Your heart is in the right place, but you gotta get your head on straight."

Cynthia breathed in deeply and allowed the reality of her termination to settle in. As she exhaled, a visceral warmth rushed from her scalp through her earlobes, down onto her neck and shoulders, the same way it had in the Navy courtroom just after her attorney and the Navy's well-dressed JAG officer approached the bench.

There had been a similar pattern of impulsive reactions to what she believed were inappropriate behaviors demonstrated by men who outranked her; impulsive reactions that eventually led to charges of insubordination, misconduct, and striking a superior officer.

But, before that hearing was five minutes old, the charges were dropped, expunged from her record, and an agreement was reached to accept an honorable, but immediate, discharge.

She was out, though, and on her own. Alone.

She realized that her impulsivity would set her back again, that she would lose all of her new friends, and that the new life that she had put together was now shattered into pieces, just like Larry's glasses.

*And for what? Just to teach a drunk loser a lesson? Dammit, Cynthia. What the HELL is wrong with you?*

On her way out of Nico's club, Cynthia hugged the bartenders and a few of the dancers. She threw a heavy forearm into the huge Samoan's chest that drew an audible "unngghh" from the thick Islander. Although he was expecting it, he lost his balance.

Junior, the bouncer, loved his job, and he would miss her the most. With Cynthia Harden around, working at Club Cheetah was even more fun.

**9**

Saturday, January 11, 1997
Downtown San Diego

A cold, misty fog hung brightly in the low sky. The reflection of the downtown lights created a white, glowing dome that covered America's Finest City, while Club Cheetah's neon exterior lights glowed in the eyes of those passing by on Harbor Drive. The northwest view, overlooking the Lindbergh Field landing strip, was stunning. To the south, the beautiful ship-filled San Diego Harbor glowed. Panning farther east, the tall, glistening images of downtown buildings were framed by the fully-illuminated Coronado Bridge and the towny hillside village of Banker's Hill that pilots guided their airliners just a couple hundred feet above on their landing pattern.

Cynthia Harden took in the view from the strip club's parking lot and laughed out loud as Junior, the Samoan bouncer, emphatically mocked the drunken pharmaceutical salesman, Larry Pangino, who had failed to collect all of his breeze-blown bills before getting dumped into a yellow cab. Junior held up a *"fitty and two fins,"* laughing as he waved the bills around before delicately placing them in the front right pocket of his extra-extra-large designer jeans.

Nico exited his club just in time to see Junior's antics. He smiled and laughed along, not seeming to mind that his favorite bouncer and his favorite ex-waitress were still laughing about the incident.

When Cynthia first took the cocktail waitress job, she had mentioned the full-time lifeguarding job that she hoped to attain. She told Nico that she would be leaving her job at the club sometime in the late spring. He took an interest then and had continued to ask her about her training, sometimes offering her his advice.

*I knew he would come out and say goodbye again.*

Wearing a long, dark coat that hung over his sharp slacks and shiny shoes, Cianfraco twisted his thick salt-and-pepper mustache with the thumb and fingertips of one hand and held a fat cigar in the other.

"So, kiddo, you're off to go kick some lifeguard ass now, huh?"

Cynthia loved his sharp accent, one that reminded her of Dennis Farina, and his fatherly way that reminded her of her daddy, Gordon.

Nico turned away from Cynthia and exhaled three clouds of smoke that hung momentarily before swirling away.

"He was a douchebag, Nico. He had it coming."

"Most of them are, princess. And, yes, they usually do have it coming. So now, with a record of three-and-oh, you're the champion of kicking douchebag's asses in my club. That's a dubious record. I'm not sure if anyone's ever going to top that one."

Nico looked at Junior and toked on his cigar, looked back at Cynthia, and continued.

"So, seriously . . . you haven't kicked enough ass to learn that it hurts you more that it does them?"

He was only half joking, and she knew it. He tipped his head down and leaned toward her. His eyes opened wider.

She held his gaze.

"You plan on doing the same thing with this lifeguard deal? You gonna march right in there and see what men you can get into it with . . . just so you can prove that they're douchebags, too?"

Cynthia looked down.

"It does appear that way, doesn't it?"

He reached for her closest arm, squeezed it gently, and said, "Cynthia, you know I say this with respect, but no shit, sweetheart, it sure does. And by the way, how's that working out for ya?"

Cynthia breathed in deeply as Nico continued his one-handed bicep hug. She exhaled and asked, "So, what do I do now?"

Nico turned and faced the tall woman who stood eye to eye next to him.

"Well, first, tell me more about this lifeguard deal. Who do you work for? What's this job pay? What about benefits? It's like being a cop, isn't it? Don't you get a *badge*?"

The way he said *baaiiddgg* made Cynthia and Junior laugh out loud. He pressed on, smiling as he bounced up and down on his toes and waved the cigar.

"I'm serious. Tell me."

Nico took three more glowing, smoky tokes and listened.

"First of all," Cynthia replied, "it's not really like a cop, even though I will have a *baaiiddgg,* eventually."

She sneered at Nico sarcastically and continued.

"The state job is more like a cop. The city job is more like a fireman. The state guys do a twenty-six-week law enforcement academy. They become park rangers with guns. The city guards don't carry guns. The city already has its own police force. Either way, it's all about ocean rescues and medical responses on the beach."

She sneered again.

"Are you still with me?"

Nico abruptly slapped the large Samoan in the chest.

Both men laughed.

"Yes, dear, we're listening. Please continue."

Once again, Cynthia sneered, this time smiling afterward.

"Okay, so after graduating from the city's academy, I'll be qualified to work as a seasonal city employee at around fifteen bucks an hour. I'll be running all over the beaches fetching weak swimmers, tracking down lost kids, providing minor medical aids, doing whatever they tell me to do."

"That's it?"

"Well, no. After a few summers, hopefully, I'll get promoted to a year-round position with benefits and a decent salary. Then I'll get trained to operate rescue vessels; make diving rescues, cliff rescues, swift water rescues; that kind of stuff. I'll get my twenty or more years . . . build a nice retirement to go along with everything my father left me . . . and that's it."

She slowly scanned the spectacular downtown view and smiled.

"Nico . . . I'm young enough to work for thirty years if I really want to. The job takes place in the greatest geographical environment I can imagine . . . San Diego's public beaches. I mean, who doesn't want to be there?"

Nico and Junior looked at each other and shrugged, agreeing.

"Thirty years of that, working my way up the city's pay scale while helping people and actually making a difference? I can definitely handle that. The job description is made exactly for somebody like me, and I couldn't be more prepared for it than I already am. At my age, with my background, the timing is perfect."

Nico nodded and shrugged.

He turned and pointed at her with his cigar.

"You got issues though, Cynthia . . . and you know what I'm talking about. You got nothing for these jerks but trouble. Why do this to yourself ?"

Nico reached again for her bicep. He pulled her next to him, and wrapped his arm around the woman who was four years younger than the youngest of his own three married daughters. He'd done this kind of counseling many times before.

"Cynthia . . . baby girl . . . listen to me. Be sweet when you show up to this academy. Be patient with these men . . . and sweet. Use sugar and honey, not piss and vinegar."

He paused for effect.

"It's gonna be pretty much all men . . . I mean . . . I'm guessing it's the men going after these great jobs with the big salaries and the full benefits, no? They're who you'll be dealing with, what . . . eighty, ninety percent of the time?"

He turned and slapped Junior in the chest again.

Junior muttered, "At least."

"Just be a teammate, right? I mean, you know how to be a teammate ..."

He looked at Junior and said, "this guy here tells me that you were a shit-hot water polo player in high school over there in Coronado. Team captain, *all-state*, he said."

He nodded toward the island, acknowledging the long, tall, brightly-lit bridge, then paused.

With his eyebrows raised, he turned his head, as if suddenly remembering something.

"Oh, yeah . . . and another thing. Junior tells me that you were a combat-rated Navy diver? Is that true? You didn't put that part on your application."

Cynthia shrugged.

"I didn't want to scare you . . . didn't want you to think I had violent tendencies."

Nico and Junior burst into laughter.

Cynthia quickly joined in.

They all looked at each other and continued laughing.

Nico howled, "Wooo . . . look, Cynthia . . . that's who you are. That's your strength. The world needs women like you . . . people like you . . . to do things that would otherwise never get done. You gotta be her again, and you gotta stop with these *jerks*."

Nico stepped back and pointed at Cynthia with his cigar.

"You never know which one of these assholes is gonna have it in for you. One misstep and you're right back here again. I'll tell you something that you can count on, Cynthia. These men will be afraid of you taking their spot . . . and they won't go down without a fight."

Cynthia flashed back to her time in the Navy.

*Duh . . . that much I know for sure.*

The trio stood silently and gazed at the downtown lights.

Cynthia turned toward Nico, her eyes welling.

"Thank you, Nico. You're a good man. My father would have loved you. I'll keep in touch. And Junior, you too, buddy. You're both salt-of-the-earth men . . . two of the finest I've ever known."

After two lengthy hugs, Cynthia left the parking lot in her sturdy 4Runner.

As she drove away, Junior sniffled and wiped a tear.

"I'm gonna miss her."

Nico cleared his throat.

"Yep, and I'll worry about her, too, that one there. Whatever it is that's eating away at her, it's in there pretty deep, and it ain't going away anytime soon."

Nico watched the 4Runner turn onto Harbor Drive and disappear in a sea of red tail lights.

"I'll be praying for you, Cynthia."

"Amen, boss. Me, too."

The Following Morning
Sunday, January 12, 1997
Marina Village, Mission Bay

Cynthia heard a pulsing buzz just before sunrise. Without opening her eyes, she reached over and tapped an alarm clock radio that showed blinking red numerals: *6:15*. Her head still beneath a soft blanket, she curled her body up and moved closer to a small electrical heating unit that purred on top of the same nightstand where the alarm vigilantly proclaimed the beginning of her day.

She appreciated the gentle rolling surge that greeted her calmly every morning upon waking, and loved living aboard the sailing vessel that her father had taught her how to pilot while she was growing up on Coronado Island.

She slid out from under the cozy bedding to the end of her bunk, her bare feet landing on a soft, furry rug. She stood into a long cat stretch then moved to the galley, turned the coffee maker on, filled the pot with bottled water, then used the head. She returned to the galley, continued making her morning coffee, and began preparing a light breakfast of PB&J on whole grain bread. As she licked the grape goo off her fingers and chased it with hot black coffee, Cynthia reviewed her training day itinerary.

Just before sunrise at 0700, she would launch from the marina and paddle on the Bay for an hour before returning to the boat for a leaner breakfast. She would spend the next two hours reading ocean lifeguard manuals and drinking lots of water and coffee, as she did on all training days. After lounging comfortably on the breezy deck of the sloop, preparing herself for her upcoming challenges, she would make herself a fruity protein smoothie, and, about 15 minutes later, she would ride her mountain bike two miles to the South Mission Beach main tower. From there, she would jog north past Crystal Pier on a long run-swim-run before riding back to the boat, where she would make herself a light lunch. After a nice rest, she would meet her trainer at a sweaty boxing gym on the North Island Naval Amphibious base, where, as a not-so-little girl, she learned jiu jitsu and other fighting skills along with her father, Gordon, and her Uncle Brady.

As she wiped the kitchen counters, replaced the jars, and moved into the master cabin to dress, Cynthia began to reflect on a day that she would never forget, a day when the tailspin she seemed to be caught in had begun.

Rolling a yoga mat onto the floor, then dropping to her knees as she began her daily warm-up routine, she further recalled the day when the team's head coach had made it clear that he had heard enough from Cynthia.

*Five years ago, Cynthia Harden was considered by many to be perhaps the best 19-year-old women's water polo player in the country, maybe the world. But she disagreed vehemently with a decision made by the U.S. women's team head coach, a man who had never really earned her respect, a man who had also grown tired of the sometimes contentious attitude of his best player.*

*As an upcoming international tournament's final preparations wound down, Cynthia, as one of the team's captains, began voicing her unsolicited opinions about what she perceived as a "passive-aggressive" coaching style that was "leaving our team uninspired and unprepared."*

*Game one of the Women's U20 World Championships was to be played in three days, and the U.S. team flight was scheduled to depart at 0800 the next morning. Toward the end of their final team meeting, however, the* evening before their departure, the head coach announced an unexpected roster change. He was replacing a very popular and highly-skilled teammate with a player who had suffered a bad hip injury and had been dismissed from the tryout program weeks earlier. The head coach rationalized his last-minute decision at the meeting.

"Bailey's hip is healed now. We need her skill set more than we need Scarlett's. Scarlett was only coming along if Bailey's hip did not recover, but it did. She's coming, and unfortunately, we can only take fifteen players to Spain. Scarlett, I'm sorry for the late notice, but as I told you earlier, you were only an alternate. It is very difficult for me to do this, but my decision is final."

Scarlett, Cynthia, and most of their teammates were surprised, confused, and even outraged. A chorus of contention grew as Cynthia and a few other 18-, 19-, and 20-year-old women held Scarlett, their weeping teammate, in their arms. Cynthia verbalized her disagreement using some choice words, but the head coach raised his hands, placed a forefinger into each ear, shook his head from side to side, and walked away.

Cynthia became more outraged and yelled, "Are you serious? You cut one of everybody's best friends and one of our best players the night before we leave for Spain, and you're going to stick your fingers in your ears like a little pussy?"

The coach did not reply. It did not matter what Cynthia or any of her teammates thought; his decision was final. Bailey and her healed hip were in. Scarlett and her powerful and accurate left arm were out.

At 0630 the next morning, Cynthia stood in a check-in security line with her teammates. All of them carried blue duffel bags with red and white trim and USA team backpacks with their names and cap numbers embroidered on them. When she was approached by her coach, Cynthia turned away, but the coach moved closer until she looked up at him. He motioned for her to join him by a bank of pay phones. He held a single airline ticket in a folded paper cover, tapping it on the back of his hand as he spoke.

"Cynthia, I knew my decision to bring Bailey back would be unpopular, but you went too far last night."

He paused, and glanced at his team that was now moving as a group through the security checkpoint.

"Yes, your scoring, your defense, and your competitiveness will be missed, but the insubordination and the lack of respect that you have consistently shown for me . . . no, that crap will not be missed. You can disagree with me, Cynthia, and we can discuss issues, like we did several times, but you cannot argue past the point of destroying everything that this team has built together. Not to mention destroying everything that you've built for yourself."

He turned to watch his team for a moment.

"That's what you did last night, Cynthia. All over something that was never up to you in the first place. It wasn't your call, it was MY call."

He bowed and shook his head.

"You never could get that part."

He nodded toward the group that had moved away from the site where Cynthia's gear bag remained behind.

"You will not be boarding the flight to Barcelona. Scarlett will go in your place, and Bailey is boarding with us now, as you can see."

The coach handed the folded paper to Cynthia.

"This is a one-way ticket to San Diego. It leaves in one hour from Terminal 3. You'll need to take a shuttle to get there. I advise that you hurry."

Cynthia uttered, "What?"

By the time she realized what had happened, her entire team was gone. Still stunned and in a daze, Cynthia heard a voice from behind her.

"Miss, are the you one who needs the shuttle to Terminal 3?"

She turned to see a smiling, middle-aged woman wearing black slacks, black shoes, a crisp white shirt, a narrow black tie, and a sharp black jacket.

"Come with me, darling, I'll take you where you need to go."

Cynthia exhaled as she released her stretch. She shook her head subtly and sighed, remembering that her amazing father, her best friend in the world, had died of lung cancer just three days later.

Clearing her head of the past, Cynthia bounded up a short staircase, headed to the storage deck, and retrieved a long, sleek vessel made of hard, shiny plastic. On the smooth, flat surface of its top deck lay a foam rubber pad that Cynthia would place her knees, shins, and the tops of her feet upon while paddling with her arms.

She hummed softly as she cautiously carried the delicate board to the end of the dock. She often used the calm, peaceful mornings of these training days to reflect and pray, as she began to do now while she took her position on the deck of the board. She pulled into the Bay using a simultaneous arm stroke, piking from her raised hips, and reached forward with both arms to full extension. Her large, strong hands angled downward vertically and formed rigid blades that pierced the water's surface and pulled directly backward. After the pull phase of her stroke ended just past her hips, her hands then exited the water, and Cynthia gracefully moved her arms upward and forward to begin another stroke.

As she drove the board forward across the glassy, orange surface of the Bay, her hips flexed rhythmically, and her rotating shoulders functioned like the wheel of a steam engine with two pistons attached.

As she gained rhythm and speed, Cynthia briefly looked up into the rising sun and said softly, "Daddy, please stay with me in spirit today. Please keep me safe and healthy. Please help me hold my tongue, so I won't speak negatively about, or toward, anyone today. I need your strength and guidance, and I need you to protect me, today and always. I miss you, Daddy. I love you."

# PART 3

Apprentice:
A person being taught a craft or trade; beginner.

Two Months Later
Day 1 of Lifeguard Academy
Tuesday, March 18, 1997
Mission Bay

To a casual observer, ocean lifeguards may be seen simply as grown-up southern California surfers patrolling the beach in rugged lifeguard vehicles, wearing dark sunglasses and white sun block. Or perhaps they may be seen as athletic and daring thrill seekers, vigilantly watching the ocean while standing on the sunny deck of a lifeguard tower in red trunks, warm and shirtless with a golden tan, calmly waiting for the opportunity to sprint across the sand and fling their body headfirst through the surf in pursuit of a struggling tourist. Then, after proudly chalking up another ocean rescue, that powerful and savvy ocean waterman calmly trots back to the tower without cracking a smile, only to do it again, and again, and again, until the sun goes down.

Although those perceptions may be somewhat accurate, it is frequently cold, windy, and cloudy on San Diego's beaches, and, even during the summer, the sun does not always shine. Those tanned, muscular lifeguards standing watch, and even the privileged supervisors who get to drive the new trucks with fancy rescue equipment on board, frequently freeze their asses off.

The average water temperature of the Pacific Ocean in San Diego during the month of March is about 59 degrees. On the first few days of the academy, Cynthia and the other cadets found out right away that during late March of 1997, the ocean would be a whole lot colder than that. Many of the cadets would not be prepared to endure the frigid conditions. A number of them would not adjust to the constricting effect that low water temperature could have on their lung capacity during intensive exercise.

If lifeguard candidates can't breathe calmly, deeply, and effectively in cold ocean water, it's unlikely that they are cut out for this kind of work. Taking the time to stabilize one's respiration rate during a rescue could easily cause a drowning. Testing potential ocean lifeguards in extremely cold water is the simplest, and most effective, way of eliminating unqualified cadets. High surf is an effective elimination tool as well, but swell size is harder to predict than water temperature, hence the annual, and almost always, cold-water lifeguard try-out academy held at the beginning of spring break every year.

Years ago, after he accepted the position of Academy Director, Lieutenant Richard Morgan learned quickly that just about anyone can swim well on warm, flat days; most applicants can provide reasonable answers during an interview; and the challenges inherent in selecting qualified individuals to staff beachfront towers are more complex than they appear. It did not take him long to decide that eliminating the weak and the timid as soon as possible was the most effective method to bring the graduation rate down to a more manageable number and raise the quality of the graduates to a higher, more reliable level. The combination of cold water and high surf quickly exposes unqualified applicants, and many job seekers quit before they even consider arguing for a second chance. While disappointed about their failure, they are often relieved to be back on the beach, safe and warm, after the sometimes intimidating and frightening tryout experience. Wrapped in a dry towel, they may gain some consolation from at least having tried to fulfill a personal dream, but still left wondering if they had really tried as hard as they could.

Sixty-six cadets completed the application process, paid their tuition and fees, and enrolled in the two-unit Ocean Lifesaving and Rescue course offered by San Diego Community College that began on March 19, 1997. Only those who graduated from the academy would receive college credit and become eligible to apply, interview, and try out for a position of Seasonal Ocean Lifeguard (SOL) at one of nine separate municipal agencies located in San Diego County.

These nine agencies collaborated, assisted each other, and formed a larger governing body called the Department of Coastal Safety (DCS), of which Lt. Morgan served as the highest-ranking officer. As the DCS's senior lieutenant, Morgan also chaired a nine-member committee that established the criteria and standards that determined the eligibility of those individuals who were hoping to provide public safety to citizens visiting San Diego County's numerous lakefront and oceanfront beaches.

Odds were very high that, if you passed the course and graduated from the academy, you would find an agency to work for your first summer. Most of the academy's cadets wanted to become a San Diego city employee, hired by the San Diego Lifeguard Patrol (SDLP), and not just because it offered the highest starting pay. It also had the longest coastline with the most diverse beaches. It was, by far, the agency with the highest need and the greatest opportunity for permanent employment. The SDLP had the greatest funding and the deepest resources in the county.

Many agreed that, if you wanted the best training, the most exposure to excitement and risk, and were willing to compete against other well-qualified individuals, the Patrol was the place for you.

For many cadets like Cynthia Harden, a long career with the Patrol was their primary goal. If they wanted to earn that privilege, however, they had to get through Lt. Morgan's challenging curriculum first.

The March 1997 class of cadets lost a handful of job seekers by the end of the first day. The first physical test they were required to complete was a timed 500-meter swim in the flat, cold water of Mission Bay. It was a pass/fail test with a 10-minute time limit, and was the minimum standard and the easiest performance requirement for the cadets to overcome.

Cynthia was stunned by the number of poor swimmers that showed up on that first day. She immediately noticed an overweight, pink-skinned male who looked as if he'd never even been to the ocean before.

*He's probably here on some kind of dare.*

Once he waded into knee-deep cold water and felt the muddy, slimy bottom of Mission Bay, he quickly realized that he wasn't born to become an ocean lifeguard. He never even got his swimming trunks wet, but it took him a while to get all of the dark, sticky mud out from between his toes. A young female who looked healthy enough, but had obviously spent very little time learning how to swim, almost sank to the bottom of the Bay, gasping for air before she was quickly rescued on a longboard by Senior POL and Chief Instructor Bryce North.

North was a positive, enthusiastic, and encouraging mentor for countless former and current cadets, and none would likely ever forget the loud and determined energy he brought all day, every day, constantly demanding, "Find another gear!"

Another cadet that Cynthia took notice of that first morning was a tall, athletic-looking Latina who began the third and final heat of the swim test very competitively. She stayed with the leaders of the group, but, before reaching the midway buoy, 250 meters out in the middle of the lagoon, Cynthia noticed that the young woman was now keeping her head and face completely out of the water as she stroked. Her raised head position caused her hips and legs to sink beneath the surface, which increased frontal resistance and created tremendous drag. The quickly-fatiguing cadet slowed down considerably and dropped well behind the pace of the leaders. A small group of young cadets who had already completed the swim test began yelling, and encouraged her to put her head down, but she continued to swim with her face out of the water.

When the director of the academy began yelling out the time remaining for her to pass the test, her crowd of supporters relayed the information loudly. Still, her face remained above the cold Bay water.

"Twenty seconds!"

Mr. North arrived at her side on his rescue board and attempted to motivate the struggling job seeker.

"Get your face back down in that water and get your ass across the line. Do it now! Find another gear, Cadet!"

Still watching closely, Cynthia shook her head.

*It's not that hard. Obviously this one can't find another gear.*

Then she noticed a particularly handsome cadet shouting louder than the others.

"GO, Coach Escobar, GO!"

The swimmer immediately put her head down, kicked furiously, and wheeled her arms through the water. Everyone screamed support, even the lieutenant.

"Go! Ten . . . nine . . . eight . . ."

The entire academy joined in exuberance as she crossed the line in time.

People were fired up. Cadets offered her, and others that had passed, congratulations and encouragement.

"Great finish . . . way to stay with it . . . quality effort . . ."

When the young woman exited the Bay, she had a relieved smile on her face, but shook her head from side to side, repeating, "It's sooo cold . . . I couldn't breathe . . ."

Cynthia observed a smaller, more intimate group of swimmers that quickly gathered around the woman and began chanting softly, "Si, se puede . . . si, se puede."

She kept her opinions to herself.

*Are they serious? That was pathetic. She'll be gone in no time; what a poser.*

She caught herself quickly.

*Observe and don't judge. Stay positive, Cyn. Find somebody here that demonstrates qualities that you admire. Someone you can trust, like that kid right there.*

Cynthia stared at the well-developed body of the attractive black male that she had noticed earlier, right after she had finished one place behind him at the end of their own heat of the 500-meter swim.

Cynthia then wondered if this young Hispanic female was more than just some poser that barely passed the swim test. She could see that the young woman had both athletic ability and strength, and that her swimming stroke was long and efficient.

*Maybe I shouldn't judge her so harshly. It is pretty freaking cold out there.*

She looked more closely at two other athletic Latinas, two muscular Latinos and, again, the handsome black male who stood nearly a head taller than the entire group.

*His voice was the one that she responded to. There's something special about him.*

Cynthia admired the young man's athletic, conditioned physique and couldn't help noticing that he was completely ripped, with almost no body fat. He had a tall swimmer's body with long arms, large hands, and big feet. His impeccable chest, chiseled abs, rounded shoulders, bulging and veiny arms, large v-shaped back, slim waist, and powerful-looking hips, thighs, and calves, testified to countless yards in the swimming pool and mile after mile of hard running on the track and stadium stairs.

Cynthia looked him up and down, taking in the uniqueness of his captivating physical form, before allowing a long second glance at the front of his tight Speedo. She turned away quickly, slightly embarrassed, after she noticed that he was looking right at her, aware of her curious eyes.

She could tell that he was very connected to the curvaceous young woman who had just barely passed the swim test. As she watched them walking together, side by side, Cynthia pondered their relationship.

*Maybe they're dating.*

The young woman seemed to be the leader of the small group. Cynthia wondered, however, about the leadership provided to a group that had all easily accomplished what their leader had struggled to achieve.

*What are they going to do when she fails the next test?*

Day 3 of Academy
Thursday, March 20, 1997
Mission Bay

The academy's difficult physical testing and repetitive training in frigid, stormy weather continued to take a toll on the cadets. Of the 55 men who began the testing, 11 were now preparing their résumés for a different employer's review, and of the 11 females who began, only five remained, and the cadets still hadn't left the flat water of Mission Bay. That would change tomorrow.

The changing venue did not intimidate Cynthia. Her challenges were not about the surf, the currents, cold water, or the crappy weather. Her challenges were about developing trustworthy relationships and performing well enough to be promoted quickly, as she did in the Navy.

After completing several trials of mock rescues during the morning of the third day of the academy, the cadets were given 10 minutes to recover before the next activity was scheduled to begin.

Thus far, Cynthia had introduced herself to none of the male cadets unless she had to. She assumed that none would feel very good about finishing behind a woman, and, besides, she didn't have an abundance of respect for men who couldn't keep up with her. The young man she heard instructors calling "Jackson" quickly became someone she felt drawn to. She noticed that he seemed to interact almost exclusively with his small group of friends. Cynthia continued watching him closely, hoping for an opportunity to introduce herself.

From across the beach, she saw him drying his body with a damp towel, then pull an academy-issued parka over his broad shoulders. He left the parka unzipped, partially exposing his ripped abdomen and sculpted chest. When Cynthia noticed that he was standing alone, she cautiously walked toward him, and when their eyes met, she said casually, "Hey, Jackson . . . you're killing it out there. Nice job."

Jackson appeared a little nervous, not expecting her to address him, but he turned and replied politely, "Thanks. You too."

"Do you swim in college?"

Jackson laughed.

"Noooo. I'm still in high school. I will graduate in June."

"Really? Damn, if you're still in high school, you must have done very well at the CIFs this year."

"Yeah, it was pretty cool. We had five swimmers from our team make it all the way to the SoCal championships in Mission Viejo."

He nodded toward the academy's pop-up tent.

"That's my coach over there, and those are my teammates with her by the tent."

Cynthia didn't have to look; she knew to whom he was referring.

"Oh, yeah, I noticed her. She had a rough first day. But you and your teammates seem to be doing very well. I can tell that you're a very close-knit group."

"Yeah, we are. Coach Escobar is really good about building team chemistry. She's been encouraging us all year to try out for a job working on the beach, so here we are. She knows how important it is for all of us to get through the academy. She's been really helpful . . . she's a great motivator."

"That's awesome. I'm sure she's an excellent coach."

*Whatever,* Cynthia thought, but she looked away and reminded herself to avoid making a sarcastic remark.

*Easy, Cyn, bite your tongue, stay positive.*

"Well," she said. "We still have a ways to go, and I think the easy part may be behind us."

"I know, and it's only the third day. They definitely aren't making it easy to get this job . . . and we haven't even been to the ocean yet. Have you checked the surf?"

"Yep. Big, and supposed to get bigger . . . and colder . . . and more rain, too. I sure do wish the sun would come out."

"Damn straight, that's what I'm sayin.'"

They turned toward each other, and Cynthia nodded.

"By the way, my name's Cynthia Harden."

"I'm Latrelle Jackson. Nice to meet you, Miss Harden."

"Oh, my gawd, Latrelle, stop. Call me Cynthia. I'm not a school-teacher."

"Oh, my bad. I guess it's kind of a habit."

Cynthia smiled.

"Well, *Mister Jackson*, I think it's a nice habit. You're a very polite young man and one hell of an athlete. I think you'll be an outstanding lifeguard, too."

"You do? Thank you . . . and I already know who you are, by the way. Everybody does by now."

Cynthia chuckled.

"Seriously? I wouldn't have guessed that."

They stood quietly gazing at the choppy and wind-blown Bay, both appearing unsure about what to say next. Latrelle shifted and moved slightly away from the athletic woman. He turned to her, smiled, and noticed that she was very tall, maybe three inches shorter than he was. He snuck a longer peek at her blue eyes and smiled again. He looked at his watch, then turned toward where his coach was standing with all of his teammates. Cadet Escobar was staring at him, her eyebrows raised, and her hands on her hips.

Latrelle thought, *I knew she'd be watching me. She's gonna say something, too.*

Cynthia noticed him looking away and said, "I know you're tight with your team and all, but I was thinking that, you know, maybe we could partner up? You're really strong, and so far it looks like you know exactly what you're doing."

Latrelle turned toward Cynthia and tilted his head.

"You think I know what I'm doing?"

"Absolutely."

"Really? You want me to be your partner?"

"I do, and I'd feel much safer with you close by. You've like, totally beaten me *every single time*. C'mon, Latrelle, you and me."

Latrelle chuckled, humbly accepting Cynthia's acknowledgment, and silently considered her proposal. He looked over his shoulder again and saw one of his high school teammates laughing and pointing at him.

Latrelle grimaced.

*This is so embarrassing.*

After allowing the moment of embarrassment to pass, Latrelle considered Cynthia's offer again. He turned toward her and met her eyes with an easy, Denzel Washington kind of smile. His smooth brown skin and rounded white teeth, strong cheekbones, and manly rigid jawline were softened by his light-colored eyes.

When Cynthia looked closer, she noticed the presence of unique green pigments floating within mahogany irises. Around the irises were razor-thin, dark grey rings that created a barrier that seemed to protect Latrelle's irises from the ocean-drenched, bloodshot whites of his eyes. Cynthia continued looking at the handsome young man who, until now, she had only been able to see from a distance.

*Gawd, he's good looking.*

After several moments, Latrelle replied, "Okay. I think I'd feel better with you close by helping me too."

"Let's do it. Let's go kick some ass, okay?"

Latrelle chuckled as he shook her hand.

"Deal."

Cynthia almost gushed.

"We'll do great together, I'm sure."

Latrelle's easy smile beamed.

"Fuh sho."

They both laughed, and Cynthia raised her right hand. Latrelle paused for an instant before he recognized the high five, then slapped her hand.

Cynthia continued unabashedly.

"Well, whatever's next . . . I'm sure it will be demanding. And definitely very wet, which, uh, I don't usually mind being wet, but I'm kind of over being wet right now."

Cynthia felt a rush of embarrassment when she said the word "wet" for the third time.

She laughed nervously, hoping that Latrelle had not noticed.

Latrelle looked down at the grass, slightly blushing. He knew he would have been just as embarrassed had he blurted out "wood" or "hard."

He moved past the awkward moment quickly, then looked up and smiled at Cynthia. When she smiled back, Latrelle thought, *She does have a cute smile.*

Cynthia intimidated him somewhat, as she did most of the cadets, but his response was empathetic and aimed to soothe her obvious embarrassment.

"I'm a little over being wet myself. Hopefully we can stay right here, dry and warm, for just a few more minutes."

It worked. Cynthia relaxed, smiled, and said softly, "Yeah, that'd be nice."

Latrelle's coach, however, did not appear pleased that her young protégé was interacting with Cynthia. She began walking briskly toward the prodigy that she had trained, mentored, and protected after the death of Latrelle's father. As she approached, she looked angry, but before she was able to get close enough to say anything, the shrill recall whistle and the loud voice of Instructor Bryce North thwarted her intentions.

"Muster here on my mark in two minutes, people! Break time is over!"

Cynthia had noticed Escobar approaching them, and that Latrelle's coach was glaring at her with contempt. She directed Escobar a deliberate, cocky smile first, then reached over, placed her strong hands on Latrelle's shoulders, and squeezed his aching trapezius muscles. Latrelle stiffened, stood taller, and arched backwards. He groaned as Harden attempted to squeeze the lactic acid out of his swollen muscle fibers.

Cynthia leaned in, her body touching his from behind, and said softly, "So much for 'just a few more minutes.' I'll see you down there, Jackson. I'll take care of those shoulders later if you want. You can do mine, too. See? Training partners."

Latrelle grinned modestly.

"Yeah, that'd be cool."

As Cynthia jogged away, she shook her head and scowled at Escobar. *Pfff . . . whatever. Stare all you want, wench. What are you gonna do about it?*

Cynthia secured her gear and turned to find Lt. Morgan. Her focus now would be on the director's commands for the remainder of a very cold Day 3, and, as she located her gear, she reassured herself. *You're good. Stay positive. You've got a great partner now, a teammate, just like Nico said. Sugar and honey, Cyn. Don't screw this up.*

She spotted Lt. Morgan and took two strides toward him before she turned and noticed that Latrelle was already jogging toward the lieutenant. *Damn he's fine,* Cynthia thought.

**13**

Day 4 of Academy,
Friday, March 21, 1997
La Jolla Shores, La Jolla, California

The surf was not yet huge on Day 4, but it was challenging. Low tide sets of four-to-six-foot sandy wave faces slammed into the novice cadets, sending their rescue boards in all directions, drawing "ooh"s and "aah"s from Morgan, North, and Chief Instructor/SDLP Senior POL Alejandro Pena, one of the Patrol's most talented experts on rescue board technique.

Earlier that day, the cadets had trained and practiced various rescue techniques in the ocean south of the Scripps Pier. Now, their last task of the day would begin at the end of a long and impressive row of La Jolla Shores beachfront homes. With nothing but a swimsuit, rash guard, and bare feet, the cadets would be required to run approximately one-half mile to the north side of the Scripps Pier, then enter the water and swim through the surf and around the pier. The course would require them to swim in to the beach and then run back to the start/finish line.

Cynthia and Latrelle were part of a small group that had dominated the event. Latrelle grabbed stick No. 3 after sprinting like a track star on the second leg of the run and finished just 10 seconds behind the two leaders. Cynthia grabbed stick No. 4 twenty seconds later. Latrelle's Lincoln Heights teammates all finished in the top half, but their coach had struggled to get out through the surf line and dropped to the rear of the pack on the cold swim course. With the aid of her strong running ability, however, Cadet Escobar made the cutoff time with a minute to spare.

The instructional staff did not make it any easier for the cadets during this particularly cold academy, and most of the cozy indoor classroom work had been completed by the end of Day 2. By the end of a fourth consecutive demanding day, most of the cadets were spent. A number of them, including Cynthia, had already lost weight, and many had developed irritating rashes where their wetsuits, trunks, and fins had rubbed against, or tugged at, their sensitive skin. Their bodies were just beginning to acclimate, but now nearly every cadet had at least one painful ailment. They were cold from the moment they arrived at a different remote location each wet and windy day, and they remained cold until they took a hot shower or found a soothing hot tub to jump in after they were dismissed.

During late March of 1997, the sun had shone brightly during the afternoon of Day 1, but an off-shore weather system from the north brought steady rain, gusting winds, and dark clouds that blanketed the Southern California coast. Over time, the storm brought in colder temperatures and the waves and currents increased in strength, so that, by 1400 hours on Day 4, the wind was howling and the rain was coming down almost horizontally. Every piece of clothing and equipment on the beach was either flying away, soaking wet, or covered in sand. Nobody was smiling. The most commonly-heard comment from the purple-lipped and shivering cadets was, "I've never been this cold in my life."

At the end of Day 4, Cynthia was pleased to learn she was ranked fifth in overall points, just behind Latrelle Jackson. As she walked off the beach toward the parking lot, she thought, *Thank God we get the weekend off . . . four days down . . . only six to go. Keep being cautious . . . and keep kicking ass, Cyn. You can do this.*

Cynthia piled her gear into the cargo space of her 4Runner and climbed into the driver's seat. After allowing the engine to warm up for a few moments, she turned the heater all the way up and directed the airflow to her shriveled, bluish feet. Instead of feeling comfort, though, she felt a sharp, stinging pain. She flinched and pulled her feet away from the hot air. When she looked down, she noticed that the top of her right foot and the back of her left heel were bleeding. She sighed, reached for her shoulder harness, winced in pain, and groaned as she slowly pulled the seat belt across her trunk, then clipped it into place. She looked over her left shoulder and began to turn the steering wheel, preparing to pull into traffic, then stopped and cursed loudly, "Ouch!"

The skin under both of her armpits was red, swollen, and inflamed. A painful, irritating rash had grown where her triceps had been pounding against her lats in the coarse, salty ocean for the past four days.

As she placed her right foot on the gas pedal, Cynthia straightened the wheel and adjusted her body. When her pain began to subside, she spoke softly, "Daddy, I need your help. I know you're up there with God . . . will you please ask Him to make it stop raining. And ask Him to make the sun come out too. I am freezing out there Daddy. I miss you so much."

Despite her prayers, thick, heavy raindrops pounded the windshield, and within minutes, the street was covered with flowing rainwater. Tears welled up in Cynthia's eyes, and she sobbed softly while concentrating on the dark road in front of her. Holding back the tears, trying to gather her wits, she completed her prayer.

"I need you, Daddy. I don't know if I can do this alone . . ."

**14**

Day 5 of Academy
Monday, March 24, 1997
South Mission Beach, San Diego, California

When the remaining 46 job-seekers reported for training on Day 5, they were divided into small groups. Each cadet was then required to act not only as an effective first-responder to various mass rescue scenarios, but also to role-play as a struggling victim out in the frigid water for lengthy periods of time. The rescue scenarios were complex, the ocean conditions were harsh, and the criteria for advancing was extremely challenging. It was still stormy and very cold that day, and the wind and stinging rain made it very difficult for rescuers to communicate and work together. Spotting and reaching the cadets who were acting as victims provided challenges that were made even more difficult by the wind swell, strong rips, and fierce lateral currents that constantly changed the victims' positions in the ocean. This was a tiresome task that required every cadet to be in and out of the water, rescuing or being rescued, for up to three hours without getting a break.

After the event was over, the cadets ate lunch and rested on a grassy area just behind the main tower at South Mission Beach. Latrelle and Cynthia sat with a group of three cadets that were senior water polo players from Coronado High School. The young champions had each accepted athletic scholarships from different colleges, and were ranked first, second, and third in the academy. The boys were also engaging, charming, and filled with amusing stories that resulted in loud rounds of laughter. Coach Escobar and her swimmers, Cynthia noticed, had decided to join the group, and laughed along with the other cadets.

The group enjoyed a rare opportunity to relax while the clouds parted and the wind rested. Cynthia's prayer was answered, and the sun poured warmth onto the shivering group. She was grateful that Lt. Morgan allowed her and the other cadets an extra 15 minutes to dry their equipment, sun themselves, and rest. Cadets curled up beneath towels and parkas and napped, or lay still on their backs, dozing, while watching seagulls that circled overhead looking for food to pillage.

The extended rest period ended abruptly with North's recall whistle. He allowed the cadets a minute or so to shake themselves back to reality, many groaning at the prospect of what lay in front of them. He then yelled enthusiastically, "Suit up! PT number eleven starts at 1320. Five minutes to get ready people. You're competing for sticks again!"

As if recalled by North's signal as well, the clouds returned, the breeze began blowing sharply onshore, and the incoming tide rose rapidly, making the afternoon's swim courses even longer. The level of focus and determination required to overcome the harsh conditions was increasing by the hour.

North and several other instructors reminded the cadets of the academy's harshest testing requirement, and shouted in unison, "NO WETSUITS!"

**15**

Day 6 of Academy
Tuesday, March 25, 1997
Ocean Beach, San Diego, California

Even though the swell had increased overnight and the surf was now taller, heavier, and more powerful than on any of the previous days, none of the cadets failed at Ocean Beach on Day 6. During the morning, the wind settled, the skies cleared briefly, and with the luxury of a body-warming wetsuit, the pier jump drill was exhilarating and fun for the cadets. From 35 feet above the surface, they jumped in the ocean and swam to the beach, navigating their way through 8- to 10-foot rolling waves that peaked and broke about 250 yards offshore. While being pushed along the surface by a rapidly-moving wall of water, the cadets practiced maintaining a streamlined body position, and learned to ride in front of the waves until the waves finally overtook them, forced them downward, and tumbled their bodies in all directions.

That afternoon, the group received training on the use of masks and snorkels and practiced rescue diving. Using 50-foot sections of yellow nylon rope to remain connected, the cadets executed search and recovery line sweeps. Their small groups of five or six cadets were challenged to locate and retrieve one of several large truck tires that Mr. North and an intern had dumped from a sled attached to the back of a powerful

WaveRunner. The visibility that day was poor, and most of the searching needed to be done by hand. The challenging conditions required the groups of cadets to feel along the cold ocean floor for nearly 30 seconds at a time before surfacing. Then, the groups would overlap backwards a few feet and repeat the sequence. Their task was not completed until a guard on the line made contact with one of the tires and the group retrieved, rolled, or carried their "victim" up to a designated spot on the beach, where a practice dummy awaited their trials of CPR.

Cynthia's group had selected Latrelle as their line leader, and he successfully managed the cadence, duration, and starting position of each of his crew's dives. After a few rounds of diving as a unit, the three boys from Coronado all surfaced together, and, sounding like excited 10-year-old boys on Christmas morning, yelled enthusiastically, "We got one! Latrelle! We got one!"

Their team was the first to recover a "victim" from the bottom, which allowed their group plenty of time to rest and warm up on the beach while the other groups continued the worst-case scenario drill.

Lt. Morgan was congratulating Latrelle and the rest of his squad when SDLP Senior POL Randy Shields exited the Ocean Beach main tower. Shields walked directly toward the group and met the lieutenant with a smile, a hearty handshake, and a one-armed bro hug. Morgan introduced his close friend to the slightly intimidated, respectful group of cadets, who became noticeably quiet as soon as the tall, warmly-dressed, uniformed patrolman approached. Keeping his arm around the back and shoulders of his close friend, Morgan turned to the cadets and said, "I'd like you all to meet Randy Shields, a great waterman and one of the finest ocean lifeguards you will ever have the pleasure of working next to. This guy may have someday played right field in the big leagues, but he loves the ocean so much he gave it all up for us."

Shields smiled and played along for a moment, reminiscing briefly about being drafted out of high school in a late round by the Minnesota Twins. Instead of signing a contract, however, he chose to begin working on a college degree while improving his skills and his draft position. He held onto the dream until an over-used tendon in his left elbow failed him during his junior year at UCSD. The injury prevented Shields from being drafted a second time, and, after that, surfing became the skill that he devoted most of his free time to. Still smiling, he addressed the cadets. "Lt. Morgan overstates my abilities as well as my potential. It is a pleasure to meet you all. I understand how difficult this training is, especially in March, but the nasty weather and this big swell have obviously made this a very demanding academy. If you make it through this afternoon and the remaining . . . what is it . . . four days?"

He paused for a moment and glanced at Morgan, who nodded and extended the four fingers on his right hand.

"Yeah, so if you make it through the next four days, you should be ready for just about anything. Not many cadets get challenged like this during their academies."

Randy held the attention of the group, but realized that he wouldn't have their ears for long, so he offered only a brief bit of advice.

"Drink lots of water, eat well, and take care of your feet. Get to bed early, and get some sleep. And be careful. One mistake out there can be very costly. Just stay focused, and it will be over before you know it, and then, you'll be cashing paychecks." His smile grew. "Good luck to you all."

His unwavering smile broadening, he shook hands with the three amigos from Coronado whom he knew, then looked over his shoulder and noticed that Lt. Morgan was standing with Cynthia and Latrelle. Morgan motioned for Shields to join them.

"Randy, this is Cynthia Harden."

Morgan paused and turned.

"And this is Latrelle Jackson. They both want to work for us this summer."

Randy nodded his approval.

"Excellent. I've actually had the pleasure of meeting Latrelle."

Latrelle replied politely, "It was my pleasure, sir."

Morgan and Shields smiled.

Shields continued.

"I saw you surfing on Arias' board last summer, right? Then again that day I gave your coach those job-posting flyers. It looks like you've been training very hard. Good for you, Latrelle."

"Yes, sir, I have been, and thank you for your encouragement. It's nice to see you again, Mr. Shields."

Randy chuckled.

"Please, Randy is fine."

"Yes, sir, of course."

Shields continued, turning toward Cynthia.

"And, Cynthia Harden, didn't you play water polo at Coronado High a few years back?"

"Yes, sir, that's correct. It's been a little longer than just a few years, though. I actually graduated in '91."

"Ah, yes. Coronado's girls won the championship like ten years in a row or something, right?"

"The streak actually ended at nine. My senior year was the last year of the streak, but they've won it a few times since then, too. Now these grommets here are killing it on the boys' team."

Cynthia nodded toward the three athletes she first met as giggling nine-year-old junior lifeguards who then, like now, dominated their competition. Randy acknowledged the boys with a knowing smile and pointed at them before returning his attention to Cynthia.

"Didn't you play in college, too?"

"Yes, I did, but that's a long story. I played my freshman year at UCLA, but then I left college and joined the Navy. After I got discharged, I considered going back to get my degree, but decided to start on a different career instead . . . so, here I am. I may still go back to school, though. Lifeguarding during the summers should make it easier to do that."

"Indeed. That's what a lot of us did before we got promoted to POL."

Randy continued as Morgan listened closely.

"You're definitely not the first to leave the Navy to join us."

Shields smiled, realizing that his time was up.

"I'm sure we'll have plenty of time for you to tell me the rest someday while we're on a vehicle patrol together. I look forward to it. Good luck to you both, and if there's anything I can do to help, don't hesitate to stop by the tower and ask."

Morgan walked with his good friend and shared his satisfaction with the group's overall performance and his optimism about their potential. He offered Randy a heads-up about a short list of cadets that he hoped would be heading Randy's way that summer. Harden and Jackson were first and second on the list.

The two men said goodbye, and Morgan returned to the beach so he could observe the remaining groups attempting to recover one of the sunken tires. He was thrilled when three of the groups recovered their "victims" within 10 minutes and watched proudly as the last two groups combined their efforts. Lt. Morgan watched closely as Cadet Marisol Escobar organized and led the combined group's diving repetitions. He continued watching Escobar giving commands as her group located, recovered, and rolled the last two bulky, cumbersome tractor tires up the steep, sandy beach.

Morgan made a note in his mental file.

*She definitely knows how to lead and give orders. Mayor Peete will be pleased.*

**16**

Tuesday, March 25, 1997
Ocean Beach

The two physical tests on Day 6 were extremely demanding, untimed, completion-only challenges. Most of the cadets completed the courses with little regard for their finishing positions, instead focusing cautiously on ensuring their completion of the events. The tall wave height, combined with the short interval of time between each wave, made the courses extremely difficult to navigate. Spotting the buoys in the huge surf was next to impossible, and maintaining an accurate course and direction toward them required the cadets to look up constantly, slowing their pace and frustrating them.

Mitchell Brennan and Colin Cantrelle, two of the Coronado water polo players, dominated a three-lap run-swim-run course that required the cadets to use fins and a rescue buoy. Latrelle, again, finished the event in front of Cynthia after she missed the same wave that he rode all the way in, his forearms and chest resting on the hard red buoy that he used like a boogie board. Once on the beach, he sprinted across the wet sand and grabbed stick No. 3, finishing only a couple of strides behind Colin.

Latrelle rested briefly with his hands on his knees, slightly disappointed that he still hadn't captured stick No. 2. He stood up, rested his arms on the top of his head to help lower his respiration rate, then turned to see Cynthia stroking in through the shallow water. He began encouraging her when he noticed that Andrew Ramsey, the third member of the Coronado trio, was gaining on his training partner.

"Go, Cynthia . . . Goooo!" Latrelle shouted.

Cynthia was slightly annoyed that Latrelle had beaten her again, but when she heard him shouting support, it soothed her ego immediately. After exiting the water well ahead of Andrew, she sprinted to the finish line where Latrelle, Colin, and Mitchell all met her with enthusiastic two-handed high fives. While she leaned forward, resting her elbows on her knees in an attempt to catch her breath, Latrelle offered her praise and encouragement.

"Way to finish strong, Cynthia. That's an excellent job. We only have four more days. Keep it up."

Cynthia offered similar words as they patted each other on the back and arms. Colin, Mitchell, and Andrew joined them and did the same as the top-five-rated cadets all stood at the finish line cheering and high-fiving their classmates who lunged across the deep sand and reached for the tongue depressor with the next lowest number on it, hoping to increase their chances of being hired, as well as to move up just one rung at a time on the Patrol's ladder of seniority.

Despite being the only African-American cadet enrolled in this academy, after venturing away from his Lincoln Heights teammates, Latrelle appeared very comfortable among the much larger group of Caucasian cadets. He seemed particularly comfortable around Cadet Harden, and others could see that she was totally into him as well.

Even though Cynthia knew that Latrelle was much younger, she couldn't deny the chemistry she felt. She thought about how close she and her training partner were becoming. *Six years difference is not a big deal. He's going to grow up into a hell of a man, and he's already an unbelievable specimen now.*

She caught herself though, and redirected her own thoughts. *Stay focused, and do not get distracted. One thing at a time.*

Cadet Escobar was still on her way out to the buoy on the final lap at Ocean Beach while Latrelle, Cynthia, and several other cadets stood at the finish line. Only a small group of cadets trailed Escobar when she plucked stick No. 31 out of Instructor Pena's hand. Cynthia shook her head subtly and snorted, then headed up the beach toward the pop-up tent where her gear was stored.

Just after Cynthia walked away, Cadet Colin Cantrelle moved in quickly beside Latrelle and said, "Are you guys hooking up or what?"

"Nah man, we're just friends. She's pretty cool, though, huh?"

"She's a legend in Coronado, bro. Everybody loves her over there. She's got a hell of a past, though, from what I hear. I heard a rumor that she got pregnant during her junior year and had an abortion. You might want to look into that . . . I'm just sayin'."

Latrelle stared at Cantrelle and said nothing. He then turned to look for Cynthia and spotted her standing next to the flapping pop-up tent that looked as if it might get blown away by the gusty winds. She looked back at him and considered her new partner. As she retrieved her towel, she again heard Nico's voice.

*Just be a teammate, right? Be nice to these men . . .*

She liked the thought of being Latrelle's teammate . . . and of being nicer to him. When she noticed that he was still looking at her, she smiled and waved enthusiastically.

At first, Latrelle did not smile, but instead, he looked at her with a confused expression on his face. After a moment, he waved back, then turned away and rejoined the group at the finish line.

Tuesday, March 25, 1997
Ocean Beach

Gathered around their cars parked in the OB lot, Cynthia, Latrelle, Mitchell, Colin, Andrew, and a few others discussed where to go for dinner. Colin turned away and walked toward the street.

"Dude, I'm fine with a carne asada burrito right here at El Rodeo."

A voice from the crowd offered an alternative plan.

"Let's all go someplace warm where we can sit down and get waited on. There's an awesome pizza place over in Point Loma on Midway. They have hot sandwiches, great burgers, and a massive salad bar, too. I need a good meal."

There was some discussion about money and how far it was to drive, but a group of 15 or so gathered in various cars and prepared to head out. Latrelle was already sitting shotgun in Cynthia's 4Runner when Marisol and his Lincoln Park teammates approached the vehicle. Gustavo peeled away from the small group first, then shook hands with his close friend.

"Sup, homie? You killin' it out there, dawg."

"You too, ese."

"You goin' to eat, bro?"

"Yeah, a pizza place just over the hill, down in Point Loma, I guess."

Gustavo turned and looked at his coach and the rest of their group standing on the curb. Before he could speak, Latrelle invited his team.

"Coach, bring them all to eat with us. Just follow Cynthia."

Marisol resisted the urge to blurt out, *That'll be the day*, but she looked at her team members and shrugged.

"Is that okay? Is that what we want to do?"

The group replied in the affirmative, and moments later a caravan left the lot, arriving at the restaurant 10 minutes later. The cadets finished ordering their dinners, and, one by one, excused themselves to the restroom.

Cynthia was washing her hands in a vanity sink, a large mirror hanging on the wall in front of her, when Marisol cautiously walked in. Cynthia looked up and met Marisol's eyes in the glass for a long count before she looked down and turned up the hot water.

A few moments passed before Cynthia muttered, "Escobar."

Marisol replied as she headed into one of the stalls, "Harden."

Cynthia continued washing her hands while Marisol sat behind a neglected and poorly-painted white plywood wall that displayed names, phone numbers, and a few sophomoric images written or drawn in various colors of Sharpie ink. As her bladder emptied, it made a discernible hissing sound that resounded in the small, quiet room. Cynthia heard the paper holder turning before the toilet flushed loudly. Marisol unlatched the lock, pushed slowly on the shabby door that was held in position by an old, squeaky spring, then moved to the vanity. The two women stood side by side, their shoulders less than a foot apart. Neither spoke as Cynthia looked in the mirror and ran her wet fingers through her tussled hair. With a scowl, Cynthia glanced briefly at Escobar, then turned and stepped toward a paper towel dispenser that hung on the wall behind them. Marisol watched through the mirror as Cynthia ripped away three sheets of paper, one at a time with one hand, while aggressively cranking the handle with the other. She noticed Cynthia's wide back muscles flexing through a tight, long-sleeve t-shirt, and thought, *She looks like a man. What could Latrelle possibly see in her?*

Cynthia dried her hands, tossed the bundle into the can, and just as she reached for the door handle, Marisol said, "So . . . Harden . . . I hear you were some kind of fully-trained diver in the Navy before this. That must give you a hell of an advantage out there, no?"

Cynthia didn't reply.

"I mean, you're like a pro already. It's pretty obvious."

Cynthia turned slowly and said, "I'll take that as a compliment."

Marisol snorted. Without looking up, she said, "So, why aren't you still in the Navy? What happened? Why are you here? You couldn't keep up with the real men?"

Cynthia laughed. "Haven't you been watching? That, Escobar, has never been a problem for me."

She was about to continue but stopped herself.

*I am definitely not going to discuss anything personal with this poser.*

Cynthia redirected the conversation.

"I went in on a Navy college program. I only signed on for four years. Why do you care?"

"Mmmm, well, that's nice. Good for you . . . and I really don't care. I was just curious. It doesn't really seem like much of an upward movement to me, though. I'm just wondering why you want to be here so badly. You're obviously over-qualified for a seasonal lifeguard position . . . at least physically you are."

Cynthia remained silent and crossed her arms. She tilted her head, an amused, thin-lipped smile forming.

Marisol kept her back turned, looking down as she rinsed her hands.

"You know, Harden, people with physical advantages don't always turn out to be the best leaders. Leadership ability is different from those physical gifts that one receives at birth. True leadership ability is learned. That's what they're looking for in this agency . . . you know, true leaders . . . people like me."

Cynthia frowned.

"What?"

"Yeah, leaders . . . people who lead other people. People who gather people together. People who actually speak to other people and inspire them. You're obviously not interested in any of that."

With her forearms still folded across her chest, Cynthia leaned against the door, glaring at Marisol.

"Oh, this ought to be good. Go ahead, Escobar. Enlighten me."

"You *could* be a leader, though, but it seems like you just don't care. Can you not see how distant you are? Especially toward the other women, and to me, in particular. I don't get it. Why is that?"

Cynthia raised an eyebrow, but remained silent.

"As women, we have to support each other, or we have no chance against all of these men. The men obviously have an unfair advantage, not only physically, but socially, too, with decades of bias directed against us. Just ten years ago, women wouldn't have even considered a job like the one you and I are going after. Not to mention the fact that the entire hiring and promotion committee is still comprised entirely of men."

Marisol turned and faced Cynthia.

"Do you understand what I'm saying?"

Cynthia replied calmly, "What unfair advantage? Obvious to whom?"

Marisol changed her tone, snarky. "Oh, my bad, I forgot, you're Scuba Cindy . . . a real life superhero. You're not like the rest of us . . . you can do the job better than any man can, right?"

Cynthia shrugged.

Marisol continued.

"I understand how you feel. I feel the same way, just not about the same kind of job."

Cynthia said nothing.

"All of my swimmers have been trained in organizational leadership. Actually, I trained them, but we are *all* going to get promoted quickly. It is *our* time to become leaders in this city."

"What I've noticed, Escobar, is that a bunch of *people* have failed already. Men *and* women. There's nothing unfair about that. And if I were you, I wouldn't think too much about a position of leadership just yet. We still have four days left. Let's see if you and your *organizational leaders* can make it to graduation day."

"We will, don't you worry. And don't overlook the fact that you're just a woman as well, Harden. Even though you may look the part, these men aren't going to take you seriously. Eventually, you're going to need somebody else's support to get what you want. You might want to consider that approach instead of making yourself an island to everyone in this academy except Latrelle Jackson."

Cynthia sighed and shook her head. *There it is. I knew that's what this was all about.*

"Look, Escobar, I have no idea what you're talking about, so . . . whatever. And who I make myself an island to is none of your business."

"Latrelle Jackson is my business. Let's be clear about that."

Cynthia glared at Marisol. *Are we really going to do this? Right here in the freaking restroom?*

"Look, Escobar," she said. "I've only got two things on my mind right now: food and sleep. So, I'm done with this."

Cynthia turned away, opened the door, and said, "Nice chatting with you, Marr-ee-sole."

Marisol replied sarcastically, "Not really."

Cynthia froze. She looked down at the floor and closed her eyes, trying very hard to remain calm. She turned toward Escobar, looked up, and glared at her for several long, silent moments. Then, with contempt in her eyes, she slowly looked down and noticed a pair of expensive, bedazzled sandals and brightly painted toenails.

She snorted, "Pfff," looked up into Marisol's eyes, shook her head from side to side, then turned and walked through the bathroom doorway.

**18**

Late Evening
Tuesday, March 25, 1997
Morgan Residence, La Jolla, California

Lt. Morgan sat with his wife on their back patio, enjoying a grey and orange, cloudy sunset. The Morgans' two Rottweilers were taking turns retrieving tennis balls that Morgan's wife, Linda, tossed across the lawn when Richard picked up a ringing wireless phone handset and extended its antenna.

"Hello, this is Richard."

"I'm hoping to get a positive update on Marisol Escobar."

Mayor Peete hadn't spoken with the lieutenant about the academy since one week before it began. After their meeting that day, Peete had reiterated the importance of Marisol Escobar's success. He had also mentioned how impressed he was by the information Morgan's secretary had forwarded to him about Cadet Harden.

Morgan recalled the conversation with Peete about Cynthia Harden. *"A Navy dive team member with two commendations, an E-6 rating, AND a former All-American at UCLA? How did we find her, and what's she doing here?"*

*"She found us, sir. I've been wondering about that myself, but we're*

*obviously very fortunate that her path somehow led to us. She may be the female leader that we've been looking for . . ."*

The mayor's voice snapped Morgan out of his reminiscence.

"Richard, are you there?"

"Oh, I'm sorry, sir . . . Escobar. Well, she's still with us."

"That's not a ringing endorsement," Peete groaned.

"Sir, to be frank, she hasn't really earned one yet. She came very close to failing already. The weather is terrible, as you know . . . so, this academy has been extremely tough, and it isn't getting any easier. She may not make it. Nearly twenty cadets have already failed, and I'm guessing we'll lose a dozen more if the weather gets any worse. She picked the worst time possible to go through our tryout program."

Morgan heard the mayor sigh.

"Do all that you can, Richard. We need her to make it to graduation."

"I understand, sir, but that's not up to me. That's up to her."

Peete breathed deeply again. Sounding concerned, he said, "I was hoping she'd be stellar out there."

"Stellar, sir? No . . . not in the ocean, at least. She has aced every written assignment, has done well on the practical medical exercises, and she has shown strong leadership abilities. She's assertive, strong-willed, and she definitely has the respect of that group from Lincoln Heights. What she has demonstrated so far is consistent with the briefing you offered, but I am concerned about her level of competence out there in the ocean, Eddie. Swimming in these ocean conditions is absolutely nothing like swimming in a pool. It's beaten a lot of very good swimmers over the years, sir."

Peete did not reply.

"If you want to see stellar, though, you should come out and watch Cynthia Harden. Seriously, not even in my finest hour could I keep up with this athlete. She's the real deal. Her résumé is legitimate. She's very talented . . . special."

Peete remained silent.

"Mr. Mayor?"

"I'm thinking . . . and I'm not sure what this Escobar family has gotten me . . . uh . . . *us* into. If you're telling me that Marisol may not graduate . . . well, we're definitely going to hear about it from her mother, I guarantee you that. I can't afford that."

"Well, sir, I guess we'll just have to cross that bridge when we get there."

"No, we need to make sure that she gets over that bridge now, Richard. I'm confident that you'll do everything that you can to get her and every one of her team members from Lincoln Park Aquatics through graduation day and onto our payroll sheets. You understand me, right?"

Mayor Peete continued before Morgan could reply.

"I've asked you for how many favors since we met, Richard?"

"Only that one."

"And how'd that work out?"

Morgan paused and said, "Better than I expected, sir."

"And how much of a sacrifice did you have to make to see those results?"

"As it turned out, not as much of a sacrifice as I thought it would be . . . just as you had assured me from the beginning."

"Well, Lieutenant, this a second favor I'm asking of you, and you should expect the same result."

Peete allowed Morgan a few moments to digest the request, which the Lieutenant had already realized was a demand.

"Richard, I am going to need the votes this woman's mother holds in her hands. I'm the only Republican that she's ever endorsed, but that's only because her husband endorsed me, but more importantly it's simply because she hasn't found a mayoral candidate that her party believes in . . . not yet at least . . . but when she does . . . this gig of mine may be up."

"Wait, she's a Democrat and she's supporting your campaign, I think I may have missed that part."

"That's correct Lieutenant. Let's just say it wouldn't be prudent for her to come out into the open and announce to the world that one of the Democratic party's most outspoken activists is donating, and getting others to donate, to various 501C groups and that those funds are being designated as campaign contributions to the man who defeated their party's candidate."

"Sir, I realize that you didn't share very much about your campaign strategy, and you obviously didn't need to, but you didn't make it clear to me just how important this woman is to your success."

"I didn't think I would have to. Richard, you're the only city employee I've ever mentioned this to . . . and I'd like to keep it that way. I'm not pleased that it has come to this either. I'm hoping that she doesn't make me any other offers like the one she's already made."

"Sir?"

Morgan heard the sound of ice clinking on glass and the mayor swallowing.

Peete breathed in deeply and exhaled loudly.

"Richard, this woman locked onto one of my first campaign promises, back when I was still on the city council. I was very outspoken about upgrading our parks and recreation facilities and programs. She approached me long before the election with an offer to support my campaign and offered to help us upgrade our aquatics program in particular . . . as long as her daughter would receive the first right of refusal to become the director of those new programs."

Morgan listened closely.

"Dr. Villareal told me that her group had enough money set aside to completely rebuild the facility down in Lincoln Heights. She and her husband have a foundation that underwrote nearly half of that project's funding."

Morgan interrupted, "Eddie, that has to be over a million bucks."

Peete laughed.

"You underbid, Richard."

"Holy crap."

"Yeah . . . exactly. They made it an anonymous donation, so it would look like I was responsible for finding those dollars, and obviously so that Marisol would be protected from scrutiny. In a manner of speaking, she and her husband made me an offer that I just couldn't refuse. It was a sweetheart of a deal for me and for the city, but most importantly, it was designed to pave a smooth road for Marisol's not-so-distant future in politics."

Morgan sighed, "Well, you did say that she has done a good job."

"Yes, she has, but they can still pull their support for me faster than you can recite the alphabet, Lieutenant. I promised them that their daughter would continue to move up quickly."

Morgan remained silent and listened closely.

"As you know, Richard, there is a vast void of female leadership under your command. Marisol now has an outstanding résumé and she has built for herself a solid reputation as a leader. She is going to become a much bigger part of this city's future, Rick, and a much bigger part of your future too."

Peete paused and took another gulp.

"Do you understand me?"

Morgan stared across the lawn at Thunder and Boomer who were now playing tug-o-war with a thick-knotted rope. His face was expressionless and his tone was flat.

"Of course, Mr. Mayor. I'll do my best, sir."

**19**

Day 7 of Academy
Wednesday, March 26, 1997
Imperial Beach, California

On Day 7, the surf in the South Bay was even bigger than the previous day in Ocean Beach. Just after sunrise at 0700, the cadets met at the foot of the pier on Imperial Beach, many of them staring out at the tall waves that caused the ground to shake when they broke onto the foamy, swirling ocean surface. Following a short safety lecture, they were ordered to put on their wetsuits, grab their rescue equipment, jog to the end of the pier, and execute another jump onto the tops of tall, rolling waves.

They lined up in pairs along a wooden rail on the south side of the rustic pier and prepared to execute tandem rescue board victim retrievals. The cadets who played the role of victims jumped in first and gave the all-clear sign that indicated that they were ready to proceed with the drill. Six at a time, the "rescuers" carefully dropped their long, soft-top rescue boards over the railing and jumped in. After retrieving their boards, the rescuers paddled to their victims and assisted them onto the decks of the boards. The rescuers were instructed to slide up in between the victims' legs and place their own chests directly on top of the victims' buttocks to secure the victims' bodies in place on top of the board.

Cynthia and Latrelle were in the second group and watched the first group of rescuers struggle as they climbed on top of their victims. Latrelle looked at Cynthia, who shook her head. She smiled and asked him the obvious question.

"You want to get on top of me first, or should I get on top of you?"

Latrelle replied quickly without smiling.

"Oh, no, you go first. You have more experience than I do."

Cynthia thought she noticed a different tone in Latrelle's voice, and looked at him quizzically, but did not reply as they listened to Instructor North describe the drill to the second group.

Their challenge would begin just outside the surf line, where the rescuers would paddle their victims in through the tall, closed-out waves on the south side of the pier, and would end when the duo landed safely together on the beach. Only a few cadets completed the mock rescue effectively. More frequently, boards and bodies flew in all directions, both rescuers and victims bailing out and diving beneath the tall waves with no regard for their long, sturdy piece of rescue equipment. Their boards now swept onto the sand, the cadets were required to swim in from over 100 yards offshore, retrieve the board, jog to the end of the pier, and start over again. The cadets quickly learned how demanding and dangerous it is to operate a rescue board in heavy surf. Morgan and North shook their heads and discreetly giggled or groaned. Expert paddler, Senior Instructor Alex Pena, remained stoic as he watched cadet after cadet being thrown over the falls. Fortunately for everyone that morning, the group avoided any injuries, the worst fear of the academy's director.

After a while, Pena saw it was time to demonstrate proper technique to the group. He grabbed a 10-footer and an intern, and they sprinted to the end of the pier. Swiftly, the duo leapt over the rail. Pena pulled his victim onto the board in an instant and began rapidly paddling. He timed his entry into a tall wave perfectly and guided the board into ankle-deep water, where both watermen popped up and bounded across the wet sand. Pena, wearing only trunks and a sleeveless neoprene top, laughed with satisfaction as he exited the water. After observing this display of skill and athleticism, most of the cadets, including Cynthia and Latrelle, shook their heads in admiration, realizing how much they still had to learn.

Since so few in the group had gained proficiency under the severe practice conditions, Morgan shut down the rescue board training session, and the testing scheduled for later that morning was postponed. Morgan, North, and Pena knew that they had pushed harder than they should have, but the lesson provided an outstanding example of what not to do.

Pena gave the brief lecture.

"One drowning is ALWAYS better than two. If the conditions require the rescuer to stand down, and the victim drowns . . . well, that is a decision that must be left up to the rescuer. Jumping off the pier with a board to make a rescue *might* be your best option, but bringing that victim in through tall, heavy, closed-out surf is definitely the *worst* option."

He paused hoping to add clarity.

"Once your victim is secured on the board, the emergency is over, right? Unless your victim is unconscious, not breathing, or is bleeding heavily, you can wait out there all day for a long lull in the surf or for a rescue vessel to come out and assist, right?"

He stopped and looked around the semicircle of cadets as they attempted to warm themselves in their already-damp parkas and towels. He paused another moment to let the lesson settle in.

"If you practice and learn how to handle a board in the surf like I can, then go ahead. Otherwise, just take a can and fins and swim your victim in under the wave. Don't get tossed over the falls and lopped in the head with your board, like these three kooks from Coronado did."

Pena playfully mocked and pointed at the three amigos, who had also struggled that day. Colin Cantrelle was the finest paddler in the group, and his trial was one of the few solid performances. He had nailed his wave mid-face with the tail down and the nose up perfectly, and was cautiously guiding the board toward knee deep water when his victim got anxious, lost his balance, and pressed down on the front rails of the long board. The nose of the board sank instantly and sent them both tumbling forward off the board and into the shallow water.

Pena's attempt to lighten the moment succeeded only briefly. There was some light laughter from the group, but the cadets were all humbled by the surf, the weather, and the dangerous training exercises the academy's director required them to complete. Nobody was in the mood to laugh for very long on Day 7.

**20**

Wednesday, March 26, 1997
Imperial Beach

The previous three days on the oceanfront had included heavier, taller, and more powerful surf conditions than Lt. Morgan could remember during any previous academy. He was well aware of these unique circumstances, and his chest swelled with pride at the remarkable and determined group of cadets he directed.

The day's training Morgan prescribed was a triangular course of three laps of swimming around the Imperial Beach pier and three laps of running through the soft sand from Elkwood Avenue, north about a quarter mile, to Dalia Street. Morgan knew that his expectations were very high, but his instincts told him there was wisdom in his decision to continue pressing. Using these conditions, he hoped to determine which cadets had the right stuff to become major contributors to the long-term success of his agency. He also knew that by pushing them too hard, he could lose a few exceptional candidates. If that happened, those who were truly committed to getting a job as an ocean lifeguard could try again at the next academy, during the fall when the water would likely be much warmer and the waves would almost certainly be smaller.

Morgan's appraisal was affirmed before the cadets began their second lap, when one of the cadets refused to enter the water. She didn't want to stop, but she was shivering uncontrollably, her teeth were chattering, and her lips had turned bright purple. She was obviously freezing cold, frustrated, dejected, exhausted, and very angry.

"Lieutenant Morgan, this has gone way beyond ridiculous. These tests are no longer reliable for this tryout program, and they've become redundant and unnecessarily dangerous."

The lieutenant had been monitoring the course, looking at the ocean with binoculars, so he did not recognize the voice. He lowered his glasses and turned to see Cadet Escobar standing at his side.

"I've trained lifeguards myself, Lieutenant. This is unacceptable, and you know it. You're going to get someone hurt. What are you trying to prove?"

Lt. Morgan was taken off guard. He could not recall being addressed so aggressively by a cadet, and was unsure how to respond. He paused and squinted at her, carefully considering the words he would use in his reply.

"Marisol, this is an untimed event. If you need to take a little extra time to collect your wits, then do so," he began. "Like any other PT, however, if you do not complete the course, I will be required to dismiss you from the academy. Those are the rules you agreed to when you registered for the academy. You signed the form. The choice is yours." He paused, turned and looked out at the ocean, scanned from south to north and back, looking for trouble. Seeing none, he turned to Marisol and continued. "I have at least a dozen instructors and interns out there on the course, so if you get in trouble they'll pull you out. It's up to you, though. If you want to continue your pursuit of this job transfer that you said you wanted, then there's the course. Complete it, and you'll move on to the next day."

Escobar didn't hesitate.

"Who do you think you are? You can't be serious. How many people have you failed already? Do you even care about them?"

Morgan did not reply.

"Look at how badly these people are struggling. Everyone is exhausted, Lieutenant. They're freezing. This is absurd. Nobody goes swimming on a day like this anyhow. There's nobody out there to rescue!"

She pointed toward the end of the pier.

"I'd like to see you go out there."

Morgan didn't flinch.

"Miss Escobar, I've already passed this academy and many other advanced lifeguard training programs that were much more demanding than this one. These conditions are nothing I haven't handled before. But this isn't about me. It's about you and the other cadets. That's my only focus today."

Escobar scowled and shook her head.

"Do you even know who my mother is, Lieutenant? Is this really where you're going to draw your line?"

Morgan still hadn't met the important woman Mayor Peete had briefed him about, but he figured now that a meeting might be coming soon. In the meantime, he remained calm and professional.

"No, I do not know who your mother is, and at this moment, it doesn't matter."

Escobar, with contempt in her eyes, shouted angrily, "You're an arrogant ASS, Lieutenant. I'm not putting myself out there for a man like you. But you'll be hearing from me again, and very soon. I promise you that."

Escobar then removed her academy-issued rash guard and threw it directly at Lt. Morgan, the wet garment glancing off his left shoulder. He held his ground, but said nothing. Her behavior left the few cadets who had witnessed the meltdown somewhat dumbstruck. Tiny Claritza Montoya had also refused to continue, and while standing by her coach and mentor, with a less-aggressive underhanded motion, she also tossed her rash guard directly toward the lieutenant.

A third cadet, an exhausted and overwhelmed male who continually finished toward the bottom of the pack, finally reached his breaking point. He could barely speak when he approached Morgan and muttered softly, "I'm giving up, Lieutenant. I no longer want to be a lifeguard."

Cynthia and Latrelle missed most of the dramatic scene, but as they ran across the sand, they could see three cadets gathering their gear, preparing to leave the beach. When Latrelle recognized Escobar and Montoya, he broke his stride, startled.

"Wait. What happened to them? Did they quit?"

"Looks like they did . . . that's a bad decision."

Cynthia concealed her next thought. *I knew she would quit. Bye bye, Coach.*

Resuming their pace, they made eye contact with the lieutenant, who yelled loudly toward them, "Harden! Jackson! Is it too cold out there? Are those waves too big? Should I stop this event?"

Cynthia slowed her pace and turned to face the academy director. She stopped and rested, placing her hands on the top of her head, fingers locked.

"Lieutenant, if you require me to do it, I'll do it. If you tell me to stop, I'll stop. Is it cold out here, and is the surf ridiculous? Well, yes . . . but I will complete the assignment."

She looked at Latrelle and nodded.

"And so will he."

"Very well then, we'll continue, and you be careful out there."

She turned, smiled at Latrelle, smacked him on the shoulder, and barked playfully at him, "Let's go, Stallion! One more lap, and don't let me beat you this time. Loser buys lunch."

She pushed him away from her to gain a lead, then turned, sprinted, and dove beneath the first incoming wave. She made it around the end of the pier first, then turned and sprinted cautiously into the surf. Latrelle was just two strokes behind when Cynthia caught a big wave and rode it all the way in to the beach.

In the huge surf at Imperial Beach, where she learned how to surf as a little girl, Cynthia finally beat Latrelle to the finish line. She waited there for him to finish, and teased him playfully when he arrived.

"I gotcha, suckah!"

Latrelle laughed and congratulated her, but still had a perplexed look on his face, as if he was wondering about the abortion rumor that Colin had mentioned yesterday.

As Cynthia cheered for the remaining cadets, Latrelle silently gazed at the ocean with a blank look on his face.

*How am I supposed to ask her about that? And where is the guy who did that to her anyway?*

**21**

Early Evening
Wednesday, March 26, 1997
Mission Valley, San Diego, California

The academy's afternoon schedule moved the cadets north to the wide, sandy beaches on Coronado Island, then onto the naval base and the private beaches of North Island to complete their day. Four cadets had suffered injuries in the violent shore break at North Island, and two of the injuries were so severe that it required Morgan, North, Pena, and some of the limited North Island staff to run a real-time medical call, ending with Instructor North transporting the injured cadets *Code 3* to the hospital. The incidents disqualified all four cadets.

And so the group of cadets shrank again.

Later that day, while seated at the bar at Bully's Restaurant, Morgan, North, and Pena reviewed the remaining 39 names on the roster. Morgan shook his head as he reviewed the names of the former cadets.

"There's a bunch of studs that have failed or quit."

North chimed in, his mouth full.

"Yeah, and one serious bitch."

Morgan nodded.

"No comment."

The lieutenant took a sip from a bottle of Coors Light before he said, "I will comment about these conditions, though. I can't believe this storm just keeps growing. I'm not happy about those injuries today either. That sucked."

He turned and looked at Pena.

"If they could only handle a rescue board before they got here, right?"

Pena nodded.

"It's a hard skill to develop, no doubt. Very dangerous. I'm sure after what happened today they aren't looking forward to taking one out in surf like that again."

The three men sat quietly for a few moments, each lamenting the injuries and the significant number of cadets they lost on the treacherous day in the South Bay.

Morgan changed his tone, sounding almost bitter.

"That was a bad choice those two girls made. They should have stuck it out."

North grunted.

"Ahhhhh . . . let 'em go, LT. Fuckin' crybabies."

"I'm not so sure this time, Bryce. I may have to answer to somebody about this. Those injured cadets may not go away quietly either."

North answered, "Shit happens. That's why we do this, to find out who's got what it takes and who doesn't."

Morgan shook his head.

"Nah, I think I may have raised the bar too high today. That was definitely the toughest day I can remember at any rookie tryout."

While listening to the lieutenant, Pena monitored the weather report on the television behind the bar. He revised the director's assessment, pointing at the large screen.

"Until tomorrow. Look at that radar image."

All three looked up and noticed a thick green and yellow swirling mass that covered over 300 miles of coastline between Santa Barbara and Tijuana. They remained quiet as each considered how the radar images would translate to conditions on the beach and in the ocean tomorrow.

After a few wordless bites of dinner, Morgan set his fork down on his plate, wiped his mouth with a napkin, took a deep breath, and sipped his beer.

"I haven't said a thing about this Cadet Escobar's family yet, and I really can't go into it too deeply with you guys. I will tell you this much, though. She's not going away without a fight. We haven't heard the last of her."

North declared, "She quit. How's she going to fight that?"

"It's not that simple. She showed me something today. The things she said could very easily be portrayed as the truth. She's not entirely wrong."

"Yeah, well, she's no waterman either. How many times did she finish in the bottom half?"

Morgan shook his head.

"She made it, though . . . every day until today . . . and even then, she quit, she didn't fail. She took a position, and she made a stand. She didn't really fail. She's protesting what she believes was a bad call on my part . . . she questioned my methods *and* my judgment."

North and Pena noticed that their lieutenant, a rock-solid decision maker that rarely expressed any doubt, had an uneasy look on his face.

Pena attempted to pick him up.

"Lieutenant, listen. We all know that pool swimmers have to learn the hard way. It takes a little something extra to become an ocean lifeguard. This is the only way to reveal that difference. The academy exposes their weaknesses. Swimming and running ability alone are not enough. This storm is offering us an opportunity to find some really high-level talent, you said so yourself. We can't back off now."

All three men nodded in agreement. Despite the bothersome drama that was certain to come along with Escobar's appeal, Morgan was still determined to find out precisely how qualified this group of cadets could become. Filling a high number of recently-created permanent positions increased his need for a larger pool of raw talent. He had already recognized a handful of cadets who had that talent. Morgan reviewed the short list of names in his head that included Jackson, Harden, and, as per Eddie Peete's instructions, Marisol Escobar and the swimmers from Lincoln Park Aquatics. The lieutenant considered Escobar's role in the future of his agency, a future that Mayor Peete had told him to do everything that he could do to ensure. Anxiously, he began to put the pieces together.

"Even before she said those things when she quit, I could tell that she had her own agenda. She wants to step in and take over as much as she can, as soon as she can. She's not here to serve, she's here to lead and make changes."

North appeared confused.

"What?"

"Yeah, from what the mayor told me, that's exactly what Escobar did as an aquatics supervisor. She created new operations policies and took over hiring, training, and promotions for all of the city's pools. She promoted as high as she can go, and she earned all kinds of awards and recognition along the way, too. That department is dialed in now. She's actually done a good job."

Pena laughed.

"She's got brown skin, too, Lieutenant, just like me . . . *and* she's a female. You know how that makes a difference these days. It finally helped me, I ain't gonna deny that."

North disagreed.

"Ah, bullshit Pena. You promoted because you're a professional, and you make gnarly rescues like very few others in this agency . . . not because you look like Erik Estrada."

Pena chuckled.

"Oh, you're hilarious."

Morgan and North laughed.

North continued.

"Hey, we all know that you shouldn't have gotten passed over the first time. That was BS."

"I know, but that's my point. Those guys that were promoted before me were all white boys, including you, Bryce. So, they *had* to give the next one to me, and we all know it. I would have filed some kind of a grievance if I had been passed over again, so they moved me up just in time. Things have changed, yes, but not as much as they're going to."

Morgan interjected, "I wasn't the Lieutenant then, and you know that I would have promoted you way before this comedian."

He nodded toward North, who said, "That is fucked up . . . even though it is true."

They all chuckled, ate and drank for a few moments, then Morgan continued.

"I'm not concerned about color or gender. I want athletes who think and react quickly like you guys. Whoever they are, they need to be strong, fast, and decisive in the ocean. Period."

"Amen," North offered. "That's the way it should be."

"I want tough-minded rescue personnel who will save lives in harsh conditions like today's, if necessary, and I want team players who are willing to learn and serve together. I haven't seen enough of this Escobar woman to determine if that's who she is yet, but after today, it would appear that she's neither."

He sipped his beer again and watched the television.

North stared at the food on his plate.

Pena broke the silence.

"Enough about her . . . whatever. There's plenty of good news, and we should be focusing on that, right?"

Morgan smiled, raised his bottle, and nodded at Pena.

"You're right. We get to select, train, and hire thirty new permanents, a dozen new sergeants, and at least two new lieutenants over the next decade. *They* will be the next generation of policy makers, and *you* guys are sure as hell going to help me find the right people to fill those spots."

"Well, she's your girl then, Lieutenant. Cynthia Harden can go the distance," Pena said.

North chimed in with his mouth full of rib eye steak and cheese enchilada.

"Affirmative, and that brother from Lincoln Heights is just as good. A woman *and* a black man, see that? And you guys think I'm just a backward-ass Okie from Muskogee. Nuh uh. Not true."

North chuckled, Morgan snorted, and Pena rolled his eyes. Morgan then pointed toward the television screen as the bartender handed him the bill.

"Well, pardon my French, boys, but by tomorrow afternoon, it looks like Black's Beach is going to be a *motherfucker*. We'll probably lose a few more. Be sharp tomorrow. It's going to get ugly out there."

He handed the bartender some of the academy's petty cash, told him to keep the change, waited for the receipt, and stood up to leave while his two subordinates continued eating.

North turned to his good friend, calling him by his nickname.

"LT, aren't you going to finish your beer?"

"Nah, I have to call Peete, and I don't want to say something I might regret."

Morgan stood up and excused himself, his head filled with thoughts about the harsh words Cadet Marisol Escobar had said to him earlier in the day. He was still unsure about what course of action she would choose to take, but he was certain that he and Mayor Peete were going to have a long talk about it tonight.

**22**

Later that Night
Wednesday, March 26, 1997
Morgan Residence

L t. Morgan considered stopping at his office to make the call, but he was too tired from the long day. He just wanted to get home to his family and their two dogs. Upon arriving, he gave them each hugs, kisses, or pats on the head, then went directly into the master bathroom to take a long, hot shower.

He felt much calmer after the soothing therapy and exited the shower stall refreshed. He stood in front of a mirror drying his body with a soft towel and looked himself in the eye, considering what he might hear from the mayor. He moved into the bedroom and, sitting on the bed, pulled on a pair of cozy pajama bottoms. He stood up, took three steps to his chest of drawers, and removed an XXL long-sleeved Chargers t-shirt as his wife Linda entered the room.

"Honey, Mayor Peete called while you were in the shower. He wants you to call him back tonight."

Morgan groaned softly, "Great."

He threw on the t-shirt, slipped his feet into warm slippers, and walked into the kitchen. He poured himself a small glass of cold milk and grabbed three chocolate chip cookies from the pantry. He removed the wireless phone from its base on the countertop, headed into the backyard, and closed the sliding glass door behind him before the dogs could escape to retrieve one of several stinky toys spread about the lawn.

As the Rotties sat staring through the glass, wagging their tails, Morgan calmly stared out at dark clouds hovering along the coast. He devoured the cookies, dunking each one into the milk before gulping it down and wiping his mouth with a shirtsleeve. He finally looked down at the handset and slowly punched in Eddie Peete's number.

Peete answered after one ring.

"This is Eddie."

*He was sitting by his phone; waiting for me to call,* Morgan realized.

"It's Richard."

"Ah, Lt. Morgan . . . I was hoping you'd call me back tonight. It's pretty late though. I thought I might hear from you a little sooner after today's events."

Morgan sighed.

"It was a long day, sir, but I'm fine. I assume you've been briefed already."

"I heard a few things. My secretary tells me the parents of a cadet that broke his wrist this afternoon are filing a grievance against the academy, the community college, the City of San Diego, and the North Island lifeguards. They claim that the conditions in North Island were brutally unsafe. They believe that your requirement to have the cadets paddle out into that big surf was the cause of this injury. They claim that you exposed their son to a hazardous risk. They say the injury was obviously unnecessary."

Morgan breathed in deeply before responding, "How many injuries have you heard of that were necessary, sir?"

Peete said nothing.

Morgan continued.

"All of the cadets sign a waiver and a hold harmless agreement. They accepted the hazards and the risks voluntarily. Imagine if one of them was attacked by a shark . . . would we be liable for that too, sir?"

Peete chuckled and said, "Those waivers aren't worth the cost of the recycled paper that they're printed on, Richard. You know that."

"Yes, sir," Morgan replied. "I'm taking care of it. I was on my cell with Risk Management and the cadet's father, while one of my instructors was transporting the injured cadet to the ER in Hillcrest. This kid is a little older, and he's no longer on their health plan. The emergency room bill alone is likely to set him back nearly a thousand dollars."

Morgan drew in a deep breath and waited for the mayor to reply.

Peete said, "My secretary also told me that this young man is going to have surgery . . . that both bones in his forearm snapped, and he's going to need metal plates to stabilize the joint. Did you talk to the boy's father about that?"

"No, sir, I did not. That is new information. I'll have Gabriella follow up with the orthopedist as soon as we know who that is."

Morgan paused. He could hear the sound of ice cubes tinkling on glass followed by a gulp.

Peete exhaled a long breath and asked, "What about the others?"

"I'm not sure what their course of action will be. We were also concerned about a cadet who hit his head falling off a rescue board. Concussion tests were negative, though. He was treated for dehydration and released. No concussion. My chief instructor drove both of the cadets to the hospital in one of our SUVs."

Morgan inhaled deeply.

"The other two injuries were treated at the scene. One was a dislocated thumb, caused by holding onto the straps of a rescue board for too long in the surf. We have a paramedic on staff, so he popped the thumb right back into place, taped it up real tight, and told the kid he should get an X-ray as soon as possible. The other cadet sprained his wrist after tripping on the lanyard of a rescue can. He'll be fine, too. All four were told that their fees will be waived if they want to return in August."

"Fair enough. Shit happens, I suppose. Just a really bad day, huh?"

"Yes, sir, it was. Thank you for understanding."

Both men were procrastinating. Injuries and minor grievances were nothing new, and they weren't very interesting to two of the highest-ranking men in San Diego County.

Morgan turned toward the sliding door when he heard Boomer's claws scratching the glass. He reached over and slid the door open, and his two tail-wagging best friends sprinted toward the first available toy.

Morgan knew that the mayor would start eventually, so he waited. Moments later, he again heard the sound of the tinkling glass, followed by another gulp.

He heard Peete take in a deep breath and exhale slowly before saying, "This tryout of yours is suddenly gaining a lot of attention, Lieutenant. My office received three separate phone calls today. All of them mentioned something about mandatory participation in unsafe conditions."

Morgan tilted his head downward, stared at his concrete patio deck, and rubbed his forehead with his fingertips. He breathed in deeply and took an inventory of his thoughts.

*No risk, no reward, Richard. These are only slight damages. The payoff will be worth it. Stay calm. Do not get defensive.*

"Yes, sir, it was pretty rough out there today. It has been all week, and it's likely to get worse tomorrow."

Peete replied quickly, almost pleading.

"Can't you tone it down a little bit, Richard? Give them a day off, and let this storm pass?"

*I could, but not just yet . . . one more day,* Morgan thought.

"Eddie, you know how I feel about the future of coastal safety. You and I share the same vision. This is just a simple ten-day tryout. If they can't make it through this, what good are they to us? Our beaches are way overpopulated, sir. We've discussed this many times."

"We have, but how does this storm have anything to do with our overcrowded beaches?"

"Sir, you've got to let me figure out how to find the right people to keep these crowded beaches safe. The bigger the crowds get, the higher the number of poor swimmers there are. My men and women are running ragged all summer. Hell, all year long. Our staff members are expected to be superheroes out there, they really are. You should come out in late July or early August. Sit for just an hour during a decent swell at Tower 2 in OB, or go down to Mission Beach and watch from the main tower."

"I know all about the number of contacts they make in a day, Richard."

"Hundreds, sir . . . in a single day, by a single rescuer. Do you know how many miles of sprinting across the sand that can be? Not to mention the toll cold water takes. It's very stressful to sit in those towers. We need more relief guards, Eddie. My full-time seasonal guards are working six, sometimes eight, hours straight without a break on hot, crowded summer days. And then they're picking up extra shifts, and working overtime to fill the duty roster some weeks. We simply don't have enough qualified bodies to give these crewmen the support they need, sir."

The line went silent except for the sounds made by ice gently touching Peete's scotch glass.

"I need to find people who can fulfill those roles, Eddie. This group I have now is loaded with them. I can push them harder still. Then I'll know who I can follow closely and perhaps promote sooner, rather than later. This year's group is going to provide a significant upgrade to our beachfront staff."

"I understand all of that. I get it, Lieutenant."

"I apologize, sir. I didn't mean to come across as condescending."

"You didn't . . . and I support what you're trying to accomplish. My primary concern, however, above all, Richard . . . is that Marisol and one of her female colleagues apparently will not be graduating on Saturday. Is this true?"

Morgan sighed.

"It is, and like you said, it was a really bad day. I attempted to convince her to keep trying . . . I really did. It seemed to me that she was more interested in questioning my methods and judgment than she was in accomplishing the task assigned to her. She was very bold, Eddie. It did not appear to me that she lacked experience questioning authority."

Peete took a long gulp of scotch and exhaled loudly.

"Ahhhh . . . I thought we would get through this thing easier. Jesus, Lieutenant, it's just three more days. That was the best you could do?"

Morgan paused, grateful that he didn't finish his beer and have a few more, like he was tempted to after the stressful day.

"Richard, that wasn't quite what I meant to say . . . but I thought we agreed that you would get this young lady and her constituents through this academy."

"We did, and I tried. It just didn't turn out that way. The conditions were brutal today, and she still almost made it. She quit, Eddie. She said it was too cold and the waves were too big. She said that it was too dangerous out there and that my methods were no longer a reliable measurement for qualifying seasonal ocean lifeguards. She called me an '*arrogant ass*,' then she dared me to swim out there."

The mayor laughed, heartily.

"If I had a dollar for every person out there that thought I was an arrogant ass, Richard, I would leave public service a very wealthy man."

Morgan barely skipped a beat.

"She dropped the *'Do you know who my mother is?'* comment on me, too."

Peete groaned, "Uhhhh . . . She said that?"

"Yes, sir. She looked right through me and laid it on me. She put on quite a display after that, and she took another girl with her. They both could have completed the course. It would have taken them a while, and they would have struggled, but they could have finished. They quit, they didn't fail. They chose to walk away when thirty-nine others kept on going."

The mayor paused to finish his drink.

"Ahhhhh . . . dammit. I'll figure out a way to take this hit somehow. You need to be prepared though, Richard. Dr. Villareal will definitely be coming after you. She smells your blood in the water, and she knows that she can squeeze me to get to you. She's going to make a demand that I will absolutely have to comply with. You know that I will have to pass that right on down to you."

"Fair enough, but whatever demand she makes, it cannot be for this summer, sir. Marisol quit. She'll have to pass the next academy in the fall."

Peete plucked a single large ice cube from a small bucket on his desk, dropped it into his glass, then poured another ounce of 12-year-old

Balvenie over the ice. He swirled the cube around in the glass for several moments, took a long sip, and spoke again.

"By the way, Rick, how's that other woman . . . the Navy girl? How's she doing?"

"Cynthia Harden? Don't even get me started. I could go on all night about how strong she is. We'll never get another one like her. She's the one, Eddie. She'll be our first female sergeant. She could make lieutenant. Hell, she could make chief someday."

"Just like her father, Richard . . . He was a master chief."

"Sir?"

"Yeah, Chief Harden . . . I didn't recognize the name that day when you sent me the fax, but I knew this girl's father. I actually served on carriers with Master Chief Gordon Harden. His crews serviced the Blackhawks that I flew in. He died while he was still a very young man, though . . . It was very sad and tragic . . . He is dearly missed by many."

"Wow. What a small world."

"There's a reason she's here. I'm not sure what it is yet, but I've no doubt it's something significant. Maybe it's to balance out this damn Escobar deal that I got myself into . . . I don't know. Whatever it is, though, you take good care of Cynthia Harden."

"That, sir, will not be a problem."

The mayor paused.

Morgan waited, knowing that it wasn't his turn yet.

"Richard, I don't have to remind you about the confidentiality that I depend on, right?"

"No, you do not, although I shared briefly with two of my senior instructors a little bit about Escobar's background with the city. And that we might hear from her again."

"That's fine. But let's be sure that our conversations about these two women . . . Escobar and Harden . . . and what we have discussed about their future roles in the DCS never comes up outside of me and you. I need both of these women to succeed quickly, Lieutenant, and I need it to look as if they both *earned* it."

"Roger that, sir. That certainly will not be difficult for Harden.

Escobar, however . . . that remains to be seen."

Peete chuckled.

"Yeah, well, that's not the only thing that remains to be seen. You just wait, Lieutenant, and you won't have to wait long either. We're going to find out just how delicately you can handle this woman's mother very soon. You will be tested, I guarantee you that. She's going to want to meet with you ASAP."

"I'll be there, sir, and I look forward to you directing me through it."

Peete gulped down the remainder of his third glass of scotch and breathed loudly.

"I need some sleep, Lieutenant, and so do you. I'm pretty sure we'll have to start dealing with this bright and early. You have a good night, Richard."

"Thank you, sir. Likewise."

Morgan hung up the phone just as Boomer dropped a wet, filthy tug-o-war rope on his thigh, took one step back, and barked at his master. Thunder hurried over and snatched the rope from his lap first, however, and scampered away, inspiring the large former football lineman with the crotchety knees to get up out of his chair and go teach those boys some manners.

**23**

Day 8 of Academy
Thursday, March 27, 1997
Black's Beach, San Diego, California

Against the hopes and prayers of every cadet, the swell picked up overnight, just as the forecast had predicted. It was rainy, cold, and windy at Black's Beach, and the cadets were informed that they would be required to complete a three-lap rectangular circuit from the high sand out to and around two barely-visible blue buoys located at least 250 yards offshore, 100 yards apart from each other. It would be an untimed, completion-only event.

To Morgan, this felt like a playoff game day from when he played college football. He knew that everyone had to perform their best to be successful today. He assembled his team of instructors and cadets safely away from the foot of the unstable rocky cliffs, about a mile south of the Torrey Pines Golf Club. Wearing navy blue parkas with gold trim, the group of cadets huddled together in a semicircle, three-deep, in front of their leader.

Lt. Morgan spoke firmly. He wanted to be sure that every cadet, as well as his staff, clearly understood that Ocean Beach, Imperial Beach, North Island, and every other location assignment that had preceded today's, were merely warm-ups for the challenges they would confront this afternoon at Black's Beach.

"I'm sure you all enjoyed being dry and warm in the classroom this morning. I appreciate how well you all did on your CPR and spinal board skill exams . . . congratulations. That concludes all classroom activities until the final exam on Saturday, which, as I stated before, requires a score of 80 percent or better in order for you to graduate."

Morgan paused and looked into the faces of the cadets, acknowledging each one.

"It's time to get wet again."

The group had learned to expect Morgan to be unrelenting, and even though they all knew that the time was coming for them to get back into the water, there was still a loud groan of disapproval. Many cadets were hoping for a reprieve, some complaining in small, quiet groups that Morgan's requirements had already become too much to endure.

He discerned their apprehension.

"Remember . . . days like today are the ones when even the most talented and experienced watermen might falter out there. These conditions place a particular demand on rescue personnel, a demand that exceeds all others. You may be expected to swim out into conditions like this for a number of reasons. This is the type of day when you will save the life of somebody that nobody would have expected to become distressed out there, and then need one of *us* to go out there and get them. It takes a hell of a waterman to want to be out in surf like this, but that type of person might someday need somebody to save his or her life. Today, you will prove to yourselves that you not only have that ability, but whether or not you have the willingness to put yourself in harm's way."

He stopped and pointed at the ocean.

"Right out there. Today."

He turned back, faced the cadets, and said, "Focus on your training. Be very sharp, and keep your eyes on the surf at all times."

He considered the huge surf for a moment before he pressed forward with his agenda.

"We'll go through a few rounds of unconscious victim retrieval, worst case scenarios . . . bleeding, broken bones, head injuries, heart attacks, diabetic emergencies . . . lots of trauma. Serious stuff, people . . . and we're going to do it methodically, efficiently, and properly. Then we'll do one PT at around 1500 hours."

Groans could clearly be heard over the loud surf.

Morgan nodded his head, empathetic.

"I understand, people, but I never promised any of you that this would be easy. Suit up, and muster with Mr. North at 1305. Good luck to each and every one of you this afternoon."

As the group began to break up, Morgan could still sense apprehension and fear in his cadets. He turned and faced the thundering surf, and realized that even he felt intimidated by the scene. He knew that his brief pep talk had not accomplished all that he had wanted it to. He watched the group move slowly and deliberately to the pop-up tent where they would change into their wetsuits.

Morgan whistled loudly three times, and immediately, the cadets reassembled in front of him at attention.

He said sternly, "Today, you will find out what you're really made of, and, so will I. Today, you will find out if you have what it takes to become one of the finest watermen the DCS has ever hired and trained, and, so will I. People . . . you are without a doubt the best group of rookies we've ever had. Do not let this day be the day that beats you! Work together, be patient and wise, and do things the right way. But, most importantly, be safe out there, and get this thing done! Good luck."

Morgan then turned, walked to his truck, and climbed into the driver's seat to get out of the rain. He allowed his cadets plenty of time to prepare themselves for the inevitable gauntlet that awaited them.

**24**

Thursday, March 27, 1997
Black's Beach

After the completion of several well-executed rescue drills and a 15-minute rest period, Mr. North called the group of cadets together and reviewed the run-swim-run course. He and his safety crewmen then entered the ocean to monitor the event, and at 1515 hours, Lt. Morgan sent the cadets into the ocean.

Twenty minutes later, nearly half of them were still struggling to get outside of the surf line on their first lap. Two cadets had already walked out of the water; they had given up trying. They did so at about the same time that Mitchell Brennan had exited the water, 250 yards south of the start/finish line, having completed the swim portion of lap one. Latrelle, Colin, and Andrew exited the water together about a minute later, and, as a group, they began a steady jog north across the wet sand.

On her first lap, Cynthia dove deep and dug her fingers into the sand in order to hold her position there. She clung to the bottom for at least 20 seconds, then kicked and pulled her way beneath and through the swirling energy of the first wave she encountered. After surfacing briefly, then diving beneath four huge waves, one at a time, repeating the technique to move beyond each wave, she made it outside of the surf line and swam quickly to the first buoy, where she made a left-shoulder turn and cruised south, along with the current. She rolled over and swam backstroke, so she could breathe easier and lower her heart rate. When she reached the second buoy, she rolled over and swam freestyle, picked her head up, looking forward every three or four strokes, and cautiously navigated her way in through another set of huge waves. She exited the water two minutes behind Latrelle, and, as she ran north across the beach, she noticed that there were two cadets standing together on the high sand, wrapping themselves in their towels and putting on their parkas.

The first time Cynthia dove beneath a wave on her second lap, she realized that her heart and respiration rates were now too high, and she could not stay underwater long enough to reach the bottom. She had to kick and pull against the incoming force of several large waves at or near the surface, while, at the same time, attempting to maintain the correct course and direction. Determined to get outside again, she dove as deep as she could, kicking and pulling with any residual strength she had, pushing the limits of her cardiovascular system, until she finally made her way out to the first buoy, where she rested, floating on her back, and allowed the strong current to assist her on her way to the second buoy.

She was extremely cold, shivering, and dehydrated. But her experience in the ocean gave her an advantage greater than brute strength or exceptional swimming ability could provide. Cynthia's courage helped her maintain focus in a potentially life-threatening environment, and despite the difficulty, she was pleased to find out how calm she had remained during the first two laps of the course. She was also very grateful for the months of training she had put in prior to attending the academy.

While running across the sand on her second lap, still in fifth place, she noticed that the group of cadets that were standing together on the beach, those who apparently had quit, had grown in number. Cynthia shook her head, thinking the same thoughts that she had at Imperial Beach the day before. *How can you come this far and just quit?*

**25**

Thursday, March 27, 1997
Black's Beach

Cynthia hesitated before she entered the ocean to begin her final lap. While briefly resting at the water's edge, she noticed how far most of the cadets had fallen behind, and that many of them were scattered about the course or had gathered into small groups of four to six. She could barely see Mitchell, who was swimming way outside the giant waves, heading south, approaching the second buoy on his final lap. He was at least 200 yards ahead of Latrelle, Colin, and Andrew, who swam together on their way out to the first buoy. Scanning the beach, she noticed that Lt. Morgan was standing tall in the bed of one of the academy's trucks, using a large pair of binoculars to visually sweep the entire area. He appeared anxious to Cynthia.

North was on the WaveRunner with a crewman, who precariously clung to the rescue sled, and four instructors, including Pena, patrolled outside the surf line on rescue boards. Several other interns, suited in neoprene from head to toe, were equipped with rescue buoys and fins, swimming along the course, ready to assist if needed.

Cynthia, feeling less confident and courageous, turned and waded into the pulling, frigid, knee-deep water. She felt intimidated when she noticed a giant set of waves approaching, so she decided to wait at the water's edge until the set cleared. She knew that attempting to get outside now was foolish and would quickly become counterproductive. She would waste all of her energy trying to maintain a steady position, only to end up way down the beach to the south. From there, she would have to run all the way back to where she stood now, just to try again.

Cynthia watched closely as the three cadets directly in front of her attempted to make their way outside of that approaching set of waves. The first wave had already risen to 15 feet in height and was still over 200 yards offshore, way out by the north blue buoy. Cynthia noticed that two of the cadets had barely made it over the foamy white lip of the growling wall of dark water. The third cadet looked to her to be in the worst possible position, and she feared that he didn't stand a chance against the wave. Her heart skipped a beat, and she felt a lump in her throat when she realized it was Latrelle.

*Oh my God, dive, Latrelle!*

Cynthia watched the wave's thick lip accelerate and curl, then land where Latrelle had taken his last stroke and hastily attempted to dive to safety. She heard the roaring wave face pound the surface and felt the ocean floor shaking beneath her feet as tons of seawater dumped on Latrelle and held him under so long that Cynthia, alarmed and frightened for his life, started running and yelled loudly, "Latrelle!"

Finally, she saw Latrelle's head and hands pop up through the foamy surface for a moment, when a second, larger wave crashed into him. Three more huge waves held Latrelle under water for 20, 30 seconds at a time, and drove him back inside and way down the beach to the south.

Cynthia was concerned that nobody else had witnessed the event and was convinced that she would be required to rescue Latrelle. But then she noticed Instructor Pena standing upright on his board, riding a giant wave like Laird Hamilton would have, had he been there. Cynthia realized then that Pena would assist Latrelle if he really needed to be rescued. She stopped running, slowed her pace to a jog, then walked toward the distant scene. She noticed that Latrelle's head now remained safely above the water's surface. She breathed a sigh of relief and said softly, "Thank you Daddy, I knew you'd be there for him."

She turned her attention back to the swim course and jogged well north of the first buoy, then skipped into the water, put her head down, executed a sequence of repeating duck-dives, and hoped for some help from a flashing rip current to take her out through the tall, crashing surf. As she swam out toward the buoy, Cynthia tried to remain focused, but, even though she knew he was out of harm's way, she could not clear the image of Latrelle getting pounded by the huge surf.

**26**

Thursday, March 27, 1997
Black's Beach

Latrelle found out the hard way that he still lacked mastery in ocean swimming. From the beginning of the final lap, he had blindly followed Colin and Andrew, determined to stay with them until reaching the sand, where he planned to sprint past them and finally snatch stick No. 2 at the finish line. As he settled into stroking toward the first buoy, he failed to consistently look up to see if any incoming waves were approaching. By the time he did look up, as Cynthia had witnessed, it was too late; that huge approaching wall of water had risen to nearly 20 feet, curled into a giant C, and crashed directly on top of him.

From Latrelle's perspective, the wave's impact had forced him down toward the ocean floor and tumbled his body in several different directions. Disoriented, he pulled with his hands and kicked with his feet, attempting to determine in which direction the surface was so he could breathe, but he could not escape the pulling mass of water. He was winded and vulnerable, afraid that he would not be able to make his way back to the surface. As he continued to tumble and spin, he wondered if he was starting to experience the first stage of drowning.

Latrelle's fear of being unable to get back to the surface and take another breath subsided slightly when the wave's grip released, and had offered him an indication as to which direction was up. But, before he could ascend, he was dragged down by another swirling eddy. He pulled and kicked with all of his remaining energy and restrained his growing instinct to inhale. A few seconds later, he broke the surface and gasped for air, having just enough time to take a second breath before he saw the next wave had already broken into a tumbling, swirling mass of water. Latrelle curled his body into a fetal position, hoping to protect himself from harm, but when the wave struck him, his shoulders, hips, and lower back were flexed beyond their normal range of motion. Latrelle felt muscles straining and severe pain radiating throughout his body as the wave imposed its will upon him.

He was pushed at least 10 feet beneath the surface, driven downward by the wave's inertia. He kicked and pulled until he felt himself moving upward through the swirling water. Piercing the surface, he gasped deeply, preparing himself for the next wave. He noticed that a third wave had already broken. He had time to take only three breaths, but enough to turn and dive toward the shore, hoping for the wave to push him into shallower water. Again he curled, this time holding tightly to his legs. He rolled like a ball, pushed by the 10-foot thick mass for several yards, but remained in control, aware, safe.

When Latrelle surfaced again, he was able to catch his breath, even as more incoming waves sunk him and held him down for several seconds. A couple of minutes later, he gratefully felt the bottom with his feet, bounced, and drove his body upward, toward the shore. Latrelle kicked and rode a smaller wave inside to a sand bar, where he knelt in the shallow water.

As Latrelle hung his head and rested his elbows on his knees, coughing and gagging on saltwater and foam, a surging inside wave knocked him over, sending him sprawling in the shallow water only yards from the beach, frustrating him further, causing him to yell out loud, "Enough! Stop it! You FUCKERS!"

Pena stayed close enough to Latrelle to assist if needed, but Cadet Jackson uprighted himself and began walking through the shallow water on his own. His heart and respiration rates were still quite elevated, and he was visibly shaken, but he was okay. But he still faced the challenge of completing the course.

Latrelle took about a dozen steps across the beach, then bent over at the waist and fell to his knees in the soft sand. He leaned forward and vomited several times until he regurgitated only clear bile. He began shivering violently and noticed that his head was pounding, and his ears were ringing and burning. He groaned loudly and reached up with both of his arms, gently curling his neck and tucking his head down between his forearms.

Latrelle stayed in the same position until he stopped vomiting. He lifted his head and chest, but remained on his knees and breathed in deeply. He wiped his face, exhaled, and raised one leg to stand, but was unable to. After several moments, he was able to use both legs and stood up. Eventually, he began walking toward the start/finish line, nearly 300 yards away.

As Latrelle approached the line, he noticed a group of cadets that were standing together, each wearing a parka. He was confused about how long he had been caught in the set of waves, and, for a brief moment he wondered if those cadets had completed the course ahead of him. His confusion cleared when he moved close enough to identify some of the individuals in the group that he knew and concluded that they had suffered a similar fate.

Lt. Morgan had been watching Latrelle closely, seeing him getting pummeled by the waves. It was only when he saw Latrelle stop vomiting and then stand up that Morgan removed his binoculars from his eyes. As Latrelle approached the lieutenant, Morgan was prepared to encourage one of his finest and favorite cadets to take his time while attempting to finish the required third lap, but when he noticed the ghostly color of Latrelle's skin, the rising and falling of his chest, his trembling and shaking, and the raspy, crackling sounds coming from his lungs, the lieutenant stopped himself. When he looked into Latrelle's sullen eyes, it almost brought tears to his own. It was obvious to the lieutenant that Latrelle Jackson would not re-enter the Pacific Ocean, and that his dream of becoming an ocean lifeguard was about to go "poof."

Latrelle could barely mutter the words.

"Lieutenant . . . I can't go back out there. Does that mean I'm out?"

Lt. Morgan placed both of his hands on Latrelle's shoulders and looked him in the eyes.

"Are you okay? Do you know where we are?"

"Yes, sir. Black's Beach. My head hurts, though."

"Did your head hit the bottom?"

"No, sir, I don't think so. My head hurts, though."

"You just said that."

Morgan recognized symptoms that caused him concern, and immediately brought Latrelle to the truck. He retrieved a large, dry towel and wrapped it around the young man's shoulders, then guided him into the climate-controlled front passenger seat. Morgan took a penlight from his breast pocket, checked Latrelle's pupils several times, and asked him a few more questions. After examining him for two minutes, he handed him a fresh, one-gallon bottle of water, a granola bar, and two extra-strength Tylenols.

Morgan stood close by and continued to monitor Cadet Jackson's condition.

"You caught a really bad break today, son. I'm really sorry. You're without a doubt one of the most talented cadets I've ever seen. Sometimes these things happen, especially on a day like today. You'll be fine though, just don't give up."

Morgan was betting on Latrelle's character, and he hoped the day's events would educate and prepare the developing waterman, and not discourage him. He had learned quickly that Latrelle had the heart of a champion, and wanted to persuade him to try again and not give up on his goal.

"Come back and try again this fall. You've got what it takes to compete for the Honor Guard award. You can finish number one at our next academy, Latrelle, and then I want you to come work for us right away."

Latrelle stared through the windshield and muttered, "Maybe."

The lieutenant sighed and patted Latrelle on the shoulder, then turned and placed his binoculars to his eyes and focused on the cadets that were still battling the harsh conditions.

Thursday, March 27, 1997
Black's Beach

Latrelle remained seated in the cab of the truck and took a long nap. When he awoke an hour later, the course was clear. During that time, the incoming high tide had peaked, a long lull had settled in, and the size of the sets had decreased, making it a little easier for the remainder of the cadets to complete the difficult course. High up on the beach, the successful cadets had gathered by the finish line, each of them proud and exhausted.

Latrelle exited the vehicle and could clearly see the group he had intended to be part of. Lt. Morgan, a bit more relaxed now that all of his personnel were present and accounted for, addressed the group of survivors. Latrelle attempted to listen, but the background noise from the heavy surf and the stiff onshore breeze made it nearly impossible for him to hear anything the lieutenant said.

Morgan was fired up as he congratulated the 30 surviving cadets. "In all the time that I have served as the director of this academy, what you just completed this afternoon was without a doubt the toughest physical test I have ever put a group of cadets through. The last two days were no picnic either. The water temperature is still only fifty-eight degrees, and we've seen the sun what . . . *TWICE* in an entire week?"

As Morgan spoke, he secured his floppy hat with one hand and leaned into the harsh and howling wind.

"That surf today had consistent ten-foot faces, with a couple of sets that were almost twice that size. I'm impressed. I mean it. You all need to take a moment and recognize what a feat you accomplished today. Look out there."

He waved and pointed toward the outside peaks that were still thundering. As far as they looked in either direction, the cadets saw tall white rollers lined up, one in front of the next, surging toward the beach like the blade of a giant bulldozer.

"I was a little anxious today, and I promise you this, I will never require any cadets to put themselves through what I just put you all through this afternoon. If it ever gets this big and this cold again, I will definitely shut it down. Nobody is ever going to be required to complete a PT like this one again, including—and most importantly—you all."

Morgan paused, turned his eyes toward his vigilant instructors, pointed at them, and said, "I'm sure they were thinking the same thing."

Then Morgan smiled at his ace instructor.

"How many times did you take that board out through that surf, Mr. Pena?"

The group howled and began chanting in unison.

"Pena, Pena, Pena . . ."

Each cadet had developed respect and deep admiration for the uber-waterman, who appeared to have much colder blood in his veins than they did. Pena smiled and nodded. He shook his head subtly, then took a step back after the acknowledgment, for he believed that this was the cadets' moment to be acknowledged, not his.

Morgan appreciated Pena's humility, nodded, and smiled at him.

He turned back toward his cadets and addressed them.

"Mother Nature isn't usually this harsh and relentless. I feel bad for those nine who didn't make it today. Getting dropped on day eight is a hard pill to swallow. I'm proud of all of them, however, for having the wisdom to stay on the beach and not go back out there. It may have cost them a job temporarily, but it did not cost them their lives . . . AND . . . they did not endanger the lives of anybody else."

Facing the stinging incoming drizzle and steady, cold onshore wind made focusing on the lecture challenging, and Morgan realized that the cadets' attention span was limited, so he raised his voice and increased his tempo.

"I saw a lot of caretaking out there and a lot of collaboration. That's what it takes to be an excellent waterman. You have to know your own limitations first. One lost life is always better than two."

He paused. He had their full attention again.

"You have to realize that you didn't create your victim's emergency. The victim did. We are not about getting dead while trying to save some citizen who just did something really foolish. We do not make that sacrifice. We are not soldiers. We are lifesaving men."

He paused again and pointed to the solo female cadet and beamed with pride.

"And you, Cynthia Harden, are a lifesaving WOMAN!"

The cadets and instructors roared their approval, but Morgan quieted them quickly and refocused their attention by raising his right arm, his hand open.

"People, listen. I am proud of you all, and it will be my privilege to work alongside any one of you. If you continue the way you have begun, no matter where you go, I believe it will be very difficult for human resources decision makers to look past you. I will give each and every one of you my endorsement, and if you choose to interview with the Patrol, I will hire you. Provided, of course, that you pass your final exam on Saturday."

The cadets shivered and their teeth chattered, and most of them were likely thinking only of the nearest hot tub or shower. Morgan knew this, and with an overwhelming sense of relief and the realization that he had pushed this group precisely to the threshold of their abilities, he felt satisfied as he dismissed the group.

"I'll see you lifesaving men and woman tomorrow at 0730 at the Del Mar main tower."

The lieutenant paused after noticing Pena shifting uncomfortably and hearing Mr. North loudly clear his throat.

"Disregard my last. Zero-EIGHT-thirty. You've earned an extra hour of sleep. Two more days, people. You're almost home."

Morgan nodded to Mr. North, who stepped to the middle of the group and shouted very loudly, "What kind of day is it?"

The cadets' response was as thundering as the surf and their cadence was impeccable.

"IT'S A GREAT DAY TO BE A LIFEGUARD, SIR! HOORAH!"

Cynthia Harden now knew for sure that she would make it to graduation. She had proven over the last eight days that there was no better-qualified female candidate for any lifeguard position, and she knew that leadership responsibilities and promotional opportunities would certainly come quickly. *Finally, I'm back on my way to the top, and this time, I'm staying put.*

But she first needed to reach out to the young man that she already missed having by her side. He was halfway up the hill, and she would need to be quick about it if she wanted to reach him before he drove away and out of her life.

**28**

Thursday, March 27, 1997
Black's Beach

Latrelle had heard just enough of the lieutenant's address to deepen his feelings of disappointment. His head wasn't hurting as badly, and, after drinking half of the water in the bottle and nibbling on the granola bar, he was beginning to feel a little better. He moved away from the truck and fetched his backpack from the tent. While walking off the beach, he attempted to feel some sense of gratitude for at least being alive, but sadness still overwhelmed him. When he heard the cadets' loud cheer, his disappointment turned into discouragement, and then grew into anger. He felt as if he'd been screwed. *Nine cadets failed today. All of my teammates failed. This is so unfair . . . If I had only seen that set coming . . . Dammit.*

Latrelle wasn't blind, but he rarely considered racial or cultural bias as a cause for success or failure. His mother hadn't raised him to think in those terms, and she wouldn't tolerate it anyhow, but this time, as he continued climbing the long hill from the beach, he became convinced that something was wrong. As he reached the top of the hill where his car was parked, he realized that the remaining cadets all had something in common. *They're all white. No minorities will be hired to work this summer.*

*That ain't right. Coach Escobar will know what to do.*

Latrelle unlocked the driver's side door, climbed in his car, and threw his equipment on the passenger seat. He reached into the glove box and retrieved his cell phone. He was just about to push the "send" button when he heard a voice calling his name. Latrelle looked into the rear view mirror and saw Cadet Harden running toward his car, waving her arm over her head with an expression of concern on her face. Cynthia was winded, and breathed heavily as she reached out and leaned onto Latrelle's forearm.

"Latrelle . . . I'm so glad I caught up with you. Are you okay?"

"I'm fine, but I'm not sure what to think right now. I feel like I should be given a second chance. I just couldn't go back out there, though. I couldn't breathe, Cynthia, and my body was like . . . frozen . . . I thought I was gonna drown. I really did."

Latrelle paused and took a breath.

Cynthia looked directly at him and remained quiet.

"No way I could have gotten back in that water . . . but I still think I'm way stronger than most of those guys."

"Latrelle . . . you *ARE*. You have to believe that. This is just a horribly unfortunate learning experience for you, and really . . . like Lt. Morgan told everyone else . . . you can come back in August and do it again. You will be rewarded then."

Latrelle looked down and leaned against the inside of the open car door. Cynthia reached out slowly, stopping just before touching his face. She lowered her hand and said, "I know you're disappointed, and I know how much you were looking forward to working this summer. Believe me, Latrelle, I've been through things like this before, and I'm telling you, you've got what it takes to overcome this. Don't let this get you down or cause you to get a negative attitude. I've never heard you say anything negative before, so don't start now. Really, Latrelle . . . it's just one summer."

Latrelle looked into Cynthia's eyes for a few moments before looking back down. Cynthia reached up, gently placed her fingers beneath Latrelle's chin, and raised it until his eyes met her own bloodshot, but still bright, blue eyes.

"By next summer, you won't even care about what happened today . . . *AND* you will be a better person for conquering this. Ninety percent of the world would just quit, Latrelle. They would make excuses and blame somebody else for their failure, too. You are not a quitter, you do not make excuses, and this was nobody's fault."

She waited for him to nod in agreement.

"I will not let you fail again, and I'm pretty sure that Lt. Morgan won't either. This is just a blip on the chart, Latrelle."

Latrelle was a little surprised by how interested Cynthia appeared to be in his life. His spirit lifted, and he thought, *Man, she is so nice to me, but this still sucks. Now I have to work for Marisol at the pool again this summer . . . and for half the pay I'd be making out here.*

He inhaled deeply, and as he exhaled, some of his feelings of bitterness and discouragement escaped. When he breathed in, he felt trust. He bowed his head at the thought of his mother, and the conversation he would soon have with her. Then he looked up, inhaled sharply, and blinked, causing one tear to drop from each eye. Cynthia moved to wipe away the tears, but Latrelle quickly used a sleeve to dry his eyes.

"My mother is going to be so disappointed."

"Oh, Latrelle . . . you are so sweet. I doubt that your mother has ever been disappointed in you. I am sure that she is proud of you and loves you very much. No matter what happens."

She moved closer to Latrelle, placed her hand softly on his chest, and felt the strong and steady beat of his heart.

"You *will* graduate from the next academy. I'll train with you all summer if you want me to. You *will* get hired, Latrelle. It's just going to take a little bit longer than you hoped."

After experiencing his vulnerability, the obvious love he had for his mother, and his passion about the job, Cynthia knew that she would support Latrelle Jackson no matter what. *I'm not letting him get away.*

Cynthia made sure that Latrelle entered her phone number into his phone, and then programmed his number into hers. She reached out with both arms, wrapped them around him, pulled him to her, and embraced him for several long moments before gently kissing him on the cheek. The taste of his salty skin enticed her to pull his face back and do it again, this time way more fully.

"Mmmmmmmmmmwaaah!"

With a beaming smile, Cynthia turned to leave, and Latrelle's eyes followed her. After several steps, Cynthia turned back, lifted her thumb toward her ear, and extended her pinkie toward her mouth. Very softly, she whispered, "Call me."

**29**

Late Evening
Thursday, March 27, 1997
Lincoln Memorial Hospital, San Diego, California

Vanessa Jackson gently flipped her cell phone closed. The message she had just listened to was uncharacteristically negative. Latrelle's voice was tainted with disappointment. She bowed her head and silently prayed for her son.

Vanessa had already experienced enough heartache to last three lifetimes, but she never complained about it to Latrelle. Her support, courage, and determination to make things right for her youngest son were not lost on him either. He had always made his mother feel proud. He never let her down or hurt her through a lack of effort or gratitude, unlike her husband and oldest son frequently had.

Latrelle never made the same mistakes his impulsive older brother made, and he succeeded by listening to and learning from his mother. Latrelle was much brighter than his big brother, Marquis, and he learned very early that Vanessa set a much better example than his father. He learned a sense of right and wrong from her and a sense of who could be trusted. Latrelle never acted like a fool, and he always made good grades, especially in subjects where creative thinking and self-expression were a premium. He had a voracious appetite for reading, and books and magazines were always nearby. From an early age, he devoured colorful and easy-to-read children's books, and left them lying around the house like candy wrappers that other kids his age would leave behind for somebody else to pick up.

Fortunately for Latrelle, the Lincoln Heights Library was stocked with thousands of books that Vanessa could borrow. When his mother brought home Robert Lipsyte's *The Contender*, a story that reminded him a lot of his brother, Latrelle's choice of reading material matured, and he consistently began taking longer journeys into the world of fiction, imagination, and unlimited possibility.

Marquis, with his limited imagination and closed mind, continued to fail at finding the courage and discipline it took to do the right thing, like Alfred Brooks finally learned to do after being treated so kindly and fairly by the demanding boxing trainer, Mr. Donatelli.

Latrelle grew up under his mother's protective wings and discreetly avoided his resentful father, his intimidating older brother, and the rest of the posse of uncles, cousins, and nephews that roamed Lincoln Heights and other nearby San Diego neighborhoods, drinking, drugging, and looking for trouble. Latrelle was sensitive and protective of his mother. He promised her when he was a very young boy that someday they would leave the neighborhood and find a much better place to live. Vanessa's friends called him sweet and loyal and smothered him with affection, while the Jackson men called him a momma's boy.

During late night drunken tirades, Latrelle's father would often declare that his son and his wife were stuck in some "Oedipus complex." Anthony Jackson would spout off to his wife, "Why don't you two just go on someplace and get a room?"

He quickly moved his rants from his wife to Latrelle, pointing at and pushing his son away.

"Man, get on out the house and get your own goddamn woman. This one's mine, nigguh."

Anthony's death in an auto accident was tragic, but Vanessa and Latrelle both benefited from his absence.

During the year of his father's death, the small neighborhood park next to the Lincoln Heights Library received funding for expansion and improvement. The city added a new playground, lighted soccer and softball fields, a two-court basketball gymnasium, a large and fully equipped weight room, and an Olympic-sized swimming pool. A private endowment operated and maintained the new pool, where admission was free to low-income families like Latrelle's. The City of San Diego hired a young, attractive, and enthusiastic Hispanic female to fill the newly-created position of Aquatics Coordinator and paid her a nice salary.

Latrelle enjoyed the activities at the Aquatics Center. Coach Escobar was an excellent swimmer, and she knew how to teach all the different strokes. While most of the kids from the neighborhood spent their time in the gym running full-court five-on-five games or in the weight room wearing wife-beater tank tops, showing off new tats and acting like gangsters, Latrelle quickly became a skilled swimmer. He adored his coach, and quickly made new friends with the kids who learned to swim along with him.

Latrelle decided to devote himself to serious training. Soon he realized that he was much faster than anyone else in the neighborhood, and, like Alfred Brooks did in the sweaty boxing gym in the Bronx, he enjoyed the feeling of completing a difficult workout. When he raced for the first time against swimmers from other neighborhoods, he found that he was faster than most of them, too. During the summer, Coach Escobar took Latrelle and his teammates to several swim meets in other communities around San Diego County. Latrelle dominated those meets, winning blue, red, and white ribbons and gold, silver, and bronze medals that decorated the walls of his bedroom.

During Latrelle's junior year of high school, his swimming coach and a small group of influential women met with his school's principal and athletic director. Coach Escobar's committee persuaded the Roosevelt High School administration to create a competitive CIF-sanctioned high school swimming program, and her committee offered the use of the nearby Lincoln Park facility as its home pool. Soon after, Latrelle Jackson became Roosevelt's newest and brightest star. He and several of his teammates began training with Coach Marisol on a year-round basis, getting out of bed at 5 a.m. to meet their coach for 90-minute workouts. Latrelle was the group's fastest and strongest swimmer, but the skills and fitness levels of his teammates were also improving.

Not only did Marisol develop workouts that emphasized strong conditioning, she was excellent at diagnosing stroke problems and providing the accurate feedback, instruction, and demonstrations that enabled her athletes to improve the quality of their strokes. She did an outstanding job of on-campus recruiting, promoted her program at school assemblies, and printed colorful flyers that she and her team members placed around Lincoln Heights and other nearby neighborhoods, hoping to recruit further talent. By the beginning of Roosevelt High School's second season of CIF competition, Marisol had successfully persuaded 18 new girls and 11 new boys to join the team, enough team members to complete a full meet lineup. Their home dual meets quickly became a very popular school event, attended by dozens of Roosevelt students, parents, faculty members, and administrators. Latrelle and his teammates were frequently the only minorities at their meets, and, like Georgetown University's rugged men's basketball teams of the 80s, their team was comprised of not a single Caucasian student-athlete, and also, just like the Hoyas did, Marisol Escobar's Roosevelt Panthers competed with a very hard edge.

During his senior year, Latrelle won the league championship in both the 100- and 200-yard freestyles, qualifying him for the CIF Southern California regional championship meet in Mission Viejo. Two of his teammates, Gustavo and Yvette, had also qualified for the big meet in Orange County, where Latrelle finished third in the 200 and sixth in the 100, while his teammates both qualified for the consolation finals.

Coach Escobar hosted her team's awards banquet at her mother's beautiful ranch house in Bonita a week after the high school season ended. Amanda Villareal had the event fully catered and paid for shiny plaques and trophies that Marisol presented to each of her Roosevelt High swimmers. In the enormous room of her mother's house, Marisol stood confidently in front of a crowd of student-athletes and family members.

She wore a beautiful black dress, her neck, ears, and wrists adorned with expensive and tasteful jewelry, her long hair coifed meticulously. Marisol was well-prepared for the event and addressed the crowd like a seasoned public speaker.

The last award of the event was presented to Latrelle for the accomplishments that made him the team's most valuable swimmer. Marisol had prepared a thoughtful introduction and spoke proudly and at length about the lasting value of the close relationship that had developed between her and her most gifted student-athlete. She praised him for his unconditional support of his teammates and his strong commitment to her program's values. She called him "an ambassador and an inspiration for all minorities to participate in the sport of competitive swimming," and proclaimed a "deep level of trust, and even love," for Latrelle Jackson. She had spoken sincerely about how much he meant to her, and trembled as she described how Latrelle was now a part of her family and she a part of his. And when she called his name to come and receive his award, she became choked up, appearing overwhelmed by her strong feelings about the shy boy who had become a confident young man.

Latrelle's mother and Marisol's mother both cried tears of gratitude, thankful that their son and daughter had come into each other's lives at such a critical time for both of them. Both mothers were fond of the relationship that had developed between their children, but neither overlooked the level of intimacy that had grown between them. When Latrelle came forward to receive his award, Marisol embraced him tightly and held him closely for several long moments. Marisol then placed both of her hands on Latrelle's cheeks and attempted to kiss him lightly on the lips, but at the last moment Latrelle turned his head, just enough for her lips to land on his cheek instead. Undeterred, she then embraced him closely and whispered into his ear, "I love you, Latrelle, and I always will. You are the most special young man I have ever known. I am so proud of you, and I will always be there for you, wherever you are, whatever you need."

Latrelle, slightly embarrassed, even confused, offered a simple, "Thank you," then returned to his seat with the beautifully engraved crystal trophy.

Two years prior to that moment, Latrelle and a handful of his teammates had set the goal of earning both academic and athletic college scholarships. They spent hours together each week preparing for the SAT exam, and Vanessa Jackson used money from her modest savings account and hired a tutor that knew all the test-taking tricks. Latrelle's strong math and science scores indicated engineering or medicine, and his language and reading comprehension scores were even stronger. He and his teammates' high SAT scores and outstanding résumés eventually earned them college scholarships at distinguished universities with competitive athletic programs, like USC, Cal-Berkeley, Notre Dame, and the University of North Carolina.

At that time, too, Marisol Escobar was rewarded for her achievements and excellence. Her presence on the deck during swim meets was impressive. She knew all the rules of swimming and all of the scoring and officiating protocols. Marisol developed a very solid reputation and had quickly become one of San Diego's most successful coaches. Her year-round aquatics programs became a benchmark for municipal parks and recreation departments all over Southern California, and her leadership and administrative abilities were exceptional. She quickly became a trusted leader and a valued mentor, not only in the Lincoln Heights community, but all over San Diego County. With the support of her strong and influential family, she began to develop a formidable political presence. She had quickly built two strong programs that had not previously existed, and her success did not go unnoticed by the school district, the State Athletic Association, the San Diego media, or, most importantly, San Diego Mayor Eddie Peete. Marisol Escobar had received coaching and leadership awards from all of them.

Marisol Escobar's deepest commitment, however, was to instill new values, ideals, and goals into young minds that might not have experienced what she was able to show them. During the summers, many of the young, low-income swimmers from the neighborhood gathered into two nice, new Econline vans provided by the city, and Marisol and her assistant coach drove them to Ocean Beach for open water training and fun beach activities. Few of the children had ever visited the beach with their families, and not one of them had ever stood up on a surfboard before they met Coach Escobar. For most of the group, it was the first time they had even been in the ocean.

Latrelle and the others quickly learned how to body surf, boogie board, and eventually stand up on surfboards that they borrowed from the lifeguards in Ocean Beach. During those summer days, he and a handful of his teammates frequently set out on long open water swims, and eventually, they found the courage to swim all the way out to the end of the Ocean Beach pier. While they were apprehensive about sharks, they would not allow their fear to stop them. They relished the challenge and the opportunity to overcome their fear while developing new skills, and swam to the end of the pier at least a dozen times by that summer's end.

One day, SDLP Ocean Lifeguard Randy Shields approached their group and handed Marisol a thin stack of job announcement flyers. Shields encouraged Escobar and her older team members to attend the academy during the spring break of their upcoming school year. That night, Latrelle told his mother about the great job opportunity and how much money he could earn before starting college.

"Fifteen dollars an hour? That's almost twice what you make lifeguarding at the pool. Son, please . . . that's a no-brainer."

That fall, Escobar shifted her team's goals and began prescribing specific ocean activities to the finest athletes in her group. She researched and described the exciting jobs that came with higher seasonal wages, and the opportunities to gain long-term careers offered by various municipal agencies in San Diego County. Marisol and her mother, Amanda, also considered that it might be best to transfer her out of San Diego's Department of Aquatics and Recreation to begin climbing the organization chart of the more distinguished San Diego Lifeguard Patrol.

For Escobar, a high-ranking officer's position with the Patrol would provide more credibility than she could ever earn in Aquatics and Recreation. In order for her to be taken seriously enough to reach her ultimate goals in city and state politics, she would need a legitimate work history to strengthen her already impressive résumé. She was a UCSD political science graduate and was well on her way to earning a master's in business and public administration from SDSU. Although she and her well-connected mother both felt very good about her current Aquatics and Recreation position, both were beginning to become frustrated with, what Amanda began to refer to as, "A dead-end department with a low ceiling and very few minds that can keep up with ours."

And so, Coach Escobar and her athletes then began to prepare for the opportunity to become ocean lifeguards.

Vanessa Jackson stared at her phone, unsure about what had happened to her son. After several moments, she flipped the phone's cover open again, retrieved the voicemail a second time, placed the phone to her ear, and listened to her son's disappointing message. With a heavy sigh, she deleted the message, placed her phone on the shelf, and gently closed her locker. She said another silent prayer, then returned to the nurse's station to complete her shift.

Latrelle hadn't stopped thinking about Cynthia Harden chasing him down and reaching out to him. He felt some chemistry between them, and he wanted to reach out to her. She had planted a seed of inspiration that was flourishing inside of him. He wanted very badly to get close to her, so she could help that seed grow and blossom into something rewarding.

Latrelle attempted to call her several times over the next two days, but each time he felt overwhelmed by apprehension as soon as he saw Cynthia's name on the screen, and he couldn't find the courage to push the button. He would get lucky instead. All he needed to do was answer the phone when she called, and it didn't take very long for Cynthia to make that call.

Before the end of April, Latrelle and Cynthia met in Ocean Beach several times for soft sand runs, buoy swims, coffee, and lunch. They also had enjoyed dinner and a movie in Mission Valley on a warm Friday night. Before their date, though, Cynthia drove to his mother's house, introduced herself, and asked Vanessa if it was okay to take her son out to dinner.

"Girl, you better get on in here and tell me a thing or two about yourself first."

Vanessa led Cynthia inside, and 45 minutes later, the three of them exited the front door, laughing and smiling. Cynthia turned and hugged Vanessa, then kissed her firmly on the cheek. *Oh my gawd . . . I love them both . . . what a family.*

As their relationship developed, Cynthia felt calmer and gained confidence about her future career, and Latrelle began to feel connected to the many lifeguard colleagues that Cynthia had introduced him to. He also felt much more prepared for the next academy.

Latrelle informed his mother that he would be accepting the full scholarship offer from USC. He would begin training with, and competing for, the Trojan swim team in the fall and would major in clinical psychology with a minor in forensics, just as he was advised to do after telling his guidance counselor that he someday hoped to work for the FBI.

At USC, he would live in a dormitory for athletes during his freshman year, but he knew that he would come back to San Diego at least a few times each semester. He would miss his momma, but his priorities had shifted, and he was inspired to come home for more reasons than just his mother making dinner and doing his laundry.

**30**

Richard Morgan depended upon coffee more than most coffee drinkers. It helped him remain calm and stay focused, and he could drink several cups a day without becoming jittery, nervous, or overly chatty. It also helped curb his voracious appetite so he could keep his weight down, which he had begun doing very well. Morgan excused himself from the table and bounded up the stairs to the barista's counter. He ordered another tall dark roast for himself and a second, smaller cup for his guest before proceeding to the men's room, where he began to review the conversation he and Cynthia Harden had just concluded. At Morgan's request, the two had met at a quiet coffee shop in North Pacific Beach.

Morgan and Cynthia had been sitting on a small front patio for nearly 30 minutes, watching bicyclists, skaters, and guys and girls walking with, or without, surfboards, many on their way to the nearby beach. Their conversation had flowed smoothly, and Richard now knew for sure that Harden was not only the most athletic and physically-qualified female applicant he had ever seen, she was also the most well-trained and professionally-prepared candidate, regardless of gender, that he had come across in several years. Her personality was engaging, she was confident but not arrogant, and she sat calmly and attentively while listening to, and sharing information with, her newest supervisor.

Morgan was still a little curious about Cynthia's past, in particular her hasty departure from UCLA after such an incredible freshman year. Her abrupt decision to also give up playing water polo at the very highest level of international competition also seemed inconsistent with her résumé. In spite of the apparent anomaly, the lieutenant was determined to help guide her future plans, hoping to align them with his own, in particular, to achieve his and the mayor's goal of finding the right woman to finally become the first-ever female sergeant in his agency—the woman that may ultimately become the first female lieutenant as well. The choice to be made had to be the right one; the woman selected had to be near perfect.

*Harden's very close.*

Half a decade before the end of the 20th century, the mayor's critical support and Morgan's determination helped the SDLP secure a large portion of the state of California's 10-year, multi-million-dollar increase in funding for qualifying municipal coastal safety agencies servicing southern California's booming public beaches. With approved, budgeted dollars that would provide personnel, payroll, equipment, and facility expansions, Lt. Morgan had essentially become the general manager of the San Diego Lifeguard Patrol.

Under his direction, the agency had quickly evolved from a small fraternal community of local watermen into a prominent emergency response team with a top-tier professional reputation. The SDLP was no longer considered a minor league operation, and Morgan was committed to recruiting, hiring, and developing big-league talent. Now, with the mayor's and governor's support, he would be able to pay his talented watermen what they were really worth and hire more of them.

Traditionally, Morgan selected a very small and specific group of cadets from each academy's graduating class to watch closely. He would monitor those with exceptional skills and character as had been demonstrated during the academy. These skills and qualities would help him predict their long-term potential in the Patrol's deck of professionals. Harden looked as if she had the makings of not just a queen, but of an ace. She was his first choice, and Morgan was hoping to rely upon her to help lead his organization for many years. Cynthia knew this, Morgan's closest allies knew this, and it was also obvious to the other cadets in her class.

In their conversation, Morgan had described to Cynthia a future that included several female senior POLs, female sergeants, and eventually a female lieutenant, under his command. He had recounted for her the Patrol's history, and had described the unique problems he had observed and experienced regarding the advancement of females in the SDLP.

*"Cynthia, the Patrol has never had a female sergeant—not yet. Very few females have even interviewed for the position. The outstanding females that became qualified were simply victims of bad timing. They interviewed along with better-qualified male candidates with higher seniority and more advanced training.*

*"I can remember at least four women that were qualified to promote to sergeant. They all ran the beach well, executed medical ops professionally, and effectively made rescues in all seasons, under any conditions. They were great with the public; all were excellent training officers, highly effective administrators; and every one of them was an outstanding athlete. All four of them got married and became mothers, though. Each and every one resigned or took early retirements before making sergeant."*

Morgan nodded as he stood in front of the urinal, pleased with his efforts, and continued to recall the conversation.

*"It's ironic too, Cynthia, because the sergeant's job description is actually much better for a mother . . . in my opinion. Sergeants are mostly removed from the front lines of emergency response, and they aren't required to spend nearly as much time devoted to strenuous operational training. The likelihood of a debilitating injury, or worse, is greatly reduced with the promotion.*

*"I can't say this as a matter of policy . . . that would be discriminating against women who have children, which I am not . . . but, based on historical data and the choices made by the exceptional women I just told you*

*about, it would appear on the surface that motherhood and long-term success in ocean lifeguarding do not seem to support each other. At least not in this agency's history."*

As he stood in front of the mirror washing his hands, Morgan looked into his eyes, convinced that he was investing in a product that could very easily break that trend. He realized, though, that anything might happen, and that Cynthia could be a complete flake who just happened to have a powerful body, amazing athletic ability, and a stellar résumé.

*Not likely.*

He left the bathroom, retrieved the two coffees, and returned to the patio where he began describing to Cynthia the privileges that she had earned as the highest-ranking cadet to accept employment under his command in the SDLP. (The three amigos had all accepted jobs on Coronado Island, and Latrelle, well, his time was yet to come.)

"You can select any station you wish, and any seasonal schedule. You can skip the nonsense that sometimes goes on at the Mission Bay stations if you like, and go directly to the oceanfront to begin your training there."

Morgan knew that the Bay stations would frustrate Cynthia, as they were sometimes staffed by overzealous and inexperienced rookies and out-of-shape veteran guards, who still failed to meet the moderate yearly requirements of the oceanfront qualifying exam.

Cynthia already knew where she wanted to be assigned, and she did not hesitate.

"Ocean Beach, then. I'd like to work there."

"An excellent choice. You'll have a great summer on Sgt. Moreland's crew. He's one of the best. Randy Shields will be there, too. Together, those guys will teach you everything you need to know. They are two of the very finest in this agency."

Morgan couldn't have planned it better. His two best friends had attended Point Loma High with him and would mentor her closely all summer. Bobby Moreland was the oldest and the most protective, Shields was the youngest and the best athlete, while Morgan was the strongest, the brightest, and the most ambitious. They each began working for the Patrol the summer after their college-playing days expired prematurely due to injury.

Morgan. Knees.

To that point, none of the three men had ever had a "real job" in their lives. They had grown up surfing and swimming at nearby Ocean Beach, and all three of them had the realization that ocean lifeguarding was not only the closest thing they could think of to being a team sport, but also the thing that each of them would be very good at and enjoy.

Since then, the Patrol had become a lot like Richard Morgan's little kingdom, and Bobby Moreland and Randy Shields were the first and second knights at his table. Bryce North and Alejandro Pena were both aligned with Morgan and his ideology, and each held a seat at the proverbial table as well. With very little interference from the fire and police chiefs, Morgan was able to put his own pieces in place when and where he wanted them. He was fair about it, and he was very good at it.

Morgan directed his newest subordinate.

"I'd like the four of us to meet at noon tomorrow at the OB tower. Does that work for you?"

"Yes, sir."

"Excellent. Randy will be your training officer, and Bobby will do your evaluation at summer's end. You'll be on the clock when you get there, and I probably won't see much of you after that. You just keep kicking ass, okay?"

"I will, Lieutenant."

"I know you will."

Morgan waited for a polite goodbye and a cordial handshake that would leave him free to take on the many tasks that he needed to complete by the day's end, but it would be a little while longer before he could get started on that.

**31**

Saturday, April 5, 1997
North Pacific Beach

Cynthia did not get up from her chair as Lt. Morgan had expected her to. He was prepared to scoot his chair back, stand up, extend his hand to shake hers, and say, "Good day," but he noticed that Cynthia might have more to say. He sat still and waited for her to speak, which she did right away.

"Sir, I'm very grateful for the way things have worked out so far, and I appreciate the offer to begin my training in Ocean Beach tomorrow."

Cynthia paused.

"But, before you go, would you mind if I take just a little bit more of your time?"

Lt. Morgan shifted his body, took another drink of the hot coffee he thought would be "to-go," and readjusted his attitude. He was pleased that she wanted to continue a conversation that might offer him information about her past.

"Of course, go ahead. Take all of the time you need."

Cynthia believed that this man would help her. She had been watching him very closely during the academy. His judgment regarding the dangerous ocean environment and the expertise with which he deployed his personnel, while requiring all of the cadets to participate in the harshest of conditions, had garnered her attention. His management of safety protocols and his entire instructional staff's quality, detailed instruction, and the inspiring and motivational speeches he gave so effectively led her to quickly develop a deep trust in him.

She realized that he was just as masterful at leading and directing as any of the men that she had competed for while playing for the Bruins in Westwood, in Colorado Springs, while trying out for the 1992 Barcelona World Games team, while training for the Navy dive team in Florida, or while deployed on combat missions. She had also realized that she was perhaps the finest job applicant that Morgan had ever seen.

*Why else would he have called me here?*

Cynthia sipped her drink and carefully placed the insulated paper cup on the table, off to one side. She leaned forward on the table and rested comfortably on her forearms. She looked directly into Richard Morgan's eyes and began telling her story.

"Lieutenant, my father died after my freshman year at UCLA. He had lung cancer. He smoked even before joining the Navy at seventeen. He was way too young to die, but he just wouldn't stop smoking."

She shook her head subtly, bowed her head slightly, and inhaled deeply.

"Never in the house though . . ."

She leaned back and allowed her eyes to scan the neighborhood and continued without looking at the lieutenant.

". . . Once in a while, in the truck with the windows rolled down, but not until I was a teenager. On the base or out at sea, he pretty much smoked one cigarette after another all day long. He told me he would go through two, three packs a day sometimes. Lucky Strikes, Camel unfiltered, or Marlboro Red."

She stopped scanning the neighborhood and looked back at Morgan before continuing, without showing much emotion.

"He was a beast, too, Lieutenant . . . Such an amazing and powerful man. You would have loved him. I loved him more than anything. He was everything to me."

She paused again, remaining unemotional, but increased the cadence of her speech.

"He hung on long enough to see me complete my first year at UCLA . . . He loved coming to my games."

Cynthia looked across the wide intersection of Cass and Loring Streets. She observed the bicyclists cruising by in all directions, the pedestrians carrying surfboards to the beach, and a middle-aged couple walking their dog.

"After he died, as his beneficiary, I got a life insurance settlement and his pension from the Navy. He set me up very nicely, and he took care of his only sister, too. My Aunt Claire now owns and operates the Harden family farm in Indiana, and she's the only surviving Harden besides me. All of the men in my family are dead, Lieutenant. Claire, her two daughters, and I are all that's left of Harden blood."

She paused to take another sip.

"Just between you and me, Lt. Morgan, and I seriously do not plan on sharing this information with anybody but you, I own stock in the family farm, and I have a limited partnership agreement in a nice auto shop and garage down in Imperial Beach. My dad owned half of that place. He also owned the duplex that I grew up in—in Coronado. Both units are being rented to Naval officers with young families, and their rent money goes directly into an IRA account in my name. The mortgage on that place was paid off before he died, too. I have full equity."

She stopped and took another sip of the hot coffee.

"I live on my dad's old sailboat in Mission Bay now . . . I'm not suffering financially, Lieutenant. I'll be fine with or without this job."

Cynthia stopped talking when she realized that she was almost bragging and noticed that her tone had become slightly defensive. She breathed in deeply and held her breath for several moments before continuing.

"My point, Lieutenant, is that the financial security I have isn't now, and never will be, enough to make me truly happy. I'm way too young to stop working . . . and I'm not the type to use that money to become a day-trader or a real estate investor. And, San Diego is my home. It always will be. I'm staying right here for the rest of my life."

She stopped to take a drink of coffee.

"Lieutenant, I played water polo for as long as I can remember, and I just knew that it would be the focal point of my entire life. It was my passion. That game was everything to me. My coaches, my teammates, the trainers, they were all my family. From the time I was a little girl on Coronado Island, all I dreamed about was playing in college national championships, the Olympics, the World Games, and any other international competition. That was going to be my life."

She paused and tilted her head. She scowled and squinted her eyes.

"Not playing for the United States on the Barcelona team in '92 was the biggest disappointment I've ever had. But it was more than just disappointment, Lieutenant, it was unfair, and it was wrong that I wasn't on that team." She paused. "You probably don't know that the team finished eleventh in the world that year. They should have easily made it to the semi-finals. We could have won that thing if I were there. I still don't know why they selected that jerk to be the head coach. He got replaced right after that tournament."

"You think you should have been on that team?"

"Absolutely. There's no question. I was easily one of the top five players in the country."

"Then why were you left off the roster?"

Harden flinched slightly.

"I assume you've already read his comments. It is public information, after all, it was a national program."

"I saw only a brief notation about a personality clash. But almost every player in the program had similar remarks in their files."

"Well, I can tell you for sure, Lieutenant, he was totally incompetent, and I told him so. He was embarrassed, he was defensive, and he was wrong." Harden paused, then continued, "I said something that I shouldn't have said, I was right . . . but I realize now that I should have kept my mouth shut. It was his team, not mine."

She shook her head again, and gazed away for a moment.

"It's really hard for me to say that, even now, after all this time. Part of me still feels like that was my team. But there's no doubt about it, I was way out of line."

Morgan knew nothing about the incident she was referring to; it had not appeared on the document that he had reviewed. He figured, however, that there was something amiss when a player with her accolades was not included in a program that was designed to compete against stronger international opponents.

"What did you say?"

It was easy for Cynthia to recall the events accurately.

"At the very last minute, this head coach cut one of our players without telling anybody that he was considering making a roster change. She was one of our best shooters, too, a big tall girl named Scarlett Embry. She was an All-American from Stanford, and she was one of my best friends. She could also play goalie if we needed her to. She was CLEARLY one of our best players. He replaced her with this girl who had already been cut, and he did it the night before we left for Barcelona."

She glanced at Morgan, a chagrined look on her face.

"She missed weeks of preparations and then, wham, just like that," she snapped her fingers, "he put her back on the team."

Morgan nodded.

"She was, like, one of those *rah-rah* chicks that supported everybody and made everybody feel really good about themselves. I'll give her that much. But then I found out that she was from some tiny, stuck-up college on the east coast . . . Bucknell, or something like that. It turned out to be the same college that our head coach had graduated from. AND, she was the daughter of this guy our coach played with at Bucknell, classmates. The dad was a major financial contributor to the program. He chartered all of our buses, set us up in hotels, and got us meals when we traveled that summer."

She looked up and stared blankly out toward the street again.

Morgan nodded.

"I've seen that happen before. It's not all that uncommon, unfortunately."

"Yeah, you're right."

She looked away for a moment, then continued emphatically.

"Well, after he made the announcement, everybody freaked out, but he just walked away. He actually put his fingers in his ears and ignored everybody . . . Then he went into his office and locked the door."

Harden looked down and shook her head.

"So, then I go over to his office door and start pounding on it. I mean like, loud, and I just kept doing it until he finally opens the door. I told him that he was an idiot for letting Scarlett go and that *he didn't know shit* about leading an elite program. All he really knew about was nepotism. I told him that it was obvious he wasn't committed to winning, and that he had no idea what it took to be the best. I already knew more about water polo and becoming a champion than he ever would . . . pfff . . . I called him an asshole, a loser, a narcissist . . . I went on and on. Every one of my teammates could hear it."

She paused, then snorted.

"I finally told him that if he was so concerned about spirit and team morale, maybe he should try coaching cheerleaders instead."

Morgan laughed out loud, but stopped quickly.

"I'm sorry. I wasn't laughing at you. I was just imagining the look on his face when you said that."

"Yeah, it was one of my best lines, for sure, but certainly not my best moment."

Then she grimaced, exhaled, and shook her head.

"The next morning, I was dismissed from the team, at the freaking airport, in front of all of my teammates, and, of course, Scarlett was placed back on the roster in my spot. I was the idiot. Ironic, huh?"

She closed her eyes, bowed her head slightly forward, and held it there for several moments.

"Bailey never scored a goal in Barcelona. Seven games, zero goals."

Cynthia looked up at Morgan, her eyes slightly welling with tears.

"I flew home to Coronado, and then my father died three days later. My stupid outburst didn't just end my water polo career, it actually killed my father. I think it broke his heart when I told him why I was cut. He had already booked a Navy flight to Spain. He was coming to watch me play."

Cynthia bowed her head again.

"My entire life up to that point, and my dad's life, too, had been all about water polo. That coach, Bailey, my stupid outburst, and then my father's death, that all changed everything in my life. I didn't know who I was, or what I was doing after that, Lieutenant."

**32**

Saturday, April 5, 1997
North Pacific Beach

Cynthia had been looking away from Morgan for several long moments before she turned back toward him. Her face suddenly showed signs of frustration.

"My father lied to me though, Lieutenant," she said softly.

Morgan did not reply but shifted, discerning Cynthia's anxiety. He did the best he could to open a space for her to feel comfortable and relaxed. Safe.

Cynthia's face lightened as she continued.

"From the time I was a very little girl, he was elusive about my mother. I never knew her. She was gone way before any of the memories I have about my life developed. I have no childhood memories of her at all."

She shook her head, as if she were embarrassed.

"When I was in the first grade, he told me that she died . . . after lying to me for years about her moving back to Ireland to take care of my sick grandma, who, of course, I never met either. From the time I was six years old, I thought my mother died from some disease you could only get in Ireland."

She paused again, thinking about how naïve she had been about the strange Irish flu that she had feared for so many years.

"The night he died, my father told me my mother's maiden name. *Meckenzie Callahan*. He was certain that she was living somewhere in northern California."

Cynthia reached into her backpack and removed an amazingly well-preserved 25-year-old Polaroid photo of her father and his bride standing on an oceanfront balcony at sunset. Before the following sunrise, Cynthia was conceived.

She handed the photo to Morgan.

"This picture was in his will, along with a long letter about how they met and then married right after she got pregnant. Apparently, she never wanted to get married, but agreed so my birth would be handled by military doctors. She left forever, just a couple of months after I was born. My father told me that he never heard from her again."

Morgan returned the photo, and Cynthia stared at it.

"This was the only thing I had that connected me to her. Isn't she beautiful? And look how young and handsome he is. Gawd, they look happy."

She returned the photo to the Ziploc bag and replaced it in her backpack.

"Anyway, the night that he died in his sleep, he told me that he had received a message from her during my freshman year at UCLA. He said that it was the first time he had heard from her since she left us."

Cynthia paused and noticed how attentive the lieutenant was.

He asked, "You never met your mother?"

"Well, not up to that point in my life, but I'll get to that in a second. So, anyhow, it was just after one of my very best games, the Pacific League championship game at Stanford. I scored the winning goal with three seconds left . . . best backhand I ever shot . . . goalie never saw it coming . . . game over. Afterward, a local TV intern interviewed me, and went on and on about what a great future I was going to have."

Cynthia chuckled.

"It was a little weird. It was like she was hitting on me. I still have the videotape. It's a crack up. My entire team and the coaches gave me a really hard time about it, but whatever."

Cynthia took a sip of coffee.

"So my real, live mother . . . this Meckenzie Callahan . . . she saw the TV news broadcast while she was lying in bed that night. She says now that she knew then, right away, that I was her daughter. It was the first time she had seen me since I was a newborn, but she knew instantly that it was me. She then recognized my name, Harden. She told my dad that it was like seeing herself in the mirror.

"I couldn't stop thinking about her though, you know . . . once I knew that she was alive. My first thought was, how did she come back to life? I thought she died from the Irish flu . . . I mean, it took me weeks to get that straight in my head. I had to completely reprogram my thinking about my mother, and accept the fact that she never went to Ireland in the first place. She was alive and well in San Francisco the entire time that I was growing up in Coronado. It was hard to digest. He died right after telling me all of this . . . that same night."

"I'm so sorry, Cynthia."

"Thank you, Lieutenant. It's okay though. It was a long time ago. Anyhow, I had a name, and I knew that she was somewhere close enough to Stanford University to see me on local TV. That's all I knew, but it was enough to get me started."

Cynthia stopped and took another sip of the drink the lieutenant had sweetened with raw sugar and half and half creamer. She turned the cup in her hand, inspecting it, before taking a second, longer gulp.

"Mmmm . . . Thank you, Lieutenant, that's pretty tasty coffee."

Morgan smiled, but said nothing.

"So, I had to find her. When I got cut from the Barcelona team and Daddy died, like I said already, it really changed everything. I decided to stop playing for the Bruins and quit school. I moved back to Coronado, and for the next four months, all I did was sleep and mourn my father. After he died, it took me a while to get the money transferred into my own accounts, but after that was set up, I decided to hire a private investigator to find my mother."

She smiled and shrugged.

"He found her . . . like almost right away. She's a pretty big part of my life now. She's actually an amazing woman."

Cynthia chuckled and shook her head from side to side.

"What is it?" Morgan asked.

"Well, I was right back where I started again. I had finally found the mother that I thought was dead, but she had her own life, you know, and there I was without one. I had given up on water polo, and dropped out of college to find her, and after all of that, I realized that I had no mission. I was a part of nothing outside of myself. You know?"

Morgan nodded.

"I had money and a nice place to live, and I could do whatever I wanted to, but I had nobody to do it with . . . and nothing to do that mattered or made a difference to anyone. I was alone, Lieutenant, but even worse than that, my life had become completely irrelevant."

"Where is your mother now?"

"She's still in up the Bay Area. She's a partner in her husband's law firm, in this adorable little town called Menlo Park. She still has a beautiful, thick Irish accent. I love listening to her speak. We talk once in a while on the phone, and I visit during holidays, but really, after all this time, it's kind of hard to just recreate 'Mommy.' You know?"

Morgan didn't really know, but he nodded anyway.

"Well, long story short, I started spending time with some close buddies that my uncle and I grew up surfing with and hanging out on the beach with down in IB. One of them used to be a SEAL team member— the guy who owns The Anchor down there. Have you ever been in that place?"

Morgan had been in there several times, over many summers, and he knew the place quite well.

"That can be a rough crowd. It's always a good idea to go in there with at least a few friends."

Cynthia laughed out loud.

"Yeah, there's no doubt about that. My uncle bartended there for years . . ."

She stared out across the street with a blank expression on her face. Appearing distracted, perhaps by a painful memory, she looked down and inhaled. She cleared her throat, looked up, and continued.

"As I was saying, it was the SEAL, this Kevin Marker guy, who talked me into enlisting in the Navy to get dive team qualified. He helped teach me how to surf when I was growing up, and I always admired and trusted him. He said he couldn't think of a better career for a woman like me. It made sense, and it provided me with another mission, and it definitely offered a high-level challenge. I mean, I knew it wouldn't be easy, and it wasn't, but it really helped me move past the whole water polo thing, made me a part of something again, ya know? More importantly though, it allowed me to let my father rest in peace."

Morgan smiled, appreciating her wisdom and maturity.

"I thought for sure that the Navy would be a good fit for me after growing up on a naval facility, and for a while, it was . . . until Commander Kent Windsor showed up."

She looked up and met the lieutenant's eyes and shook her head subtly. "He was like that U.S. team head coach, but much worse. This guy was full-on hateful."

Cynthia stopped and redirected herself. She breathed in deeply through her nose and exhaled slowly from her mouth, pursing her lips while very subtly shaking her head from side to side. She remained silent for several long moments. Lt. Morgan raised one eyebrow and tilted his head to the side.

"Are you okay, Cynthia?"

Cynthia breathed in again, repeating the sequence before she replied, "Yeah . . . I'm fine. I think I've said enough though. Maybe the coffee is getting to me. I'm rarely this open about my past, certainly not this open about my worst failures."

The lieutenant smiled and replied softly, "It's okay, Cynthia. I've seen it first-hand already, not only what you're capable of, but what you're made of. We've all got people or incidents from our past that, let's say, redirected our futures."

"Yeah, you're right about that, but really, before I tell you any more about my failures, just let me get started in Ocean Beach. I'd like to show you how well I can succeed first."

"Fair enough. And, Cynthia, there's no requirement for you to share anything about your past with me, or with any other personnel in the Patrol. You understand that, right? This is not an inquiry or an interview. I just asked you here to share a few things with you that I thought you should know."

"I appreciate that, but I do have one more thing to say."

"Go ahead."

"Well, what I'm trying to get to is this, Lieutenant. I've received just about every award a high school student-athlete can, and I earned a full scholarship to attend UCLA. I feel like I was dropped from that U.S. National team not really by my own doing, and certainly not because I wasn't one of the best players in the country. I received a Navy commendation, along with seven others in my unit, on a salvage and recovery mission in hostile North Pacific waters before my twenty-third birthday, and then *that* path to excellence got blocked by something out of my control as well. I have always enjoyed living close to the edge, with the highest expectations possible, but this time I want to stay put, Lieutenant. Do you understand what I'm talking about?"

"I think I do."

"I've lost my passion and my mission a couple of times already, and each time it felt just like it did when my dad died; that something was taken away from me. It really wasn't by *my* doing. Now, I'll admit that I made a few mistakes, but those mistakes were a reaction to somebody who had authority over me, treating me, or somebody else important to me, unfairly."

She paused and stared directly into Morgan's eyes.

He did not shift his gaze.

"Promise me right now, Lieutenant, that this Patrol of yours isn't a *men's only* organization, and that you're not one of these guys who takes care of his friends and family at the cost of others. Promise me that you'll play fair, Lieutenant, and that you'll treat me justly, all the way to the top, sir . . . and then, you and I will have a long-term deal."

The determination in Cynthia's words was unmistakable. Morgan had never before experienced a woman with so much passion, and he definitely had never met a woman this physically capable.

*She is going to be a phenomenal leader in this organization,* he thought. Morgan took his time to respond.

"I hope you realize how committed I am to avoiding any and all perceptions of unfairness. My primary concern is about finding, hiring, training, and promoting the very best, Ms. Harden. I see that in you. I don't see just a woman, although between you and me, I *need* a woman with your ability, skill, background, and competence to move up quickly through our ranks. But, even as talented and prepared as you appear to be, not only will I treat you fairly, I will just as surely not give you any preferential treatment either. You're going to *earn* each and every privilege you receive."

He paused, becoming more focused, intent on delivering the appropriate message.

"If you don't make it to the top of this organization, it will be because somebody better than you beats you to it. Period. If you are indeed the best, you will get there first, each and every time you attempt to get to the next level. I *promise* you that."

He smiled and sat back, satisfied with his response. He could tell that Cynthia was very earnest about being taken seriously, and that their morning meeting affirmed his beliefs about the extraordinary potential she possessed.

"You are wise and prepared beyond your years, Cynthia. You will find that many of the men and women that I have selected and trained will be the finest and the most professional you have ever worked with. The Patrol is an extended family, and we have a mission, a statement of values, and a common belief. Our goal is to develop and maintain the greatest skills possible and to work together as professionals so that every beach patron goes home safely every day. People might get sick, and other people might even get injured, but nobody is going to drown. That's the mission, Ms. Harden."

"I won't be offended if you call me 'Miss,' Lieutenant.

"Actually, I would prefer to call you 'Cynthia' from now on, if you don't mind. I never served in the military, so for me, first names are not a sign of preferential treatment."

"Touché, but if it's okay with you, I'll keep calling you Lieutenant."

"Of course."

Lt. Morgan relaxed and smiled before continuing.

"I am blessed to have two great families, Cynthia. My own, and the Patrol. I enjoy a wonderful life here on these beaches in San Diego. Mister Shields and Sergeant Moreland will share that sentiment with you as well."

"That's why I'm here, Lieutenant, and I do not intend on going anywhere for at least twenty-five years."

She smiled, replaced her sunglasses over her eyes, and stood.

"I'll see you at noon tomorrow in OB, Lieutenant."

"I look forward to it, Cynthia."

Sgt. Moreland, POL Shields, and SOL Harden met with Lt. Morgan in Ocean Beach the next day, and the summer began early for her. By the time her class of rookies began working their seasonal 40-hour schedules during the third week of June, Cynthia had already logged over 240 hours of beachfront tower ops and all 10 required hours as a personal watercraft crewman, qualifying her to begin personal watercraft operator training. Before the summer of '97 began, she had been checked off on *Code 3* vehicle driving, spinal board extraction technique, CPR, defibrillator operation, and emergency radio codes; had memorized a long list of district street names and locations; and nervously enjoyed many training hours with POL Shields seated right next to her up in the Ocean Beach main tower, observing and commanding the entire beachfront staff.

Cynthia had moved quickly into position A, right where she was the most comfortable.

# PART 4

Discrimination:
To make distinctions in treatment;
show partiality or prejudice.

**33**

Two Days Later
Early Morning, Monday, April 7, 1997
Dr. Amanda Villareal's Ranch House, Bonita, California

In 1940, Kenneth Clark became the first African-American to earn a Ph.D. in psychology from Columbia University. Two years later, Dr. Clark became the first fully tenured black professor at the City College of New York. In 1966, he was appointed to the New York State Board of Regents and was the first African-American to become the president of the American Psychological Association.

Dr. Clark conducted an experiment in the early 1940s to prove the negative psychological, emotional, and social effects of segregation on black children and society at large. His primary subjects were young black girls. One group was comprised of girls that attended segregated public schools in Washington, D.C. A second group attended integrated public schools in New York City. The data revealed a disturbing trend of internalized racism that was demonstrated by both groups. More disturbing, however, was the data showing an almost unanimous trend of low self-esteem, and even self-hatred, in the group that attended segregated schools. Dr. Clark's findings were confirmed decades later in the 21st century by Kiri Davis, a young high school student and documentary filmmaker. Several other American academic and social organizations conducted their own versions of Clark's inquiry, and their conclusions were just as convincing and alarming.

Clark interviewed young black girls and then placed two dolls in front of them. One doll was like a Barbie doll, a buxom blonde, white female adult. The second doll was a structural duplicate of the first. The skin tone, however, was dark chocolate brown, and the hair was jet black. Many questions were asked. The subjects were instructed to point at or pick up the doll that they believed to be the answer to each of the following questions:

*Which is the pretty doll? Which is the smart doll? Which is the good doll?*

Nineteen of the original 22 black female subjects pointed at or picked up the white doll each time.

Then they were asked:

*Which is the ugly doll? Which is the dumb doll? Which is the bad doll?*

All 22 picked up the black doll.

*Which doll do you want to be like?*

Again, nineteen of 22 picked up the white doll.

*Finally, which doll is most like you?*

All 22 immediately pointed at or picked up the black doll.

What did it mean? Good question. No simple answer.

*Brown v. Board of Education,* however, utilized Dr. Clark's testimony to support Brown's position regarding the benefits of desegregation, and in 1954, the U.S. Supreme Court ruled that segregation in American public schools was unconstitutional. These and other lessons learned from Clark about segregation bias have served to guide legislative, judiciary, and executive branches of American governmental organizations, beginning with federal and trickling down to state, county, and municipal agencies for half a century. Due to the increased awareness that followed the new legislation, Americans began to slowly embrace integration. As the arrival of the new millennium approached, a new paradigm called *multicultural diversity* appeared. The identity conflict facing young black Americans was not unique to them, however, and young children from many non-Caucasian cultures, regardless of their skin tone or their native language, were impacted by the social and cultural biases that had been occurring, and were continuing to occur, in 20th century America.

Many employers and their employees had to learn hard and costly lessons about their own forms of workplace discrimination that had not only been tolerated, but even encouraged, by colleagues, peer groups, and supervisors. Their inappropriate, and now illegal, behaviors had been creating a hostile workplace environment for many Americans, for many decades, and regardless of their race or gender, countless victims had no legal recourse to do anything about it. Victims of discrimination were forced to "turn the other cheek" to remain employed, or, if they chose to fight back, they would almost certainly be chastised, disciplined, or fired.

"Discrimination occurs in various forms and will no longer be tolerated" became a battle cry for workers who were finally beginning to feel safe in the workplace and free to make a living without being harassed or bullied. Public and private employers were suddenly tasked with providing new, mandatory training seminars to educate government agency employees (from top to bottom of the chain of command) about new diversity laws. Difficult to enforce on the streets, these new guidelines were intended to instill a growing attitude of tolerance and an ability to embrace differences in values and cultural characteristics among colleagues. It wasn't an easy task, by any means, but by identifying and eliminating many of those previously accepted behaviors, the fight against discrimination eventually became a more manageable problem in American workplace environments.

Dr. Amanda Villareal was an outspoken and highly-educated expert on the topic of American social inequities, and was very familiar with Dr. Clark's work. She had earned her undergraduate degree in political science, business, and public administration from the University of Mexico City before moving to America and quickly completing the process of becoming an American citizen, years before meeting her future husband, the American-born son of a wealthy Columbian immigrant. Standing in front of three U.S. Customs agents, charming Amanda sang the National Anthem and correctly recited both the Preamble of the United States Constitution and the Pledge of Allegiance. She then correctly answered all 25 multiple-choice and true-false questions about the U.S. Constitution and U.S. history. After the exam was graded, her family took photos, she signed the government-notarized documents, and Amanda Villareal became an American citizen in Washington, D.C., on July 5, 1965.

She moved west and settled briefly in El Paso, Texas, where her retired parents, both former professors on the large and prestigious multi-national campus in Mexico City, purchased a 40-acre ranch by the Rio Grande River. A few years later, Ms. Villareal moved to Flagstaff and earned her master's degree in sociology from Northern Arizona University before returning to Texas in December of 1975. At UT-Austin, she defended her Ph.D. dissertation on the subject of *Minority Hiring in American Municipalities: Before and After the Death of Dr. Martin Luther King.*

Dr. Villareal then moved to San Diego, where she became a fully tenured professor and was eventually promoted to the position of director of sociology at UCSD, the first female and the first minority to hold the position. She purchased her own sprawling ranch house with fairway views in Bonita two years before meeting Marisol's handsome and athletic father at Jack Murphy Stadium on a warm October Monday night, while cheering on her adopted Chargers as they destroyed the hapless Oakland Raiders.

After becoming pregnant during the second year of their relationship, she married the charismatic and powerful Victor Trujillo-Escobar. Escobar's expansive estate helped Amanda establish non-profit organizations and created generous endowments for programs that she believed in. She learned very quickly how to maintain a private, behind-the-scenes lifestyle, and very effectively promoted her social and political agendas. She found out that, much like her husband's family had been doing successfully for a very long time, she preferred supporting her handpicked political candidates to accepting the responsibilities, headaches, and conflicts of interest that came along with holding public office.

Amanda was well-respected and powerful to begin with, and although her marriage to the dark, mysterious importer and coffee tycoon ended in an amenable divorce before Marisol's 10th birthday, it provided Amanda with both great funding and deeper support for her causes. She was on the board of several associations and served as the president of the city of San Diego's recently-created Women's Council for Diversity. Her council met with the San Diego mayor once a month, and their agendas frequently included matters related to his ongoing re-election campaign.

This "little problem" confronting her daughter and her daughter's swim team members would not present much of a challenge for Amanda to overcome. She had quickly learned that it would be all about one man: an apparently "quasi-tyrannical," long time San Diego city employee, the SDLP's director of personnel and its chief policy maker, Lt. Richard Morgan. If the problem was going to be resolved, she knew that negotiations would be with him. After researching his background, Amanda realized that the lieutenant's job description seemed to have very few checks and balances written into it. It appeared to her that this longtime lifeguard supervisor could hire, fire, train, and promote pretty much anybody he wanted to. Additionally, it appeared to her that he had been doing just that for years without any person, and certainly no oversight committee, guiding and evaluating his most important decisions.

She delicately explained to her daughter how they were to proceed.

"Marisol, escuchame. Eso es facil."

**34**

Monday, April 7, 1997
Bonita, California

According to Dr. Villareal, Marisol Escobar and her Lincoln Park Tiburones swim team members—Yvette Chavez, Gustavo Guerrero, Claritza Montoya, and Abel Navarro—became victims of illegal discrimination when they were dismissed from the March 1997 San Diego County Ocean Lifeguard Academy. Their dismissals left them ineligible to receive seasonal employment as oceanfront lifeguards during the summer of 1997. These young job seekers, however, had outstanding high school transcripts, supportive letters of recommendation, and experience as pool lifeguards under Marisol's direct supervision at a city facility. They, and their parents and relatives, were prepared to meet at City Hall with pickets as soon as Dr. Villareal told them to.

Marisol Escobar had submitted a claim of discrimination, and she and her group were being represented by her mother's close friend, Joshua Stein, a prominent civil rights attorney with an extremely successful settlement record. Stein had won lawsuits against several California counties and municipalities, and a few cases against the state itself.

Latrelle Jackson's name, however, did not appear on any of the documents that were filed at the city courthouse. Marisol had contacted

Latrelle and had described the petition she was also forwarding to a high-ranking representative from the EEOC. The claim also focused on the educational nature of the required ocean lifesaving and rescue course offered by San Diego Community College, arguing that the emphasis should be on improvement and adjustments made after instruction and feedback were given.

Latrelle listened quietly as Marisol described how the criteria for passing the academy had created racially- and culturally-biased graduation rates.

"The punitive nature of the timed pass/fail events that might result in the immediate dismissal from the program of a job-seeking candidate contradicts an essential educational principle. The tryout is for entry-level, flat-water bay lifeguard positions, and the criteria being used are not reliable. The program director's willingness to subject job-seeking novices to deadly ocean conditions demonstrates reckless and negligent behavior."

The academy's methods were not the only matter being called into question.

"The program director's willingness to overlook the sensitive cultural and demographical shortcomings in the graduation data demonstrates egregious discrimination. This most recent episode of eliminating these five outstanding minority cadets, just two days before graduation day, is reprehensible and illegal. Additionally, any other municipal agencies in San Diego County that support the decisions of this academy's director will also be demonstrating illegal discrimination."

Looking out across wooded fairways and a small running creek, Marisol paced across the large redwood deck attached to her bedroom. She held a thin, blue, flip-cover Erikson cell phone to her ear, leaned back against the deck railing, and spoke with confidence.

"Latrelle, you are the single most important subject in this action. You are the one who has been the most unfairly treated. You are obviously more qualified than any of us, and you are also more qualified than ninety-five percent of the other cadets who were enrolled in that academy. Your teammates and I all should have passed that course, and we should all be working on the beach this summer."

Marisol paused, expecting an enthusiastic proclamation of support, something like, *Oh, hell yeah!* Instead, all she heard was silence.

"Latrelle! Are you listening? Sign the petition, stand next to me, and help lead us."

Latrelle finally broke his silence.

"No, thank you."

"What? You need to think about this for a second, Latrelle. This Lt. Morgan obviously discriminates against minorities, and *you* are a minority, Latrelle. Help me change their policies so more people like *us* can be hired."

Latrelle hesitated, considering Marisol's choice of words.

"People like *us?*"

"Yes, Latrelle, people like us. Not white people, apparently the only kind this guy will hire."

Latrelle hesitated again, now considering his own choice of words.

"Coach, I don't think it matters that I'm black, or that you and the others are Latinos. So what if the only cadets who graduated were white. I thought about that for a while, Coach, but then I let it go."

"How can you let that go, Latrelle? You don't think that all of us are qualified for those jobs?"

"I got beat, and that's why I'm not qualified. Period. I got beat by the ocean, and I beat myself because I swam right out into that set without even knowing it was coming. I screwed up, Coach . . . I almost drowned out there. I failed. I wasn't a victim of discrimination. I just wasn't ready for that challenge yet."

Latrelle softened his tone.

"Listen, Marisol, I appreciate how you feel, but I truly don't believe that I got beat by an unfair system. I failed to complete that course, the others failed as well, and you and Claritza *quit* that day in IB. So, just like you used to say at practice, 'If it was easy, everybody would do it.'"

Marisol did not reply.

"Thirty people made it through that academy . . . and it wasn't unfair . . . it was just the most difficult challenge I've ever faced. I'm not going to back away from a challenge, and go around it some other way. I'll be more prepared next time because I failed this time. I just wasn't ready for that responsibility yet. Now I am, and I will not fail again."

"Well, you shouldn't have failed this time either. That's my point."

"Coach, maybe not everyone is cut out to do that job . . . did you ever think of that? Don't take this wrong, but maybe you're not cut out for this. Do you really think Claritza wants to spend her summers out there in big waves? It's scary out there, Coach; it's not for everyone. I know it is for me, though, and I'm going to prove it in August."

Marisol felt a sense of pride as she listened to the young man that she had admired for years. She felt even more strongly about the needs of the entire group.

"Latrelle, listen, I appreciate your humility and your commitment to excellence. I always have . . . but this is about fairness and an equal opportunity to get hired. These are entry-level jobs, and this Morgan guy is demanding too much expertise way too soon. *That* is not fair."

"Coach, I'm all for fairness and equal opportunity, but I still think you're wrong about this. If he hires somebody that's not truly qualified, well, who knows what could happen. It's a much more serious position than your claim is taking into consideration. This job isn't like working at the pool, Coach, so, like I said already, count me out. I don't need the EEOC to help me get that job. I will earn it, just like I've earned everything else."

Escobar yelled into the phone, "Ayyyyyyeee, Latrelle! Tu no entiendes!"

Silence . . . then the sound of a few long, deep breaths from Marisol before she continued in a defeated tone.

"Well, good luck, Latrelle. Your positive attitude doesn't surprise me, although the fact that you're still so idealistic and naïve does. It also doesn't change the fact that their policies are way off-base. That academy's evaluation system is just not fair. With you or without you, I'm going to make them change their ways."

"Well, good luck to you, too, Coach."

Latrelle did not say goodbye. He simply pulled the phone away from his ear and pressed the *end* button. He was a bit shaken by the intensity level and even some anger that he perceived coming from his coach. He had never heard that from her.

Latrelle and Marisol didn't speak again that spring. He did not return to the Lincoln Park pool to work that summer, and he did not resume his training with the Tiburones. Instead, they agreed that it would be best if he transferred to another city pool to earn a full summer of spending money to take with him to USC in the fall.

During that summer, however, it was Marisol who started to recognize just how much she missed and admired her young protégé. *I know that pinche gorda, Cynthia Harden, has something to do with this . . . She's totally brainwashing him. I can't let her keep doing this to my Latrelle.*

**35**

Tuesday, April 8, 1997
Mayor Peete's Office
Downtown San Diego

The first time Amanda Villareal showed the film of Dr. Clark's original test to her only daughter, Marisol Escobar was just five years old. Before she showed her the old, well-preserved reel of film, Amanda administered her own version of the test to Marisol. The young Escobar girl was dark-skinned, she had black hair, and her eyes were dark brown. She was confused about nothing, however, and she knew her identity. Marisol demonstrated no self-hatred or negative bias against the dark doll and, while giggling, she selected the white doll when the negative adjectives like "bad," "dumb," and "ugly" were used in the question. When her mother explained afterward why so many other minority children like her answered the same questions to Clark's test differently, Marisol became confused and concerned.

It was then that Amanda began to educate her daughter thoroughly about marketing images and economic exploitation. She filled her daughter's young mind with lectures about economic bias, racial profiling, a global history of religious persecution, and all forms of ongoing intolerance. At an early age, Marisol learned about "white America" and the "haves" and the "have-nots." It didn't take her long to figure out that

almost all of the "haves" were white, but that she, her wealthy and powerful father, and her highly educated and politically prominent mother, were obviously exceptions. Before Marisol had even started middle
school, Amanda also described to her intelligent and interested daughter
the psychological conflicts related to gender identity and sexual orien-
tation, and offered graphic examples of hate crimes. Long before most
American adults had heard anything about "multicultural diversity" and
the "value for embracing differences," Marisol Escobar was not only bilingual in Spanish and English, but was also fluent in social and psychological themes that most high school graduates had neither the maturity
nor the intellect to grasp.

Marisol thought of Dr. Clark's doll test only sparingly before she
quit the academy, but soon afterward, it caused her to think about its
implications more deeply.

*Just how many dark dolls ARE working as ocean lifeguards in San Diego?
I was just denied my chance, and every single one of the athletes I coach wasn't
good enough either? WTF?*

Marisol and her mother researched hiring data related to many ocean
lifeguarding agencies in California. The data was staggering, and on the
surface, it provided undeniable evidence that minorities were somehow
being excluded from employment opportunities in the field of ocean
lifeguarding. From 1965 to 1995, their research found that 94 percent
of all oceanfront lifeguards hired by government agencies operating in
San Diego, Orange, and Los Angeles counties were Caucasian males.
The next largest subgroup, 3 percent, was comprised of native Pacific
Islanders. Hispanics and blacks each comprised less than 2 percent of the
overall employee pool during those years.

Amanda's first call after collecting the data and drawing her
conclusions was to San Diego Mayor Eddie Peete. Peete listened intently
for several minutes as Dr. Villareal reviewed the data and outlined her
claim.

"Eddie, this cultural bias unfairly benefits individuals that grow
up near the ocean. That's precisely where the opportunity to develop
the skills, knowledge, and entry-level abilities required to become an

oceanfront lifeguard are abundant. These white coastal families raise their children on the beach and participate in ocean activities year-round. They obviously have easier access to attaining the required skills that will lead directly to these employment opportunities, and eventually to the lucrative careers that develop later. That predisposition provides a tremendously unfair advantage over most minority and low economic groups that live nowhere near the ocean."

"Go on."

"How are individuals from non-coastal-dwelling minority cultures supposed to prepare themselves for career opportunities in the field of public coastal safety? Those good jobs carry competitive seasonal wages, great permanent salaries, and excellent medical and retirement benefits that are realistically being offered *only* to white people."

The mayor interjected.

"What you describe seems obvious to me, Amanda. It's like that in many geographical areas. People who grow up near coal mines may likely become miners, for example. The same thing might apply to the commercial fishing industry on both coasts. Harbor towns almost certainly are filled with individuals who earn their living as fishermen. Those raised in Texas might become ranchers or work on oil rigs, and those lucky enough to grow up in Aspen or Vail might become ski instructors or work for the ski patrol. What are you suggesting we do about that?"

"I'm not concerned about those other constituents just yet, Eddie. I'm more concerned about the diverse group of residents in San Diego County who can easily commute to our public beaches to earn a very nice living. I'm extremely concerned, now that I know for a fact, that the individuals who are earning that living right now are almost exclusively white males. That does not represent the diverse population of our city, our county, or of this country, Eddie."

She paused, anticipating an argument, but none came.

"The solution to this problem, Mr. Mayor, is a more aggressive outreach program and new legislation with quotas that ensure minority hiring for those jobs on the beaches. We also need to provide a living example of what we are attempting to recruit, and create a new breed of municipal ocean lifeguard to mitigate the *white doll* impact on the minorities in this county. Marisol demonstrated exemplary leadership qualities, and she quickly attained unprecedented success as a city employee, Eddie, but she and those outstanding student-athletes from Lincoln Heights *all* failed that tryout . . . *every single one of them.*"

Amanda could hear the mayor breathing in deeply, so she briefly paused.

"Now, not a single one of them is eligible to work on a beach in *your* city, Mr. Mayor . . . and every other graduate from that academy . . . all thirty of them . . . each and every one of them . . . is white. How in the world can you be okay with that?"

Peete had no choice but to agree with his major campaign contributor. *Her logic is impeccable, and her cause will support my campaign for re-election.*

The mayor politely completed the call, hung up the phone, and immediately called Richard Morgan.

**36**

Mid-Morning
Tuesday, April 8, 1997
Lifeguard Headquarters
Quivira Basin, Mission Bay

Lt. Morgan remained calm, not yet feeling the need to defend his academy's graduation criteria or the Patrol's hiring policies. "Eddie, with all due respect, if your twelve-year-old daughter, Nikki, needed to be rescued outside the surf line, who would you want to execute that rescue? A neophyte ocean swimmer that first heard about a really cool job opportunity at some random career fair just six months before his or her first day on the job?"

"A rare use of hyperbole, Lieutenant . . . effective, however. Go on."

"Sir, why recruit individuals who have little or no ocean experience and attempt to, first, convince them that this is a job or a career that they might be interested in, and second, spend valuable time and money training them just so they *might* eventually succeed?"

"Your point is well taken, Richard. However, this topic is much bigger than that."

"I understand, but we must remain focused on our imperative, sir: saving lives, preventing drownings, and avoiding unnecessary injuries.

Sir, with all due respect to you, and what I can clearly see is an extremely sensitive political issue that you are being tasked with, the logical, definitive solution is to continue to utilize the experienced watermen who grow up right here on our beaches, regardless of their cultural background, gender . . . whatever."

Peete said nothing.

"These *Barbie and Ken dolls* that grew up on the beach, sir, they clearly make the best candidates. It's natural, accomplished by attraction. There's no promotion, no marketing, and no persuasion, and we're not excluding anyone either. The ocean does all of the excluding for us. And thank God it does, sir, so others like Nikki can swim out into trouble, but still come home that night."

The mayor breathed in deeply, paused for several moments, and redirected his favorite subordinate.

"I can't disagree with your reasoning, Richard, but that's not what this is about. There are glass ceilings in place here. This woman's *imperative* is to shatter that glass and raise the roof for her community. She's serious, she's formidable, and more importantly, Richard, she's right."

Morgan knew that the mayor was between a rock and a hard place, so he decided not to press too hard.

"So, what she's saying is that our payroll is mostly white men because of a bias that has existed from a time way before the civil rights movement? She's suggesting that minorities across the board have been geographically and culturally conditioned to eliminate themselves as candidates for these jobs, and they believe that these jobs are only available to white people that grow up along the coast. Am I getting this right?"

"That is correct, Lieutenant. The latest data support the conclusion that at least sixty-five percent of American minority children still demonstrate some type of self-directed negative bias when taking similar tests to the one administered by Dr. Clark a long time ago."

Morgan exhaled fully and remained silent as Mayor Peete continued.

"This obviously goes way deeper than ocean lifeguarding opportunities, Richard, but our focus must be on how this phenomenon affects the DCS, your lifeguard patrol, and this city, now and in the future. My guess is that Dr. Villareal will look for some correlation to expand her research into all of our public safety units, and she will task me to influence their numbers as well. This is nothing new, Richard, it's just taken a while to expose the unique paradox of your specific profession. Consider that maybe you and your watermen colleagues have simply been flying under the radar, perhaps without even knowing it."

Morgan paused and shook his head.

"I hope I don't sound biased myself," he answered, "but is she suggesting that this is *my* fault? Since we, or I, rather, have done nothing specific to stop something that I wasn't even aware of, then I, or *we,* as a municipal agency, are all guilty of discrimination? Because we didn't proactively recognize and identify minority job seekers from non-coastal neighborhoods first, and then we failed to invite and prepare them to attend and complete our pre-hiring academy, we are guilty of discrimination?"

"Well, in a word, *yes.* You never disappoint me with your quick grasp of things, Richard. That's not sarcasm either. What I admire about you the most, Lieutenant—even more than your passion about providing the finest public coastal safety services possible—is your ability to expand your mind, and expand your values, too. You are probably the fairest man I've ever served with, Richard. Your character and your leadership ability will make you a very fine captain, and chief, someday. You're the best, and I truly appreciate how much I can depend on you to be reasonable and flexible when things get dicey like this."

Morgan thought silently for several moments. *The requirements are the same for all candidates, even though they are skewed toward benefitting those who are familiar with the ocean. But that's who I want to hire, that's who I need to hire. It's a lifeguard test; it's not a social experiment. Individuals who grow up close to the beach are the ones who want to become ocean lifeguards.*

*It's been that way for as long as I can remember, passed down from generation to generation, to family and friends, summer after summer . . . and even this March, with only seven or eight minorities out of 70 total cadets. But no minorities graduated, and Cynthia was the only female . . . That is a lot of white males . . . 29 out of 30. They're right, that is undeniably discriminating. Ugghh . . .*

Morgan then realized that it was time to adjust the demanding criteria for graduation from the academy and the high standards he had kept in place to get hired. It wasn't the first time that somebody had complained about the difficulty of some of the testing conditions. It was, however, the first time that somebody had suggested, and provided supporting data, that the tests were culturally biased. Lt. Morgan decided that he would not be proud or defiant, nor would he resist his mayor's suggestion.

He knew that the ocean itself would eventually determine who would make it, and who would walk away. He also knew that whomever he hired in the future would have earned it. He accepted the new reality that would present itself very soon.

*This is a low-level bureaucratic action that will provide an exemption for a small percentage of job seekers, over the course of many years. I would be foolish to get upset over this. Be fair, just like the mayor said I am, and provide the opportunity, but continue to allow the ocean itself to determine who is fit for duty.*

"Eddie, listen, the solution is simple . . ."

16 months later
August, 1998
Ocean Beach

There are many proud traditions and unique social events planned each year by the men and women who serve in the San Diego Lifeguard Patrol. The annual ocean relay competition between the three city districts is perhaps the social pinnacle, complete with a raucous party on the beach that moves after sundown to someplace more intimate, and always includes plenty of drinking and hooking up. Longboard surfing contests and distance paddling races preceded smaller gatherings that didn't get anywhere near as out of control as the relay after-party did, but they were events that strengthened friendships, developed community, and, more importantly, provided the opportunity to drink and hook up with someone you've been curious about. The one event that was certain to get the most out of hand each year, however, was the rookie party.

Traditionally, the majority of the Patrol's rookies worked an entire summer on Mission Bay before they were given the opportunity to work on the oceanfront. That being the case, the rookie party was usually held at one of the Bay stations and would continue well into the night, with blazing bonfires on the beach that burned warmly and glowed brightly until the police broke it up. The event's attendance was dominated by rookies and second-year guards. A smaller percentage of veteran SOLs and a few of the instructors and interns from the academy made cameo appearances, but usually left early and let the young revelers do their thing. What kept most of the veterans and POLs from attending each year was the outdoor venue, someplace out on the cold, damp, and windy Bay.

SOL Marisol Escobar, however, came up with a better idea during her rookie summer of 1998. After graduating from the Fall 1997 academy, as Dr. Villareal demanded, Marisol waited until May of 1998 to take a five-month leave of absence from her permanent Aquatics Supervisor position at the city's Lincoln Park pool. She was assigned to a crew of 10 that patrolled Leisure Lagoon on Mission Bay, and she thrived in the position. Her bilingual abilities were critical, she memorized locations and street names quickly, and she picked up radio codes and communication protocols sooner than most of the other rookies. She had an assertive personality, and she quickly moved into a leadership role. She rarely had to enter the water to assist distressed swimmers, and even when she did, bay rescues were a piece of cake, usually a simple matter of run, reach, and grab.

SOL Escobar enjoyed her first summer on the Bay and demonstrated excellence and professionalism, just as her city supervisors predicted she would. She showed potential for advancement, and Morgan instructed that summer's two Bay supervisors, POLs Mike Johnson and Gary Zampese, to place Escobar in positions of responsibility where she would be given the opportunity to lead. She so impressed her colleagues that they nominated her for the Patrol's Rookie of the Year award. That award, however, was given to Latrelle Jackson, who killed it during his first summer on the oceanfront while stationed at South Mission Beach. Cynthia Harden, who had received the same award in 1997, attended the semi-formal awards banquet with Latrelle, and kissed him lightly on the cheek when he returned to their table with a handsome plaque and generous gift certificate in hand.

During that summer of 1998, Marisol's father, Victor, visited his daughter frequently on the Bay, bringing food and drinks for her and her colleagues. He often brought breakfast burritos, and on weekends, he occasionally brought stacked boxes of large pizzas to feed every guard on duty. All of the Bay guards loved Victor Trujillo-Escobar, and because they loved him so much, Marisol quickly became every Bay guard's newest *bff.*

By the end of one of his routine half-hour visits in late July, Marisol had explained to her father the historical significance of the Patrol's annual rookie party. Victor enthusiastically agreed to fund a party that nobody in the Patrol was likely to forget anytime soon. Marisol did an excellent job of marketing the event, and by the time the week of the party arrived, every member of the Patrol and many members of other lifeguard agencies, north and south of San Diego, had heard about the event.

POL Zampese briefed Lt. Morgan about Escobar's role in planning the event. "Apparently sir, she's going to host quite a bash in Ocean Beach next Sunday night. Word is *everybody's* going."

Victor rented the entire outdoor patio area adjacent to The Main Tower Bar and Grill on Santa Monica Avenue, right across the street from the Ocean Beach main tower. The patio was large enough to host a crowd of at least 100 people, and Victor hired Marisol's favorite Tijuana band, *Santos Patrones*, to play all night. Victor made a prepayment of a thousand dollars to the bar's owner, and Marisol printed coupons and gift certificates good for fish tacos, cheeseburgers, carne asada fries, sodas, and 16-ounce draft beers. Margaritas, shots of tequila, and other alcoholic beverages could be purchased at the bar, and security personnel gave bracelets to those that showed valid ID. By 10 o'clock, the bar tab was dry, but that provided plenty of time for Marisol, a few of her rookie Bay guard colleagues, and a larger crew of veteran SOLs to get loose enough to jump off of the OB pier on that beautiful night with clear skies and a full moon.

Lt. Morgan, Sgt. Bobby Moreland, and POL Randy Shields all had front row seats from the stern of Moreland's 32-foot Navistar, anchored just south of the pier. In flat, calm water just above a reef, the three senior officers casually attempted to observe the party. It was their own tradition to party along on rookie night and reminisce about their advancement through the ranks. They enjoyed freshly-caught fish and icy-cold beer on Bobby's comfortable boat while listening to Jerry Coleman provide radio play-by-play of game three of a Padres/Rockies series. Each had his own pair of binos, and, just in case something extraordinary occurred, they could use Shield's camera with the special lens he used to photograph his daughter's surfing contests.

When they noticed the group of approximately 20 men and 10 women charging up the stairs that led to the long concrete pier, the three men quickly realized what was about to happen. Rookies traditionally jumped the pier on rookie party night, and occasionally, civilians joined them. The jumpers would then swim the quarter mile back to shore to retrieve the dry clothes that they had peeled off and left behind on the beach or had handed to somebody up on the pier who wasn't going to jump. This group, however, had grown much larger than the groups on past rookie nights, and Morgan did not want there to be a need for a mass rescue. But he realized that preventing the group from jumping would have been a total buzz kill. As a preventive measure, the lieutenant dialed Quivira HQ and ordered the on-duty sergeant to launch *Ocean 1*, *Code 2*, to the north side of the OB pier.

*Code 2.*

*Use urgency, but no lights or siren.*

The rescue vessel arrived just before the group reached the end of the long pier.

A few non-jumpers remained fully clothed and collected last-minute garments from the group of young men and women. The women stripped down to their panties and bras while Marisol, Claritza, and another bold, buzzed female rookie relinquished their bras just before jumping. The majority of men jumped in their boxers or their board shorts, while three young males stood on the rail naked. Each did a full and proud 360-degree turn, while some of the females gazed at their fit, strong, and athletic bodies. A few of the rookies who had already jumped into the ocean howled and shouted from the water's surface 35 feet below to the hesitant trio of streakers.

"Do it! Go for it!"

Morgan, Moreland, and Shields were standing on the bow watching and listening to their newest subordinates rallying on the pier when they heard a distinguishable voice loudly attempting to motivate the jumpers.

"Grab your balls with one hand and keep your other hand above your head. If you put both hands on your balls you'll tip over and take a header! C'mon! One hand on your balls and jump, you pussies!"

The men in the boat burst into laughter, remembering quickly that they were hoping to remain unseen. As they attempted to quiet down, they giggled like buzzed high school jocks. The voice they heard was unmistakable. There was no question that Bryce North was already in the water.

Shields cracked up, rolling on the padded stern bench.

"He is priceless. I love that guy!"

North had told his good friends earlier that he would not be able to join them on Moreland's boat that evening. He had plans to meet his ex-wife at her Bikram yoga studio in Solana Beach for a session of painful and humbling heat-induced exhaustion, followed by a stir-fry tofu dinner and what Suri hoped would be a long night of tantric lovemaking. She planned the romantic, full-moon evening to try, once again, and work things out. North, however, was still struggling to maintain his commitments with his forgiving New Age lover, and he had changed his mind. He found it much easier to relate to the young women he trained during the academy and attempted to "mentor" afterward. His habitual fraternization continued to be the undoing of his reconciliation efforts with his ex-wife, and the rookie party was the one event each year he would not miss.

Morgan immediately relaxed after realizing North was in the water with several rescue cans. Sgt. Mercer had piloted *Ocean 1* alongside the pier to escort the group through the flat surf on the well-lit and warm, dry summer night. Nobody got hurt, and the three off-duty men in Moreland's boat remained unseen and unnoticed. Everyone retrieved all of their articles of clothing eventually, although members of the opposite sex seemed to be collecting each other's undergarments, looking for the owner as if they were playing pin the tail on the donkey.

Bryce North and Mike Johnson noticed that Marisol Escobar was among the last to make it back to shore and had not yet retrieved her clothing. Johnson was lurking in the shadows, close to the stairwell the jumpers had used to access the pier, while North stood in full view under a bright floodlight attached to the exterior wall of the Ocean Beach main tower. They noticed that Marisol was a bit winded, causing her chest to rise and fall as her tall silhouette glided across the beach in the moonlight.

She had been training hard while on duty and looked very fit, her body well toned. She sauntered around the moonlit beach unabashedly, still topless, while searching for the individual who held her clothing. As she walked away from the main tower, she flipped her long, dark hair backward around her shoulders. She reached up with both of her hands to gather her hair and squeezed the water out of the thick mass. Escobar continued walking, holding her arms above her head, wrapping her locks with a hair tie that she had left on her wrist.

Mike Johnson managed to find the young partier who Marisol had given her clothing to, and relieved the intimidated girl of her responsibilities. He held Marisol's full-cupped satin bra in one hand, and her hip-hugging khaki shorts and a tight-fitting red V-neck sweater in the other. He stared as she walked directly toward him, her entire body still clearly exposed in the full moonlight. When she recognized Johnson, and noticed that he was watching her, she quickly crossed her arms and placed her hands over her breasts, covering the dark nipples that he had been looking at.

Marisol appeared disappointed it was Johnson that fate had assigned to her and spoke curtly.

"Is that my bra?"

Johnson's game plan had worked in the past, so he tried again.

"I don't know. Should I help you try it on, so we can both find out? I want to make sure this one gets to its rightful owner. This is a spectacular bra. I just had to meet the girl who puts her big tits in this thing."

"Ewwww. I'm pretty sure that you can't say that to me no matter how many beers I've had. Your uninvited comments are totally sexual in nature, and I don't want to hear them again. Johnson, give me my clothes, and stop staring at me."

"You know you want it. Why else would you have taken this thing off and pranced around the beach like that? I got to tell you, Escobar, you are real easy to look at. If you're looking for something to do later, I've got just the thing for you."

"Gross. In your dreams is the only place we'll ever do something together. Nice try. Don't talk to me again tonight. You're a pig."

Johnson made Escobar wait another 10 seconds, gazing at her abdomen and below her waist, stopping at her tiny, wet, see-through panties. He moaned loudly as he tilted his head to gain a better view.

"Mmmmm, mmmm, mmm. Neatly trimmed, too . . . just like it should be."

He teased her as he dangled the bra in front of him. When she reached for it, he pulled it away and laughed

"Not until you let me see what you're hiding."

"Fuck off, Johnson! Enough already. Give me my clothes!"

Marisol aggressively grabbed for, and retrieved, her bra. She turned away from him and secured it in place before reaching for her shorts, which he played tug-of-war with for a couple of seconds before relenting, laughing again.

"I was just playing with ya. I'm only kidding, Rook. I just wanted to be sure my favorite Bay guard got all of her clothes back. Have a nice night, Escobar. Nice party, by the way."

"Whatever, Johnson. You're going to pay for what you just did, trust me."

**38**

Sunday, August 23, 1998
Ocean Beach

Marisol Escobar turned abruptly away, disgusted by her Bay station supervisor's behavior. She jogged toward the Ocean Beach main tower. A small group of rookies had assembled by a set of double doors that Mr. North had opened, allowing the stoked young jumpers to rinse off and warm up in the tower's shower before getting dressed and returning to the party. North was standing in the doorway and had witnessed the entire event involving Johnson and Escobar. He was more impressed with how stunningly attractive Escobar was than he was by Johnson's predictable and unsuccessful attempt at seduction.

*Wow. She is gorgeous, and feisty. I thought for sure she was going to slap him. Maybe I should try to make her feel better.*

Marisol was still covering her breasts with her shorts as she walked briskly past North and declared in a near shout, "He's a pervert. I know you saw what he just did. Did you hear what he said to me? He's a predator and a pig and you know it. He should be fired."

She turned away and went to the shower, slamming the door without waiting for a reply from North.

North smiled and started to laugh, but he quickly realized that there were several drunk and impressionable rookies in the area. He straightened up and, without saying another word, walked onto the sand several feet away. He stood there and enjoyed the loud music from across the street. Escobar ignored him when she left the tower to rejoin her party.

Hopeful that the incident would attract no further attention, North secured the OB tower and returned to the patio across the street. He continued to watch closely as Escobar went directly to the bar and ordered another round of beers and several shots of tequila for her new lifeguard friends. North saw Mike Johnson walk to his Harley, fire up the engine several times as he walked the bike backward a few steps, then turn and loudly ride away.

SOL Escobar was still upset. She was offended. She felt disrespected. She was made to feel inferior.

Suppressed. Powerless.

Johnson holding her clothes like that had made her feel vulnerable. She didn't like it.

But something else was happening. She felt it not just from inside of her, a tingling, but from the outside, a frequency of energy that she could actually smell, but not like a fragrance. It was warm and damp, maybe the smell of sea salt. She wasn't sure. She just knew it was there. And she liked how it made her feel. She had become aroused by the space's clearing for sexual expression and lust. It seemed as if nobody cared about anything but finding a partner for sex that night.

Including Marisol.

Marisol noticed that Latrelle was seated in a corner booth with Cynthia Harden and two guards from Ocean Beach, SOLs Fernan and Snow.

As she handed out plastic cups filled with cold, foamy beer to a group of rookies seated at the next booth, Marisol returned a contempt-filled glare directed from Cynthia, who stood up.

Cynthia looked down at Latrelle, her hand resting softly on his round shoulder and said, "I'll be right back, Stallion." She headed toward the outdoor patio, again glaring at Marisol as she walked by, thinking, *I don't even like being in the same room with this poser. Look at her buying all of her friendships. I can't stand her.*

Although Cynthia was uncertain about leaving Latrelle's side, she had an intuitive sense about Marisol's intentions, one that she hoped to confirm tonight.

Latrelle and Marisol had hardly spoken since the call urging him to join her EEOC grievance against Lt. Morgan. During their academy training last August, nearly a year ago, they were able to work together and get along though. On the day of their graduation from the academy, they hugged briefly, Latrelle pulling away first. Latrelle saw Marisol only once after that, during Christmas break at a grocery store near his mother's house in Lincoln Heights. They spoke briefly.

Marisol, however, missed Latrelle, and never got over the rejection she felt when he refused to sign her petition. She still badly wanted some form of validation from him. The alcohol and the captivating energy in the room had her head spinning, and her thighs tingling.

*I wish it would have been Latrelle who was holding my bra tonight.*

Latrelle saw Marisol look directly at him as she downed a shot of tequila. He saw her shudder slightly, then shake her head briefly. He did not look away as she slipped a lime wedge between her teeth, wrap her lips around it and suck the juice out while pulling the fruit from the peel with her perfect teeth. He watched her take a deep breath then look away, down at the table top from which she retrieved a foamy cup of beer, lifted it to her lips and gulped down the top two inches.

He quickly looked away, hoping she wouldn't approach.

She approached.

Latrelle reluctantly turned his eyes to Marisol. Their eyes met. She smiled and, without hesitating, she slid into the space Cynthia had vacated. Marisol turned toward him, and moved closer until she touched his body. She didn't wait for him to speak, and did not allow him to move away. She subtly slid a hand beneath the table and tugged at the inside of his thigh. She leaned in closely until her breasts pressed against his shoulder.

Latrelle looked across the table at Fernan and Snow, their eyebrows raised, jaws dropped.

Marisol placed her mouth close to his ear. She spoke in a low sultry voice that only Latrelle could hear.

"You are so attractive, Latrelle, I can't stop myself. I am so proud of you for everything you've accomplished. You are such an amazing man."

Marisol then paused, noticing that Fernan and Snow were staring at her. Curtly, she said, "Do you mind?"

Fernan and Snow said nothing, each leaned back against the cushioned booth, but neither looked away, eyebrows still raised, mouths open.

After adjusting her body and moving even closer to Latrelle, Marisol's lips softly touched his ear. She whispered, "I've been thinking about you a lot. I miss you, Latrelle. I want us to be together tonight. I know a place where we can go and be alone. We can talk."

She rested her forehead on his shoulder, beginning to realize that the tequila was catching up. She giggled, raised her head, and sloppily winked across the table at Fernan and Snow.

She turned to Latrelle, used both hands and grabbed his closest bicep. She stood up and pulled against his body weight. She was easily strong enough to slide his body across the cushioned bench seat to the edge of the booth.

Marisol implored him, this time loud enough for several people in the room to hear her say, "Come with me to my car, Latrelle. Let's go. C'mon."

**39**

Sunday, August 23, 1998
Ocean Beach

Escobar removed her hands from Latrelle's bicep and weaved her way across the dining room floor toward the front door. Latrelle sat motionless at the edge of the booth, his feet and shoulders turned open toward the room. He looked stunned and unsure about what had just happened. Although Escobar looked back, beckoning with a come-hither finger gesture, Latrelle did not move. After several long moments standing alone at the door, Escobar showed a pouty lower lip and a sad face for Latrelle to see, but she did relent. It appeared that her attempts to persuade Latrelle to leave the party with her were over.

For now.

Marisol returned to the bar and was quickly joined by a host of Bay lifeguard rookies who instantly began admiring her beauty and embracing her generosity.

Cynthia observed the entire interaction between Marisol and Latrelle. She watched Escobar take a seat at the bar and waited until Marisol turned her back before returning to Latrelle at their booth. She kissed him on the cheek as soon as she arrived. Fernan and Snow laughed and shook their heads in disbelief at the unexpected behavior of their usually refined, and always in control, colleague.

Latrelle started to shift nervously when he saw that Marisol had turned her stool and was staring at him. She stood, left the bar, and stepped toward their booth. Cynthia stood, having already noticed. Before Marisol arrived at the booth, Cynthia stepped toward her. She shook her head and spoke loudly. Several heads in the dining room turned.

"No! He's not interested in you, Marisol. Not since that day you showed your *ass* down in IB. Your true colors glowed that day. We both know what a fraud you are, and everybody else here that hasn't figured it out by now . . . they'll figure it out soon enough."

She glared at Marisol and scowled.

"And good luck finding someone to scratch that itch of yours, Escobar."

Cynthia turned, kissed Latrelle on the lips, and said, "We're outta here, let's go."

Holding her hand, Latrelle followed Cynthia out the door. Upon exiting the building, he said, "That was really uncomfortable. Thanks."

Cynthia laughed.

"You're welcome, Latrelle."

She turned to face him, brought her arms around his shoulders, and kissed him, prying his lips open with her tongue, searching for his. She held the back of his head in her strong hands, and rolled her neck as he reciprocated.

An aggressive, passionate kiss.

She pulled away and looked Latrelle dead in the eye.

"I think I have an idea about how you can show me that appreciation."

Over the course of the past year, while Latrelle was at USC, his contact with Cynthia consisted mostly of late night phone calls, but upon his return to San Diego during the summer following his freshman year, they began spending more time together. While their relationship gained momentum, Latrelle found himself reluctant to move too quickly, focusing instead on developing his lifeguarding skills and swimming prowess. He liked Cynthia and was attracted to her, but their age difference gnawed at him and the story he had heard about Cynthia's teen pregnancy contributed to that reluctance. As a result, the level of physical intimacy in their relationship had not developed much beyond hand-holding, back rubs, and tender kisses. While this frustrated Cynthia, she never pressed him and she never complained.

This evening would be different.

Upon leaving the rookie party, the couple climbed into Cynthia's 4Runner and headed directly to her sailboat at Marina Village. Cynthia brought Latrelle onboard and led him into her master cabin. He watched her undress, finally stepping out of her panties, then did nothing to resist when she gently pushed him backward onto her bed. She crawled toward his groin and removed his shorts. Now he was naked too. She satisfied her curiosity while pleasing him for several minutes. Feeling his body tighten, she stopped and she looked into his eyes. She smiled, and kissed him on the belly. His skin was thin, the muscle beneath it firm. She kissed up his torso, then sat up and placed her hips on top of his. Latrelle moaned with pleasure, then suddenly rolled sideways and pulled away from her.

"What's wrong?" Cynthia asked.

"What if you get pregnant? Shouldn't we use a condom?"

Cynthia chuckled.

"Well, I don't have a condom, and don't worry about it. I've been using birth control for a long time. Trust me, Latrelle, getting pregnant is the *last* thing that I want to happen . . . at least not anytime soon."

Latrelle said nothing.

Cynthia asked, "Are you okay?"

"Yeah, I'm just a little nervous, I guess."

Cynthia laughed.

"Relax. I know what to do."

"Yeah, well, that's what makes me so nervous."

Cynthia laughed again.

"Don't be scared, Latrelle."

She held his face in her hands and looked directly into his eyes, their noses almost touching.

"I know what Colin Cantrelle told you during the academy."

Latrelle's eyes opened wide, but he said nothing.

"Eventually, a lot of people in Coronado found out what happened to me. That is not an easy community to keep a secret in. Colin's big sister, Chelsea . . . well, she and I played water polo together. My teammates were the first to figure it out . . . so . . . obviously her little brother must have heard about it, too. It's not such a big secret anymore, but it was a long time ago, Latrelle . . . I mean . . . who cares now?"

Latrelle wasn't expecting to hear any of that, as he had no idea that she knew that he knew.

He sat up, but said nothing.

"Latrelle, it's all true . . . it happened during my junior year."

Latrelle squinted and tilted his head.

"An abortion?"

Cynthia breathed in, sighed, and bowed her head.

"Yes. My childhood Navy doctor performed the procedure. He's my godfather . . . Colonel Blew."

She paused.

"His wife counseled me afterward, she's a doctor, too . . . a civilian psychiatrist. I still see her once a month. She was basically my mother during my school years. She came to a lot of my junior lifeguard events, swim meets, and water polo games. She has always been there for me. She still is. She was at my baptism . . . she's my godmother. My dad's old business partner in their garage down in IB, Chief Fitzpatrick, he knew about it, too. He and my dad were like brothers. They all looked after me when my Dad was away on deployments."

"Did you tell your father?"

"No. And neither did they. Not back then at least."

"They were the only ones who knew?"

"Yep."

"Who did you live with back then . . . when your dad was gone? You didn't live by yourself did you?"

"No. I lived with my uncle Brady. He's my dad's little brother. After my grandfather died in Indiana, Brady moved in with us. I was six. He was like, thirteen at the time."

Cynthia looked away, as if remembering something, then said, "When my dad went on his first deployment, Brady was my legal guardian."

"How old were you when your dad left?"

"Freshman year of high school."

Latrelle nodded.

"That's when my dad died . . . my freshman year at Roosevelt. Car accident."

"So that's what happened to your dad . . ."

"Yeah, sorry. I never talk about it."

"Latrelle, *I'm* sorry."

"The accident was head-on, about a mile from my house. My mom and I both heard the crash. It woke me up."

"Wow, that's insane."

"Yeah, we waited up together until about four a.m. when the police finally knocked on the door. We both knew why the cop was there."

"Oh, my God, Latrelle. That's horrible. I am so sorry."

Cynthia reached and hugged him, then held him in her arms as he continued speaking.

"The next day my mom went to the morgue to identify his body. She told me that there was nothing left but an empty bag of skin. I'm glad I didn't see it."

"Poor Vanessa."

"Yeah . . . but he and my brother would sometimes be so mean to her. It was actually more peaceful around the house . . . and my neighborhood, after Marquis went to jail and my father died. It really was; I can't lie about that. My mom and I both gained a lot of strength from all of that. She is the strongest person I know."

"I love your mom. She's awesome."

"Yes, she is."

There was a long moment of awkward silence before Latrelle said, "Do you want to tell me about the abortion?"

Cynthia sighed and said, "I know it was the right thing to do, but it still hurts deep inside." She pointed to her stomach. "I mean . . . she was in there."

"She?"

Latrelle's eyes welled.

Cynthia blinked repeatedly.

"Doctor Blew wouldn't tell me at first, but I begged him. I told him I wanted to know who it was in there . . . and who we were going to . . . kill."

Latrelle said nothing.

"I know she's in heaven with my Dad now . . . her grandfather. I still love her . . . I always will. It wasn't her fault."

Cynthia nodded her head several times.

"With all of the support I had, I finally moved past the self-hate and a pretty deep depression. It took me a while to get there though. I was pretty fucked up . . . sorry . . . I mean, I was pretty messed up for about a year. I had made up a story in my head that I was an unworthy person. I really let my dad down, too, and all of those people who supported me while he was away serving his country. I felt like a complete loser, and a liar, too . . . an unforgiven sinner. The guilt just ate me up. For months, all I did was cry."

"I don't know what to say, Cynthia. I can only imagine how difficult and dark that time must have been for you."

Cynthia sniffled, then breathed in deeply. She wiped her eyes and exhaled.

"I felt awful. And I was very angry at the guy that did it to me." She tilted her head down. "I didn't stop him though, Latrelle. And then we did it again and we kept doing it until I found out that I was pregnant. We never did it again after the day I found out though, and I never told the guy, I just like, broke up with him."

"What happened to him?"

"He moved away from Coronado the next year. I haven't seen or heard from him since then."

Latrelle looked into her teary eyes, his own eyes filled with empathy and asked, "Did it hurt?"

"Did what hurt?"

"The abortion."

"No, I mean, not really, but it was invasive and humiliating. I felt so ashamed . . . I had a terrible water polo season that year. I missed like half of the season. I got really sick after the procedure, I missed a lot of school, and my grades totally sucked. I was sure that I had blown everything . . . college, water polo . . . and that I had lost the respect of everyone who believed in and looked up to me."

She shook her head, a chagrined look appearing on her face. Then she snorted softly and said, "I did a little better my senior year though. I got into UCLA, but I was still pretty depressed. Playing in college really helped me move through it, so I'm mostly healed from it all now, but it left a pretty deep bruise on my soul."

Latrelle asked, "Who was he?"

"Who?"

"The guy."

"Oh. It's not important. He's gone. It was all wrong, obviously. If my dad had been there, and not deployed, none of that would have ever happened. I strayed pretty far without my dad around, Latrelle . . . I really did. I started drinking, smoking pot, ditching school . . . I was totally misguided, but this guy . . . he made me feel like I was cool. I'd never felt that way before. I never felt that confident around people, except for when I was in the water. That's the only place I ever felt confidence. But out of the water, I was always just the big, ugly, water polo player."

"Oh, stop. There is absolutely nothing ugly about you, Cynthia. You're beautiful."

"You're so sweet, thank you . . . I don't feel ugly anymore though, not until I think about the abortion that is, and I try not to do that."

She shrugged and Latrelle nodded.

"So, my dad was away on three separate deployments while I was in high school. I'm actually pretty lucky that I didn't screw my life up even worse than I did. But I dug a pretty deep hole for myself, and I barely climbed out of it." She smiled. "But I did."

Latrelle tilted his head and looked up, then nodded, as if he remembered something. Then he said, "My brother, Marquis, he actually got a girl pregnant . . . but she had the baby. She never told anybody about it though. She barely showed, so nobody could tell until it was too late. That's when she told Marquis, and then he told my mom. My mom said she would help them if they needed her to, but Marquis never did anything about it. He just told the girl that it was her problem, and said that he wasn't the father."

Latrelle shook his head from side to side.

"I don't know what happened to Marquis . . . he was so cool when I was a little kid . . . he just changed. He's in prison now."

Cynthia gasped slightly and uttered, "Really? Prison?"

"Yeah. He and another kid that I grew up with robbed the liquor store in my neighborhood. The guy behind the counter recognized both of them and just laughed, but then Marquis pulled a gun and hit the guy in the head with it, took all of the cash out of the drawer, raided the liquor, and trashed the place. They got arrested that night. Apparently they'd hit a few other shops before that. They got convicted on a few counts. He's still got like eight more years to go."

"Wow, that's a long time. Do you ever visit him?"

"Yeah. I used to go with my mom every month, but he doesn't really want us to come anymore. She goes once in a while, but I haven't seen him in over a year."

Cynthia just listened and allowed him to continue.

"The other guy that he got sentenced with got stabbed less than a year after he went in. He's dead. He was only twenty years old. I'm afraid that might happen to Marquis, too, but he lifts weights all the time, and he's in a gang in there . . . he's pretty hard now. It's pretty scary when I go there to talk with him . . . that's why I don't go anymore."

He looked up into Cynthia's eyes.

"I've seen my share of bad choices and ugly incidents. Cynthia, I'm not going to judge you. I get it. You did the best you could at the time. It's okay."

Cynthia's eyes leaked tears, but she smiled and said, "My God, Latrelle, you are like the perfect man."

Latrelle laughed.

"Thanks, but that's a little too much pressure for me. I'm just saying . . . it doesn't matter what you did then. I'm glad though, that you told me.

After Colin said that to me, I was a little confused about who you were . . . it just didn't add up for me."

Cynthia smiled, then said, "Tell me about your dad."

"My dad? Well, when he was sober, he was a good man. He played center field in Triple-A for ten years before he got called up to the bigs, so he was never around. He played for the Oakland A's in the seventies. I've got pictures and VCR tapes of his games. He was good. You ever hear of a player named Reggie Jackson?"

"Wasn't he a Yankee? Home run guy?"

"He was, but after he was an A. My dad collided with him chasing a deep fly ball in a game at Fenway. It knocked him down hard on the warning track, up against the fence, but he hung onto it. He ran, like, forever, to get there. He could fly. It was an amazing catch. He could chase down fly balls like an all-star, and he stole a lot of bases. He had a cannon for an arm, too."

Latrelle chuckled.

"He said he couldn't hit a big league slider though, so he didn't get to stay with the A's past that one season."

He shook his head, a disappointed look appearing on his face.

"He drank too much, and he used to chase women in every town that he played in. He cheated on my mom all the time . . ."

Cynthia placed her palm on Latrelle's cheek, then moved a finger to his lips.

"Shhhh. You don't have to tell me anymore if you don't want to, okay?"

Latrelle looked up into Cynthia's eyes and said, "Okay."

"But thank you for opening up to me, and thank you for listening and not judging me. You are such a good person, Latrelle. I am sooo lucky I found you."

Latrelle blushed and looked away for a moment, but Cynthia was on him. She kissed him gently, then rolled him onto his back and they made love for the first time, for a long time.

Cynthia left the bedroom and returned with two Chaco Tacos.

They talked and laughed while they devoured the delicious chocolate, creamy, crunchy, frozen ice cream treats.

Then they made love again, for a long time, again.

After, Cynthia rested her head on Latrelle's chest and whispered softly, "I think I'm falling in love with you, Stallion."

When she heard no reply, she looked up, and saw that Latrelle, with a satisfied smile on his face, had fallen asleep.

**Early Morning**
**Monday, August 24, 1998**
**Lifeguard Headquarters**

Senior POL Bryce North debriefed with Lt. Morgan first thing the next morning. After informing the lieutenant of the exchange between Johnson and Escobar, he began to describe Marisol's exit from the ocean that night under the full moon. Morgan stopped North when his description began to focus below her neck.

"That's enough. Anything else I *need* to know?"

"No, but Escobar is right about one thing."

"What's that?"

"Johnson is a predator."

"True. It's probably a good thing *you* didn't find her clothes first."

"Haha! Listen, LT . . . I know you're married to a good Christian woman and all that, but really, you should have seen this chick's body. Dude . . . Escobar is HOT!"

"I get it. I was there, remember? We were right there in Bobby's boat with the big eyes and Randy's surf lens. Escobar is obviously very proud of her body. She knew what she was doing, and she knew that every man within visual scanning range was going to check her out, too. She just wasn't counting on Johnson being the guy that paid the most attention, and I guarantee you that she wasn't counting on exposing herself to me."

He paused.

"She surprised me last night. That was the last thing I ever expected from her. She's obviously got another layer beneath the surface that none of us knew anything about. Apparently, after she takes a few pops, her personality adjusts a bit. I wonder what Mayor Peete knows about that."

He paused again and redirected, careful to respect the confidentiality he promised Peete.

"We sure got a good laugh from you, though. What happened to your date with Suri?"

"Don't ask."

Morgan snorted playfully, thinking, *Same old story.*

North stood and prepared to leave the office. A rescue boat operator like Sgt. Moreland, he was on his way to the docks to begin his shift. Before leaving, however, he turned and reminded the lieutenant of something he overlooked.

"Oh, yeah, LT. There is one more thing."

Morgan did not look up from his desk.

"I'm listening."

"Escobar had more than just a *few pops* last night."

Morgan looked up.

"And?"

"Rick, she could barely walk and there was no way she could drive. I made sure she got home safely though."

"Made sure how?"

"Well, I escorted her out of the party; I could tell that she was wasted. I was surprised that she didn't really have a wing man, so I stepped in."

Morgan smirked and shook his head.

"Do I really want to hear this?"

"Oh, c'mon, Rick. It's nothing like that, at least not with this chick. I know better than that, especially with what you've already been through with her."

"Fair enough. I apologize, go on."

"Well, we stopped and got a burrito, then I drove her out to Bonita by your grandparent's place. Big gated house with a huge wall around it . . . looked like a freaking compound. Her mother was standing at the top of the driveway with some guy wearing a suit when I pulled up. She is not a very friendly woman. She didn't want to talk to me at all."

"Were you alone with Marisol?"

"Oh, no, sir. Martin Arias was there, too. He came along. He actually knew how to get to her house. I guess their parents are friends or something. She slept pretty much the entire way there."

Morgan nodded.

"Okay then, nobody got hurt. Nice work, Bryce."

"We'll see today, I guess, but Escobar should be fine."

North then laughed.

Morgan asked, "What's so funny?"

"Well, she ate like half of a bean burrito at Ortega's. But then she was in the restroom for about ten minutes. She threw up several times. We could hear it . . . the whole place was cracking up. One too many shots of tequila apparently."

"Good thing it was you and not some rookie with a hard-on that drove her home . . . or to his place instead." He shook his head. "Marisol freaking Escobar, Lord help me."

"Yeah, I think you might need a higher power to help you out on this one."

"Copy that. I'll talk to you later, Bryce."

North nodded, turned, and exited the office. Morgan bowed his head, rested his elbows on his desktop, and massaged his scalp with his thumbs and fingertips.

*I thought sending Johnson to the Bay for a summer would mellow him out, and now I have to deal with both him and Escobar? This is going to be about as much fun as getting a freaking cold sore. Who is this woman, and what the hell does she really want?*

**41**

Ten Days Later
Wednesday, September 3, 1998
Lifeguard Headquarters

When Lt. Richard Morgan began directing the academy and hiring rookie lifeguards, he learned quickly that some years the crops were almost barren of raw talent, and he had to try to "make chicken salad out of chicken shit," as his good friend Randy Shields would often remind him. Cynthia Harden's rookie crew was metaphorically full of lean chicken, though, and the March 1997 group quickly enhanced the quality of the professional watermen that staffed San Diego's beaches. Several of her classmates moved up quickly, and even though they did not advance as rapidly as she did, their rate of progress was well beyond the norm.

Morgan delivered on his intentions, and in unprecedented time, SOL Harden received advanced training. While on duty, she reacted effectively and professionally time after time. She recognized weak swimmers and neophyte tourists as soon as they arrived on the beach, and often greeted them warmly, then accurately described to them every hazard they might encounter before directing them to a safer area on the beach. Of course, many tourists, as well as locals, thought they knew more about the ocean than the female lifeguard did, and the result was that, while Cynthia made rescues repeatedly throughout the day, she often rescued those she had already warned, and even then, she might have to rescue the real dumbasses a third, maybe even a fourth, time in a single day. True story. Common story. *Serious dumbasses.*

Cynthia ran medical calls like a paramedic, handled intoxicated and drugged-out "outdoorsmen" (lifeguard code for homeless person) like a well-respected police officer, and offered encouragement and mentoring to younger, less-experienced seasonal guards. She never faltered, impressing each of her supervisors. She received the difficult-to-achieve certifications for main tower observation and PWC operator before completing her 18th month as a seasonal employee. Those accomplishments made her eligible to interview for a POL position. Her Navy training provided all of her advanced emergency medical certifications, as well as advanced dive rescue and dive instructor ratings. Cynthia breezed through the interview, outscoring the entire field of 13 candidates on her first attempt. Then, along with three white males, she accepted one of the newly-funded and highly-coveted positions that Lt. Morgan received from the DCS. The four new supervisors were then sworn in as San Diego peace officers, each receiving their very own heavy and shiny *baaiiddgge* on September 3, 1998, right about the time Marisol Escobar finally recovered from the hangover she "earned" after hosting the 1998 rookie party.

# PART 5

Subterfuge:
Any plan or action used to hide or
evade something.

Five Days Later
Monday, September 8, 1998
Lifeguard Headquarters

Despite the one and only smudge on Escobar's résumé, Lt. Morgan complied with the mayor's directive to fast-track her. Since Marisol had performed so well on the Bay, Morgan had no choice but to facilitate her transition to the oceanfront, starting next summer. After an eventful and productive summer for Harden and Escobar, it was actually Mike Johnson who looked the most like "chicken shit" to Morgan. As he reviewed the tall stack of summer evaluation reports on his desk, he scoffed out loud at his own thoughts.

"I should transfer them both to Mission Beach next summer . . . Johnson and Escobar. Maybe that will get rid of at least one of my headaches."

Morgan knew better, though, and he separated them immediately. He knew for sure that there was no lifeguard station in San Diego big enough for both Mike Johnson and Marisol Escobar. He also knew that if they worked side by side, Johnson would keep trying to get into Escobar's bikini and he would become more belligerent as she continued to reject him. Johnson was still an asset to the Patrol, however, and despite his shortcomings, he always ran his station effectively and kept his beaches safe. Morgan tabled the thought of reassigning his newest duo of adversaries to the same station.

*No. You can't set them both up to fail like that. Not yet at least . . .*

During his debriefing with Mayor Peete, Morgan had been directed to use the Johnson-Escobar incident as an example of sexual harassment and to send a strong message to his watermen. Morgan agreed to suspend Johnson for one week without pay, and then transferred him back to the oceanfront. He decided to say nothing to Escobar about her topless pier jump. He did inform the mayor, however, that there were several eyewitnesses to Escobar's display of "inappropriate" behavior at a Patrol-related event that evening. Morgan also mentioned that some very incriminating photographs had somehow made their way across his desk.

The mayor appreciated the information and praised his favorite subordinate.

"Good work, Lieutenant. You seem to have a way of catching good cards right after a bad hand. Let's hold onto this for now, though, just in case we need it someday."

"Of course, sir."

"And keep pressing on with Escobar. Despite her *revealing* night out on the town, she's still earned a shot at the next level. Her evaluations are solid; you told me so yourself."

"They are, and I will."

"And, Lieutenant . . . you might want to ask one of your most tactful sergeants to pull Miss Escobar aside and have a little off-the-record chat with her about discretion. And have that sergeant be clear. She needs to understand that even though there was no police intervention, she broke a few laws with her jump—not to mention unauthorized entry to the Ocean Beach tower—along with all the others that did the same thing."

"Of course, sir."

"We need to keep this as leverage, if needed."

"I couldn't agree more, sir."

During the first week of September, however, on Marisol's first attempt at qualifying for oceanfront status, she missed the cut-off time on a one-mile run/one-mile swim course. The ocean was very cold on that blustery morning. It was also very choppy, with a slightly above-average swell. After running a very strong mile, once in the ocean, she kept her head mostly out of the water, and her swim back to the finish line took 18 seconds longer than the exam allowed. When Lt. Morgan provided a two-minute adjustment for the swell and the water temperature, however, she and all 11 of the Bay guards that had missed the 32-minute cutoff time were given a pass.

It was pretty cold and windy that day. Morgan was a reasonable man. Fair. 32:00, 34:00, what's the difference?

He informed the mayor later that evening.

"That's what I'm talking about. Nice work, Lieutenant."

Marisol's next assignment would be to a beachfront station where she would work side by side with many long-term veterans who cared primarily about the safety of their patrons and the professionalism of their crews. Most of them knew very little about Marisol Escobar's abilities as an ocean lifeguard, but many had heard something about her impressive display of partying skills that night in Ocean Beach. Most of them had also heard about her EEOC grievance and how she had become the woman that convinced Lt. Morgan that his academy's curriculum was too hard and unfair. Morgan knew that many of his supervising personnel would be leery about getting too close to Escobar, and he assumed that many of his training officers would be intimidated by her reputation for questioning the methodology of those above her in the chain of command.

Before choosing her 1999 summer oceanfront assignment, Morgan placed a call to his good friend, city councilman Scotty Meyers. Morgan found out that the Escobar family's master plan was to have Marisol complete her law degree while working for the Patrol, and once she passed the state bar exam, she would use her credibility as a high-ranking peace officer to maneuver her way onto the city council and then into the city manager's office.

Councilman Meyers elaborated on Escobar's plan.

"Once there, they'll launch Marisol's preferred career into state politics. Their ultimate goal, according to people I know that keep their finger on the pulse of the most prominent San Diego democrats, is to have her sitting in Washington, D.C., as a house rep or a senator. They're grooming her, Rick. Her mother and father have contributed more money to their causes than I've ever heard of . . . and . . . they both support a very popular African-American mayor, even though he's a Republican. They're in a very unique and powerful position. They're working both sides of the aisle."

Meyers paused, and Morgan could hear a deep breath being exhaled before his friend continued.

"I've been told more than once, Rick, that from the time that Marisol was a little girl, she's dreamed about, talked about, written about, and has been very committed to becoming the first female president."

Morgan was confused.

"President of what?"

"The United States, Richard. She wants to be the first female president of this country. I think they're serious, too, and I'm starting to see that they just might have the means for her to become a legitimate candidate. She could start as governor or state senator and get on a ticket as VP first, then run her own campaign after that. President Marisol Escobar . . . Commander in Chief."

Meyers paused, almost choking on the embellished image that he allowed to slip out. He had taken the conversation perhaps an extra step forward, but retreated only slightly.

"Listen, Richard, if you ever underestimate the bureaucratic or political power of somebody in San Diego County while thinking that you have the support of Mayor Peete when you really don't, just make sure it is not the Escobar family that you're underestimating. They are connected in ways deeper than I care to know about. Be careful with this one, Richard. Draw your line somewhere else."

Neither man spoke for several moments. Morgan cleared his throat and adjusted his position at his desk.

Meyers continued.

"I'm serious. This family has some kind of hold on the mayor, and I'm pretty sure that the governor's in their pocket by now, too. They will take you down, or anybody else who opposes them. I mean they will really hurt you, Rick."

Morgan snorted, slightly amused.

"What, you mean, like *Goodfellas?*"

"Dude, listen to me. Her old man might be involved in something like that from what I hear. I know people in the South Bay who are convinced that he's brokering more than just his family's coffee with the shipping and trucking company he owns. Seriously, Rick, if you get in his daughter's way, you might end up in the trunk of a car on the wrong side of the border."

"Shut up! You can't be serious! You come up with some of the craziest ideas I've ever heard."

"Maybe . . . sometimes I may get caught up in the moment a little too much, but not this time. Look, Rick, I have no proof, and I haven't heard anything about any criminal investigation. All I know is what these people told me. It was enough to convince me, though, that I will be very careful about opposing any agenda that woman or her *Women's Diversity Council* puts on the table."

"Wow. That IS serious. I can't believe this is going on here in San Diego. Holy crap, Scotty, this is going to get real, isn't it?"

"Yeah, I guess you could put it that way. Very real."

"Why the heck did she have to become a swimmer? This is going to be a clusterfuck."

"It already is, and it has been for a while. Escobar steamrolled everybody in parks and recreation, and that's a huge department. None of them were tough enough to take her on. Her father wrote the first check to get that pool at Lincoln Park built, and less than a year later, she was named the director. She's an irresistible force, Rick. Let somebody else be the immovable object that gets in her way."

Morgan exhaled loudly, "Damn . . ."

"You've worked too hard, and you're far too important to this city. Just be patient and let them do their thing. It's her mother, bro . . . Dr. Villareal . . . she's the one that's calling all of the shots. She's pulling all the strings, and Marisol is her puppet, so to speak."

"Yeah, I learned that right away. I learned that they're both pretty smart, and good at what they do, too."

"Indeed, Rick, and don't forget about the old man. Those two women may be the brains of the operation, but he is definitely the muscle . . . and the bank."

"Ahhhh. I can't get rid of her. She's all-in, isn't she?"

"I think so, Rick, but I also think that she'll be gone in five, six, maybe seven years if their plan works. It's not going to take her ten years to pass the bar and put her name on a ballot, trust me. Let her go, hell, help her get there faster so she'll be gone sooner. I'm telling you, man, if you get in her way, you could feel the consequences for the rest of your life."

"So, just stay out of her way, and let her have whatever she wants?"

"You asked me for my advice, Rick. This is my advice to you."

**43**

Monday, September 8, 1998
Lifeguard Headquarters

Still seated at his desk, Morgan remembered the meeting with Dr. Villareal that the Mayor had ordered him to attend just after the completion of the March 1997 academy. At that meeting, he had been instructed by Marisol's mother to adjust his graduation criteria and to personally ensure her that each and every member of Escobar's group would graduate from the next academy, and that each of them would also be hired immediately thereafter.

*"I expect them all to receive their certificates and to be placed on the city's payroll this fall. Am I clear enough about that? None of those kids should have failed to begin with. Each should be a city employee earning that high seasonal wage already. You're very fortunate that Mayor Peete holds you in such high regard, Lieutenant, otherwise I would have proceeded with a claim of lost wages for the entire summer for all six of them, and I would have named YOU personally responsible, Lt. Morgan."*

Remembering the humbling, *"Yes, ma'am,"* and, *"Thank you, ma'am,"* he'd offered that morning, Morgan winced. He knew exactly where things stood with Escobar.

*Once she's qualified and interviews, the mayor will require me to adjust my criteria. Again, there will be no rejecting her.*

Morgan was intelligent enough to realize that Marisol would be taken much more seriously after a career as an officer in emergency response than she ever would in aquatics and recreation and that their plan, although still not entirely feasible, was certainly logical.

The lieutenant set Marisol's file on his desk and considered his options. He knew better than to cross Dr. Villareal again, and now, after hearing the councilman's stern warnings about this young woman's father, his thoughts went directly to his own family. He shuddered after imagining his wife, Linda, his two sons, Brandon and Robert, and his only daughter, Tiffany, bound with duct tape and gagged with a reddened cloth, huddled in the corner of a dark room somewhere.

He shook his head and instantly erased the images, instead focusing on an outcome that would protect the Patrol without further delaying the Escobar family's master plan.

He would heed Councilman Meyer's advice and began to consider that maybe the solution was to pave her path with the least resistance possible. If he placed her in too challenging of an environment it would certainly reek of a setup, but if he assigned her to a station that was less challenging, well, if she struggled to get by there, then it would quickly become obvious to everyone that the Escobar plan had a root flaw.

It then became obvious to him; Marisol's ocean-front training would have to take place at La Jolla Shores, a virtual playground compared to the Patrol's other stations.

Public contacts would be available all day, lost and/or found children were abundant, minor medical aids came frequently, all of which would be right down Main Street for Marisol. Large swells and huge rips were less frequent at the cove-protected beaches of La Jolla Shores. Escobar would do well there during the summer as a seasonal guard . . . but once she promoted to POL and was required to work year-round, there would come a day when the waves would grow large and the water would be breathtakingly frigid.

On that day, she would be the first rescuer required to charge into the ocean to retrieve a swimmer in distress.

*Then we'll see how badly she wants to use our program to embellish her résumé . . .*

Without looking up from her cell phone, Marisol started to answer.

"I think that ocean lifeguarding in San Diego is . . ." then was interrupted by the vibration and ringing of her phone.

"Excuse me, Lieutenant."

She turned her head and answered the call.

"Que hondas, amiga?"

Marisol shot a sardonic smile at Morgan and held her hand up with one forefinger extended. Morgan reclined into the back of his chair and looked away. He snorted softly, closed his eyes, and subtly bowed his head. He rubbed his eyebrows and temples with the thumb and two middle fingers of his right hand. He grimaced and attempted to ignore the casual conversation Marisol seemed to be enjoying with one of her girlfriends. She ended the call quickly though, and returned to the table with a warm smile.

"I'm sorry, Lieutenant, where were we?"

"The job."

"Oh yeah, that. Well, you see, I've wanted to be a lifeguard since the very first time my father took me to Watson's Water World down in the South Bay . . . I think I was eight years old. I loved those red suits . . . and the whistles they twirled around their fingers. Those girls were so cool . . . and super cute, too."

She paused and smiled.

"The thing that really got me though, was the little white cross that was on all of their gear. It just seemed to me like it was a really important job, especially with all of those little kids running around without their parents paying very close attention. I decided right then to become a good swimmer so I could someday become a lifeguard. My dad took me to join the swim team at the Chula Vista Country Club that week, and one thing led to another, so here I am."

Morgan raised his eyebrows.

"I believe there's a little more to it than that, Marisol."

"Well of course there is, I just wasn't sure if you had assumed that something like that might be the whole truth."

"I try to avoid assumptions, Ms. Escobar. I've learned they usually create more problems than solutions."

"Indeed they may, Lieutenant."

Escobar glanced at the cup of tea in front of her and said, "Ever since I was a little girl, I have also wanted to be a leader in my community . . . a pioneer, so to speak. So I became one, and now my commitment is to being a living example for people of all cultures to follow and learn from. My goal is to demonstrate that stereotypes, glass ceilings, and other perceived barriers can all be destroyed. Hopefully, people will learn that the limitations they falsely believe are there, the ones that are holding them back from having what they want . . . those people will learn that the barriers aren't there at all."

Escobar paused, removed the wooden sticks that held her tea bag in place, and allowed the overstuffed bag to drop into the hot water.

She looked up at Morgan.

"And getting back to assumptions for a moment . . . I've also learned that assumptions can lead to some very interesting, and even overwhelming, conclusions. Like the assumption that I had about your agency's hiring records . . . the assumption that led my mother and me to do the research that we did. And actually, Lieutenant, we found out that our assumption wasn't as bad as the facts turned out to be."

Escobar offered a satisfied smile and leaned back in her chair.

"So, having said that, I'm going to *assume* that a minority female being placed on the Department of Coastal Safety's board of directors, someday in the not-too-distant future, will set an extraordinary precedent that will benefit thousands of young minority men and women."

She sipped her tea and said, "That's my primary goal, Lieutenant."

Morgan nodded.

"That is an admirable goal, Marisol. Do you mind if I call you Marisol, or do you prefer Ms. Escobar?"

"I don't mind at all, especially since you've shown me the respect of learning how to pronounce it correctly. Most white people butcher my name."

Morgan shrugged.

"Well, I guess I'm not like most white people then, for whatever that's worth."

"Maybe you're not, and that's worth a lot to me. We'll see. Honestly though, my first impression during the academy was that you were just another *gabacho*."

Morgan smiled, thinking, *She's definitely not afraid to speak her mind.*

"*Gabacho?* I heard that word in a movie once . . . umm . . . *Stand and Deliver*, right? What's that guy's name? The teacher?"

Marisol tilted her head and smiled.

"Edward James Olmos . . . Lieutenant, I'm impressed."

"I actually asked around about that word. It's slang for a white guy who only cares about what happens on his side of the border . . . or something like that, right?"

Marisol nodded.

"Yeah, like a xenophobe."

*Damn, she is consistent.*

He sipped his coffee.

Escobar sipped her tea.

Morgan exhaled after taking a long gulp. He wiped his lip and nodded his head.

"That was a good movie. My kids loved it."

"Yes, it was."

She smiled at Morgan but said no more.

Morgan continued.

"Anyhow, I've already noticed that you are a leader, Marisol, and I agree that you set a fine example for your community, for any community actually. My primary goal, however, is saving lives, not just inspiring people to create new avenues that will help them overcome their perceived weaknesses. I see plenty of those types in every academy. I think I've got that covered."

He paused and sipped his coffee.

Marisol glanced at her phone.

Morgan pressed on.

"Marisol, how much thought have you given to making ocean rescues in cold water and large surf during the winter? Have you visualized a scenario where you are alone, and you are the last chance to save somebody's life at, say, eight o'clock in the morning, or just before sunset? You might be the first, or last, guard on duty, and backup could be at least five minutes away."

"I'm not worried about that. I know what it takes."

Morgan nodded.

"What about on a day like that one when you quit, down in Imperial Beach? What happens then?"

Marisol paused before answering and spent the next several moments gently dunking her tea bag beneath the hot water's surface. She pulled the bag out of the water and placed it on top of a folded paper napkin. She picked the cup up and moved it toward her lips and gently blew on the surface of the drink, took a couple of sips, then placed the cup back onto the tabletop.

"I agree with you about the beautiful day, Lieutenant . . . and so many healthy and happy looking white people out here already this morning."

Morgan squinted.

*Again with the "white" thing.*

"Look, Lieutenant, I know what you think I am. With all due respect, you're wrong, and despite the fact that you subjected hundreds of untrained cadets to unacceptably dangerous ocean conditions over the course of your career, I still think that you are very good at what you do. You obviously take this job very seriously. You and several of your *lifesaving men* have quickly earned my respect."

Morgan was puzzled, thinking, *Where is she going with all of this? Everything she says contradicts itself. She's good.*

"I may have slightly underestimated the difficulty of attaining this job, yes, and I may have been a bit hypercritical of your methods, Lieutenant, but here's something else I've learned as well. Now that I've completed my first summer, it's really not as tough as you preached about during . . ."

At that moment, Marisol's cell phone rang again and she took the call without hesitation.

Morgan shook his head and rested his chin on his chest.

*She's about to lose me . . .*

Marisol looked sternly at Morgan and then signaled to him to stay. She stood up and briskly walked away.

During the three minutes that the call lasted, Morgan shook his head, laughed quietly, and reminded himself how formidable this young woman's mother and father were. He sat patiently, sipped his hot coffee, and waited for her to return.

As she sat down, Marisol smiled.

"Lieutenant, I apologize, I had to take that call. I realize how important this conversation is, too. Can we start over? Do you mind?"

Morgan recognized an almost flirtatious tone that surprised and challenged him. He noticed that her smile was charming, and watched her tilt her head and purse her lips. She sat up in her chair, pulled her shoulders back, and leaned forward, displaying her tanned cleavage as she reached into a Louis Vuitton bag and removed a small rectangular tube of lip gloss. She continued to offer him a coy smile, and instantly the image of North's description of her body walking across the beach appeared in his mind. The brief view that he caught through the powerful binoculars as she prepared to jump from the pier topless, and the two photos of her moonlit silhouette that Shields delivered to his office in a sealed catalogue envelope, recurred in his mind.

He took a gulp of coffee, and attempted to clear the images. Yet he couldn't help but notice that she was now dressed in a short, white skirt and a tight V-neck sweater. She was wearing very stylish Tory Burch sandals and had finely-pedicured and meticulously-painted toenails. He glanced at, but quickly looked away from, her long, dark, and toned legs. He looked up but could not avoid noticing a diamond charm that hovered tantalizingly between her round breasts, and as he returned his eyes to her face, he saw her glossing her pouty lips with bright pink moisturizer. Large silver hoop rings hung delicately from her ears, and an expensive pair of Chanel sunglasses added a sense of maturity and sophistication. Reflexively, he closed his eyes, turned away feigning a cough, and cleared his throat before turning his attention back to the stunningly attractive young woman. As he glanced into the shiny lenses that covered her eyes, he thought, *She sure doesn't look the part of an oppressed minority that's been deprived of equal opportunity.*

He then refocused on the conversation at hand, reminding her, "The job. In big surf and cold water, just like that day in IB, and *you* making a solo rescue on a day like that. That's what we were talking about, Marisol."

Escobar quickly replied, "Of course."

She smiled and sipped at the tea.

"I don't really get that though, Lieutenant. It's not about overcoming intimidation or some fear of the ocean for me. That doesn't inspire or motivate me. You know . . . with Instructor North and his *what a great day it is to be a lifeguard* and *find another gear* crap. Military behaviorism is all that is, just superego and testosterone. To me, that's like a compensation for things that most men lack, like sensitivity, compassion, and most importantly, intuition. Present company excluded, sir."

She smiled, and took another sip.

"If you really want to know what this job is about for me, Lieutenant, then I'll tell you. It's about the hundreds of thousands of minorities living in San Diego County who want good jobs with good benefits. City jobs working for the government. That's what your agency has, but apparently you're only offering them to white men."

She paused to take a sip of tea.

"I know how many of those new jobs you have to offer, Lieutenant. There's more than a handful each fiscal year, and I'm told that you have eight years left to fill those positions."

"Those new positions aren't breaking news, Marisol. And what does that have to do with you making rescues? What's your point?"

"My point, Lieutenant, is that I'm here to set an example, to become a leader in your agency, and my *commitment* is to seeing a high number of minorities receiving those positions. Lieutenant, out of all of the men and women in San Diego, you can't find fifteen minorities that can become qualified for a long-term career in coastal safety? That would fill thirty percent of those new positions. That's what I would call a fair and equitable hiring record."

He breathed in, and calmly replied, "Marisol, if those individuals are qualified and meet all of our standards, of course it would be appropriate to hire and train them. But like I've already told you, I'm focused on selecting qualified human beings, regardless of their background, ethnicity, or gender. The individuals who enroll in the academy are all I get to choose from."

Escobar removed her sunglasses.

Smiling, she politely asked, "Why can't you personally recruit more minorities and then teach them the skills they need to become ocean lifeguards? If you made it a priority to visit these communities, and *you* spoke passionately at school assemblies, just like I did to build my swimming programs *and* to find my pool guards, then you could become a part of the solution. But instead of you going personally, or sending some of your finest, like maybe, Shields or Pena—you know, nice guys that are intelligent and might actually make a difference—you send unprepared seasonal employees who wear tattered red trunks, faded uniform tops, and flip-flops. They offer canned speeches and do stupid skits that don't inspire any of those kids. I've been at those assemblies; I've seen it myself. It's embarrassing, really. All those seasonal guards seem to care about is getting some easy off-season hours. It really does make your agency look second-rate, if I can be open with you, sir."

Morgan stiffened at first, but realized that she was reciting a version of the truth.

"Go on. I'm listening."

"So, there indeed could be the perception that you just wait for them to come to you instead, and when they don't, you have no choice but to hire these white guys, over and over, each and every year. That perceived lack of interest in finding candidates from these less affluent, minority neighborhoods only strengthens the cultural bias. I know you can see that."

Morgan did not reply. Escobar paused and leaned back. She lifted her cup, drank more of her hot tea, then replaced the cup on the table.

"Look, Lt. Morgan, I appreciate how familiar with the ocean your lifeguards need to be, and I understand how proud you are of the strong, outstanding athletes you've selected. Reading was the first skill I developed as a child, and is still my favorite activity, but being good at sports is a close second. My father was a great soccer player, an All-American before he graduated from college. He still plays now, even though he's in his fifties, and he's still very good. My mom played on the LPGA tour for two years before she met my dad. She left the tour, but she still plays all the time."

Marisol paused then tapped her chest with her forefinger. "It's in there, Lieutenant. I've got the heart of a champion, learned from two champions. All I've ever done is win. It's what our family does."

She shook her head subtly and said, "I'm no different than you. I appreciate hard work, determination, and the value of raw talent. I did very well as a competitive swimmer in high school, and I played on the volleyball team all four years at USD. I was an all-conference hitter my senior year." She leaned back and paused, then smiled as if she was reminiscing about something.

"You ever spike a volleyball off somebody's head or chest, Lieutenant? I mean hit it perfectly."

Morgan raised his eyebrows but said nothing.

He shook his head.

"I am passionate about winning, Lieutenant. I coach my swimmers very hard, just as you do with your cadets. I am not just a wealthy, spoiled, minority girl from the South Bay with a chip on her shoulder and something to prove . . . even though I get that perception exists in your world."

Morgan nodded.

Escobar sipped.

"I didn't get to where I am without working very hard, and I didn't build winning programs by waiting for qualified participants to find me."

Escobar leaned back and smiled at Morgan.

"Getting back to your original question about a day like the one in IB, there are many guards in this patrol that will make rescues faster and easier than I can. I accept that."

Morgan shook his head.

"You shouldn't, and I won't, but as of now, I'm not convinced that you'll ever develop the skills and abilities that I expect from my year-round crews. I can't have one link in that chain break. And I sure as hell can't throw that chain out there when I know there's a weak link, Marisol. That's how people die. I know you understand that."

Marisol nodded.

"I do understand, and I don't entirely disagree with you. I know that's not where my strengths are, Lieutenant, but that's because I didn't grow up on the beach . . . that's my point."

She sipped her tea.

"I didn't get a ten-year head start by body surfing and spear fishing, so my strengths are in other areas, but I'm very good at what I do well, and I'm getting much better at what I don't."

"Better may not be good enough, Marisol."

"You underestimate me, Lt. Morgan. I already have a Bachelor of Arts in Public Administration, my master's thesis will be completed in December, and then I'll start working on my law degree. I have supervision, leadership, and motivational abilities like very few others on your entire staff. I've given lectures about the characteristics of social and cultural subgroups that contribute positively and negatively to an organization's productivity, and I know how to utilize effective conflict resolution techniques for workplace issues like sexual harassment, bullying, and racial bias like the back of my hand. How many of those *awesome* local surfers that you hired can say that? Besides, those guys are so territorial that they make it worse."

"Not all of them."

Morgan stopped and reconsidered her statement.

*She does have a point though.*

Escobar softened her tone.

"Maybe not all of them, but certainly many of them. I've seen it. I've worked with them."

They both remained silent.

They each took a long drink before Marisol said, "But this isn't necessarily about them, it's about me, right? That's why you wanted to meet with me, so let's get back to that. I have been a great communicator and an outstanding administrator from the beginning of my tenure with the city. As a supervisor, I am fair, but stern in my approach, and that makes me a very powerful leader. People listen to me and I get things done . . . just like I did all summer with those rookies on the Bay. They trusted me like I was their mother before the summer ended."

Morgan nodded and smiled, thinking, *I doubt their mothers would have gotten drunk and taken their clothes off at a party.*

Marisol scowled and shook her head, then pointed across the table.

"I know what that smile is for, Lieutenant. I'm not naïve. I made a relatively bad decision that night, but I'm not going to apologize for it. I was having fun . . . trying to embrace the *beach culture* you guys promote. I was doing a pretty good job of it, I might add, until Mike Johnson showed up."

Morgan replied, "Fair enough. That's all behind us anyhow. I believe you had more to say about leadership."

"Exactly. What I'm really getting at, Lieutenant, is how many unique, original ideas do you think your current leaders and policy makers can generate, when all you keep hiring are white boy surfers?"

She stopped, but Morgan knew that she was not finished.

"Lieutenant, your Patrol needs an assertive minority female, like me, to help make policy. I already know for a fact that Mayor Peete has directed you to promote a woman into one of those new sergeant positions. You know that with my background and my community support I am a perfect fit . . . just like that old wetsuit that you surf in all winter."

Morgan scoffed, "Marisol, c'mon. You might be overstating your qualifications just a bit."

She shrugged.

"Maybe, but I'm not worried about that. All you have to do is train me, and don't you dare hold me back like you did by making that academy so unreasonably difficult. *Thirty-six* cadets failed that spring, that's more than half of the entire class, and I lasted longer than most of them. I don't feel so bad about that. You said it yourself; that was the most difficult academy ever, and you admitted that it was unsafe and unrealistic. That academy is the only thing I've ever failed, and even then, I didn't really fail, Lieutenant. I know now that I can make it through whatever challenges you put in front of me."

Escobar's phone vibrated and rang again.

This time, however, she quickly pressed "decline" and returned her attention to Morgan.

"I have no reason to hold you back, Marisol. You will be given every opportunity to succeed and you will be treated no differently than any other member of my staff."

Escobar squinted, then said, "Earlier you mentioned something about America's finest city. Right?"

"That's what I said, yes."

"Well, how about America's most *diverse* city, and more importantly, how about America's most *diverse* payroll sheets? How can you not be inspired by that possibility? You can set a precedent, Lt. Morgan, and be in the very front of a county-wide, and maybe even a state-wide, coastal safety trend. It's inevitable, so why wait? The time is now; it's *our* turn."

She paused, smiled, and subtly pointed a finger in his direction.

"You could be *that guy*."

Morgan chuckled.

"Maybe."

Emphatically, Escobar said, "Why should every single person that comes to the beach have to be conditioned to believe that the only people good enough to wear those uniforms, and go out into the ocean to save lives, are white boys? Why, Lieutenant? That's all they're seeing now."

Morgan said nothing.

"The city of San Diego needs me, and us, to shatter that perception. The mayor needs me to show the city that he is committed to equity. Lieutenant, *YOU* need me."

When Marisol mentioned what she thought he needed, Morgan choked slightly on his coffee. He abruptly sat forward as liquid entered his trachea, and unable to restrain his gag reflex, he coughed for several moments.

"Nice, Lieutenant. Now you're mocking me?"

"No, I'm not. I'm sorry, Marisol, please continue. I am listening."

Marisol paused, tilted her head, and grimaced at Morgan for a moment.

"Now is the perfect time, Lieutenant, and I am the perfect woman. I'll be qualified to interview for POL before you know it. After that, it will be an easy transition to administrative sergeant; you know that I'm already qualified for that position based on my experience in aquatics."

Morgan breathed in deeply and exhaled before he replied, "Marisol, regardless of the logic of your vision, there is still a lot of hard work for you to do before any of that can happen. If you earn what you speak of, you'll receive the benefit. That is all I can tell you."

"Fair enough, Lieutenant, but you already know that I'm the only option you have."

"Uh, that's debatable, Marisol."

"Whatever, I know she's everybody's all-American, but she's still white, Lieutenant, and she grew up on the beach, too. She quit college, and she won't be getting a degree anytime soon, if ever. She's got nothing unique to offer your agency. Not like I do . . . there's no comparison between Cynthia Harden and me."

At that moment, Morgan stood up.

"Well, I can't say that I disagree with that. There *is* no comparison between the two of you, and if I can be frank, Marisol . . . Cynthia Harden is not only more qualified than you, but she has almost two years of seniority over you as well. I really don't think you should set your sights on advancing beyond her. That's not a reasonable goal."

He smiled and extended his hand.

"However, you're a bright woman with a clear vision and relevant ideas. You express yourself very well. I learned a lot of things that I did not know about you today. I appreciate that. Don't let my opinion stop you from trying."

Marisol chuckled, "Oh, trust me, you don't have to worry about that."

Morgan smiled and nodded as Escobar stood and shook his hand.

"Lieutenant, the fact that you listened to me shows me a lot about your character. You're a very easy man to talk to as well. I also appreciate that you were candid with me about Cynthia Harden. I look forward to competing with her, and proving myself to you, Lieutenant. I will earn your respect."

"You already have, Marisol. Don't kid yourself. But as I stated, you have a lot of hard work in front of you."

"I understand that."

She cleared her throat and shifted her body.

"I do respect you, sir, and the excellent group of lifesaving men and women that you've selected. I'm proud to be a part of that."

She drained the remaining tea with a final gulp.

"Thank you for the tea. And thank you for assigning me to the Shores. I'm looking forward to that."

Morgan nodded.

Marisol turned away, and dialed her phone as she returned to her Audi convertible parked along the curb, top down.

**45**

Saturday, September 13, 1998
North Pacific Beach

L t. Morgan was now convinced that Escobar knew what she doing, and he knew that with all of her support, it was very likely that she would accomplish everything that she had just declared she would. Still standing on the outdoor patio, he dialed his cell phone and waited for an answer.

"Hi, Trisha, it's Richard Morgan. Is Mayor Peete available?"

He paused, then said, "Okay. Will you ask him to call me as soon as he can, please?"

Morgan hung up and bounded back inside to order another black coffee. He used the restroom, retrieved the tall cup, and returned to the table. His cell phone rang before he was able to take a second, hot sip.

"Thank you for getting back to me so quickly. I just finished meeting with Escobar, as you suggested. She laid it all out there for me . . . even mentioned you a couple of times."

"And you're surprised by that?"

"No, sir, I guess I just never thought she was that serious. I mean, I still don't think she really has any idea how brutal it can be out there. She's in for a hell of a ride."

"And like we agreed, Richard, you're going to have somebody there to catch her when she falls."

"Understood, sir."

"What's the most realistic timeline before she's eligible to interview for that sergeant's position?"

"Sergeant? Cynthia Harden isn't even ready to interview for sergeant yet, and Escobar is *at least* three years of training behind her. Marisol is not even ready to get through the POL academy. That program lasts thirty days, and it's ten times harder than the rookie academy. I just don't see her becoming eligible to even interview for a permanent position, not for a very long time . . . and you're already talking about sergeant? It could take her ten years to become eligible for sergeant, and that's assuming that she'll get promoted to, and maintain a POL spot. You never said anything about Sergeant, Eddie, this really is absurd. "

"I figured you could do the math, Lieutenant. I told you what the stakes were a long time ago. These people got me elected, and they will again, so, you make sure that she's eligible to interview for a permanent position quickly. Remember what we agreed to, Richard . . . velocity. Your timeline is not an option, and I don't really care if you think this is *absurd*. She's nothing to me unless she makes sergeant, and they can burn me down if she doesn't, so, you need to get busy . . . three, maybe four years is all you get."

"There's no way, sir. She'll never be ready by then."

"If you make it priority one, there's still time for her to drastically improve her status and actually *earn* it . . . she's going be Sergeant Escobar long before the end of '02."

Morgan said nothing.

"Richard, listen to me. It has to be this way. You already know that . . . so, let's just keep on keepin' on. Okay? You get out there and train her yourself if you have to."

Morgan breathed in and exhaled a heavy sigh.

"Yes, sir."

# PART 6

Patrol:
The act of going around or
through an area, in order to make sure it is safe.

**46**

Twenty Mostly Drama-Free Months Later
Tuesday, May 30, 2000
North Pacific Beach

After the rookie party incident, Lt. Morgan exiled Mike Johnson to the mostly-secluded beaches in North PB, and only assigned salty veterans like longtime crew mate, Gary Zampese, to share shifts with him. After being disciplined, Johnson had become a model employee, and he demonstrated the changes in attitude and behavior that Morgan had outlined on paper and required him to agree to and sign. Johnson wisely avoided trouble, and he and GZ worked together as well as any duo in the Patrol. The two watermen had long ago established their own protocols and standard operating procedures that every supervising sergeant had eventually learned to accept. If a newly-promoted POL, like Marisol Escobar, were to succeed at their station, she would have to quickly learn how to operate on Johnson's and Zampese's terms, just like Cynthia Harden and three other young POLs had already shown the ability to do.

And well.

The six-member crew enjoyed working together, and after reviewing a stack of documents outlining numerous challenging rescues and well-run medical calls containing not a single negative report, Morgan declared that Harden and the others had all passed the unofficial Mike Johnson training exercise, and so had Johnson.

After a year in North PB, Morgan transferred Harden to Mission Beach, and her three colleagues to other stations. To fill those vacancies, Morgan considered transferring probationary POL Marisol Escobar and three other probationary POLs to North PB. Seated at his desk while still weighing his options, Morgan closed his eyes and rested his forehead on the palm of his hand.

*You're better than this and you know it . . .*

Escobar's promotion to POL seemed premature to most of the Patrol's personnel, but many of them realized that she was likely the beneficiary of a new hiring philosophy that focused more on gender equity, and they didn't question the lieutenant's judgment for very long. But her assignment to North PB caused many, most notably Mike Johnson, to question their lieutenant's motives.

Johnson was now alone with Marisol Escobar for the first time since the rookie party, and the two colleagues prepared for their first vehicle patrol together, a mandatory assignment that would require them to sit side by side in the cab of an emergency lifeguard vehicle for an extended period of time, rolling slowly across the sand, up and down the beach. The assignment could last as long as an hour—depending on who was sitting in the driver's seat—and, if there was poor weather, or small crowds, maybe longer.

Vehicle patrols for Johnson were often nothing more than an opportunity to admire the occasional seasonal female that rode next to him in the wet seat. If he was lucky, he might cast his bait, set his hook, and lead the young lady to his bed sometime during the summer. Johnson coveted being alone with the young women that he outranked, and none had ever outranked him before. Marisol Escobar, however, had become a threat to do that. Nonetheless, Johnson had been looking forward to a vehicle patrol with her for a very long time, and as he opened the door on the driver's side of Unit 24 and entered the truck, he turned to Escobar and said, "So, how do you like having a badge and a real uniform now?

You been playing dress-up at home in front of the mirror? You got any fantasies you want me to help you out with?"

Escobar was expecting him to say something right away.

"Don't you dare start with me, Johnson. How do you know I'm not wearing a wire and this whole thing isn't just a setup to finally get you fired? You're still a pervert and you obviously haven't learned a thing. Don't talk to me about anything other than this beach and what I need to know about it."

Johnson chuckled.

"A wire? Really? Hmmm . . . I never thought of that. That is good. And where would you conceal that device anyhow, Ms. Escobar?" He raised his eyebrows. "I bet I could find it. I bet I could find a few places you might be hiding something."

He could barely stop himself from looking over at the young lady that had been the object of his lusty desires from the moment he first saw her in a wet, one-piece swim suit on the Bay.

He wasn't giving up just yet, regardless of her grievance against him. He saw how drunk she was that night at the rookie party and he still hoped, somehow, someday, he might be in the right place, at the right time, when she got that loose again. Maybe, just maybe, he could get another close look at those breasts and then finally get up in between those thighs. He'd seen it before, and had been patient enough to gain the opportunity to sleep with several women whose first impression of him was similar to Escobar's.

*Just a one-time hate fuck, Marisol. As they say, there's a thin line . . .*

Johnson said nothing more though.

They arrived at the far end of the Tourmaline parking lot and he backed the truck into a low drainage area behind a tall, sandy berm. He parked and exited the vehicle and hiked up the short hill where he met three shirtless surfers. There were several other men and women getting into or out of their wetsuits, preparing to enter the water or securing their boards on their vehicles at the end of a surfing session on the peaky waves at the Tourmaline Surf Park. On a mostly sunny, warm spring day, they stood alongside a concrete bench in the corner of the parking lot.

One of the three strong-looking men moved forward to clasp Johnson's hand and briefly hugged him with his other arm.

"Sup? Quién es esa Choc-oh-lat?"

"That's the chick from the rookie party."

"No shit? That's the home-girl bitch that got you suspended? In your truck right now?"

"In the flesh, Holmes."

"Day-umm. She's fly Esss-aaye."

"Unh huh. I told you."

The crew laughed out loud. They stared and pointed at Marisol, who was still seated in the truck. She was well aware of their leering eyes and was hoping that Johnson would return to the driver's seat and continue the uncomfortable patrol. The dark, inked-up man spoke again, this time louder.

"Hey, Betty Boop. Step on outta that truck and let us all take a *look-see*. Don't-chew wanna come out and meet all of Mr. Johnson's homies?"

Pablo, a dark-skinned, inked-up vato, bounced back and forth, holding his groin with one hand while emphatically waving the other. He was tatted all the way up his neck, onto his ears and cheeks, and beneath one eye, two small teardrops had been delicately placed. A highly-skilled artist had engraved a tall wooden cross that held a limp body in place on Pablo's wide, toned back. The dead man's head bled inside of a thorny crown, thick spikes were driven through his feet and hands, and a gaping red incision tore across his emaciated waist. The crucifixion scene on his back was as threatening and unnerving to those who were unsure about its meaning as it was prophetic and comforting to those who believed in the resurrection of man.

George, one of the other men, was a pretty damn good long-boarder, even though he weighed at least 260 pounds. He remained stoic as he moved in behind Pablo to gain a better view of Escobar. His greaser-style jet-black hair, dark black sunglasses, thick bones, and two full sleeves of ink made him the most intimidating man in the group. The third man, Pence, was the tallest and gangliest of the three, with huge hands and thick forearms that looked like steel suspension bridge cables covered in blond hair.

Most locals knew better than to surf when and where Johnson's crew did. They learned that they had to earn their way into the lineup by killing big waves and being humble about it. If they hadn't earned the privilege of being in the lineup yet, and they dropped in on one of the crew's waves, they might end up in Pence's firm grasp with George and Pablo nearby, ready with heavy fists and heavier feet. Johnson's boys had put their fists and feet through several surfboard decks, and George actually had taken a bite out of a tourist's surfboard one long-ago summer day.

On that day, Johnson was working at Windansea Beach when the novice surfer came running to show the lifeguards his damaged board. The damage looked like a shark bite, except it was made by a large human mouth. The tourist wanted the lifeguards to paddle out into the lineup and arrest the huge black-haired male who had knocked him off his board, ripped the leash off of his ankle, and took his thin-railed board away from him. The indignant surfer described how George had growled like a pit bull as he chomped through the rail, then spat out a chunk of fiberglass yelling, "Don't ever surf here again you fucking kook. I'll take a bite out of your throat next time."

The three men were scary fuckers, and everybody was well aware that they were Johnson's boys. He had deals with these cats that nobody else in the Patrol knew about.

Johnson was enjoying his attempt at humiliating Escobar, and it seemed to be working. At first, Escobar ignored Pablo's taunts and sat meekly in her truck seat, saying nothing. Then she suddenly exited the vehicle and walked directly toward the four men. Her feet were bare and her tanned and muscular thighs were only partially covered by her navy blue duty shorts. Her torso and chest were concealed beneath a blue cotton polo shirt and the red one-piece that she wore beneath it. The polo shirt that had her name embroidered in gold above her right breast appeared to be a size too small.

Pablo blurted out, "Mamasita! Chi-Chi's grrrrrrrandes!"

The other men roared their agreement with Pablo's observation.

Escobar stopped by the tailgate of the truck and shook her head. She held up one hand, signaling her disapproval as she waited for the catcalls to stop.

"Johnson, this is totally unacceptable. Can't you do anything professionally? I mean, really, you are sooo predictable."

Pablo strutted slowly toward Escobar, then walked around her and looked her up and down.

"Holmes? You got to see this creation of eck-stuh-see with her clothes off ?"

Johnson nodded.

"Hey girlfriend, homeboy here tells me that you got some chocolate-covered cherry nipples on top of those cantaloupe titties. When you gonna start wearing a two-piece, sister, so I can see them, too?"

George chipped in, "Yeah, and I'll bet that little coochie down there tastes like Kahlua, too."

Pence was next.

"No doubt. Hey, girlfriend, you ever hear of a train? Let's see if my locomotive can fit into your tunnel."

The three surfers laughed and continued making comments as Escobar stood still and shook her head. She glared at each man, disgusted, but unafraid, and memorized the faces in the crowd. Johnson said nothing as he stared at Escobar through the dark lenses of his sunglasses, looking satisfied. He began walking toward the truck and said, "Hey! You guys leave my trainee alone. Be polite to Mizzzz Escobar. You guys know better than that. Didn't your parents teach you nothing?"

He turned to Escobar. "Really, I think that's what they call *reprehensible behavior,* right? We don't allow that kind of shit around here no more. Besides, I got training I need to provide to POL Escobar, now that she's part of our crew. We ain't got time for you lowlifes. Let's go Marr-ee-sole . . . Say goodbye to your new friends."

Marisol glared at the men, scowled, and turned away.

Pablo shouted as she walked to the truck.

"And be nice, girlfriend . . . You never know when you might need one of us."

Pablo, George, and Pence continued to chuckle as they waved at the young woman they had heard so much about, but until now had never seen. Pablo pumped his fist up and down in front of his groin, arched his head and neck backwards to one side, and pretended to be at the climax of an orgasm when Marisol turned away and re-entered the vehicle.

47

Two Days Later
Thursday, June 1, 2000
North Pacific Beach

"He made you wait right there, in front of his buddies like that?" Escobar pointed toward the large concrete drainage culvert adjacent to the parking lot.

"Right up there. Just on the other side of the parking lot. I'm going to drive up there. I want to see if those losers are here again."

Randy Shields was seated in the wet seat, as Morgan directed him to be every time he and Escobar patrolled together. Shields would respond to any rescues out in the ocean, and Marisol would operate the unit and monitor the radio.

Shields knew the area well and the men Escobar had described.

"You mean those guys?"

George and Pablo stood on the sidewalk, expressionless, and did not turn to look toward the two lifeguards in the truck.

"Yeah, that's them . . . and a tall white guy with curly blond hair and a nappy beard who's apparently impressed with himself."

Shields laughed, but not because something was funny.

"Yeah . . . Pence. Not likely he's at work today, though. He'll be around sometime, probably after making a drug deal or stealing something from somebody's vehicle while they're on the beach."

Shields turned to face Escobar.

"He's a real dirtbag, keep your eye on him. He's an ex-con too, by far the worst of the bunch. He did, like, seven years for burglary and assault and battery. He beat the hell out of an older couple in their mansion up in La Jolla Farms and got away with about a hundred grand in jewelry. They didn't catch him for over a year and then the trial took forever while he was out on bail."

He turned back and looked at the men on the sidewalk.

"If he was there that day, then I'm sure it got pretty ugly. I'll help you submit the paperwork to Sergeant McIntyre, and he'll expedite your report to Lt. Morgan. You're right though, Johnson's been getting away with stuff like this for way too long, Marisol. But you understand, of course, that they will have to speak to him, too."

"He'll lie again, just like he did after the rookie party."

"It's not likely to be the last time either, Marisol. You picked the right person to come to, though. I've got my own list of issues with that asshole. We'll make it right this time. He's been on a third-strike plan for a while. Just let the process work. He'll hang himself eventually."

Escobar apparently was not impressed.

"Process? You mean like last time? One week? No. I want him fired."

She paused.

"Do the right thing, Shields, and tell your buddy Morgan to fire that animal. He may actually do something about it if he hears it from you."

**48**

Ten Days Later
Tuesday, June 11, 2000
Pacific Beach, California

Richard Morgan was taking a rare turn at sitting behind the wheel on a vehicle beach patrol. Since he was promoted to lieutenant, he no longer wore his red trunks beneath his uniform, nor did he carry his rescue fins with him wherever he went all day, not like the on-duty rescue personnel that served under him. As a lieutenant, he was no longer expected to be a first responder, and the uniform he wore on a daily basis was designed for formality.

On days like this one, however, he typically left his polished duty boots in the cargo compartment of the Navigator, and hung his uniform top and neatly pressed pants on a hanger above the driver's side rear door. While on one of these rare vehicle patrols, however, he wore loose-fitting navy blue cargo pants over his red, size 42 Birdwell trunks, an XXL navy blue polo shirt, and black, size 15 flip-flops that revealed the pale white skin on his Fred Flintstone-like feet.

Morgan made himself available to patrol his beaches at least a few times each year, and over time, as the Patrol's only senior lieutenant, he had participated in several rescue scenarios that required his assistance.

He relished the opportunity to activate his status to "on-duty rescue personnel."

During the random patrols, he also took advantage of the opportunity to have a private moment with a member of one of his crews.

On a typical June gloom afternoon, Morgan drove south along an uncrowded stretch of sand on Pacific Beach. He cautiously maneuvered the Navigator high above the water's edge as he inquired about the incident involving Escobar. The lieutenant became silent, then Mike Johnson turned and looked directly at him.

"I understand, Lieutenant, but that's not at all how it went down. I never said a word to Escobar."

Morgan showed no reaction and continued driving, his eyes on the beach in front of him, both hands on the wheel.

"Wait, I take that back. I actually did tease her playfully about her new POL uniform and her badge. I suppose she might have taken offense to that."

Johnson paused, but Morgan allowed him to continue.

"So, yeah, guilty as charged I guess. But seriously, LT, it was a harmless comment. Hell, I said way worse things to Harden while she was here and she either laughed out loud or replied with some of her own trash talk. Sir, Escobar has like, rice paper for skin. Seriously, she is not cut out for this job. I was just trying to break the ice during an obviously awkward moment."

"Fair enough," Morgan said, "However, Escobar was also pretty detailed in her narrative about what was said to her by a group of men that you took her to meet at Tourmaline."

"What group of men? What'd she say?"

"Why don't you tell me your version of what happened first, Mike?"

"Nothing happened. We were on an area familiarization patrol when I stopped at the lot to meet some of the locals. I tried to introduce her but she wouldn't even get out of the truck."

"She claims that she did."

"Well, yeah, after some guys from the surf club started calling out to her to come up and say hello. She was totally rude to all of them. Looked right down her nose and scowled at them like she was disgusted. They tried kidding around with her, but she pointed at them and made, like, a stop sign with her hand. She looked like a kindergarten teacher, like she was disciplining bad little boys."

Morgan snorted but said nothing.

"She didn't care who they were, how many years they had been surfing that break, or how dependable they could be when the shit hit the fan. She had no clue about what I was trying to accomplish by bringing her around a group like that."

Johnson paused and nodded at Morgan.

"You know how those guys can be, and first impressions can be lasting impressions. She brought it on herself. Hell, I had to make them stop, they were getting pretty brutal. She should be thanking me, and this is what I get instead? This is just a complete overreaction on her part. She's weak, Lieutenant. Useless."

Aware that Escobar was not as weak as Johnson proclaimed, the lieutenant knew that continuing with any type of interrogation about the incident was futile. He had heard enough and he knew enough about both of them to realize that the truth about what had happened was likely to be somewhere near the middle.

"You've always been clever, Mike, I'll give you that. Most of the newbies are afraid of you, so they never say anything about it, but we both know that you push the envelope way too hard. This Escobar is a totally different type of person, though. Apparently you still haven't figured that out. She's afraid of no one and she's not going to back down until she takes another piece of you or finishes you off completely."

"Pfff, if I didn't need this job so bad, Lieutenant, you and Escobar both would have heard a lot more from me after that bullshit rookie party grievance. All due respect, LT, you gave me the shaft on that deal, and you know it. Sexual harassment, my ass. It was a fucking party, she was drunk and she stood there naked, right in front of me. I never even touched her. That was bullshit."

He took a deep breath, shook his head, and continued.

"Fuck her, Rick, and fuck the horse she rode in on. I took my medicine just like you ordered me to. I shut my mouth and I never said another word to that bitch. Not until *you* transferred her here. I never expected that, you didn't give me a heads-up, and I'm still not sure what you're trying to accomplish. Are you testing me, or are you testing her?"

Morgan turned and said, "I think you know the answer to that question, Mike."

"It must be her, but what did you expect me to do, bow down and treat her like the fucking queen that she thinks she is?"

Morgan chuckled and said, "All I wanted was to see was if she was ready to deal with guys like you. I think she showed that maybe she is. What do you think?"

"No comment."

Morgan laughed, but did not reply.

He pulled the SUV forward in an arc to face the ocean, backed it up until it was a few feet from the boardwalk, and parked it on high sand in front of World Famous, a Pacific Beach restaurant that was a great place to enjoy hot clam chowder and fresh fish tacos while watching the sunset from a large, heated patio with glass walls.

Morgan opened his door and stepped out of the SUV, looking back at his wet seat as he exited.

"Let's go. I need a coffee."

He grabbed his Sabre radio and keyed the mouthpiece. Using his call sign, he radioed his coffee break status and location.

"PB tower, 21 Lincoln."

The tower guard responded immediately.

"Go ahead, Lieutenant."

"Tower, I'll be on a *Code 7* for about twenty minutes, PB Drive."

*Code 7.*

Meal break.

"Copy, 21 Lincoln. *Code 7.*"

Morgan started across the deep sand, lieutenant's bars pinned to the collar of his blue and gold polo shirt. Johnson, at 6-foot-3 with a wide, solid frame that was covered only by red trunks and a tight-fitting blue cotton duty shirt, carried a pair of black Reef sandals as he followed. His body looked very much like that of a college linebacker in his prime, while the larger lieutenant in front of him maintained the appearance of an aging former college offensive lineman, which he was.

As the two men reached the thick concrete barrier that separated the sand from the boardwalk, Morgan stopped and placed a palm on the top of one of Johnson's rounded shoulders. He held him in place until the two men faced each other.

"Mike, listen to me. You're a good man, and one hell of an ocean lifeguard . . . most of the time. You've had an outstanding career making rescues and running our beaches safely, and I'm hopeful that will continue. I know how hard you work to support your ex-wife and your three kids. I appreciate how much this job means to you, and I know how much you value earning your full retirement benefits. Don't think for one second that my intention is to take any of that away from you unfairly."

Johnson was moved by his lieutenant's sincerity, right up until the last word.

"Unfairly?"

"Yeah, as in, somebody else's agenda will be your undoing. I will do my best to prevent that from happening."

Johnson turned and squinted at Morgan.

"Sir? That sounds like a loaded statement."

Morgan nodded.

"You're right, it is."

Morgan released his grip and slid over the 3-foot-tall barrier. Johnson quickly followed and crossed the wide concrete boardwalk, checking both ways for approaching skaters or bicyclists, and headed for the front door of the restaurant.

"Mike, I can't control your inappropriate behaviors though. Nobody can, nobody has ever been able to, but more importantly, I can't tolerate them anymore. This isn't like the old days; we can't say and do the same old shit that you and a lot of the other guys . . . hell, even me when I first started . . . have been taking liberties with for years. You're going to have to evolve, Mike, you know, survival of the fittest. You understand that, right? Evolve or die, in a manner of speaking."

Johnson squinted again, his focus acute. He answered with conviction in his voice.

"I can see that, and I've changed. I think I've adapted and evolved rather well."

"Well, when people are watching, you have . . ."

Johnson nodded. He knew better than to dispute Morgan at this point and was fully aware of the habitual indiscretions he took when nobody was looking.

"That has to end or you're done, Mike. You've got to be cleaner than everybody now, and absolutely compliant to the letter of the law. You're on a tight leash from now on, and you'll need to demonstrate the utmost of professionalism at all times. Period."

The two men reached the front door of the restaurant. Morgan opened it, allowing Johnson to pass in front of him. As they entered the doorway, now clear of the distracting, steady onshore breeze, Morgan lowered his voice while maintaining a stern tone.

"I've given this a lot of thought, Mike. The mayor has given me his input as well."

Johnson stopped in mid-step.

"The mayor?"

"Yeah, my boss. Mike . . . Escobar has become a legitimate contender for any promotion that she seeks and the mayor is in her corner. If there's a conflict of any type between you and Escobar again, it will be a no-contest. You'll lose this job . . . Consider this a heads-up. Now, let's take a seat, get a coffee, maybe a fish taco or two if you're hungry, and allow me to educate you about how you are going to get through the rest of your career when Marisol Escobar becomes your supervising sergeant."

Johnson turned abruptly, an expression of dismay on his face, while Morgan placed a hand on his back and ushered him through the doorway. Johnson continued into the lobby with his head down and his shoulders slouched, shaking his head while Morgan patted him firmly on the back.

The thick, heavy wooden door swung closed behind them.

**49**

Six Weeks Later
Saturday, July 22, 2000
Mission Beach

Richard Morgan listened closely as Cynthia Harden elaborated on her experiences in the Navy. She had shared a few stories with him years before during their meeting at the coffee shop in Pacific Beach, but she had stopped herself from revealing too much. She decided then that it might be wiser if she waited until a much later time, long after she proved herself worthy as an ocean lifeguard, to tell her story about the ending of her career in the Navy. Her premature dismissal was not an easy story for her to tell; it was complicated and she still felt strongly that she had been cheated.

The time had come, however, and Cynthia was ready.

As she began, Morgan was empathetic.

"Listen, Cynthia, you really don't have to continue if you're not comfortable."

"No, sir, I'm fine. I've wanted to set the record straight for years, and I clearly believe that you're nothing like the man I'm about to tell you about, so what I say here won't hurt me."

Seated side by side in the lieutenant's Navigator, Morgan and Cynthia patrolled south across the deep sand of Mission Beach. She looked out through the passenger-side window, observing and assessing the safety conditions for a large number of beach patrons who were enjoying various ocean activities.

"Things were going very well for me in the Navy. I had received my special ops rating eighteen months prior and my team had already completed three separate classified dives. My unit commander, Captain Aaron Reed, was one of the greatest people I've ever known. He was awesome. We had a very close relationship . . . open . . . friendly . . . almost like equals, but we both knew better than that. I never asked him for any special treatment and he never offered. We just respected and understood each other, so we got along very well. Kind of like you and I do, if you don't mind me saying so."

"Not at all. I totally agree."

"The only difference, really, is that we served together on a team every day on base and on tactical operations, and you and I, well, you're never at the beach, and that's the only place I'm ever *deployed*, as they say in the Navy."

Morgan laughed and playfully sat taller, puffing his chest.

"Hey! What are you trying to say? I'm deployed here on the beach right now."

Cynthia smiled.

"You know what I'm saying."

Morgan smiled and drove.

"Our entire unit was tight, but then our base's executive commander retired. He was awesome, too, another true leader, another amazingly gifted soldier by the name of William Erving. He was special, but when he was replaced everything changed. I had just completed four years of service, but I promoted so rapidly that I opted in for six more. I had my sights set on master chief . . . *E-nine*."

Morgan glanced away from the beach for a brief moment and made eye contact.

"*E-nine*, as high as you could promote because you didn't complete college, right?"

"Exactly, and I would have been fine with that. I would have gone twenty-five, probably thirty years in the Navy. I would have loved every minute of it, too. Master dive chief would have been the best ranking possible for somebody like me."

She stopped smiling.

"But Erving's replacement for base commander was this *jackass* colonel, Kent Windsor. Three months into his command, he started questioning everyone."

Harden paused and focused on a group of waders that bounced up and down in shallow water, turning their backs to incoming waves, getting knocked around and swept off their feet, over and over. She scanned farther south and noticed dozens of waders, body surfers, and boogie boarders playing in a wide no-surfing zone. She quickly assessed that they were all in good shape and continued telling the story.

"The entire course of my life was unquestionably changed again because of a . . . well, a prick, sir . . . a prick that knew less about what we were doing than I did, but a prick who outranked me. Just like the water polo thing I told you about. I got screwed over again, but much worse this time." She paused, "I'm sorry to make it sound like I was a helpless victim, but this time I really was."

Cynthia paused again, drew in a deep breath, and looked across the cab at Morgan.

He noticed her apprehensiveness and a hint of vulnerability in her eyes. He reassured her again.

"Cynthia, if you'd rather stop . . ."

"No, I'm fine."

Her tempo increased.

"I've just never told this story to anyone before. It's a little harder than I thought it would be."

She breathed in deeply and exhaled.

"When Windsor came in, immediately he disapproved of what he called an 'unprofessional communication style' and 'inappropriate body language' consistently demonstrated within our unit. But he also singled me out."

She shook her head and grimaced.

"I had served with Captain Reed for nearly three years. He was right next to me on those missions I mentioned earlier, always as our team leader. There was nothing going on between us, and I never even thought about having a sexual relationship with any of my crewmates. Windsor was sooo out of line with his accusations. He manipulated the truth against all of us. Nobody knows why either. Just another insecure douchebag with authority, I guess."

She looked across the cab at Morgan.

"No offense Lieutenant; you're certainly not insecure or a douchebag. I was just, well, I mean, about the authority figure thing."

Morgan laughed.

"No offense taken. Proceed."

Harden scowled.

"He destroyed the entire unit. Each of us is either out of the Navy like me, or is still serving, but isolated somewhere. This fucking guy thought he knew everything and he didn't know shit. Sorry."

"Cynthia, stop apologizing to me, will ya?"

She continued shaking her head, but smiled.

"He was a hateful redneck from Mississippi. He told me that females had no place in combat units. He hated it that I was trained to do things that he could only dream of doing." Harden turned toward Morgan, her tone sincere. "He was so unlike Reed and Erving, it was absurd. *They* were soldiers. Windsor was completely the opposite in personality, character, ability, leadership style . . . everything. He was a punk, too, a tiny little man that leaned on his family's reputation and the legacy they all created for him at Annapolis. This guy was a real tool, Lieutenant. I mean really."

As they approached the Mission Beach main tower, Cynthia observed a growing number of waders, swimmers, boogey boarders, and surfers in an open area. She kept her eyes focused on the surf as she continued.

"Windsor claimed that I had been receiving preferential treatment that led to my rapid promotion. Then he accused me of sexual misconduct with Captain Reed, which was total BS. It was his personal, two-headed witch hunt against me, the competent female combat operative with confirmed kills, and Reed, the well-respected black officer who showed me how to do it."

She grimaced again.

"Windsor . . . he was a relic from a much worse time, Lieutenant, a real redneck southerner . . . I hope that bastard has an ugly death, too, I really do. I'm sorry, Lieutenant . . . I'm having a hard time forgiving that asshole. But, as an old friend once told me, I'm still young. Maybe someday I'll finally let that one go."

The lieutenant raised his eyebrows.

"Wow. That is harsh."

"Yeah. I was livid. I guess you might say I still am . . . toward this bastard. He was transferred out about a month after his investigation flopped, right after Reed and I were exonerated, but the damage was done."

Harden paused and shook her head.

"And then I made it worse."

Morgan stopped the SUV when a Frisbee rolled and spun to a stop directly in the vehicle's path. A sunburned teenage boy ran and hopped into the sand like a long jumper, quickly retrieved the disc, and scurried away to continue playing catch with his dad. Morgan returned his eyes to the path directly in front of the Navigator, a large and relatively clumsy vehicle that was not built for driving across deep sand.

"Cute kid; he's going to need some sunscreen though," he said.

The lieutenant put the vehicle in park and exited. He waved and smiled at the father of the boy who retrieved the Frisbee. The father approached and the boy's small group of siblings followed their daddy toward the lifeguard who was smiling and waving.

"Good afternoon, sir. How are you?"

The father smiled broadly, gathering his oldest boy, who was still holding the Frisbee.

"Oh, hello, officer. That was my bad, a horrible toss."

The men laughed and shook hands.

"Yeah, I'm going to need to talk to you about that."

The father halted, but Morgan quickly tapped him on the arm and said, "Naaaah, I'm just playing."

Everybody laughed.

"I will say something about these kids and their red skin, though," Morgan said, as he reached into a side pocket of his cargo shorts and pulled out a 4-ounce bottle of SPF 45 sunscreen and handed it to the kid's father. "This will get you through today, but get some more of this as soon as you can."

The father nodded after noticing his children's reddened shoulders, earlobes, and noses.

"Oh, yeah, look at that."

Morgan smiled at the kids, reached into a different pocket, retrieved small decals and rub-on tattoos with SDLP logos and slogans on them, and said, "Here, you guys take these."

He squatted, nodded to the group of children, held out his thick, long arms, and corralled them into a smaller circle.

"Okay, so you're all having fun on the beach, right?"

A slowly developing chorus replied, "Yeeuuhh."

"Well, we want you to have fun *and* be safe. Right?"

"Yesss."

"Always swim near a lifeguard, okay? See the towers there . . . and there?"

He turned and pointed out the towers with the numbers *15* and *14* painted in tall black numerals on their sides.

"If you always swim in front of one of those, you will always be safer."

"Oa-Kaaeey!"

The group giggled as the lieutenant shook their daddy's hand again.

"Thank you for the sunscreen, officer . . . you know how kids are with that stuff."

Morgan smiled.

"Yes, I do. Enjoy your stay in San Diego, sir. You let us know if you need anything. We'll be happy to help."

Morgan returned to the Navigator. Cynthia hopped out immediately and briskly walked around the vehicle before the lieutenant realized what she had done. As she moved back inside the cab and closed her door, she looked at Morgan and said, "Clear."

Morgan smiled and said, "Oh, thanks, once in a while I forget to do that now that I'm a lieutenant. Besides, with these knees it takes me a couple minutes to walk all the way around this boat."

He placed a finger across his lips.

"Shhh, don't tell anyone."

Harden smiled as the lieutenant resumed their patrol. Cynthia was about to continue her story, but a voice from the Navigator's radio interrupted her. She and the lieutenant listened to a routine call being made by a seasonal guard in Tower 15. He was calling the Mission Beach main tower, declaring that he was on his way out into the ocean. He needed to make contact with several young boogie boarders that had been sucked into a rip current. The current had pulled the group of boogies about 30 yards to the south, away from their families, their pop-up tents, beach blankets, and lawn chairs, just as it had been doing most of the sunny day.

Morgan and Harden watched the shirtless, tanned, muscular guard in his early twenties leap from the deck of his tower and run fluidly across the sand past the Navigator. He carried a pair of blue and orange swim fins in one hand and a red rescue buoy in the other. Twenty-five yards in front of the SUV, he reached the water's edge, began shouting commands, and pointed to the north with the buoy. He skipped into waist-deep water, released the tethered buoy, and allowed it to float near him. He turned away from the incoming surf, squatted down and quickly placed the fins on his feet. He then began diving under waves and swam rapidly to the large group of boogie boards, arriving there in about 30 seconds.

While treading water, he instructed the group of young boys to catch the next wave in and to stay on it until they could place their feet on the ocean floor.

"Then turn left and walk north," he shouted.

He swam past several boys who complied and continued toward a smaller group of four neophyte boogie boarders who failed to make progress toward the beach, struggling to paddle in against a large flashing rip current.

Harden removed a baseball-sized handset that was mounted to the dashboard and called to the tower.

"Mission Beach from Lincoln One, we're watching one guard assist a group of boogies. Am I clear to assist?"

The main tower guard replied quickly, "Copy Lincoln One, you're clear to assist."

Morgan squinted as he watched the seasonal guard shout instructions at two of the drifting boarders. The pair had apparently lost confidence in their ability to make progress across the water on top of their cheap foam boards. With no leashes attached to their wrists, they had abandoned their boards and were now attempting to swim in against the strong current without the benefit of a floatation device.

Cynthia looked at Morgan and winked.

"I'll be right back."

She cautiously exited the vehicle, dropped her cargo shorts, peeled her polo shirt off, threw them both onto the seat, gently placed her sunglasses on the dashboard, and moved quickly to the rear of the vehicle. She reached up to the roof rack and released a strap that secured a 10-foot rescue board in place. She tucked the board under one armpit and moved briskly across the wet sand into the water. She mounted the board on both knees and paddled across the inside surf, directly out through the rip current where the waves diminished in size due to the deeper water beneath them.

While the first lifeguard was rescuing three older boys, Cynthia had arrived at the area where the two preteen boogie boarders, who had abandoned their boards, were barely keeping their heads above the water, one showing signs of serious distress and very poor swimming ability.

She grabbed the closest boy, pulled him across the deck of her rescue board until his waist was completely out of the water, and instructed him sternly.

"Hold onto these handles and don't let go. Stay on this board no matter what. I'm a lifeguard and I'm going to help you and your friend get back to the beach. Relax buddy, everything is going to be fine."

She then turned and looked at the smaller boy who was approximately

25 feet away. She watched as his head, then one hand, and quickly the other, disappeared beneath the surface of the ocean.

The boy on the board screamed, "He's drowning! Get him! Hurry!"

Cynthia checked for incoming surf, then took three quick strokes and dove directly toward the spot where the boy went under. She immediately spotted him, grabbed one wrist, pulled gently, reached around his torso, and placed her other hand under his armpit. Securing his body, she placed her bare feet on the bottom and pushed against the ocean floor. She quickly reached the surface, and heard the young boy crying and gasping for air.

"Atta boy. Breathe."

Noticing a growing set of approaching waves, she shuttled him back to the rescue board where the first boy watched closely.

"Listen to me carefully," Cynthia shouted and pointed, "You need to move all the way up onto the front of the board. Put your head there and put your feet right here in the middle. Hang onto those straps and don't let go."

The boy on the board adjusted his position as directed.

"And you, my little surfer friend, you and I are going to lay right on top of him, okay?"

She pulled him onto the board with one hand and steadied it with her other. She cautiously straddled the rear of the board, leaned forward, and then pushed the smaller boy between the first boy's legs. She adjusted her position and spoke softly into the little boy's ear as he continued to cry.

"Now, grab onto his trunks and don't let go until we're on the beach, okay."

The boy stammered between gasps, "Oh, oh, ohhh, kay."

The first boy noticed the approaching waves and yelled, alarmed, "Waves are coming!"

Cynthia pressed her weight on top of the boys and paddled furiously, directly toward the first rising wave. She reached the wave's face just before it broke and the board glided over the peak to the other side, Cynthia yelling, "HOLD ON!"

The board slammed down onto the wave's arching back, but the trio remained securely in place. The boy perched in the front yelled again, a tone of laughter in his voice.

"That was awesome! Here comes another one!"

Boy number two, however, was not as stoked, and began squirming. Cynthia barked immediately as she stopped paddling, grasped his arm, and held it tightly.

"No! Stay put. One more wave and it will be over. Relax. I got this!"

The boy put his head down on the other boy's back and cried again.

The lookout, perched up on the nose of the board, yelled, "Here it cooomes!"

Cynthia paddled rapidly, glided the board smoothly over the second wave, then immediately sat up, moved to the rear of the board, dropped her feet into the water, and used an eggbeater kick to turn the board 180 degrees. She quickly readjusted the boys' positions on the board, pulled them back about a foot, and began paddling directly toward shore. The third wave of the set caught up to them, lifted the rear of the board, and propelled them down the wave face. Cynthia continued paddling rapidly across the breaking surface of the wave until she maintained the right speed and allowed the wave's energy to do the rest of the work while she guided the board by holding its rails and pressing downward against the deck with her hips.

The boy in the front was now totally stoked and screamed as the board glided smoothly, and swiftly toward the shore, "AWESOME!!!"

The little boy stuffed between them finally looked up, stopped crying, and smiled. As they were ordered to do, the boys remained in their positions until the board glided to a halt on the sand.

Cynthia gracefully hopped to her feet and allowed the board to remain where it had stopped. She scooped up the boys, taking one under each arm, then dropped to her knees and looked back and forth, making eye contact with each one of them several times, asking them, "Are you guys okay? Talk to me."

The taller boy was all words.

"That was sooo cool. Oh my Gawd, that was amazing. How'd you do that?"

The small boy was reticent, and said softly, "That was scary. I thought I was going to drown."

Morgan was standing barefoot at the water's edge, holding a rescue can and a pair of fins. He smiled and shook his head as he looked at the two lifesavers and their five rescued boys, all standing together. Three sets of parents arrived, after sprinting across the sand. The seasonal lifeguard nodded, smiled, then gathered his fins and buoy and said, "Have a great rest of the day you guys, but stay away from that rip current."

He pointed with his red rescue buoy and instructed the group, "Go way up there to the north, all the way up to that tower with the number 15 on it, okay? Stay in front of that tower and you'll be safe. Be sure to keep looking in toward the beach to check your position. When you notice that you've drifted, come in to the beach, then walk back up to the tower before you re-enter the water."

He turned, jogged back to his station, and retrieved a towel. While drying off, he reached for his hand-held radio and called the main tower.

"Tower 15 clear. Back in service."

The main tower guard replied, "Copy that, fifteen, nice job."

Cynthia returned to the Navigator, retrieved her towel, and stood in the sun for several long moments catching her breath. Morgan continued to smile, but said nothing as Harden secured the board on top of the Navigator, wrapped her towel around her waist, pulled her polo shirt over her head and shoulders, reset her sunglasses on the bridge of her nose, and climbed back into the wet seat.

She exhaled, looked at Morgan and said, "Now . . . where were we?"

They both cracked up, then Morgan said, "Cynthia, really, you *are* all that and a bag of chips. You and Newman were both amazing. Smooth and calm; a thing of beauty to watch."

Cynthia rolled up her window to avoid the chilly on-shore breeze and continued to smile.

"Yeah, Lieutenant, that was a blast. That kid's feet were on the bottom; he was done. I can't believe how fast that happened."

They were both calming down, each reflecting on how badly the scenario could have turned out. Neither spoke as Morgan pulled away from the scene, thinking, *Right place at the right time. Just another day at the beach.*

Morgan grabbed the mic from the Navigator's dash and called, "Tower . . . Lincoln One clear. We're *Code 4.*"

*Code 4.*

No further assistance required.

"Copy, Lincoln One, *Code 4.* That was one hell of a rescue by your wet seat, sir. Very nicely done, Harden. Tower clear."

Morgan didn't mind the prohibited name-dropping being broadcast over the city's emergency frequency and agreed silently. *That was a hell of a rescue.*

Cynthia looked out toward the ocean, scanning for others that she might need to respond to.

"So," Morgan said, "you were just about to tell me more about that *Windsor* guy."

Cynthia paused. She felt great energy and was happy, right where she wanted to be. Satisfied and challenged, but more importantly, trusted, appreciated, and utilized. She wanted to feel this way forever, and learn to avoid those thoughts and feelings about a much darker time and place. And the resentments that came along with them.

"You know what, Lieutenant, this moment is too perfect. I don't want to spoil it by talking about that jackass. Maybe the next time we patrol together, I can tell you what I did to that pathetic little man."

Morgan chuckled then reached across the cab and gently placed his hand on Cynthia's shoulder.

"I will be looking forward to that, and, Cynthia, I can't think of anyone I'd rather have in that wet seat, or *any* wet seat for that matter, than you. You truly are one of those at the very top, among the finest that we have."

**50**

Three Months Later
Monday, October 23, 2000
Mission Beach

Like many newly promoted POLs, Marisol Escobar sat anxiously in the hot seat, isolated and alone, way up there above the beach in a glass-enclosed observation deck. Perhaps not as complicated as the job of an air traffic controller, the primary responsibility of a main tower guard is managing up to, even over, 50 personnel and an entire network of operations that provides public safety and the prevention of drownings for more than a mile-long strand of beach. The task can be extremely stressful. The challenge of remaining focused, undistracted, calm, vigilant, and decisive can at times be overwhelming and mentally fatiguing. Certain personalities thrive in the position, others, not so much. Escobar, while vigilant, undistracted, and focused, at times had difficulty remaining calm. Like many other inexperienced main tower guards, Marisol sometimes struggled with making accurate assessments of ocean conditions and deciphering potentially complex rescue scenarios. She, among many other newer tower guards, had a tendency to act quickly. If there was any doubt, as they were trained to do, they sent someone out. Better to have someone there and not need them, than to need them there and not send them, right?

But that puts a lot of miles on your seasonals' legs, and shakes their confidence if they're not allowed to make their own assessments. It's definitely a learning curve. Some get it quickly—others, not so fast.

Thousands of human bodies, young and old, strong and weak, big and small, neophyte swimmers or experienced watermen, are cluttered in small areas relatively close by, or scattered across a vast expanse of swirling ocean currents, bouncing and thrashing, ducking and floating, swept in and out by waves and rip currents, or knocked off their feet in crashing shore break. Then, add hundreds of surfers, boogie boarders, SCUBA divers, spear fishermen, and drunken boaters, not to mention the thousands of landlubbers that remain on the beach that can suddenly have a diabetic emergency, heart attack, stroke, or fall from the edge of a cliff, and indeed, the job of overseeing beach operations from a single location, by yourself, isolated up in the main tower, might seriously stress you the fuck out.

Add in alcohol and drugs on the beach, and well, you do the math on that one.

Giving decisive orders to the personnel under your command about where to go, whom to assist, and how to assist them is not a task for those who lack knowledge, experience, good judgement, or confidence. Add to that the fact that those orders are broadcast over an emergency radio frequency being closely monitored by several of your supervisors, and even personnel from other agencies . . . simply put, the pressure that comes with that responsibility can be exhausting. In the slow winter months, perhaps not as tough; but during the dog days of summer? Believe it.

*The hot box.* Aptly named.

Relieved that her 90-minute rotation in the Pacific Beach main tower was completed, Escobar then took on a less stressful role as the wet seat in a patrolling vehicle. As a wet seat she wouldn't be expected to make as many complex decisions. If she were needed now, she would be told what to do by either the main tower guard who just relieved her, or by the driver of the patrol vehicle she rode in. The driver of that vehicle, however, was Cynthia Harden, and this was the first time they had patrolled together. Escobar was nervous as she rode alongside the now almost-legendary Cynthia Harden. She was intimidated by her superior and knew exactly how capable Harden was.

Feeling insecure, Marisol hoped to gain some of Cynthia's respect, so as they rode along together on the beach, she began telling Cynthia about *her* accomplishments.

"So, I taught them all how to swim. I actually built two programs from scratch, and in the last five years over two dozen of my minority athletes have been accepted to college. Twelve, maybe more, are now working somewhere in San Diego County as ocean lifeguards. That would have never happened if it weren't for me. They would have never received those jobs."

Harden replied sarcastically, "Good for you, Marisol."

Escobar noticed the tone in Cynthia's voice.

"Whatever, Harden. I should have known that you wouldn't care about programs that serve other's needs. My programs have been acknowledged by community leaders, like the mayor and the city council. The mayor called my programs, '*a template for all municipal organizations to learn from.*' I'm just getting started in the Patrol. There's a lot of work for me to do here, but I've got a specific plan designed to straighten this agency out so it can finally function appropriately in the new millennium."

She paused and grimaced before she continued.

"That day in Imperial Beach was the most embarrassing moment of my life, and is the only time in my life that I have ever quit something. I don't even like thinking about it. I'm not even sure why I'm speaking to you about it now. Even so, that arrogant Lt. Morgan had to change his tune after I proved how unfair his methods were. Totally unfair, and it cost me an entire summer of seniority too. He would have kept on excluding qualified people for who knows how long if it weren't for me."

Harden rolled her eyes.

"Do you realize how many times you just said 'me'?"

Marisol flicked her tongue against the roof of her mouth, making a disapproving and condescending sucking sound.

"See, there you go again, just like the conversation we had in the restroom that night during the academy. You just don't care about making a difference, do you? Maybe you could actually learn something from *me*."

Cynthia tilted her head to the side and shot a blank stare across the cab before returning her eyes to the path in front of the vehicle.

"It's obvious," continued Escobar, "that all *you* care about is beating every man that you can. All you want is to prove that you're better than they are at making rescues. That doesn't help anyone, Cynthia; that's all about *you*. You're the one with the *me, me, me, I, I, I,* attitude. You couldn't care less about anybody else."

Cynthia laughed.

"Really?"

"Yeah, really. Again, Cynthia, mine is a much grander vision than yours."

Marisol paused when a small child abruptly ran away from her mother and into the path of the truck. Harden gently applied the brakes and allowed the tot to safely pass 20 yards in front of the vehicle. The mother waved at Cynthia and retrieved her child. After the course was clear, Marisol abruptly changed the subject and Harden resumed the vehicle patrol.

"And there's one other thing that's been bothering me for a while."

"Oh, I can't wait to hear this."

"After you and Latrelle hooked up . . . he became like a totally different person. I'm sure you don't care about this either, but he played a very important role in my family's life for a very long time. He still does and he always will. He feels the same way, too. He just doesn't want to hurt your feelings by telling you the truth."

Escobar turned and noticed that Harden was laughing.

"What, you don't believe me? I've known him since he was a skinny and frightened little boy. I helped him grow up after his father died, and I care more about him than you ever will. Have you even met his mother?"

"Are you serious?"

"Whatever, I'm sure Vanessa feels the same way I do. The academy was when everything changed. After that week, suddenly everything was about you."

"I'm not sure what your point is, Escobar."

"My point . . . Cynthia . . . is that he's not like you, and you're not like us. You have no idea what it's like. Latrelle and I can connect in ways that you can never have with him. He's just too young to understand that he's living out some adolescent white girl fantasy. He'll grow out of it soon enough."

Harden laughed again.

"How do you even come up with this shit?"

"You know it's true, and you're afraid I'm right."

"Okay, Marisol . . . since you began this, I'm going to be just as frank with you about some things that *I* know are the truth." She paused, making certain that she had Escobar's attention. "You're nothing but a spoiled brat. You make something out of everything, and you obviously cannot just accept things for the way they are. Instead, you look for things to complain about, and then you state how things should have been done differently. You focus on going around, instead of *overcoming* the challenge, just like you did to get this job. You don't actually solve anything, you just find ways to create little loopholes so you don't have to do the same work that everyone else does. And then you make it sound like you discovered some biased job requirement, or a flaw in the job description."

Cynthia slowed the truck, realizing that she was becoming too distracted to continue driving safely.

"You've had some success, yes, and I won't deny that you've changed a few things for the better. I've been screwed over by a couple of men in my past, and I'm right there with you concerning gender equity and harassment. But here's the thing, Marisol: You throw enough crap at the wall, sooner or later some of it is going to stick. Any bureaucrat can do that, and really, that's all you are and it is all you'll ever be. You're a talker, you're not a doer. You're the one that doesn't get it. You're out of place here; the Patrol is way out of your league. You should have stayed at the pool. You made a huge mistake, Escobar."

Escobar replied quickly.

"You're sooo wrong about that . . ."

Cynthia cut off Escobar abruptly.

"Shut up, Escobar. You listen to me. *You're* the one that is the most concerned about skipping over people. *You're* the one who wants to prove that she's better than everyone else . . . but really, all you care about is looking *smarter* than everybody else. You put a lot of effort into making everybody look dumber than you, like they all don't know shit. But you're really not that smart, Marisol, you're just very good at magnifying problems that don't bother anybody else."

Escobar was about to say something, but Cynthia stopped her.

"It's still my turn."

Harden placed her foot firmly on the brake pedal and stopped the vehicle. She turned to face Escobar and said, "The truth is, you're only looking out for yourself, and your discrimination and diversity claims are BS."

"Whatever, Harden. You're entitled to your own opinion, which I will never care about. Your opinion is irrelevant, and you, ultimately, will be irrelevant, too. You're beneath me, and I'm going to prove that when I become sergeant. You make rescues, Harden; that's what you do, and you're good at it. You'll stay right here on the beach making rescues where this agency needs you. You're a rock star out here. I can see that, everybody can. But I make policy, Harden; I educate, and I lead people. That's exactly where I'm needed and that's exactly where they are going to place me, right in a position to do that."

"Whatever."

"I'll make sergeant first, way before you do, then lieutenant. You'll see soon enough."

Harden scowled, then scoffed.

"Over my dead body."

"Oh, is that some kind of a threat?"

"I don't make threats, Escobar."

"Whatever, Harden. Nice try. You'll be working for me before you know it."

Harden laughed.

"Wow. You're more full of yourself than your boy, Mike Johnson, is."

Escobar scowled.

"That's disgusting. He is so not my boy. And by the way, he'll be the first to go."

Cynthia laughed.

"At the rate you're going, Johnson will be long since retired before you even make it out of your probation. You're not even a full POL yet, and you're talking all this shit about sergeant? You'll never make it, Escobar. I don't care who you think you have in your corner. It ain't gonna happen."

"No, not true. You wait and see. And you won't have to wait long either. Hopefully by then, Latrelle will have pulled his head out of his ass and stopped sleeping with his first and only white girl. Then he can come back home where he belongs."

Cynthia laughed, but quickly stopped and her mood turned serious. She looked at Marisol and waited until their eyes met. Her tone was filled with venom.

"I'm only going to say two more things and then we're done. One, don't *ever* speak to me about Latrelle Jackson again."

Marisol shifted nervously in the wet seat, appearing to lose confidence, and avoided Cynthia's gaze. Harden remained intense, staring until Marisol looked into her eyes.

"And number two. Like I said before, *over my dead body* will you *ever* outrank me!"

She continued to stare at Marisol, who eventually shrugged her shoulders, turned away, looked at the ocean, and said softly, "We'll see."

Cynthia waited several moments before slowly turning away. She glanced quickly at the dashboard, placed the truck's transmission into park, and released her foot from the brake pedal.

She exited the vehicle and completed a slow and deliberate walk-around to confirm that no person or thing had found its way into the path of one of the vehicle's wheels, then resumed the patrol. Neither woman said another word.

"She told you that she was going to be a lieutenant?"

"Sergeant first, then lieutenant. Oh, and she said she's coming after you as soon as she's promoted."

"What a bitch. Do you see what I've been talking about?"

"I always have seen it. I saw it before you did, at my academy. She's a problem, and she's going to be a bigger problem if she makes sergeant. Somebody has to stop that from happening."

"Nobody wants to stop her more than I do. If she makes sergeant, she'll be all over me. Morgan would never promote her if he wasn't going to support her decisions afterward. I can't afford to lose this job."

"Well none of us wants to lose our job, Mike."

"No, Harden, you don't understand. I have an ex-wife and three kids that I *have* to support. They get a piece of everything I make. My youngest is still in kindergarten and my oldest will be a freshman at Claremont next fall."

He paused and looked over his shoulder toward Cynthia.

"If she's coming after me, then she's also coming after my kids, and she doesn't even know it. Do you think she cares about my kids? I mean, don't get me wrong, I'm counting the days until I get to stop paying alimony to my ex-wife, but the money I send every fucking payday is keeping clean clothes on my kids' backs and good food in their bellies. This South Bay whore is fucking with my livelihood *and* my family's well-being. Fuck her."

He paused and his tone lightened.

"And she's still coming after you because you took Mr. Africa away from her before she could set her hook. She wants him back . . . you *know* that."

Johnson gazed at the ocean through the truck's windshield.

"She is pretty fucking hot, ya know? You'd be wise to keep an eye on Mr. Africa at all times."

Harden shook her head and said, "Why do you have to call him that?"

Johnson chuckled.

"It's a whole lot better than calling him Mr. Nigger, isn't it? I know how you feel about the N word. It's like a sign of respect for you, Cynthia. Look how evolved I am since you and I have been working together. You're like a social mentor to me now."

"You're still an asshole though, Mike, and you know it."

"Just trying to make ya laugh."

"It's not funny. Racism makes me sick. People are people; I don't care about their skin color."

She looked over at Johnson and shook her head.

"Enough about Latrelle."

"Fine. No more talk about your dark chocolate lover."

Harden sighed, scowled at Johnson, then guided the conversation back to Marisol.

"But I do agree with you about Escobar. I'm not going to sit around and wait for her to promote and start working her agenda."

She paused as two young boys with boogie boards sprinted in front of the truck without looking. Johnson cautiously slowed the vehicle.

"I didn't know you had kids. You've never mentioned anything about a family."

Johnson rested his right wrist on top of the steering wheel and his left forearm on the open window frame as he slowly drove the truck across the sand, past a group of surfers out in the water. He inhaled deeply, exhaled slowly, and began telling his story.

"It was our twelfth anniversary. I never saw it coming. Bitch set me up and had the whole thing planned to a T."

Johnson turned and glanced at Cynthia briefly, then returned his eyes to the sand in front of him.

"We had dinner at Mr. A's that night—small table next to a big window, watching the airliners land and takeoff. You know that place?"

"I do. My dad and I used to go there on my birthday, if we didn't go to the Brig. I actually like the Brig much better. Mr. A's is kind of stuffy."

"Yeah, but Debbie loved it there. She would get all dolled up and make me wear a suit and tie every time . . ."

Johnson paused, then smiled.

"We actually had sex in the elevator that night, on the bottom floor of the parking garage. Just pulled her dress up and we did it right there. Debbie loved public sex after a couple of bottles of red wine. She is still the horniest woman I've ever known. From the first time we saw each other, our attraction was way more than just chemistry—it was fucking electricity. I mean lightning bolts. Even after she knew that I had cheated on her, all she cared about was me putting it inside of her. That part she never got tired of . . . and neither did I."

He turned toward Cynthia.

"I guess I kind of took that for granted, huh? I should have known something was up when she stopped kissing me during sex."

Cynthia stared at the group of surfers who sat tall on their boards, looking out toward the horizon, scanning for approaching waves.

"I have no response to that."

Johnson cracked up. "Well said, Harden. Gawd, you're such a great chick, I swear. Seriously, why the hell couldn't we have met twenty years ago?"

"Uh, I was like seven years old. That's gross."

Johnson cracked up again.

"Oh, yeah, I forgot."

Cynthia shook her head, smiling as Johnson continued to chuckle.

"Anyhow, now she's living with some guy that she met at the elementary school our kids went to. He's the principal or some goddamn thing; a fucking skinny, pencil-dick triathlon guy with a Ph.D. and a closet full of linen pants, pink and yellow Polo shirts, and loafers. This guy doesn't even surf, he plays golf and tennis. I swear he's a faggot, too. I guarantee you that he's running up to one of those clubs in Hillcrest a couple nights a month . . . fucking homo . . . whatever."

Cynthia shook her head abruptly but laughed when she visualized the flamboyantly dressed schoolteacher in the woods, just off the fairway, with another man's penis in his mouth.

"You're a real piece of work, Johnson. Seriously . . . even in the Navy I never met anyone quite like you."

He laughed and shrugged.

"See? Like I said, just trying to make you laugh. I guess you're okay with fag jokes then."

Cynthia laughed, then stiffened.

"I never said that, and no, I'm not. Don't twist my words."

They drove quietly and sat calmly until a couple of tourists flagged them down after spotting a pod of dolphins they had mistakenly identified as sharks. Johnson placed the truck's transmission in park and briefly educated the tourists about the shape of dorsal fins, undulating swimming motion, and pods. He waited until the couple walked away before he continued his story.

"Debbie was pretty pissed when she first found out."

"Found out what?"

"That I cheated on her."

"Oh, yeah, that."

Johnson breathed deeply and accelerated the truck only to a crawl.

"It was an old high school flame that I ran into on the beach. It took a while, but this chick would not leave me alone. She got to me eventually. During the winter, when nobody was around, she would lay out there on a towel, right by the main tower in North PB. As soon as

I went on a break she would come up in the trailer and give me head. I mean, who says 'no' to a blowjob?"

He looked at Cynthia, shrugged, and smiled.

"You know what I'm saying?"

"Gross."

He laughed.

"So . . . I ended up fucking her at her place a couple times, but it got old fast. She wasn't worth it. I was an idiot; she was just a nasty whore."

"Ewww, grosser."

He laughed, then shook his head and scowled.

"I screwed up. Debbie knew her. They had common friends, so it was pretty easy for her to find out. I was stupid and I was very lucky that she forgave me that time, but then a couple more of these hotties threw themselves at me and it just got a little easier, you know? Tourists, unhappily married moms who brought their kids to the beach . . . that kind of shit."

He shrugged.

"I was still trying to hide it, thinking that she had no clue, but she knew. This principal guy was all ears and she was singing to him like the fucking Mormon Tabernacle Choir. She never said a thing to me, though."

He chuckled and began shaking his head slowly, as if he still couldn't believe what he was saying.

"Apparently, Debbie was sleeping with this guy the whole time, and *I* never had a clue. They educated themselves about California's no-fault, community property divorce laws and then they launched their plan. Now they're the fucking Brady Bunch."

Cynthia chuckled, but said nothing.

"It turns out this asshole actually earns less than I do. Poor son-of-a-bitch went to college forever and I got this job right out of high school. Can you believe that? That's why it's so fucking cutthroat around here. I couldn't even imagine working some other shit job and trying to survive on that salary somewhere nice in San Diego. Everything I have is because of this job . . . I have a lot to protect."

Johnson's tone softened.

"I wish the kids were with me more often. I miss them, but they're actually doing pretty well now. They've been living with Debbie and Mr. Pencil-dick for a few years now, but they won't get married . . . so I gotta keep paying her alimony. He's got his own alimony to pay, but not near as much as I do, and he doesn't pay child support because his two kids live with him. His ex is a total fuck-up. She's on meds or something. So I'm actually supporting all five of those kids . . . and Debbie. They get two grand a month from me. I'm basically paying her a small salary."

Cynthia raised her eyebrows.

"Ouch. That's a shitty deal. Two grand a month? That's more than half of my take home."

"Pfff. Well, it's a good thing I've been a Senior POL for so long. My salary is as high as it can get until sergeant. It was rough in the beginning though, but it's not as harsh now; I figured out how to make it work a while ago."

"Wow, that's crazy."

Johnson nodded.

"Yeah, it was pretty ugly at first . . . swapping houses in the middle of the week was always a pain in the ass . . . homework, sports practices, and games after school. Shit, those early games on Saturday mornings always killed me. I worked almost every weekend, so it didn't really work for me at all. I just agreed to let her take care of the kids during the school year."

He shrugged.

"They come and stay with me at least one weekend a month, and then as much as they want during the summers. It's turned out okay, but it still bothers me that Mr. Pencil-dick gets to spend more time with my kids than I do, and then I get to pay more than half of his fucking bills."

He shook his head.

"I wanted to kill that fucker, and her, too. I was so pissed. I finally started seeing a shrink with diplomas from Harvard and Stanford hanging on her walls. She straightened me out . . . brilliant woman. Now I know that if I ever do anything to that fucking Freddie Couples wannabe, I'll lose everything. And, like I said before, that ain't gonna happen. I ain't losing shit."

Johnson paused and turned toward Cynthia.

"What are you gonna do, ya know? He's not *that* big of a douchebag after all, and the kids get along with him okay, or rather, they don't *hate* him. Except for Angie, my oldest . . . she might hate him a little bit. She's had the hardest time with this. Her mom used to cry about it and act all hurt, always talking shit about me. Debbie blamed everything on me and tried to get my own children to hate me. She never mentioned to them that she was fucking Freddie, and she sure as hell ain't saying shit about how much money I give her. They still don't know. I'm not gonna tell them. That is one issue that I have definitely taken the high road on. Someday I'll tell Angie what really happened, but not now. She's got her own life to live first."

He paused, then said, "It kind of backfired on Debbie though. Angie isn't as close to her mom as she was before the divorce, and she doesn't like her boyfriend at all. She still won't do what he says and she rarely talks to him. She told me that when he asks her to do something, or tells her *how* she should do something, she just says, 'Why are you talking to me? I don't have to do what you say.'"

He looked at Cynthia, a proud, content smile on his face.

"She's my girl. She's got my back. She knows who her daddy is. Fuck him."

Johnson slowed the vehicle to a crawl and gazed out at the surfers.

"So, I'll be paying for at least half of their college tuition too. I'm all in for as long as they need me. It's the right thing to do . . . gotta man-up, ya know? I ain't no deadbeat dad."

He turned and looked at Cynthia.

"The point I'm trying to make is, I ain't losing this job. I will strangle that bitch Escobar first."

Harden sensed a vulnerability she had assumed was not there. Johnson was hurt, she could feel it radiating from his heart, and smelled it as it emanated from his pores. But the strongest message came from his voice, a resounding tone of love for, and commitment to, his family.

She looked at him, taking in a perspective she never imagined she would gain regarding Mike Johnson, waited for him to return her gaze, and asked him, "So what happened after the dinner that night?"

"Well, we came home after dinner and I was still thinking everything was fine. I got up early the next morning to paddle before my shift, and when I came home after work that night, everybody was gone. It was the end of June, school was out, the sun was still up and I'm thinking, *'No big deal, they're probably at the beach, or maybe they're at the movies or a Padres game or something.'*

"But then the sun goes down and before I know it, it's like ten o'clock and she's still not answering her cell phone, and nobody's home. I finally walked upstairs into my den and found an envelope on the keypad of my computer with my name written on it. It was in her handwriting. I open it up and there's a note inside. Again it's her handwriting."

Johnson paused and took a deep breath.

"Well, to make a long story short, they were all on a flight to Providence, and then they spent the entire summer in Rhode Island with her parents. I got served with divorce papers before they came back." Johnson shook his head and grimaced. "Right there in the parking lot at Mission Beach . . . right in back of the tower. This guy just walks right up to me and he says, 'Hey bro, is your name Mike Johnson?' and I'm like, 'Yeah.' He hands me this big sealed envelope and he says, 'You've been served,' and then he turns and walks away."

He chuckled.

"Can you believe that? Just like that. Within six months, the entire thing was over. Fortunately, we hung onto our assets and gave very little to any blood-sucking divorce lawyers. Talk about slimeballs . . . those guys are brutal."

"I wouldn't know."

"Well, I hope you never find out. Anyhow, I kept the truck, my boat, and trailer, which were mostly paid for, and she got the Suburban, the canyon house on the big lot, and a shitload of equity. I got about sixty grand in cash from the settlement, which I've already doubled with some nice investments. We bought that house right after we got married in '84, so by '95 it had almost doubled in value. She's sitting on her retirement right there; it's been appraised at a half a million already. She rents that place out while she lives in the fucking schoolteacher's house. She's golden already, so I get to keep *all* of my retirement benefits and I contribute the maximum, which the city matches, before she gets her piece. I negotiated that first."

"Nice."

"Yeah. We both made out well. I could have been a real prick and she could have been a real bitch, but neither one of us hired one of those ass-wipe divorce lawyers. I'd seen enough bad divorces to know better and Debbie had, too. We both agreed right away. Besides, my kids would have struggled even more and we'd all be broke. I kept my head on straight and finally got Debbie to also. It's all good now. I'll be just fine as long as I make it to my full retirement."

Johnson paused when he noticed a young boy walking his yellow lab along the water's edge. Harden grabbed the hand-held mic that hung from the bottom of the dashboard and offered a gentle verbal reminder over the truck's PA about the beach laws, then patiently waited for the boy to realize that the lifeguard in the truck was speaking to him. The boy and his lab changed directions and immediately headed east, off the beach.

Johnson continued.

"I work for my retirement and for my kids now. I work as much overtime as possible in the summer and I always accept relief shifts in the winter. I haven't taken a vacation or a sick day in almost three years. I don't spend a lot of money and I get by on very little, actually. I'm not complaining. Those are just the facts. This is my reality, and I am not about to lose this job and start struggling to meet all of my responsibilities."

Johnson looked across his shoulder into Harden's eyes.

"Fuck Marisol Escobar."

Cynthia said nothing.

Johnson said nothing.

They both looked out toward the ocean and silently watched a skilled old man with a long, gray goatee standing upright on a blue and yellow longboard. He was killing graceful cutbacks off the lip of a nice wave that peeled to the right, before dropping back down into the wave's trough. He repeated the sequence several times, riding the wave that stood tall in front of a cloudless, bright orange sky. Foamy spray and light mist levitated above the top of the wave that grew in height with the help of a gentle off-shore breeze. The surfer made a final cutback before he dropped down just beneath the wave's narrow, lipping shoulder, completed a smooth bottom turn, walked nimbly to the front of the board, then crouched down and glided across the curling wave face for several long moments. Holding his position gracefully, he then stood up, walked to the back of the board, and turned up and over the top of the wave just before it closed out in front of him. He was belly down on his board, paddling back outside to line up for another wave when Johnson continued.

"She was right for what she did, Cynthia. I wasn't a very good husband and I deserved what I got. I've taken my medicine though, and I will keep supporting my kids for the rest of their lives. I'm counting on at least fifteen more years of this job ahead of me . . . Shit . . . I could do this job until I'm sixty . . . then Marisol Escobar can go ahead and fire me."

"I understand, Mike."

"Naaahhh. No you don't. You don't have three kids."

As Cynthia rested comfortably in the climate-controlled wet seat and gazed at the beautiful ocean scene, she suddenly realized, *He'll find a way to stop her when the time comes, and I'm sure his plan will include a direct frontal assault that will draw everybody's attention to him. That will allow me to flank her and stay under the radar . . . and I can do some serious damage from there.*

**52**

Three Days Later
Monday, October 30, 2000
Lifeguard Headquarters

Gabriella Sanchez hung up the phone, stepped away from her desk, and walked to the back of the building. She tapped lightly on an open door and stepped inside the room.

"Lieutenant, Marisol Escobar just called."

Richard Morgan looked up.

"Is she on the line now?"

"No, sir. I told her that you were away from your desk. She did, however, say that she wanted you to call her back immediately."

"Did she say what it was about?"

"No, sir. She just told me that it was urgent."

"Ugh, what now?"

As the lieutenant's secretary turned and left the office, she said empathically, "Good luck, sir."

Morgan looked at the phone on his desk, thinking, *Well, I suppose there's no time like the present.* He glanced at a staff directory pinned to a corkboard, ran his finger about a quarter of the way down the list, muttered Escobar's phone number twice, then turned and dialed.

He heard three rings, then a voice said, "Hola, este es Marisol."

"Hi, Marisol, it's Richard Morgan. Gabby said that you wanted to speak with me."

"Uhhh, yes, I do. Is now a good time?"

Morgan snorted, "No time like the present."

"Great, Lieutenant. I'd like to discuss my current assignment, at Mission and Pacific Beach."

"Okay. Is everything all right?"

"Well, yes, I mean I don't have any grievances if that's what you're asking . . . but I do have a couple of issues."

Morgan paused and exhaled.

"Issues?"

"Well, sir . . . I'm not sure how to put this, so I'll guess I'll just say it. I don't feel comfortable sharing shifts with Cynthia Harden. Mike Johnson, either."

"Did something happen that I'm unaware of ?"

"No. Nothing really happened, I mean, not since that incident at Tourmaline, but it's still weird having to work with them both."

The lieutenant sat up, intrigued.

"Weird? I'm not sure I understand," he said.

"It's uncomfortable, and I don't think it's working out. Do you think I could transfer back to the Shores?"

Morgan looked down at his desk and scratched the top of his head.

"That's a tough one, Marisol. It's policy and procedure that that all probies complete their first twelve months at a primary station."

"I understand the policy, and I realize how important it is to become familiar with each station before moving on, but, sir, isn't it possible for me to complete this assignment at a later time?"

*Absolutely not*, Morgan thought. He paused, however, and offered a more diplomatic response.

"Hmmm . . . I try not to make exceptions, you know. That sets a poor example, not a good precedent. I'm sure you can appreciate that. I mean, if I do this for you, what's to stop any other probationary POL from making the same request? Personality conflicts need to be resolved and put behind us; awkward circumstances just have to be dealt with, Marisol. These are areas of strength that you told me you possess, areas of strength that I value highly, and depend upon from every guard we employ."

Escobar pleaded, "But, don't you think there are some extenuating circumstances here?"

"Marisol, one of the reasons this agency is so effective at providing public safety is that we all put our personal feelings aside while we're on the job. This job is about collaboration and teamwork. You don't have to like all of your colleagues, but you do have to be able to trust and work with them. That requires maturity. I expect my guards to act like adults so they can get the job done."

He paused.

"This is a little bit uncharacteristic of you, don't you think? Aren't these the leadership qualities that are supposed to separate you from the others on my staff ? That's what you told me."

Escobar did not reply.

Morgan continued.

"Are you sure that you want to pursue this path, Marisol?"

"Lieutenant, Harden won't even look at me when we're on duty together, and everybody else just gives me the cold shoulder. And when I see Johnson in the tower, he just smirks sarcastically, or sneers and laughs at me. Then he'll pretend like he was laughing at something else. He is such a child. It's very uncomfortable, and totally unprofessional."

Morgan said nothing.

"Lieutenant, I shouldn't have to tolerate this kind of treatment. I've been extremely professional and I've completed every one of my training assignments. I'm trying very hard. I really am. I've been doing exactly what you told me to do, and exactly how you told me to do it."

"I can see that. I appreciate that too. Just keep your head down and keep moving forward, so to speak."

"That is my intention, but those two are obviously conspiring against me, and I'm not being hypersensitive, Lieutenant. I've worked for the city long enough to know when this adolescent nonsense is going on, and I'm telling you, it's going on at both Mission and Pacific Beach. It's obvious that they don't appreciate my effort level, or acknowledge me when I succeed, and, even worse, it feels like they're not the only ones who want me to fail."

*Well, that may be true,* Morgan thought. *She's not the first probie to feel this way.*

"Here's what I can do. I'll flip your schedule. You'll have to work Schedule A though. I'll keep them on Schedule B, so Wednesdays at PB will be the only days that you'll have to work together. But you have to stay on the strand, Marisol, and your next assignment is going to be Ocean Beach, not La Jolla Shores. That's the sequence that we set up for you when you accepted this position. We are not going to change that. You'll just have to figure out a way to overcome this. I'm confident that you can handle that. I've had to encourage other probationary POLs through this as well, Marisol. Consider that this kind of thing may be part of the trial for you, just as it was for many other POLs.

"But, Lieutenant, I just think that . . ."

Morgan cut her off.

"That's the best I can do for you. Your new schedule will start next Wednesday. You'll stay on that schedule until you complete the assignment at the end of next summer. I have to take another call now. You have a good day, Marisol."

**53**

Six Months Later, Spring Break
Saturday, April 7, 2001
Mission Beach

On a crowded day at Mission Beach, as he lay on a large towel next to his wife, Troy Neely looked out at the Pacific Ocean. He was hot, sunburned, and bored, and, although he grew up swimming in the cold lakes and lazy rivers of Minnesota, he had never been outside of the waves in the ocean. He sat up, rested on his elbows, and turned to Stephanie, his young bride.

"Sweetie, I think I'll go for a swim."

"You are? Honey, it's dangerous out there. Are you sure?"

"Yes, I'm sure. I've always wanted to do this."

"Well, okay, but be careful. Don't go too far away, all right? It's the ocean, I'm scared."

Troy laughed.

"Don't worry, you know that I can swim just fine, and I'm pretty sure that I won't get attacked by a shark either."

"Ohhh, you . . ."

She reached and playfully smacked him with a paperback novel.

"Why do you have to say things like that? Now I'm going to be a nervous wreck."

Troy laughed again.

"Honey, you're almost always a nervous wreck. Relax, sweetheart, look behind us."

He pointed directly behind them.

"That is a lifeguard tower."

He rotated over his right shoulder and pointed again.

"And see that yellow truck down there, driving toward us?"

"Yes."

"Well, there are TWO lifeguards in there. They drive around all day looking for sharks, and people who can't swim very well. So, if you see anything that looks like a shark, or anyone who looks like he can't swim very well, then you just go over there and tell them, all right?"

"You're not funny, but I still love you. And I am not a nervous wreck almost all of the time."

"No, you're not, honey. I was just kidding."

"Thank you. I'll be right here reading my book. I want you to wave at me every few minutes, okay?"

"I will, honey. See you in a little bit."

He paused.

"Here's what I'll do. Get me a ten dollar bill out of my backpack. I'll get us a snack after I get out of the water."

He took the bill, zipped it into a pocket on his trunks, and started toward the ocean. He turned back when he heard Stephanie call out to him.

"Honey, don't forget to wave at me so I know you're safe, okay?"

Troy nodded, waved, and backpedaled into the water.

"Yes, dear."

Fifteen minutes later, having finished the next two chapters in her book, Stephanie looked up. Her husband had been practicing body surfing, but he had kept his word and waved at his wife every few minutes. Now, however, she was unable to spot him. She placed her book on her towel, stood up, and shaded her eyes with both hands. Squinting into the afternoon sun, she scanned the waves, pivoting her head from north to south. Her heart began racing, her blood pressure increased, and instantly she became alarmed. She ran to the water's edge and yelled, "Troy! Where are you, Troy? TROY!!!"

She ran 20 yards to the south, and yelled again, "TROY!!!"

Beginning to weep hysterically, she ran to the north, yelling, stammering, "TRR-RR-OOYY!!!"

Then, she turned and looked toward the lifeguard tower her husband had pointed to. She noticed a young man wearing red shorts and a blue jacket, sunglasses on his face, standing on the tower's deck, leaning against a rail, calmly looking at the ocean. When the guard noticed her running toward him, he grabbed his lifeguard radio and cautiously stepped off the tower to greet her.

"My husband is out there. I can't find him. He was just there a minute ago and now he's gone! Help me. I think he's drowning."

She turned and ran back toward the water.

"TROY!!!"

The lifeguard remained calm and radioed the main tower.

"Mission Beach from Tower 13, I have a possible missing adult. Stand by for description."

"Copy thirteen, Tower standing by."

Marisol Escobar was driving Unit 22 south toward the Mission Beach main tower when she heard the call. She looked at her wet seat, a veteran seasonal guard, and said, "Let's head down there. That sounds like trouble."

Back at Tower 13, the lifeguard ran down the beach to meet with Stephanie.

"Ma'am, please calm down. I need you to answer a few questions, okay?"

"My husband is out there somewhere. We don't have time for questions. Why are you still standing here? Go out there and find him. This is what he told me to do. You're supposed to go help him!"

"Ma'am, we will help him, but we need to know who we're looking for first. Let's start with a description of him, okay?"

"He's tall and he has blond hair."

"He's white?"

"Yes, he's white!"

"About your age?"

"Yes, he's my husband! Why is this taking so long? He's out there!!!"

She turned, ran to water's edge and yelled, "TTTTRRR-ROOOOYYYY!!!"

The lifeguard followed.

"Ma'am, what was he wearing?"

"Uhhh, blue shorts."

"Was he wearing a rash guard or a wetsuit top?"

"No! Just his blue trunks!"

"Is he a good swimmer?"

"Uhhh, I guess so, yes, he's a good swimmer."

"When and where did you last see him?"

"Right out there, maybe five minutes ago. Where is he???"

"What's his name?"

"Troy, Troy Neely!"

"Okay, just try to be calm, I'm sure everything is going to be fine. He may have swum down the beach a little bit; there is a pretty strong lateral current today. Just wait here, with me."

He keyed the mic and said, "Mission Beach, thirteen, prepare for description of possible missing swimmer."

"Go ahead, thirteen."

"We're looking for a tall, white male with blond hair, approximately thirty years of age, wearing blue trunks, no top. Last seen five minutes ago, in the water, south of thirteen. Good swimming ability. His name is Troy Neely."

"Copy thirteen. Break. Unit 22, did you copy?"

Escobar's wet seat responded.

"Affirm tower, tall white male in blue trunks in the thirteen area, good swimmer."

The main tower guard continued.

"Tower 13 from Mission, do you have a spot on that swimmer yet?"

"Negative, tower."

"Copy. Thirteen, stand by there with reporting party. Unit 22 will be there in two minutes."

"Thirteen copies, standing by."

Marshall Devers was a 15-year veteran seasonal guard. Lt. Morgan had implored him years ago to interview for POL, but Devers had already received master's degrees in both chemistry and education, and held a tenured position as a faculty member at a private school in La Jolla. He continued to work every summer, however, and was an outstanding ocean lifeguard. He was very familiar with Mission Beach, and he had participated in just about every type of rescue scenario an ocean lifeguard could.

As Escobar drove toward the scene, Devers said, "Let's just hope this is another case of a guy not paying attention to the currents. What's this, the fourth missing adult since noon?"

"I don't know, Marshall. Did you hear that lady's voice in the background of Thirteen's call? She was freaking out. It sounds to me like she may have actually seen him go under."

"Marisol, they almost always freak out. Let's just get there and make that determination then."

"I'm not losing a swimmer during one of my patrols . . . I'm telling you, there's something different about this one."

Devers placed a pair of binoculars to his eyes as the truck approached the scene.

"There, at the water's edge, just south of thirteen, I can see them."

When Unit 22 arrived, Stephanie Neely immediately sprinted toward the truck. Devers and Escobar were out of the truck and standing on the sand when she reached them. She pointed at the lifeguard she had been speaking to.

"He won't go out there and find my husband. I thought he was supposed to do that. Isn't that why you're here?"

Devers replied, "Yes, ma'am. That is what we do, and we will, as soon as we're sure that he needs our help."

"I'm SURE that he needs your help; he disappeared."

She turned and pointed at the ocean.

"Right out there!"

"Okay, ma'am. I understand that you're anxious. But, please, see if you can calm yourself just enough to tell me your name."

A quizzical look appeared on her face.

"Stephanie Neely, but what does that have to do with anything?"

"Listen, Stephanie. I need you to tell me exactly what you saw, from the very beginning. Where were you, and what were you doing?"

"I was right here, reading my book and watching my husband play in the waves."

"Okay, how long was he in the water?"

"Ten, maybe fifteen minutes."

"And did you see him swim in either direction, up there or down there?"

Stephanie paused.

"Yes, that way." She waved her arm toward the south.

Devers turned to Escobar and nodded, then instructed the 13 guard to take his rescue board into the water and to paddle south.

"I want you to make contact with as many of those waders and swimmers as you can. Be discreet, do not alarm anybody," he said to the young ocean lifeguard.

"Copy that," the lifeguard replied.

The 13 guard began sprinting toward the water with his board, but Escobar yelled, "Wait!"

She then ran to the truck and retrieved a bright orange flotation buoy that was attached to a long rope with a small anchor. She handed the rig to the guard.

"Take this with you and wait for my signal, then deploy that datum. I'm calling in a *Code X* right now."

The guard looked at Devers, then Devers looked at Escobar. "What? Marisol, we can't confirm that yet. She didn't say anything about seeing him go under."

He turned to Stephanie.

"Ma'am, did you actually see your husband disappear under the surface of the water? Were you looking right at him when he disappeared?

Was he showing signs of distress or waving for help?"

Stephanie paused.

"Umm, no, I never saw that . . . I . . . I'm not sure. I was reading my book, then I looked up, and he was gone."

"How long were you reading before you looked up, Mrs. Neely?"

"I don't remember, maybe a few minutes, all I know is that he's gone."

Escobar looked at Devers.

"This is a *Code X*."

"No, it's not, not yet. He could be anywhere, walking on the beach, or out there body surfing still. There was no distress, Marisol. Follow the procedure, let the main tower make some PAs, and we'll use the PA in the truck. You know that's the next step."

In the background, they could already hear the main tower's loud PA system, *"Lifeguards are looking for a tall, white male in blue swim trunks last seen in the Tower 13 area . . . Attention on the beach and in the water, lifeguards are looking for Troy Neely. Mr. Neely, if you can hear this transmission, please walk to the nearest lifeguard tower . . . "*

Devers returned to the truck and made similar PA announcements as Escobar and the Tower 13 guard scanned the area, hoping to spot Troy Neely.

Escobar stepped toward the truck.

"This is a *Code X*, and we're wasting time. He's been missing too long already."

"Marisol, just calm down, let the main tower do his job."

"Devers, this woman is freaking out, she said she saw him disappear."

"No, that's not what she said. She said she was reading her book. And look at that current, Marisol. I guarantee you that he's down there by Tower 12. Just follow the procedure."

Escobar looked at Stephanie, who screamed, "Why are you three just standing here?" Stephanie turned to the 13 guard, "He's drowning! Why aren't you going out there?"

Escobar looked at the 13 guard and pointed to the ocean.

"Go, now!"

She turned back to Devers who was still seated in the truck, mic in hand.

"And you, too. Take the board from the truck, masks and snorkels, too. Set that datum, and start diving."

Before Devers could protest, Escobar keyed her radio.

"Mission Beach tower. This is Unit 22. I have confirmation that the swimmer was seen going under just south of thirteen. I am initiating full *Code X* procedure now."

Immediately every lifeguard within running distance sprinted toward Tower 13 with rescue equipment. Other guards arrived in vehicles and yelled at the swimmers and boogie boarders in the ocean.

"Please exit the water at this time. Everybody exit the water. We need to clear the ocean."

The main tower guard made similar PA announcements, as did Escobar in Unit 22. Three minutes later, the ocean in front of towers 13, 12, 11, and the Mission Beach main tower was cleared of citizens, but filled with lifeguards.

Within five minutes, two rescue boats had arrived, and the fire department's helicopter was circling the area. A Coast Guard helicopter, rescue boats from Encinitas and Del Mar, and the San Diego police department helicopter were on their way to assist, and two local television choppers were broadcasting live action shots to San Diego residents who watched from their living rooms, while thousands of beach patrons crowded the area and watched from the sand.

Troy Neely exited a Mission Beach candy shop with a dripping ice cream cone in each hand. After reaching the boardwalk he noticed the array of sudden activity on the beach and hurried to gain a better view. He stepped onto the sand by Tower 13 and attempted to make his way through the crowd. He noticed a woman standing by a lifeguard truck, being hugged and comforted by a female lifeguard. As he moved in closer, he could see that it was his wife.

He rushed to her side, and said, "Stephanie, what's going on?"

"Oh, my God, Troy! Where have you been?"

"Sweetie, it's okay. I just went to get us some ice cream."

Escobar turned toward Stephanie, then pointed at Troy Neely, her eyes as big as saucers.

"Is this your husband?"

"Yes, he's alive!"

Escobar froze, unable to move a muscle.

"Oh, shit."

**54**

The Next Morning
Monday, April 7, 2001
Main Lifeguard Tower, Mission Beach

Lt. Morgan stood behind his desk, his phone to his ear. "Good morning, Kenny."

"Good morning, Lieutenant."

Sergeant Kenny Mendenhall was seated at his desk on the second floor of the Mission Beach main tower.

"I assume you're calling to schedule the *drowning review*."

Morgan snorted, "Uh, yeah. What time does Escobar's shift start?"

"She's off today, sir. She's on Schedule A."

"Oh, that's right. Ugh, I'll call her at home. Let's shoot for ten a.m. Let McIntyre know. I want him there, and we better get a female guard to join us in that room, too."

"Yes, sir. I'll get Posakany, she's already here. She's in the tower now."

"All right, I'll see you guys in a couple of hours."

"Hey, Richard?"

"Yeah."

"Didn't she do this at the Shores while she was still a seasonal?"

Morgan groaned, then said, "Yep, and she was pretty indignant during that debriefing. This is not going to be pretty. Just tell those other two to be patient when we start the review. I'll guide the conversation. You three will be there, pretty much as silent observers. If you ask any questions be careful not to antagonize her, and definitely do not attempt to make any jokes. She will not respond positively to that. Make sure you tell McIntyre to go easy; you know how he can be."

Mendenhall chuckled.

"Understood, sir. I'll see you at ten."

Two hours later, Escobar arrived at Mission Beach in her Audi with the top down. Wearing a lacy white summer dress and high heels, she entered the tower and made her way up the staircase to a room where three uniformed officers and one female POL sat side by side at a long table. A single chair had been placed on the other side of the table.

Morgan waved an open hand.

"Miss Escobar, if you don't mind, please have a seat."

Marisol, looking nervous, sat down.

Morgan said, "Thank you for coming on your day off, Marisol. This shouldn't take long. I do need to inform you, however, that this review is being audio recorded. I'd like for you to acknowledge that you are aware of that before we begin."

Escobar said, "I acknowledge that this review is being audio recorded."

Morgan replied, "Thank you," then pressed the record key, then announced who was in the room and why they were there.

"Marisol, I'm going to ask you to reconstruct the sequence of events that led to you calling the *Code X*, starting from when you first heard the missing person's report that was called in by the Tower 13 guard. Then we may ask you some questions, and we'd like you to take your time before answering each one so that you can accurately recall as many details as possible. But before we do that, is there anything that you'd like to say?"

Escobar bowed her head, breathed in deeply, then looked up.

"First of all, I would like to express how grateful I am that Troy Neely is still alive."

She paused.

"His wife was so scared . . . during the secondary interview, she convinced me that she saw him drowning, so I guess I got a little bit scared, too. But I was just doing what we've been trained to do. 'When in doubt, go out.' I wasn't convinced that Mr. Neely was safe, Lieutenant. I wanted to be sure. Better to have and not need, than to need and not have, right? I think what I did was a reasonable thing to do, considering the circumstances."

"Anything else?"

Marisol said, "Well, yes. The kid in thirteen, Newman?"

Sergeant McIntyre, the duty roster supervisor replied, "Yes, Travis Newman. That is who was on duty in Tower 13 at the time of the incident. He made the initial call."

"He's still a rookie, right? I mean, technically he hasn't even completed an entire summer on the oceanfront. Am I correct?"

All four panelists shifted their bodies. Morgan kept his eyes on Escobar, while the three other panelists turned and looked at the lieutenant.

Morgan nodded slowly and said, "That is correct. He graduated from the academy a little over a year ago."

"Right. So, when I arrived on scene, Mrs. Neely immediately complained to me that Newman hadn't done anything to help her husband. She stated that she had pointed out to him where her husband was last seen in the water, but that he did nothing. When I arrived she was yelling at him, 'Why aren't you doing anything?'"

"Go on."

"Well, I wasn't confident that he knew how to spot a rescue. He looked unsure about what to do, and he was unclear about what had happened. He had seen nothing."

McIntyre interjected.

"Even though he interviewed the reporting party, and called in the missing person's report quickly and accurately, you still questioned his judgment?"

"Uh, well, he did do a good job with that, but then he just stood there and waited for me to arrive. He could have gone into the water long before we even got there."

"That's not our protocol, Marisol. He followed the procedure just as he was trained to do. He stayed with the R-P until backup arrived."

"Well, then that's a bad policy. He should have gone out into the water and looked for Mr. Neely. He knew that there was a strong current out in front of his tower, and he didn't make any warnings to move Mr. Neely or any of the other swimmers to a safer area. If Newman would have done that before Mr. Neely drifted down the beach, none of this would have happened. That woman would have been able to see her husband the entire time."

Morgan rested his forehead against his fingertips.

Escobar continued.

"That's what happened, Lieutenant. That was the first breakdown . . . in my opinion."

"What else?"

"Well, after Devers and I arrived, I told Newman right away to go out there and to start looking for Mr. Neely. Then Devers told him to wait until the main tower guard and our unit made PAs first."

Sgt. McIntyre interjected again.

"That's not what Newman or Devers reported. They both stated that Devers instructed Newman to take his rescue board out into the water and to start contacting people. They both claim that, after Devers instructed Newman to go out on his board, you told Newman to wait until you retrieved the datum buoy, and that you were going to call in the *Code X* right away."

Escobar glared at McIntyre and sat quietly.

"And, they both also stated that, after Devers conducted his secondary interview with the RP; he *could not* verify that a witnessed drowning had occurred. Devers claimed that Mrs. Neely said that she never saw her husband showing *any* signs of distress, and that she *did not* see him submerge."

Morgan glanced at McIntyre, shook his head, and waved at him to stop.

Escobar replied, "Lieutenant, is this going to be like the last time we did this at La Jolla Shores? Are we going to focus on the minutiae again? These are all minor details. That woman told me that he suddenly disappeared. This is nothing like what happened at the Shores. That was my mistake I just didn't look around the beach thoroughly before I called it in, but this time I did the right thing, the right way. The main tower made PAs, and we made PAs from the truck. There was no response."

Escobar looked into the eyes of all four panelists.

"I knew that the victim was out in the water this time, and so did Newman. He's the one who failed to do his job correctly, not me."

McIntyre again interjected

"What is your beef with Newman? He's a good kid, and a heck of a guard already."

"Gerald, enough. Let her finish. Go ahead, Marisol, the floor is yours," Morgan said sternly.

"The big picture, Lieutenant, as you have always stated, is about what *could* happen, right? That man *could* have been drowning. He was from Minnesota after all, and could barely swim, for all we knew. His wife told me that this was the first time either one of them had been to the Pacific Ocean."

The room fell silent.

Escobar continued.

"Isn't it our responsibility to be proactive? Aren't we supposed to *prevent* a drowning before it even gets started?"

Morgan smiled.

"Yes, Miss Escobar, that is our job."

He then turned to the others in the room.

"I think we've heard all that we need to hear. I'm going to discontinue this review now, and I am turning the recorder off."

He pushed the button.

"You are all excused. Thank you for attending."

McIntyre shook his head and glanced at Escobar disapprovingly while Mendenhall and Posokany left the room, their eyes fixed on the doorway. Standing in the open doorway with his hand on the doorknob, McIntyre turned toward Morgan.

"Are you really going to let her just throw that kid under the bus like that?"

Morgan's tone was curt.

"Sergeant McIntyre, that is enough. You are dismissed. Please leave this room now, and close that door behind you."

McIntyre directed Escobar a departing scowl before he turned and exited the room. Escobar winced when the door slammed behind her.

Morgan then leaned on his forearms and brought his hands together, interlocking his fingers. He tilted his head slightly, an amused smile cracking his lips. He locked eyes and said nothing.

Escobar shrugged, looked away, shook her head, and said, "Am I excused now?"

Morgan chuckled.

"Excused? No, Marisol. You are not excused."

"You said that you had 'discontinued this review,' didn't you?"

"That is what I said, yes."

"Well, then, why am I still here?"

Morgan breathed in and leaned back in his chair, unsure about how to proceed.

He sighed, and said, "Look, Marisol, what you did out there was by no means the worst thing that could have happened. Nobody got hurt, and everything turned out fine. However, like you did at the Shores, in my opinion, you overreacted."

"No, I disagree."

"I thought you might. Remember, Marisol, the rest of the beach remains mostly unguarded during a *Code X*. That left us vulnerable on an extremely crowded day."

"But still, Lieutenant, something needed to be done to help that woman."

"You understand negligence, right? Failure to provide a required duty."

"Of course I do."

"Okay, then suppose something unrelated occurred during that call, a mass rescue, up in North PB maybe, whose staff is all at the *Code X*, except for one lone guy up in the tower, and one downstairs guard. We may have been caught with our pants down, so to speak. And also, our personnel, and others' personnel, were subjected to unnecessary stress, and potential injury. Not to mention the complete and totally unnecessary waste of valuable resources."

Escobar bowed her head.

Morgan continued.

"Look, Marisol, you're a bright young woman. You really are. You have many admirable qualities, and I think there might be a high place for you in the city's org chart. I really do. But you and I both know that it's probably not in the Patrol, and that you are not likely to become a senior officer on the DCS board."

Escobar glared into the lieutenant's eyes, but did not speak.

"You have shown that you have a tendency to react too quickly during moments of crisis, Marisol. Now, fortunately, your style hasn't created any injuries, or worse, but it has created quite a financial burden for the city of San Diego and its taxpayers."

He raised his eyebrows and squinted at Marisol.

"Twice now."

"But, Lieutenant . . ."

Morgan raised a hand and calmly shook his head.

"No . . . no 'buts,' not again. The first time you called for a *Code X* we got lucky. That kid popped out from under your tower in time for us to limit the efforts, and the costs, of the other agencies that began to assist us. We were able to use the scenario as . . . I'll call it a relatively expensive drill. We were able to make some valuable assessments, but the whole thing was avoidable. And costly. Agreed?"

Escobar nodded.

"Yeah, I guess so. But I already told you that I learned a valuable lesson that day."

"Well, did you? Are you certain that you were thorough enough on Saturday? Devers is solid. He's at the very top of seasonal seniority, and if he didn't enjoy teaching so much, I would have made him a sergeant a long time ago."

He raised his eyebrows and glared across the table.

"What you really failed to do, Marisol, was to defer to Devers, even though you outrank him."

He shook his head.

"I've observed this a few times now, Marisol—situations where you have demonstrated an unwillingness to defer to the judgment of somebody more experienced than you are. That weakness has created some doubt about your ability to collaborate. And now, your decisions have become a fiscal burden. Wouldn't you agree?"

"I don't think I should answer that . . . and I don't mean this disrespectfully, Lieutenant, but what are you planning to do about it?"

"Nothing. What can I do other than hope that you'll see what I see, and that quickly you'll make a significant adjustment?"

He shrugged and frowned.

"Now *I* have to take another hit in the media. I have to answer questions, *on TV*, about how my agency can make an error in judgment like this – an expensive error that now everyone in San Diego County has either seen, or heard about."

He frowned again.

"Have you thought about that?"

"No, sir. I guess I haven't considered the public's response to something like this."

"Well, there you go . . . I guess you learned something else now, too. Public perception is a slippery slope, Marisol. I figured you to be the type that knows all about abrupt shifts in public opinion."

Escobar did not reply.

Morgan continued.

"We owe a lot of agencies a lot of money for this; they don't offer their assistance for free. This one will likely be close to fifty grand. Last time it was just under twenty. That's a sergeant's yearly salary that you've tallied up. You gonna give that money back after the mayor orders me to promote you to that position, like you told me he would?"

"You can't say that to me."

"I just did."

"That's rude and unprofessional; do you really want to go there?"

"Yes, I do. I want to find out if you'll grow up, take the feedback, accept the criticism, and actually make some changes in your approach to things around here. I thought you were making progress, I really did, but you took a big step backward today. You deflected responsibility, and you threw two colleagues right under the bus, just like McIntyre suggested."

He shook his head.

"That's not leadership, Marisol. I can live with an expensive *Code X*, but the crap you pulled just now . . . no way."

Marisol looked down. When she lifted her head, she revealed a reddened face.

"I didn't realize how much Mrs. Neely got to me until just now. I got caught up in her emotions . . . I'm sorry. Newman and Devers did nothing wrong. They just did what I told them to do. They followed the chain of command, even though they knew that I was probably wrong."

Morgan offered a grin and snorted, "Probably wrong?"

"Okay, wrong. Devers is clearly more experienced than I am. I should have trusted him, listened to him, and waited longer."

Morgan smiled.

"Marisol, that is best thing I've heard you say all day."

"I am sorry, Lieutenant."

"I actually believe you. Now listen to me. You're going to take a week off, use some comp time, and get away from the beach. Let this blow over. But when you come back, you're going to speak with McIntrye, Mendenhall, and Posokany . . . separately."

"I will."

"And you're going to tell them what you just told me. Okay?"

"Yes, sir. I will, especially the week-off part."

Morgan laughed.

"And then you're going to make amends with Newman and Devers. We're going to put this thing back together piece by piece. And like I told you and the mayor both, a long time ago, I'm not going to get in the way of your future. But if you don't rise to the occasion along the way, you're not going to reach those lofty goals you set."

Escobar wiped her eyes and sighed.

"You know, Lieutenant, I've told you this before, but you *are* good at what you do, and you just showed me so again. You're fair and objective. I probably should have just trusted you all along."

"Well, you can start right now."

Escobar nodded but said nothing.

# PART 7

Selection:
The process of choosing something, or someone,
in preference to others

**55**

One Week Later
Late Evening, Monday, April 14, 2001
Morgan Residence

Richard Morgan rested comfortably in a cushioned lounge chair on his back patio enjoying a cold beer. He had been tossing tennis balls for his two dogs to chase and retrieve when he heard his wife call out to him, "Richard, it's Mayor Peete."

Morgan sighed, "Oh, this ought to be fun."

She walked to the open doorway, handed him the phone, smiled coyly, and walked back into the house.

Morgan inhaled, exhaled, and said, "Hi, Eddie."

"I go out of town for a week and all hell breaks loose? Is that the way it is?"

Morgan chuckled.

"Seems that way, huh? Welcome back, sir. How was Montana?"

"The weather was perfect, the trout were hitting, the riding trails took us through some of the most beautiful country I've ever seen, the place we stayed was spectacular, and the food was great. I mean five-star. It was just what I needed."

"Nice. Linda and I are hoping to do something like that. We're looking at taking a cruise through the Inside Passage, from Seattle up through Alaska, maybe sometime in September."

"You should do that. You've been working hard for a long time. When was the last time you got away for a week or two?"

"It's been a while, sir."

Morgan heard ice tinkling and the mayor drinking.

"So, I understand that your week was a little more complicated than mine was."

Morgan sipped his beer.

"You could say that."

"I'm sure it pleases you, though, that Escobar screwed the pooch again, no?"

Morgan chuckled.

"Actually, Eddie, you know, this time I feel bad for her. She's trying to integrate herself, and working pretty hard at learning the job—she really is."

"Hello? Who am I speaking with? Is this Richard Morgan's number?"

"Very funny, Eddie. I'm serious."

"Lieutenant! I'm stunned. You never cease to amaze me."

"Listen, Eddie. We both know that she should have stayed at SOL for at least three more years before she promoted. Hell, she may have quit already if we had never promoted her to begin with. We knew that she wasn't ready when others were, but I don't think we considered just how unfair that promotion was to *her*. That position comes with a lot of pressure. She got smacked pretty hard the last few days, knocked to her knees, so to speak. I hope she takes a full ten-count to clear her head before she gets back in the ring. She's not had an easy probation."

"I don't understand."

"I misjudged her. I think we all did. She's actually got some earnest qualities, Eddie. She's not just an ambitious activist. She's more than that. She's not a duplicate of her mother."

"Pfff, please, there is no duplicate of that woman, and thank God, too."

"I thought she was your golden ticket, sir."

"She is, but there's only enough room for one of her in my world."

"Copy that."

"So what are you trying to say, Richard?"

Morgan drank and exhaled.

"I'm not sure, but I think I may be starting to change my opinion of her. Before, all I could think about was how to position her in places where she wouldn't hurt us. Don't get me wrong; I still feel that way, but I'm starting to think she might actually become a pretty decent leader someday. Maybe not out there on the beach in emergency response, but Eddie, she has grown up in four years."

"You've definitely got my attention now, Richard. Go on."

"She was genuine with that woman. Escobar could see that she was afraid, so she acted with no hesitation. Now, we have procedures in place that mitigate overreactions, and she ignored those, but her intentions were pure. She had compassion for that woman. She stayed by her side and held her hand the entire time. I saw it myself, Eddie. She comforted that woman. She took care of her. I did not expect that. That is an underappreciated quality that I value tremendously."

Morgan drained his beer, looked into the kitchen at his wife, and held up his empty glass.

"I think she was wise to leave aquatics," he said. "She is getting a much greater experience out here, just as they predicted she would. She's seeing much more of the real world on the beach than she ever could at that little pool. Her timeline is still way off though, and your's too, sir. She's more sensitive than I realized. She may crack, and if she does, well, that would screw up your plans. I can see that."

"Her cracking would not be good, that is correct."

Morgan changed his tone.

"I might be able to find a way to utilize her to our benefit, but pushing their agenda too quickly will end up hurting her more than it will hurt anybody else . . . even you."

"Wow, Lieutenant, that sounds like genuine concern for Marisol Escobar. Let me ask again, is this Richard Morgan?"

"I'm not an ogre, Eddie."

Peete snorted, "No, you're not, but your opinion of her has turned a hundred and eighty degrees *without* compromising your position."

Morgan laughed.

"A one-eighty? I wouldn't go that far. Listen, Eddie, the bottom-line facts are that she's called in two of those in less than two years. Both were unnecessary and costly. You're the one who pays the bills; I'm sure I don't have to tell you about that."

"No you don't, and I'll get to that in a minute, but I can't wait too long, Richard. We've discussed this many times."

"Yes, we have, but her value politically is totally overstated."

"I do not agree, and I have some new information for you, which is actually why I called. There's a young up-and-comer Democrat on the Chula Vista city council who's gaining some momentum. He's very slick . . . smart and manipulative."

"Manipulative? A politician? No way . . ."

The Mayor laughed.

"He's trying to prove that the proposal for the new baseball stadium will create an expensive eyesore and that the downtown redevelopment around it, if successful, will serve nobody but the Padres' ownership group, wealthy investors, brokers, real estate owners, contractors, business owners, and the like. He's obviously not a Padres fan, and there are plenty of others in this city who've never even been to a professional baseball game."

"Losers."

Peete laughed again.

"Don't forget, Lieutenant, forty-five percent voted 'no' on that stadium bond issue, so he's already got a huge pool of voters that he can rally behind him."

"That would suck. We need that stadium."

"Well, of course we do, and he can't stop us now. It's too late, the money is already out there being spent. The Padres will be playing there on opening day in '04."

"Go Pads."

Peete chuckled.

"He's totally underestimating the number of jobs that will be created, the hundreds of millions of dollars in city taxes that will be generated from all of the increased spending, and he's ignoring the fact that the bonds will be repaid entirely by increased revenues from hotel taxes. He's promising voters that he'll get a new bond proposal that will redirect those dollars to public education, health care, immigration reform, and public transportation. He's already stated that he will get the new bond proposal on the next ballot, and, if elected, he will veto any bonds related to stadiums or downtown redevelopment in the future."

"Wait, a Democrat is pursuing those issues? I never saw that coming."

Peete chuckled.

"Sarcasm is not a very good look for you, Lieutenant, but it is amusing."

"I'm just saying that he can't do that, or can he? I mean once the bond has passed it can't be rescinded, right? Isn't that a bold-faced lie?"

"Yes, but a lot of voters don't know that. Many voters believe what they're told, whether it's true or not. They believe what they want to believe, and he knows it, so why not make promises that he can't keep? It doesn't matter, once he's in office he can just skirt the issue and blame it on the city council. Besides, almost everybody knows that this new stadium will be the greatest financial windfall San Diego has seen since it built the Murph."

"Go Chargers!"

Peete sipped his scotch and said, "He's got voters believing in him, and our approval ratings have dropped a few points already in several precincts."

"Oh, Eddie, really? C'mon, enough with that paranoia. That guy's an under-qualified idealist, and apparently a liar, too. Meyers told me all about him. I know who you're talking about. He has no chance to become mayor . . . not a threat."

"Yeah, like the Japanese weren't a threat to Pearl Harbor?"

Morgan snorted, "Whatever."

"Richard, I'm serious. I still need Escobar to succeed. That is the only way we can maintain control of the council and the mayor's office.

I promised Dr. Villareal, *and* Victor Trujillo-Escobar, a long time ago, that Marisol would be strongly considered for a promotion to administrative sergeant. And you and I both know what *strongly considered* really means."

"Yes, I'm clear about what that means, Eddie."

"Well, you also need to be clear about something else. Dr. Villareal isn't really a big fan of this Chavez character from Chula Vista. She knows he's just a loud mouth, but she's also not convinced that she can control Meyers enough to continue supporting us. And you and I both know that the Republican party will be vulnerable without her support. If she turns her back on me, Chavez gains the power."

Morgan said nothing.

"So, instead of taking either one of those risks, she is planning on putting a resolution before the council that will legislate—if it passes, that is—that the mayor of San Diego may be eligible to run for a third term. If it passes, it becomes law, and then I can put my name on the ballot again in '04."

"So, you would run against Meyers in the primary?"

"I'll get to that later. Stay with me. This resolution for a third term will only pass if Dr. Villareal puts it on the table. And she'll only do that after I deliver on what I promised her . . . AND within the time limits that we agreed upon."

The mayor paused.

Morgan remained silent.

"You know what the timeline is, Richard. We've discussed this many times."

Morgan sighed.

"Yes, sir, but I've still not changed my position. Marisol won't be ready by then, she's not qualified, she hasn't earned it, and I've got thirty personnel more qualified for that position than Escobar. With all due respect, Eddie, you're manipulating me. It doesn't feel good."

"I'm sure it doesn't, and I'm sorry, but this is in the best interest of our city. Surely you see that. Jeezuzz, Richard, it's a freaking sergeant's position. Is it that big of a deal?"

"Yes, Eddie, it is. It's the beginning of a legacy. It's extremely important to me that our first female sergeant be the most qualified female candidate my agency has ever produced. That's Cynthia Harden, it is NOT Marisol Escobar. The city's best interest is not my primary concern, not this time. Mine is to run this agency professionally and fairly, and this, *mandate*, is the farthest thing possible from that. It's totally biased, sir. There's nothing fair about it."

"Yes, it is, Lieutenant, and no, there's not . . . I will not disagree with you about that . . . but that's irrelevant. What is relevant is that Dr. Villareal holds enough council votes in her hands to determine the outcome of that resolution before she even submits the proposal, and she also has the power to pull that resolution off the table."

He paused, then continued.

"Do you realize how much power my office will have if I'm given a third term?"

"Three terms, Eddie? Really? That's not just some BS ploy to get their daughter what she wants, and then they'll just pull the plug anyway?"

"Three terms. Twelve years, Lieutenant. They're not pulling any plugs."

"So, your plan is to portray Scotty as unprepared in '04?"

"That is the plan, yes. And he is okay with that. He's not ready to take the reins anyhow, and he's the first to say so. Dr. Villareal and many others will bury him with ideas that he's not ready to negotiate. I'm not bashing him; I like Scotty, and someday he'll be ready, but not in '04. Besides, like I already said, we're not convinced that he can beat Chavez head to head, but with some experience in campaigning during the primary election against me, he may learn just enough to beat Chavez in '08. I've discussed this with him already. He's on board."

Peete paused.

Morgan exhaled, then said, "Wow. I had no idea how many moves ahead you politicians were thinking about."

Peete laughed.

"Not many people do, but that's the way of the world."

"Not my world."

Peete laughed again.

"That's a good thing, Richard. I wouldn't wish this life on you, not ever. It's my world though, and this is how it has to be."

Morgan said nothing.

"None of these things will happen if Marisol gets passed over. She has to be wearing chevrons in time to get that resolution on the ballot, and passed. I'm talking by next year, Richard. That will give Amanda plenty of time to get that resolution on the table, and passed, and it will give me time to start my third campaign. I'll win in a landslide, and all you have to do is make sure that Marisol Escobar becomes our first-ever female, and our first-ever *minority*, sergeant."

"This is crazy. I am so glad I'm not a politician."

Peete laughed again, heartily this time.

"Well, consider that you already are, and that *your* interests will be well served if you go along with this plan. I've taken very good care of you and the Patrol, Richard, and I'll be able to take even better care of you, and all of our public safety units, if I get four more years. And that's not all."

Morgan chuckled and said, "Oh, there's more good news?"

"Yes, there is. You'll see, Richard, not only will I be in office long enough to throw out the first pitch on opening day at that beautiful new ballpark in downtown, but I will also get the ball rolling on a new football stadium for the Chargers, too."

Morgan interjected, "That would be amazing, yes, and I do support that outcome, but have you considered how it's going to make you look in the eyes of the council and the other chiefs, when you promote Escobar after she's basically opened a tab with several emergency response agencies in the county and she's like, 'Hey, the next round's on me!'?"

"That's cute, but it leads me to my next point."

Linda brought her husband a fresh beer in a cold glass. He sipped it while listening.

"Dr. Villareal called me last night. She told me all about your meeting with Marisol, who, apparently, had some nice things to say about you. Amanda told me that she appreciated the guidance that you offered her daughter . . . she said that."

"Really?"

"Yes, Richard."

Morgan chuckled.

"Imagine that."

"Well, listen to this. Dr. Villareal, actually, somehow, knows exactly how costly her daughter's two mistakes were."

"Exactly, sir?"

"Almost to the dollar, Richard."

"How in the hell did she gain access to the billing departments of those agencies, and how did she do it so quickly? How in the world does she find these things out?"

"I don't know, Richard, and I don't need to know. But here's the best part."

"I'm holding my breath, sir."

"She wrote a check, payable to the City of San Diego, for sixty-eight thousand dollars. Marisol's *tab* is paid, Lieutenant . . . And there's more, Richard."

"Oh, goodie."

"You're pretty funny tonight."

"Ahhh, I had a few beers is all, Eddie."

"Well, that might soften this blow a bit then."

The mayor paused and took a belt from his own drink.

"Richard, Amanda came to my office late last night to talk about these things."

"Mmmm, another behind-closed-doors ultimatum."

"Bingo. When Amanda wrote that check from her foundation's account, after she signed it, she held it out in front of me. When I reached for it and said 'Thank you,' she pulled it back."

"She's got stones . . ."

"Yes, she does. She looked me in the eye and said, *'I want her off the beach, Eddie, and I want her in an office where she belongs. She's been out there for nearly four years; she's already proven herself. Promote her to sergeant this summer, or, not only will this be the last check you'll ever see from my foundation . . . you can kiss that resolution for your third term goodbye.'*"

Peete paused.

Morgan raised his eyebrows, but said nothing.

"And Richard, you and I both know that she means it. She walked out of my office without a handshake, without a smile, and without even saying, 'Goodbye.'"

"Damn. She doesn't mess around, does she?"

"She never has, Lieutenant. You know that."

Morgan sighed.

"Ugh. So, that's it? You didn't say anything before she left?"

"I did. I caught up to her at the elevator and I told her that it's not time, not just yet."

"What'd she say?"

"Well, she said the same thing I've said all along, Lieutenant. Anything after '02 is too late.

"I can't believe you're actually going to make me do this."

Peete gulped down the last of his drink and exhaled.

"Look at it this way, Richard. After she gets off the beach, you won't have to worry about her calling one of those *Code X* deals again, now will you?"

**56**

Seven Months Later
Thursday, November 29, 2001
Lifeguard Headquarters

S gt. Derek Mahaffey, an 18-year veteran, unexpectedly retired in June
of 2001. He had married his girlfriend—a wealthy, attractive, third-
generation La Jolla realtor whom he met on the beach a couple of years
earlier. He told Morgan that, although he loved his job, he loved his new
lifestyle even more. His early retirement offered an additional sergeant's
position for Morgan to fill, and an opportunity to meet Mayor Peete's
and Dr. Villareal's deadlines. Morgan, however, was still committed to
rewarding Cynthia Harden for her excellence, and he wouldn't budge
regarding his decision to make her the Patrol's first-ever female sergeant.

Mahaffey's replacement was to be named after a final round of
interviews in early September. But when Al Qaeda took down the Twin
Towers on Sept. 11, 2001, things got dicey, even for the SDLP an entire
continent away.

Along with many EMS agencies from all across the country, the
Patrol sent its very finest to assist. Finding Mahaffey's replacement became
an afterthought while Peete, Morgan, several  SDLP sergeants, Senior
POLs, and high-ranking emergency responders from other agencies in

California spent weeks assisting, cleaning up, and offering whatever they could to whomever needed it.

In the aftermath, like many other governmental agencies across the country, the SDLP's normal operating procedures were disrupted for several weeks. Soon Halloween had passed, then Thanksgiving came and went, and now Christmas decorations were popping up all over San Diego County, and, to the chagrin of Dr. Villareal and Mayor Peete, Mahaffey's position had still not been filled.

Nearing the end of 2001, however, SDLP operations had returned to a quasi-normal status, and the sergeant's promotion, once again, became Lt. Morgan's first priority. A promotion ceremony had been scheduled for the second Monday in December, but Morgan still would not allow the mayor to convince him of Escobar's value, and the mayor, in turn, was becoming less concerned about the lieutenant's opinion. When he realized that he was getting nowhere, Peete abruptly halted the conversation.

"Richard, stop. This is a waste of time."

"I understand, Mr. Mayor. But this is becoming a major morale issue. I risk losing the trust of many good people if I don't promote Cynthia Harden first."

"Richard, don't speak to me like I'm an idiot. *Morale?* You think I need to be educated about morale issues?"

"No, sir, I do not, but if I put Escobar in Mahaffey's place, my crews will definitely become cynical about my leadership. They'll think I'm losing it. I can't let that happen. It has to be Harden first. Escobar cannot receive that promotion before Cynthia does, sir. This is where I have to draw my line. I'm the leader of this organization. I have to act like it."

"I understand the responsibility of leadership, Lieutenant, and I also appreciate your commitment to Harden. There's no doubt that she's the most qualified, but as I've told you all along, that is irrelevant . . . at least this time it is. Let's table this for twenty-four more hours. I want you to bring her to meet me."

"You want to meet Cynthia Harden?"

"Tonight . . . before I leave my office at eight o'clock."

"What about Marisol?"

"I already know everything I need to know about her. I need to speak with Harden."

"I'm sure she'll appreciate that."

"I'm not trying to lead you on either, Lieutenant. Timing is not a crucial variable regarding Harden. Not like it is with Escobar, you know this already. Listen, there are a few things that Miss Harden needs to know and there are a couple things that I need to hear from her before I make my recommendation."

"Recommendation, sir? Don't you mean orders?"

Peete sighed.

"Easy, Lieutenant. Don't make this worse than it already is. Bring Harden to my office . . . tonight."

"Yes, sir. I'll take care of it. We'll be there."

Lt. Morgan met Cynthia in the lifeguard headquarters parking lot and drove them downtown in the Navigator. They hardly spoke and both appeared to be a little nervous. They parked underground, walked to the elevator, and rode quietly up to the 11th floor where they were met by a two-person security team: one a well-dressed, athletic-looking man who stood by the outer-office door; another, wearing similar clothing, seated at a desk at the far end of the lobby. The man at the desk looked down at a clipboard, looked up, and nodded at Morgan, then motioned with his head toward the doorway.

They walked into the office and Mayor Peete politely greeted Morgan first, then Cynthia. He showed Cynthia a very comfortable seat across from his ornate desk, then turned to Morgan and said, "Richard, this will take ten minutes, tops."

Peete smiled and gestured for Cynthia to sit down, then bowed his head once toward Morgan. He closed the door, leaving Morgan alone with the security men in the office reception area.

Morgan glanced at his watch, then walked over to a large, comfortable-looking couch and sat down. He tapped his fingertips in a galloping drum roll on the soft, dark burgundy leather cushion of the overstuffed couch.

He sat for about a minute then stood up, both security men watching him without turning their heads. He walked to a west-facing window and glanced out at several tall buildings, the USS Midway mooring, the San Diego Bay, Coronado Island, and some twinkling Christmas lights that hung from houses located on the hills of Point Loma. He turned and scanned the office walls that were adorned with fire, police, and lifeguard departments' special recognition awards for service and bravery in the line of duty, and several large, colorful group photos of handsome, neatly uniformed personnel.

There were other, smaller photos of Peete shaking hands with, or wrapping his arms around the backs and shoulders of, various local athletes, celebrities, politicians, and a few others Morgan did not recognize. He stopped and looked more closely at a photo on the bottom shelf of one of the many pieces of polished antique furniture in the room. Morgan leaned over and picked up the five-by-seven wooden frame.

The photo was taken on election night. The six people centered in the frame were all wearing brilliant smiles. Five of them held up their right hands with two fingers extended, forming a V. Richard recognized Mayor Peete in the middle, his beautiful wife to his right, their handsome oldest son standing just behind his mother, and Peete's charming young daughter, Nikki, smiling proudly, standing just in front of her father. On the mayor's left stood two impeccably dressed and stunningly attractive Latinas.

Morgan recognized Dr. Amanda Villareal, proudly displaying a small postcard-sized flag. She held a corner of the flag with one hand, while standing next to and hugging Veronica Martinez, a popular Democrat who held a seat on the city council. In the photo, Martinez proudly held the other corner of a tiny rainbow flag while the two powerful women shared what appeared to be a rather intimate kiss on the lips.

*Wait. What?*

Morgan brought the photo closer to his eyes.

*Is Dr. Villareal a lesbian? And councilwoman Martinez is her partner? But they were married to men . . . and they both have children.*

Morgan continued staring at the beautiful female couple in the photo, realizing, *He's gathering gay and lesbian votes, too . . . I've been fooling myself all along . . . Cynthia never had a chance at becoming our first female sergeant.*

Morgan looked up at the first security man, then the other. *Wow, these guys must be some kind of Secret Service.*

He looked back down at the photo, and made a second realization. *I'll be damned, Eddie Peete has his sights set on governor, hell maybe even the White House. Why else would he be harvesting all of these Democrat's votes? This isn't about Escobar's résumé and her future in politics, it's about Eddie's future campaigns. That's the trade-off.*

Morgan set the photo down and looked up at a large family portrait of the Peete family centered on the largest wall in the room.

*He would be an awesome president, though.*

Morgan smiled at the tandem security squad.

*I would vote for him in a heartbeat . . . I don't care what party he represents.*

Morgan then heard the latch on the office door click, and he looked up to see Peete and Harden exiting the office. The mayor approached him, and offered a firm handshake.

"Thank you, Richard. I really appreciate you taking your time to do this for me."

He turned back to Cynthia.

"Miss Harden, it was a great pleasure to finally meet you after all that I have heard about you, not only from Lt. Morgan here but, like I mentioned, from your father as well, many years ago."

Peete looked at Morgan.

"Chief Harden, her dad, was a great man. I am very excited about having his daughter working for us, and *leading* our Patrol for a very long time. Just as I'm sure he's up there resting peacefully, watching over you now."

Peete then ushered them toward the elevator, the athletic security man following closely.

"Richard, have a nice weekend. We'll talk on Monday."

Peete turned and stepped inside his office just as a chime announced the elevator's arrival. As the door opened, the security man checked inside the elevator briefly, motioned toward Morgan and Harden with an open hand to enter, then offered the couple a pleasant nod as the door closed.

The ride down the elevator and all the way back to headquarters was discouragingly quiet, and when Cynthia exited the Navigator, Morgan said to her softly, "Hang in there, Cynthia, we'll know next Monday. I'll call you as soon as I find out."

Harden answered just as softly, "Good night, Lieutenant. I'll be waiting."

**57**

The Next Day
Friday, November 30, 2001
Lifeguard Headquarters

Richard Morgan wasn't expecting to hear from Eddie Peete until Monday, so the call caught him off guard.

"I can't delay this any longer," the mayor said. "I may have waited too long already. Marisol Escobar is your sergeant."

Morgan knew it was coming, but he couldn't stop himself. Not this time.

"*WHAT*? Are you kidding?"

"Richard, do I sound like I'm joking?"

"I apologize, sir, but that is just wrong."

"I understand your passion about Cynthia Harden. This was not easy for me. I wish it could be another way."

"Sir, Marisol Escobar has so much work to do. It's ridiculous that we're even considering her for sergeant. This is going to make me look like an amateur."

"I doubt that, and you told me yourself that your sergeants don't have to respond as much on the beach. I'm actually doing you a favor by redirecting her away from there, right? And besides, Harden still enjoys working on the beach, she told me so last night. She actually said that she will probably miss the action once she becomes a sergeant."

"I'm pretty sure she said that to appease you, Eddie. I know for a fact that it will turn her inside out to see Escobar outranking her."

"It doesn't matter, Lieutenant. I've already explained this to you."

"Sir, I stand to lose so much credibility here. I already have because of her *Code X* fiascos. Now you're requiring me to make her an incident commander *and* a supervisor whose primary task will be to evaluate our personnel. She's not qualified to do either, Eddie."

"And you'll have somebody there to help her, just as you have all along . . . Richard, listen to me, we needed a lot of help to get the DCS's funding approved. That was a huge amount of money that the state released to us in the name of public safety. You explained your vision very clearly and you got what you asked for. I helped you get the audience that you needed, but Escobar's family helped us get there first."

Morgan said nothing.

"The people they called in favors from are the same people whom I have depended on to remain elected. I am going to need those people to get that resolution passed, and I will also need them to get re-elected here . . . and wherever I go, whatever I do, I will need them."

Morgan did not reply but thought, *Just as I thought. He's thinking several moves ahead.*

"There were promises given and agreements were made. The hiring data they presented to me made us look bad, Rick. That was on your watch. It was pretty ugly, wouldn't you agree?"

"I can only hire who applies, Eddie."

"Well, this woman has brought in a whole new group of applicants, hasn't she? That all began with her and it will continue because of all the young men and women she taught how to swim at our city's pools. And now they work for us, on our city's *beaches*, Richard. Those kids are out there saving lives every day. That is a story that San Diegans will embrace, support, and be proud of. Can you not see that?"

Morgan replied flatly, "You already know that I can see that."

The mayor noticed his tone.

"Richard, trust me. I am not going to allow the future of my administration, and the future of this city, to fall apart because you fail to see the wisdom in this decision; blinded by a just cause of seeing a more worthy candidate receiving accolades for something that nobody is going to care about in five years."

Morgan stiffened, but remained humble and silent.

"Listen, Lieutenant, the changes I promised will continue with Escobar at the very front of what has become an extremely popular community outreach program. You put a sergeant's shield on her Class A uniform and she's going to look mighty impressive, don't you think? Hell, maybe we can put *her* in front of those cameras when the media starts asking questions."

"I'm not sure we're ready for that, Eddie, and I do just fine in front of cameras."

"Yes, you do. I'm just saying that she will also represent the image that I'm looking for, if and when she is given that opportunity, agreed?"

"Well, yes. I mean . . . whatever, Eddie."

"Don't be cynical, Richard. Employers are flocking to those job fairs now and the quality of the individuals applying for those jobs has risen significantly. Her family and friends have poured scholarship money into our Junior Lifeguard program, too. Those Lincoln Heights kids, and many others, are learning about and enjoying ocean activities while they are still very young. It is working, Richard. Escobar's group has built a bridge from those neighborhoods to our beaches. There's now opportunity for those communities, when there was none before."

"Yes, sir, that is true."

"Say what you want about Escobar as a first responder, an incident commander, or an evaluator. I don't care if she's substandard in those areas. That woman and her mother are building a machine that is helping people find good jobs. I need her to continue to strengthen and expand the bridges that she's already built, Lieutenant."

"I understand, sir."

"This all started with *you*, Richard. You set the example. You showed a willingness to appreciate the delicate nature of the paradox, and *you* made the adjustments that set this great precedent. My approval ratings will sky rocket, as soon as *Sergeant Escobar* shows up in uniform at a press conference standing right next to me.

Peete paused.

Morgan said nothing.

"The number one thing for you to realize, Richard, is that you do not have to get re-elected. Dr. Villareal can still hurt me, she really can. And her husband, well, I'm not even going there. Either one of them can destroy me and my future very easily with just a couple of phone calls. But after we promote Marisol, the resolution passes, and those phone calls will destroy Mendez instead."

"If you say so, sir."

Peete sighed, sounding almost exasperated. He breathed in, snorted out the breath, and continued, curt.

"Surely you can see that Escobar holds the stronger cards: gender *and* ethnicity. Like pocket aces, Richard. And you want me to go all-in with Cynthia Harden, who has only one ace. She's being dominated and she can't win the hand. I can only lose if we choose her, and if I lose, you may lose as well."

Morgan kept his thoughts to himself.

*You caught an ace on the flop, too. Sexuality. Three aces . . . That's a pretty good hand. You're a pretty good player, Eddie.*

"Think about Dr. Villareal's reaction if we don't select her daughter. Think about the next election night. If that resolution doesn't pass, Chavez will beat Meyers, this city will fall apart financially, and the Patrol . . . well, I don't even want to think about that."

The mayor paused, then said, "And by the way, Lieutenant, and I am not saying this disrespectfully, but nobody even knows, or cares, about who Cynthia Harden is. Her getting promoted *after* Escobar . . . Well, I'm not sure if I can put this into kind words, but . . . so what?"

"That is sooo brutal, Eddie. I absolutely hate politics."

Peete chuckled.

"I know you do, but that's just the way it is, Lieutenant. Besides, you already know that Escobar is not going to be with the Patrol for very long. Once she passes the bar, she will move into some other position with the city, or maybe the county, probably before she's thirty years old. You won't have to deal with her or her family again, except for maybe when you attend large, festive events. When that time comes, you will smile, shake hands, and pose for photos just like you always have."

"If you say so, sir."

"And if you're really talented, Richard, like I know you are, you will find a way to make her tenure here benefit both you and the Patrol. Hell, if that family is as generous to your Patrol as they were to Aquatics, you may get your new main towers after all, AND a brand new fleet of vehicles. You know, Richard, they may even be able to get you a new rescue boat. Did you ever consider that?"

Morgan raised his eyebrows.

"No, I hadn't thought of that."

"I didn't think you had. You might want to chew on that possibility for a while . . . Listen, Richard, regardless of any of that, this whole thing will be over before you know it, and like I said before, this benefits everyone, and nobody's going to get hurt."

"Cynthia Harden will get hurt and so will all of Escobar's soon-to-be subordinates who have been working circles around her for years, patiently waiting their turn."

"Harden is tough, and so are the others; we already know that. She'll get over it, they'll get over it, and you'll get over it."

Morgan pouted, "Yeah, well, what if I don't get over it?"

The mayor laughed.

"Ohhh, I admire you, Richard. I always have. You're the best at what you do and because of you, we've got the best damn lifeguard service on the planet . . . right here in our fine city where it's needed the most. I wish my fire and police chiefs were as patient and selfless as you are. The problem there is that they're both aspiring politicians, just like this young Latina that you're going to promote as our first-ever female sergeant . . . Lieutenant."

"It's your call, sir. And I do understand the value of this decision, even though I do not agree."

"Well put, Richard. That's my boy."

Morgan chuckled.

"I thought you guys didn't like the word *boy*."

Peete laughed loudly.

"Haha. You're a bold man, Richard. I like that, and yes, you are my *boy*. You're the man, too, Lieutenant, the very best. Don't let this thing get your panties all knotted up, okay?"

"I got it, sir. Harden will be next, and soon, right?"

"As soon as she wants it."

Morgan was disappointed, but he was no longer discouraged. He realized long ago that Eddie Peete was an extremely gifted politician that often left all sides agreeing about the positive outcomes that resulted from his toughest decisions. He knew that Peete was right this time, and embraced the idea of having him continue as mayor until '08, but when he thought about telling Harden the bad news, it tightened his throat and made his ears burn.

"Like I said, a couple of years from now nobody will care about who was promoted first, and everybody already knows who the finer sergeant will be. Time will sort all of that out for us. Just tell that young lady to keep her head up, and to keep fighting the good fight."

"Oh, I'm sure she will, Eddie."

**58**

Friday, November 30, 2001
Lifeguard Headquarters

L t. Morgan stood in front of Headquarters and waited for Harden's 4Runner to arrive. He greeted her as she exited the vehicle, asked her to listen patiently, and to wait until he was finished before responding. He noticed that her body language showed signs of discouragement before he even began delivering the news. She remained silent as they walked across the parking lot toward a large, grassy lawn next to large boulders securing the banks of the channel that led into and out of shallow Mission Bay.

"The official announcement will be made a week from Monday, on the tenth. Marisol Escobar will be Mahaffey's replacement as sergeant. She doesn't know yet, and she won't be told until the tenth. So, unless something happens that changes the mayor's mind between now and then, you're going to have to wait for the next go-round. Apparently, Peete not only wishes the perception of the Patrol to be that, yes, we do hire women for high-ranking positions, but more importantly in America's 'most diverse city,' we hire minority women for high-ranking positions first. It's a political campaign ploy, Cynthia, and it has absolutely nothing to do with your qualifications or your abilities."

He paused.

Cynthia remained silent as they continued walking slowly across the lot.

"I'm sorry, Cynthia. You'll get the next one."

"Really? Are you sure? I should have gotten this one. It's not so much about the timing, Lieutenant. I'm not going anywhere . . . I already told you that I'm in no hurry to become a sergeant, and like I told the mayor, I'm in no hurry to get off the beach either. But *her* before me? Seriously?"

"I'm sorry. I did everything I could."

"It's such BS. Just like USA water polo and the goddamn Navy all over again. This time it's the freaking mayor of San Diego."

Harden shook her head, grimaced, then turned and pointed her forefinger at Morgan, animated and expressive, raising her voice.

"One person can create a ripple that disrupts an entire organization, and then that organization falters, Lieutenant. Marisol causes the ripple."

Cynthia shook her head in disgust.

"But instead, she's Saint Marisol, the great community leader, the Pied freaking Piper of equal opportunity. She's such an opportunist, and now she's going to become an ocean . . . fucking . . . lifeguard . . . sergeant. What a joke! She couldn't rescue Amanda Beard in a Jacuzzi."

Morgan laughed out loud.

He shook his head and began clapping his hands, still laughing as he continued.

"Look . . . I understand, and I agree. But I am not about to allow the Patrol to falter. Trust me, I'll keep the right personnel in place to prevent that. I've been doing that since she first got to the beach."

He paused and reached toward Cynthia, gently placing a hand on her shoulder.

"I'm sorry, Cynthia, I really am. You have no idea how hard I tried to prevent this from happening. He's never done this to me before, and he won't again. I don't know what he told you last night, and I'm not sure if I want to. If he wanted me to know, he would have invited me in there with you. I actually think he's testing you to see if he can trust you. So don't tell me a thing; I don't want to know. One thing I know about Eddie Peete for sure is that if he wants me to know something, he'll tell me himself, like he did this morning when he promised me that he will never do anything to inhibit your progress again."

Cynthia stopped walking and turned to face Morgan.

"Okay, Lieutenant, whatever you say."

She shook her head.

"I think I'll take some time off. Now might be a good time for me to visit my mother."

Morgan stopped abruptly, turned his head sharply, and looked directly at Cynthia.

"Relax, Lieutenant. Not for legal advice—for perspective. She's brilliant. I'm sure she'll have something wise to tell me about how to deal with this situation. She paused and shook her head once more, then said, "She hates me, you know? Marisol does. I can't even imagine being supervised and evaluated by her. This is going to be a nightmare."

"Yeah, it sure is, and not just for you . . . go ahead, Cynthia. Take as much time off as you need."

"I'll only need a week. Besides, I want to be back in time to see the shit show, errr, I mean promotion ceremony. Should I bring one barf bag or two?"

"Haha. You might want to bring more than just two."

# PART 8

Collusion:
A secret agreement for fraudulent or
illegal purpose; conspiracy

**59**

Later That Night
Friday, November 30, 2001
Hoffbrau Restaurant
Point Loma, California

"So this is where you find all of those tramps, huh?"

"Works like a charm in the summer. Pretty quiet this time of year, but I've had plenty of luck in the winter."

Johnson smiled and tipped his beer toward her.

"You sure you won't have at least one beer? Tonight could change your life forever, you know. You and I would be perfect together, Harden. And just think . . . if we got married I wouldn't have to worry about that goddamn alimony and child support so much. I could start living off of you and your bright future."

"Pfff, please. Not a chance."

"I just thought I'd give it another try. You still don't know what you're missing."

"My gawd . . . will you ever get over yourself?"

"Not likely."

Cynthia had learned quickly how to neutralize Johnson's sexual innuendos and inappropriate behaviors. It offended her the first time he approached her while he was naked, offering a full frontal view of his pride and joy after stepping out of the shower, feigning that he was all alone in the Pacific Beach main tower's cramped co-ed locker room. Cynthia's father, however, had prepared his daughter very well with warnings about and solutions for the moments in her life when men were certain to behave badly. She took care of business that day in Pacific Beach; first slapping Johnson across the face, then pushing him back inside the shower stall and slamming the door. She remembered the stern warning she had given him that day.

*"Fuck you, Johnson, don't you EVER try something like that again. Next time it will be my fist. I'll break your nose and knock your teeth out. Believe me."*

Although the open-handed smack to his face startled and stung him, Johnson attempted to laugh it off and apologized from inside the shower stall.

*"Hey, I'm sorry, I didn't see you. Lighten up . . . my mistake."*

*"Yeah, right. Do you try to get away with that crap with every new female that comes into your tower?"*

*"What else can I say, Harden? I said I was sorry, you gonna make a big deal outta this?"*

*"No, I told you what I'll do. Here's your towel, jerk-off."*

After he exhibited some humility and remorse about the incident, their relationship quickly evolved. It was based on mutual respect and trust, and Johnson soon learned to admire POL Harden's talents and abilities. They soon joined each other on excessive, ridiculous workouts and there was no doubt in their minds that they could both take care of business if, and when, the shit hit the fan. Johnson was mostly all business, and, even in the face of an occasional distasteful display of immaturity, Cynthia actually liked him and often laughed at his off-handed humor. The Mike Johnson that many women in the Patrol knew as a pig was not the same Mike Johnson that worked around Cynthia.

As they sat across the table from each other, Johnson took a large gulp from a tall, cold glass of draft beer. He wiped the foam from his upper lip, and said, "So . . . you've reconsidered my other proposal then?"

Cynthia sipped a club soda through two tiny straws. She pushed her glass away and leaned forward. She glanced around, scanning the small dining room, and noticed a long bar with a dozen or so stools. She feared that someone might be watching her, listening and waiting for her to say something incriminating. Realizing that there were only six other people in the entire establishment, including the bartender and a single waitress, she began to speak openly.

"You've got some serious reasons to see Escobar fail, right?"

"Fuckin' A right I do. She's trying to get me fired and make an example of me. She makes sergeant, I'm done. I already explained this to you. I'm not losing this job, and even though Morgan says he's got my back, I'm starting to see that she can easily jump right over him to get what she wants. She wants me out . . . I'm out."

"You're probably right. I'm also having a hard time seeing myself serving under her. No way. She's not here because she wants to be a part of a great team, and she doesn't give a shit about ocean lifeguarding or emergency response. The Patrol has no use for her. The mayor, however, and maybe even Morgan, it seems like they do."

Johnson shook his head.

"Morgan . . . he's such a limp dick . . . Escobar fucking owns him."

Harden chuckled.

"Well, I don't know anything about a limp dick, and I don't really want to either, but there's no doubt that she owns him. She owns a lot of people in this town, but not either one of us, Mike, and certainly not Latrelle. Escobar hates me just as much as I hate her, and she's still bitter toward Latrelle because he said 'no' to her EEOC deal. She also made it clear to me how she feels about us as a couple. She's jealous, Mike. She had always intended to sleep with him someday. There's no telling what kind of bullshit she'll create to try to prevent us from being together."

Johnson nodded.

"She is a bitch. I could see her using her position to fuck with you for sure."

"Exactly, and do you think she'll stop there? After she's done messing with you, me, and Latrelle, I guarantee you that she'll go after North,

Pena, and all of those instructors who were there that day in IB. And don't you think for a second that her crown jewel won't be to take Morgan and his academy down. She'll want to run that program herself. She'll try to take over hiring and promotions just like she did in Aquatics, and then she'll be first in line to become a lieutenant."

Cynthia paused and looked around the bar, again wondering if she aroused interest.

"She'll be able to write her own ticket. I've been screwed over enough, Mike, and I have worked way too hard for this. If a woman ever takes Morgan's job, it will be me, not her. I am not going to let that happen. We cannot let that happen. No way."

Cynthia took another sip of her sparkling water. Johnson sipped his beer, listening intently.

Harden shook her head and said, "I feel just as strongly as you do, maybe even more so. Like you said to me already, Mike, I will drown that bitch first."

The couple looked each other directly in the eyes and Cynthia said, "She will eventually work her way into the highest levels of this city's government . . . Morgan and the mayor won't be able to do a thing about it once she gets rolling. Apparently her family is that powerful. Mayor Peete told me so himself."

Cynthia leaned across the table toward Johnson, rested on her forearms, and lowered her voice.

"He said to me . . . and these are his words, Mike, *'Her progress can be inhibited only by an egregious failure to perform while on duty. From the outside, she has already been endorsed and she is completely protected. Untouchable and unstoppable'* is what he called her."

"He told you that? When? Where?"

Cynthia set her glass on the cocktail napkin in front of her and said, "Last night, in his office."

"Who's office? Morgan's?"

"Nope, Mayor Peete's office . . . and he was very open with me, Mike. He's a very intelligent, articulate man, suggestive and persuasive. He was vague, almost ambiguous, but I got the feeling that he doesn't trust Marisol or her family at all. It sounded like he sold out to them for his own political gain and that he is starting to regret that. I remember him saying something I had never heard before, and I didn't understand it at first."

"What did he say?"

"He said, 'You can't un-ring a bell.' I know what he means now. He means that he made a promise that he can't take back . . . like he spoke too soon, and now he regrets it. It sounds like he *has* to promote her, and right away. He was apologetic about it. He told me that, under any other circumstances, I would easily be given that position, but at this time, he could not allow Morgan to select me . . . that it had to be Escobar. And even then, he still left me feeling like he wanted my help somehow."

She drank more of the soda, then continued.

"He also said that we have something in common—he and I, that is. He said something about removing those obstacles that might prevent us from making it to the very top of whatever it is we're doing. He said that we both have a responsibility to protect our future and to do whatever it takes to see it through to the end. "

"Strong words. So, are you ready to hear my plan then? If the mayor wants her to fail as badly as we do, then we should have no problem . . . as long as we do this right."

"I'm all ears."

"It's actually pretty simple. Remember when she called that *Code X* on a missing juvenile boy her first summer in La Jolla, right before she promoted? Do you remember that? That kid was hiding behind a towel hanging right under her tower. Did you actually hear the radio transmission she made? She was hysterical. It freaked everybody out, especially that kid's mom."

"No, I missed that, but I sure heard about it. The sergeants at Shores made it sound like it was a drill or something, right?"

"That was bullshit. She called that thing in so fast nobody even had a chance to look for the kid."

"Yeah, well that's not the first time something like that has ever happened."

"I understand . . . but then she did it again at Mission Beach while she was still a probie. That guy was out body surfing a few peaks down the beach and got out of the water to get a fucking ice cream cone!"

Johnson slapped his hand on the table and cracked up.

"You remember that day?"

Cynthia nodded. She was part of the dive team that frantically searched for Troy Neely that afternoon.

Johnson looked up and drew the attention of his buddy, Tucker, behind the bar, and motioned for him to bring the couple another round. The bartender quickly poured a pint of Stella from the tap and filled a second tall glass with ice and club soda.

"Okay, she screwed up twice, but what does that have to do with your plan?"

Johnson sat back, smiled, tipped his tall glass, and emptied the remaining half pint of beer before handing the empty glass to Tucker, exchanging it for a full one. Johnson leaned back farther and belched loudly.

"Ex-cuuuuse me . . . Damn that's good beer."

"That's gross."

Johnson smiled.

"You think Escobar can overcome a third *Code X?*"

Attentively, Cynthia sat taller and raised her eyebrows.

Johnson continued.

"She just has to be the first responding guard to get into the water, and with no wet seat. The victim will then disappear, right before she is able to make contact."

"Then what?"

"The victim will dive away and stay underwater. Use a tank and swim the fuck outta there. Escobar will be *freaking* out. She'll flash that *Code X* sign so fast it will make everybody's head spin. We'll set it up way down there in the middle of the strand, at eighteen, right where RC and that Mormon kid knocked heads going over the falls on a rescue. Both of them died that day . . . back in '87."

"I remember that. I think I was a freshman in high school. That was gnarly."

"Yeah, I was on that rescue. Not a good day at all. Shields and I got into a fist fight in the garage that night at Mission Beach. He tried to say it was my fault, but I was back-up on the beach that day. He was out in the water. He let that kid swim out and try to assist. That was all on him."

Johnson shook his head, and swallowed a gulp of beer.

"Whatever, that's history."

"Wow, you and Shields?"

"Yep, and not a day goes by that he doesn't forget it."

Neither spoke.

Both drank more.

Johnson shook his head and, with a faraway gaze in his eyes, he said, "It will be an easy sell for another swimmer to go down right there . . . Tower 18 . . . That fucking place is haunted."

"Yeah, no seasonal guards on duty in December either. You're all alone out there."

"Yep, and that's exactly what Escobar will be; right there, all alone, freezing cold, and scared shitless. The first backup guard will still be minutes away and I'll make sure that that's me. She'll be an easy target, as if she isn't already . . . an imbecile that lost a swimmer in distress . . . Nobody will ever find the body, because there isn't one . . . but everyone will think there is . . . and they'll also think there's a corpse down there starting to rot at the bottom of the ocean. There's no way they'll give her the promotion after that. She'll have fucking nightmares for the rest of her life . . . I guarantee you that she'll quit before the summer even starts."

Cynthia appeared confused.

"I'm not clear about something. How are you going to provide a distressed swimmer that turns into a drowning victim and then just disappears?"

"I'm not . . ."

Johnson leaned back and smiled before he lifted his glass. Cynthia watched him closely and noticed, as he took down another half pint, just how thick his muscular, veiny, and tanned throat was. She watched as his prominent larynx moved up and down with each gulp.

He pulled the glass away, belched again, then said, "You are."

They both sat motionless for several moments.

Johnson leaned closer and spoke softly, like a narrator telling a story about an event that had already occurred. He'd seen it in his mind countless times and he knew every detail.

"And then you're going to swim away underwater before she gets close enough to see that it was you. She'll have to signal for assistance and that will start a circus act *Code X* again. But you'll be long gone. You're the world-class diver. It'll be easy for you. I've got all the details figured out already."

Cynthia tilted her head, thinking, *I can do that.*

"Tell me more."

"I've been planning this thing for over a year, ever since Morgan took me on that patrol and questioned me about what happened on her first day in North PB. It was he said/she said, just like the first time. This time though, that dog North wasn't there to rat me out. Whatever . . . I digress."

Johnson took another quick gulp.

"I know Morgan doesn't believe me, and he probably doesn't really care about what happened, but he also warned me that day about the inevitability of her becoming *Sergeant* Escobar. She'll try to fire me someday; you can bet your ass about that, but if she goes back to Aquatics and Recreation where she belongs, both of our problems will be solved. I couldn't give a rat's ass about her aspirations after she leaves the Patrol. She can do whatever the hell she wants to then. We just need to get her the fuck out of here, and now. This is our only chance, Harden."

Cynthia removed a lime wedge that was resting on the rim of her glass and squeezed it, draining the juice into the soda water. She dropped the wedge onto the ice and stabbed at it with the straws, pushing it all the way down to the bottom of the glass, then stirred the juice into the soda, thinking, *She's going to have to do much worse than just another false Code X. Somebody in the Patrol is going to have to get hurt, and that somebody has to be her . . . or Johnson . . . but it sure isn't going to be me.*

Cynthia broke the silence.

"Well, we're going to have to move quickly then, whatever it is we do. Morgan is going to make the announcement on the tenth."

Johnson sat up abruptly and looked at his watch.

"What! The tenth? That's less than two weeks! That bitch is going to be a sergeant this month?"

"'*Unless something happens that makes the mayor change his mind,*' is what Morgan told me. I acted like I had no idea it was coming, so I threw a hissy-fit, but I knew it was going to be Escobar, even before I left Peete's office last night. I told Lt. Morgan that I'm going to San Francisco for a week. I'm outta here. We have until Tuesday, because I'm leaving first thing Wednesday morning . . . I'm taking a road trip."

"Saturday, Sunday, Monday, Tuesday . . . Fuck, that's only four days!"

"Uh, huh. Do you have it planned out that well?"

Johnson stared at Cynthia silently, concentrating.

"That's perfect then."

"What's perfect?"

"Well, your road trip is a perfect alibi, but you're going to have to leave later, because you're the only one who can pull this thing off. But if everyone thinks that you're out of town already, then you'll be off the hook. I'll be on duty that day, so I'm good, too. We can do this. Wednesday's a training day, so your boyfriend and those other two probies are headed to the river for swift water certification. We'll be short-staffed all day; it is perfect . . . fucking perfect timing. We got this, Cynthia. Escobar will show her ass again, and then it will be over. If everything goes right, I guarantee you that she'll quit. This one will break her. That cock-tease bitch is done!"

Cynthia loudly proclaimed, "Here's to that!" and finally drew the attention of the other people in the bar, including Tucker, who shouted, "Here's to what?"

Johnson replied with smile

"Here's to your mother! Now bring me another beer, bitch!"

Tucker laughed.

"Coming right up, asshole."

**60**

Four Days Later, Late evening
Tuesday, December 4, 2001
Hoffbrau Restaurant

Mike Johnson sat on his favorite barstool, hanging out with Tucker, his long time friend and favorite bartender. He shook his head as he stared at his full glass of beer.

"This chick is so hot . . . it almost breaks my heart that I have to take her down."

Tucker said, "Dude, I haven't heard you this fired up since your divorce."

"Yeah, well, *that* didn't cost me my job, but *this* could . . . and I ain't gonna let that happen."

As Johnson sipped his beer, Tucker looked up and noticed a tall, well-dressed female entering the restaurant. She stopped and spoke briefly with a waitress, who then pointed to the bar. The woman turned, walked toward them, and as she approached, Tucker said, "Speaking of hot chicks, check this babe out."

Johnson turned, then froze, startled by the sight of the attractive woman. She was wearing a lacey, low-cut, full-length, pink designer dress that was sheer enough to clearly reveal the outline of her nipples. Her hair was tied up neatly, exposing her tanned neck and lean shoulders. She was wearing black stiletto heels that clicked in cadence as she glided across the floor, and the high slits in her dress revealed nearly all of her long, toned legs with each step. She was a vision of pure beauty, oozing with sexuality.

Without turning away from the woman, Johnson said, "That's *her.*"

Marisol arrived at the bar and smiled at Johnson. She delicately extended her arm with a limp wrist and giggled.

"Aren't you going to greet me properly, and kiss my hand like a gentleman?"

She raised her hand to Johnson's face, and he suspiciously kissed the back of her hand. As she withdrew her hand, she seductively scratched his cheek with the back of her fingernails, then giggled and moved to the stool next to him. She crossed her legs, exposing all of her thighs, then turned to the bartender.

"Tres Generaciónes. Doble, por favor."

Johnson raised his eyebrows and asked, "Are you drunk?"

Escobar placed her hand on Johnson's chest and swayed toward him.

"Of course I am. Do you think I would come here sober?"

Johnson appeared confused.

"So, what do you want from me?"

Escobar waited while Tucker dampened the edge of a rocks glass and dunked it into a dish of salt. He poured more than two ounces of the tequila, then skewered two lime wedges with a plastic sword, gently hung them from the salty rim, and delicately placed the glass on a cocktail napkin in front of her.

"Here you are, beautiful. This one's on me."

Escobar blew him a kiss.

"Muchas gracias, guapo."

She turned to face Johnson.

"Cynthia told me that you might be here."

"Cynthia Harden?"

"Sí. She called me this afternoon and told me that you had a plan to undermine my promotion to sergeant, that you two had formed an *alliance.*"

"An alliance? Harden told you that?"

"Sí. I believe her too, I mean, why not? Neither one of you want to work beneath me in the chain of command."

"That wouldn't be my preference, no, but I know nothing about an alliance."

She raised the glass, looked at Johnson, and giggled.

"Whatever you say, Mike."

She licked the rim of the glass, gulped half of the drink, sucked on one of the wedges, shuddered, and exhaled a strong aroma of tequila. She set the glass down and winked across the bar at Tucker, who responded with a coy smile and an aroused look in his eyes.

Marisol looked back at Johnson

"I'm here to negotiate something myself. An alliance," she tapped Johnson's chest, "between you," she then tapped her own chest, "and *me.*"

Johnson squinted and tilted his head.

"What the fuck are you talking about?"

"I want to ruin Harden's life, Mike. I hate that slut. And if you help me do that, I'll never fuck with you again."

Escobar continued with a tone of seduction in her voice.

"And to show you that I mean it, I'll let you fuck me . . . tonight . . . right here . . . right now."

Tucker and Johnson turned and looked at each other. Tucker laughed and Johnson shook his head in disbelief as Escobar raised her voice slightly.

"Even though you disgust me, Mike, there is a place, *deep* inside of me, that I think you might actually be able to reach. I haven't found anybody man enough to accomplish that, not yet at least. On our first patrol in North PB, you said something about being able to find certain places where I might be hiding something. Do you remember that?"

She looked at his crotch, then placed a hand on his thigh.

"I haven't stopped thinking about fucking you since that day."

"Really? Hmmm. What I remember is you saying something about wearing a wire, like you were going to set me up. Pardon me for being a little suspicious."

Escobar leaned closer, allowing one of her breasts to touch Johnson's arm, and whispered, "You don't need to be suspicious. Not this time. Just meet me in the ladies room and I will show you that you can trust me."

She picked up her glass, slowly licked the remaining salt from the rim, and threw her head back as she gulped down the remainder of her drink. She placed the other lime wedge between her straight, white teeth and giggled, then bit into it, sucked on it, and seductively pursed her full lips as she slowly removed the peel from her mouth. She then took the tip of her long, pink tongue and used it to trace a slow, counter-clockwise circle around her open mouth. She directed Johnson a brief, cryptic laugh, placed her hand on his crotch and squeezed his penis, moaned, then turned and walked toward the restroom.

Both men appeared paralyzed as they watched her strut away until she disappeared around the corner.

Tucker laughed heartily.

"What the hell was that?"

Johnson looked as if he was still in a daze.

"Fuck if I know, but I'll tell you this much . . . I am definitely going into that restroom."

"You're damn right you are!"

Johnson waited about a minute before he left the bar. He cautiously opened the ladies room door, peeked inside, and saw Escobar standing in front of a mirror applying lip gloss. She turned, glared fiercely at Johnson, and snapped her words at him aggressively.

"Lock the door!"

Johnson did as he was instructed, suddenly appearing unsure of himself.

Escobar noticed.

"After all this time, you're just going to stand there cowering against the door like that? I thought you wanted to fuck me."

Escobar raised her dress, revealed that she was wearing no panties, then lifted a leg and placed the long, thin heel of one of her shoes on the vanity top.

"Now, come over here and do as I say."

Johnson looked around the bathroom, glanced under each stall, then moved slowly until he stood next to her. With both hands, he pulled the thin straps of her dress down over her shoulders, then squeezed Escobar's bare breasts. He used his mouth to stimulate a nipple, causing her to moan.

After several moments, he slithered down her abdomen with his tongue, dropped to his knees, and placed his face between her legs. Escobar moaned, "Ohhh, right there, just like that, don't stop until I tell you to."

She placed both of her hands on his head, pulled his hair, and pressed his face against her groin. Several moments later she pleaded, "Enough, I want you, now!"

Johnson stood up, grinning. He unbuttoned his jeans and before he could pull them down, Escobar grabbed his penis and moaned, "Mmmm, very nice."

Marisol guided him toward her while Johnson used one arm to pull her closer, the other to squeeze one of her breasts.

Escobar moaned, "Ohhhh, yes, yes, yes, like that, ohhhhhh, yes!"

For several long, passionate moments Johnson thrusted as hard as he could, then stopped abruptly and spun Escobar around. He bent her over so her bare chest lay on the countertop. He then lifted her dress and began thrusting again.

Escobar shouted, "Don't stop! Keep going, Mike, fuck me, harder!"

Johnson was as fully aroused as he could remember being. He closed his eyes and groaned, about to climax, when suddenly, he heard pounding on the door, and a voice that he recognized.

"Mike, are you in there?"

Johnson opened his eyes, looked up, and noticed a familiar sliding glass door that was partially covered by a thin curtain. Confused, he squinted, then rubbed his eyes. Now able to focus across the room, he recognized the entertainment center and his television, which was broadcasting a Showtime softcore porn movie.

"What the...? Holy shit!"

As he rolled off the couch and began to stand up, he noticed that his penis was uncomfortably poking against his shorts, then realized how urgently he needed to urinate.

He yelled through the door, "Hang on, I gotta take a leak, I'll be right there."

Johnson limped to the bathroom, lifted the toilet seat, and had a difficult time aiming his flow of urine into the bowl. He flushed, hurried to the door, and opened it.

"Fuck, I'm sorry, man . . . I must have fallen asleep."

Pence stood in the doorway, George and Pablo behind him.

"What the hell was going on in here? We could hear you yelling. I thought you had a chick in here."

"Oh, man. I just had the best fucking dream of my life."

"Yeah, it sounded like it. What the hell was it?"

"Never mind, we got more important shit to talk about."

He welcomed the men into his living room and said, "Now listen to me. I've never been in a jam like this before. My entire life could get fucked up real bad if we don't get this thing right."

He looked at each of his friends.

"I'm going to need you guys to do me a HUGE favor tomorrow. It's a little bit complicated, so pay fucking attention."

**61**

The Next Day
Wednesday, December 5, 2001
Mission Beach

Mike Johnson glanced at his watch. His last main tower rotation for the day was scheduled to end in five minutes. He noticed that Gary Zampese was already headed up the long ramp to the large glass-enclosed elevated platform that served as the main tower. One thing that Mike could always count on was GZ showing up a little bit early. The two performed a quick turnover, but there was nothing to see on this cold and cloudy day. Johnson was out of the tower well before 3:30. He had quite a few details to take care of, and would use the additional minutes to remain slightly ahead of schedule.

Johnson walked directly to the port-a-let behind the tower and relieved himself. He then entered the large mobile-mini storage freighter that served as an office, equipment shed, lunchroom, changing facility, and fitness center. He stripped down to his red trunks and completed a set of 25 pull-ups, then dropped to the floor and pounded out 50 push-ups. He repeated the circuit two more times with only 60 seconds rest between sets before grabbing a pair of heavy dumbbells. He grunted through a set of combination biceps curls and shoulder presses and shouted as he reached muscle failure, dropping the weights with a loud thud on a thick rubber mat that covered the floor. The entire routine lasted exactly 12 minutes, as it always did.

He grabbed a small protein drink, a canned coffee drink, and a bottle of cold water from a small refrigerator, then pulled a Ziploc bag filled with mixed nuts from his backpack. He covered his torso with his uniform top, his legs with Patrol issue sweatpants, and pulled on his warm winter service jacket. After slamming down the protein drink, he tossed the empty container into the recycling bin and walked outside into the blustery late afternoon weather. He then climbed into Unit 24 and headed north to the Tourmaline Surf Park. He drove slowly and parked the unit facing the ocean on the north side of the lot.

He checked his watch.

*Still ahead of schedule.*

Johnson sat for several minutes, alternating between sips of water and the energy drink, watching the only surfer in the water taking a not-so-nice right that flattened and paused before rising up again on the inside. The longboarder walked toward the nose of the board and maintained trim nicely across a small wave, then completed a smooth ride across the crumbling inside section that was about 30 inches high. The rider walked backwards nimbly on his deck and effortlessly turned the board inside toward the shore. He rode all the way into shin-deep water before he hopped off and scooped up his leash-less board in one smooth motion. As the surfer began to walk toward him, he glanced at his watch again and thought, *Almost 4 p.m.*

He then reached for his Saber radio and called Zampese in the main tower.

"North PB . . . Unit 24."

"Go ahead, twenty-four."

"Uh . . . I'm going to be *Code 4* on a minor med here at Tourmaline. Looks like an injury to the foot. Victim is walking toward me from the water's edge now. Stand by for further."

"North PB copies."

Up in the tower, approximately 300 yards south of the location of the call, Zampese stole a quick glance toward the water's edge and observed one male surfer in a wetsuit and hood, but no boots, carrying a longboard under his right arm. The surfer limped awkwardly toward the lifeguard vehicle that was parked well out of Zampese's view.

The injured surfer had just about reached Unit 24 when Mike exited the vehicle, lowered the tailgate, and offered the limping man a place to sit.

The surfer, a tall and lean man of approximately 40 years of age, chuckled slightly and said, "Yeah those stingrays are a motherfucker. Look at this mess."

The two men discreetly exchanged fist bumps and, even though they were out of the line of sight of anyone that mattered, they pretended that there was an actual first aid in progress. Knowing the first phase of his plan was now securely in place, Johnson walked to the truck's cab and retrieved his cell phone. He returned to the tailgate and winked at the stingray victim before returning his attention to the phone. Johnson dialed quickly and waited just a moment before the recipient answered his call.

The voice was calm.

"Bueno."

"Are you guys ready?"

"Just sitting here at Hennessey's . . . waiting to hear from you."

"Okay. Get your wetsuits on and grab your boards. I want you over the north rail at exactly four-twenty. Just paddle north and stay in the water until they come in and get you . . . which they're not going to do. Every one of us is going to get called away on an emergency, so just stay out there until you know it's clear. Trust me."

"No prahlum, Ess-aaye. I truss you."

"I'll get right with you guys later. After this all goes down, you guys gotta stay off the grid for a while . . . go surf the Cliffs or up in North County for the rest of the winter like we agreed."

"Four-twenty it is . . . my favorite time of day, homie."

Johnson let out a nervous laugh, but remained silent.

"Hey, amigo, good luck with all this bullshit, okay?"

"Thanks, Pablo. Late."

"Late."

Johnson looked at his watch.

*Four o'clock. Perfect.*

He dialed the phone again and waited, but all he got was four rings and a voicemail greeting. He hung up quickly.

Cynthia Harden felt the phone vibrating in her hand. She glanced at it, recognized the caller ID, but ignored the call. She placed the phone inside a ziploc bag on the bench seat next to her and pulled a second phone out of a backpack. Holding the phone tightly in one hand, she steered a low-profile inflatable pontoon watercraft with the other.

She was still inside the mouth of Mission Bay, slowly trolling west in a no-wake zone. Wearing a dark raincoat with the hood pulled low over her beanie-covered head, sunglasses covering most of her face, Cynthia sat low in the grey-colored vessel, nearly undetectable. She guided the skiff along a rocky seawall that curved gradually into a long, tall jetty that stretched a half mile out toward the opening of the Mission Bay channel.

Johnson was annoyed that Harden hadn't answered his call. He looked at his watch again.

*WTF?*

He dialed the number a second time.

Cynthia could feel the phone vibrating on the bench, but ignored it again. She was focused on distancing herself from the Patrol's Bay Observation Tower that overlooked Quivira Basin, while remaining out of the line of sight of the South Mission Beach main tower guard.

After making it out of the channel unseen, she returned Johnson's call on the second cell phone.

"Johnson."

"Is everything set?"

"Affirmative. I just talked to them."

Johnson walked away from the stingray victim and continued the conversation with Harden.

"They're going to jump at 1620 as planned. I'm in the unit at the north end of Tourmaline with the stingray victim. I will be unable to respond. I checked with the PB tower earlier and the rotation is set.

Shields will not be in the tower like we hoped . . . He's on patrol now, so he will be responding to the pier. We're sticking to the plan, though. I called Mission earlier and confirmed that Davis is in the tower from 1530 to 1700. Escobar will have the unit on patrol. She'll be the only one who can respond, as long as these guys jump when they're supposed to. Everything is going according to plan and the conditions are perfect. There's a strong rip pulling in front of eighteen. We couldn't have picked a better day and time for this . . . It's all falling right into place."

Johnson paused.

"Why didn't you answer your phone?"

"I have way too many minutes on it. I'm using a cheap prepaid phone I got for Christmas from my mom that I use to call her. I'm right where I'm supposed to be and I'm right on time. Forget about the phone."

He paused and took a long, deep breath.

"Are you sure you're on schedule?"

He checked his watch again.

"I'm just leaving the channel now. I'll be in position as we planned."

"Okay . . . good. Just make sure you don't pop up in that rip too early. Give those guys on the pier five extra minutes just to be safe. If Shields isn't called away from the tower to respond, you know he'll be out on Marisol's rescue right away, and then you'll have to abort. Just be patient and wait until after 1620 for sure. Okay?"

"Yeah I got it. If it looks too sketchy, I'll just dive out of there and we'll go to Plan B."

"Fuck Plan B. We cannot screw this up. Do you have both of my bottles secured?"

"Yes, Mike, I got it . . . just like we planned."

"All right then. That huge concrete block that the junior guards use to set their buoy hasn't moved since the summer. It's right at three hundred yards from Tower 18. You know where it is, and you know what to do. As soon as they call in the rescue, I'll head down there and make sure that you're long gone before any divers or rescue boats enter the area."

They hung up and, as Johnson continued treating the fake stingray injury, he glanced at his watch.

*4:07.*

He keyed the mic on the Sabre and called the tower again.

"North PB from Unit 24 . . . affirmative on stingray at Tourmaline. Patient is a thirty-six-year-old male, alert and oriented times four. No signs of allergies or swelling. Unit 24 will remain in service here to monitor victim."

"North PB copies."

Mike looked his friend in the eyes and smiled.

"We're taking that bitch down. In about fifteen minutes, the shit is going to hit the fan and then it will be over. Unzip that wetsuit, brother, let me take your blood pressure."

Johnson couldn't be sure that somebody wasn't watching him from somewhere, and if indeed any witnesses were ever asked, they would be able to recall that the lifeguard took readings and documented blood pressure, pulse, and respiration, then cleaned and wrapped the wound before taking those readings again and logging them. Johnson removed Unit 24's trauma pack, retrieved the BP cuff, stethoscope, four-inch gauze pads, Betadine solution, and Coban wrapping tape, and took his time going through the motions of a real-time medical aid. While he monitored the silent Sabre, waiting for the calls he knew were coming, he thought, *Everyone is now in place.*

Just then, however, Johnson heard Pacific Beach main tower guard Martin Arias' voice on his radio.

"Unit 23 from Pacific Beach."

Randy Shields replied, and Johnson's mouth dropped open.

"Unit 23. Go ahead, tower."

"Twenty-three, uh, I'm going to need you to head to the north side of Crystal Pier and contact two surfers on the outside for possible citations for an illegal pier jump. Uh, twenty-three. . . these guys . . . they, uh, they stood on the rail, waved their arms, and turned and looked right at me like they wanted me to see them first. They made obvious hand gestures before they jumped, and I don't, uh, I don't think they meant *we're number one* either."

Johnson's jaw dropped.

"Those dumb fucks jumped early."

Pence said, "You mean George and Pablo?"

"Yeah, those rocket scientists."

"Dude . . . you know George is always late, so he sets his watch like ten minutes fast. He probably thinks he's right on time."

"Are you fucking serious?"

Johnson stared at his watch in disbelief.

*Nine minutes early . . . dammit . . . C'mon Harden, get there.*

He quickly restocked the trauma pack and zipped it shut. He shook his best friend's hand, slapped him on the shoulder, and sent him on his way.

"Thanks Pence, I got a feeling I'm gonna be calling on you again. This could get pretty gnarly, so stay close to your phone for a couple of days. I may need you to do me another big favor. And hey . . . I'm sorry about making you go out in that shitty surf."

"Dude, no problem. I was in for like fifteen minutes and I caught a couple decent rides. I didn't even get my hair wet. Anything I can do to help, you let me know. Call me later no matter what, though. Let me know how this thing turns out."

Johnson grabbed his phone and dialed Harden's number. Again, it rang four times and went to her voicemail. This time he left a message.

"Harden, those guys jumped early. We lost ten minutes. Hurry the fuck up!"

**62**

Wednesday, December 5, 2001
Mission Beach

Cynthia throttled down as she approached the kelp bed. Faded red leaves and golden bulbs floated on the choppy surface and covered a band of underwater forest that was countless miles long, hundreds of feet wide, and from 20 to over 100 feet deep. The habitat was a very popular source of bounty for skilled line, trap, and spear fishermen.

It would help provide her cover now.

After securing the backup cell phone in the Ziploc bag, Harden geared up and prepared for the first leg of her dive. She inventoried all her equipment one last time, checked the line to the anchor, mentally reviewed the orders she created, and glanced at her watch.

*4:12.*

Just before rolling over the side of the skiff into the water, she heard a faint beeping sound that she recognized as the cell phone's voice mail indicator. She considered ignoring it, but thought better, realizing, *more information can't hurt.*

The message from Johnson was clear, and, although it slightly alarmed her that Shields might solve the pier jump caper sooner than planned, she was relieved that she was finally beneath the surface of the ocean.

As far as she could tell, she had not yet attracted anyone's attention. According to the plan, the first person to see her would be either Martin Arias or Mark Davis from one of the main towers in about 20 minutes.

But that timeline had just changed, and Cynthia knew that she had to hurry to make up for George and Pablo's gaffe.

Observing the two hooded surfers that had flipped Arias off, tossed their surfboards over the north side of the pier, then jumped into the cold ocean, Randy Shields attempted to recognize them through his binoculars. The light was poor though, and the chop provided cover for their faces, so he was unable to get a visual ID. He realized that they were not in danger and were a threat to no one. All they were was a waste of time and a pain in the ass. He had already attempted to get their attention over the vehicle's PA system several times and was frustrated by their antics. The longer they ignored him, the more he felt the urge to write them a citation for creating a nuisance.

Shields's frustration did not last long, though, and instead of dwelling on the problem, he began to focus on the peculiarity of the circumstances. Daytime pier jumpers were not unheard of, but were rarer than a winter stingray victim. Sometimes, during the summer, dudes would jump off the pier and attempt to swim away, just to see if they could do it without getting caught . . . Navy guys, Marines, Zonies, some roided-out drunks . . . but that was in the summer, when it was hot outside and warm in the water. It didn't seem right to him that it would happen today.

Something about Johnson and the stingray victim at Tourmaline also didn't seem right. Everything Shields was seeing or hearing seemed to him to be a bit contrived. The two events—the stingray victim and the pier jumpers—both seemed out of the ordinary. He was confused already, but his suspicions leapt and his heart rate bumped up when he heard a call over his radio.

"Pacific Beach from Mission Beach . . . Do you have an available guard to respond to one head in the rip at Tower 18? We're going to need to put a guard in the water to check the disposition of a . . . uh . . . possibly a distressed swimmer out there. Clear."

The call from Davis caused the hair on the back of Shields's neck to stand up, and instantly he felt a shot of adrenaline released into his blood stream.

*Now this? What is going on today?*

Shields recognized concern in Davis' voice.

"And Pacific Beach, I'm not sure where that swimmer came from. I, uh, I haven't seen anyone on the beach or any surfers in that area all day. Do you have a spot on one swimmer outside at Tower 18?"

Shields also heard concern in Martin Arias' voice from the Pacific Beach main tower.

"Copy PB . . . affirmative with visual on one swimmer in distress at eighteen. And that's a negative. Unit 23 is still responding to two jumpers north of Crystal Pier. You'll have to use Unit 22."

Davis was hoping that Shields would be available to respond to Tower 18 because Marisol Escobar was not his first choice to use as a rescuer, especially on a cold, rough day like today. Nonetheless, he had no choice; it was her duty to make rescues. Davis looked south and saw her truck making a U-turn in the sand. He keyed the mic and called her.

"Unit 22 from Mission Beach, head down to Tower 18. I'm going to need you to put a board in and check the disposition of one swimmer in the head of a rip. Break. Unit 22, make that a *Code 3* response . . . That's now an *11-59*. Repeat. Unit 22, respond *Code 3* to Tower 18 for one swimmer in distress."

*11-59.*

*Swimmer in distress. Water rescue in progress.*

Escobar kept her response brief, but not brief enough. All ears that monitored could hear the tension and uneasiness in her tight throat.

"Copy t-tower. Unit 22 resp-ponding *Code 3* to Tower 18."

Davis noticed the lights on the truck flashing, then picked up the landline and immediately called the PB tower.

Arias answered before the first ring was complete.

"PB tower, Arias."

"Martin, where the hell did that swimmer come from?"

"I don't know. I've been scanning and I never saw a thing. I've got a little bit of glare coming off my water, but my vision is fine. That head just popped up out of nowhere. There's no surfboard, no boogey board, nothing in the water . . . and nothing on the beach. No towel, no bag, nothing!"

Just then Shields called over the radio.

"Pacific Beach, this is Unit 23. I can disregard these two pier jumpers. They're *Code 4* and Tower 18 is a priority. Am I clear to back up Unit 22?"

The response came not from Arias in the Pacific Beach main tower, but from Senior POL Mike Johnson in Unit 24.

"That's a negative, Unit 23. Remain in service there at the pier to make contact with those two pier jumpers. Unit 24 is responding *Code 3* from North PB."

Shields was apprehensive about doing nothing to assist during a potential drowning, but he realized that Unit 24 could respond more quickly, and over his shoulder he watched Johnson's unit drive past him at more than 35 miles an hour.

Arias replied to Johnson, "Copy that . . . Unit 24 responding from North PB. Unit 23, remain in service at Crystal Pier for now, and stand by for further instructions. Break. South Mission from PB tower. Are you clear to have Unit 21 provide assistance at Tower 18?"

SDLP POL Alan Henderson had been parked on the beach in Unit 21, staring out at the empty ocean, waiting for his shift to end. He had been monitoring the call and realized quickly that he would be needed to assist Escobar.

"South Mission copies and that is affirmative. Unit 21, make Tower 18 your destination. *Code 3.*"

"Twenty-one copies . . . *Code 3* to eighteen."

Johnson smiled as he drove past Shields. He opened up the truck's engine and accelerated way beyond the Patrol's maximum speed limit for driving on the beach on a *Code 3*, but he couldn't care less about breaking the speed limit. He cared only about getting to Tower 18 as quickly as possible, so he could monitor, and perhaps delay, the progress of the rescue.

He made it to the scene quickly and parked Unit 24 in front of Tower 18. He flipped a switch under the dashboard to turn off the sirens, but allowed the bright, spinning lights across the top of the cab to continue flashing. He grabbed a pair of binoculars wedged between the vehicle's dashboard and the interior surface of the windshield, exited the pickup, moved to the rear of the truck, and vaulted himself onto the tailgate. Through the binoculars, he spotted Escobar and Harden's tiny heads bobbing up and down in the ocean approximately 75 yards offshore.

As he watched them drifting, Johnson mumbled, "So far, so good."

63

Wednesday, December 5, 2001
Mission Beach

Marisol Escobar had been calmly patrolling Mission Beach in Unit 22, listening to smooth jazz on the FM radio, thinking only about what she was going to do for dinner that night. Her dinner thoughts evaporated, though, when she heard Mission Beach main tower guard Mark Davis' call about a possible swimmer in distress at Tower 18. She had just patrolled the area and was aware of the strong rip current activity in front of Tower 18. She knew where to go and she knew what the conditions would be like, but she was still anxious about the situation.

This was the very scenario that Morgan had questioned her about some time ago when he bought her a cup of green tea. This was what being a permanent year-round ocean lifeguard was all about. This moment was why the lieutenant believed the tryout should be as difficult as he allowed it to be.

Marisol drove rapidly across the bumpy and undulating surface of the sandy beach, trying to gain a higher vantage point as she approached Tower 18. She arrived moments later, visually scanning for the victim as she parked facing the ocean. She quickly assessed that the waves were too big, and she would quickly lose her bulky and cumbersome rescue board in the surf. She decided, instead, to go out with just a rescue can and fins.

Faced with today's slightly above-moderate surf conditions, every other POL on duty would have used the 10-foot rescue board that was mounted on the top of all of the Patrol's emergency response vehicles.

Experienced watermen like Johnson, Shields, and Harden would have made it to the victim in less than 30 seconds. Each would have quickly pulled the victim onto the deck of their board, where both rescuer and victim would rest for a few moments and share a tension-relieving one-liner like, "Was that as fun for you as it was for me?"

The answer would almost always be "No," and, then, after a few relaxing and confidence-building breaths, the rescuer would choose a safe, easy route, and shuttle the swimmer back to the beach. Instead, with only a rescue can and duck feet fins, it had already taken Escobar more than three minutes just to get outside the surf line.

Johnson's plan was right on target.

He moved to the front of the truck and stood tall, refocusing through his binoculars. He noticed that Escobar and Harden were now side by side. He spoke loudly to himself, this time a tone of concern in his voice, "What the hell is going on?"

Escobar was acting frantically and appeared unsure about what to do next. She swam alongside Harden, who kept her face concealed, her head turned away from the beach.

Again Johnson spoke out aloud.

"I thought I could trust you, Harden. You were supposed to be long gone already."

Johnson reminded himself about how committed Harden was to ensuring Escobar's failure. *Relax. Follow her lead. Play dumb and don't say a fucking word. Nobody's going out there except for me, not for at least a couple of minutes.*

Henderson arrived in Unit 21, exited his vehicle, and, as Johnson had done moments earlier, gathered his rescue equipment. Henderson pulled on his neoprene top, grabbed his rescue board, and prepared to enter the water. Johnson, however, stepped in front of him and placed his right hand firmly on Henderson's chest.

"You fucking wait right here, Alan. This is Escobar's rescue. You know what I'm talking about, too, so just hold on. Let's give her one more minute to see if she can do this by herself."

"What? Are you serious? You know she can't bring a victim in on her own."

"We'll see. You're probably right, but let's give her a chance to show everybody just how much progress she's made."

Johnson turned and pointed.

"She's out there, right next to the victim, right now. I just watched them through my binos. She's got this, so let's just wait for that swimmer to take the can, and then Escobar will give us an *all clear* sign."

Henderson shrugged.

"Whatever you say, Mike."

**64**

Wednesday, December 5, 2001
Mission Beach

Marisol Escobar was struggling to keep her head above the water. The swell had picked up and the undulating surface of the ocean was causing her to frequently lose sight of the victim's head. She was pretty sure that the victim was wearing a wetsuit, and hoped that this would assist her in the rescue. She wondered if the victim was simply a surfer who had lost a board and had grown fatigued while trying to swim in against the rip current, or maybe an inexperienced spear fisherman who had dived too deep, too many times, and was now exhausted.

She was beginning to hyperventilate, and, as her body rapidly got colder, Marisol was becoming concerned for her own safety. She had already used most of her strength getting out through the surf line, her heart was pounding, and her breathing was shallow. Her trachea was burning and her ears and head were screaming in pain.

Completely fatigued, Escobar reached back and pulled on the lanyard that was connected to her flotation buoy. She brought the device to her chest, wrapped her arms around it, and remained buoyant. For an instant, she reflected on the time when she first swam in really cold water—during the academy that she had dropped out of. She still hadn't gotten over how distasteful that experience was for her, and ever since, when she was required to put her face in the ocean, she questioned herself and the path she had chosen. But Amanda had been so supportive of, and so instrumental in, setting up Marisol's fast track in the Patrol that it was not an option to let her mother down by quitting, simply because cold ocean water sucks and big waves are scary. So she kept going, every day wondering, *How much longer do I have to wait to become sergeant? Is this really going to work as fast as she said it would?*

Just then, the victim appeared from beneath the water's surface, right in front of her, wearing a neoprene hood and a full wetsuit. Marisol gasped as she spoke, while a soothing warmth spread throughout her body.

"Oh m-my God . . . I'm s-s-so glad it's you. I thought I was going to have to make a r-rescue and that I had lost a v-v-victim. Should I give an all clear sign?"

"No . . . we're not clear. There is a victim. I saw him go under right here. I think he's on the bottom. I just got here, too. Now take off your belt and let go of that buoy. I need you to dive to the bottom with me."

Escobar was startled. Seeing Cynthia Harden confused her. She looked at Harden suspiciously.

"Wait. What are you doing here? I thought you were leaving town this morning."

Cynthia looked briefly toward the shore to see if a second rescuer had begun paddling out. Seeing no second rescuer, she turned to face Escobar, continuing to conceal her face from anybody looking out from the beach.

"I decided to catch some fresh fish to take to my mom before I left town. We don't have time for this, Marisol. We have to dive now. Together."

Escobar was still unconvinced.

"Are you sure somebody's down there?"

"Yes! A surfer fell on his board and hit his head. I saw the whole thing just a couple of minutes ago. Let go of the rescue buoy, Marisol. We need to dive now."

Escobar was still resting on her rescue buoy and did not release her arms from it, but Harden was unrelenting.

"Marisol! Now! He's down there and he's going to die if we don't bring him up. Do you remember when you asked me to be a leader? Well, here I am. Now do what I say!"

Marisol reluctantly reached down with her numb fingers and attempted to remove the spring-loaded safety clip that locked the belt around her waist. Trembling, even the slightest movements were causing her great difficulty. After removing the clip, she returned her hands quickly to the red buoy and rested. Her breathing continued at a shallow and rapid pace.

After a moment, Marisol reached beneath the water's surface again, pulled the overlapping Velcro belt away from her stomach, and released it to the ocean. Lacking confidence, she looked at the familiar face and anxiously prepared to dive to the bottom.

Before letting go of the buoy, however, Marisol raised her right arm overhead and began waving it toward the beach for assistance. Then she crossed her arms above her head, making the sign of a large X.

Cynthia mentally reminded herself of the urgency.

*You're going to have to work fast, Cynthia . . . and you'll only get this one chance. Stay focused. One step at a time. Get her underwater, NOW!*

Escobar prepared to dive, and took several deep breaths while Harden called out a quick cadence. She rolled forward, pulled with both arms, and headed directly toward the bottom. She cleared her ears to equalize the building pressure at a depth of about 10 feet and continued kicking very hard with her finned feet. She made rapid progress and for a moment was unaware of the cold water temperature, focusing only on spotting something that looked like a body on the bottom of the ocean.

Marisol felt calm and confident. She was proud of herself and suddenly felt like part of a highly-skilled team of professional athletes, a team that would pluck a surfer's body off the bottom and bring the body back to the surface before loading it onto the deck of a rescue boat. The surfer would then be given CPR and his heart would be shocked back to life. He would be transported quickly to a hospital where he would receive advanced medical care and everything would be fine.

As Lt. Morgan commanded, that surfer would continue to live his life as he should. Morgan's inspiring words resonated in her head.

*"Nobody is going to drown on our beaches today!"*

**65**

Wednesday, December 5, 2001
Mission Beach

Mike Johnson grinned when he saw Marisol crossing both of her arms over her head in the sign of an *X*. Called into action by her signal, he quickly threw on his neoprene top, gathered the rest of his rescue gear, and headed down the sloped beach with his rescue board in tow. Johnson's board sailed upward abruptly after being caught by a rising gust of wind, halting his progress across the wet sand. He quickly adjusted, tucked the 10-footer back beneath his armpit, and resumed his sprint into the ocean. Upon reaching knee-deep water, he prepared to paddle out through the incoming waves. Henderson had retrieved a small, bright colored buoy from his service vehicle and ran with it through the shallow ocean water toward Johnson, shouting, "Johnson! Catch!"

Henderson heaved the object that was wrapped in yellow nylon line and attached to two small diving belt weights. Johnson caught the device, but had to leave the deck of his board to do it and splashed into the cold water like a teenage boy making a diving touchdown catch in a backyard pool. Johnson spoke out loud as he climbed back onto the deck of his board, "Shit that's cold! Nice toss, Henderson, you dipshit."

Johnson secured the small rig between his knees and paddled over the next set of waves. He made rapid progress toward the two women and quickly arrived at the location where he expected to find Escobar alone on the surface, still clinging to her hard red rescue buoy. He extended his body upward as high as possible and searched for his adversary. He shrugged his shoulders backwards, flexed his chest outward, and held his hands out in front of him, palms up. Maintaining his balance while twisting his trunk back and forth, he scanned the ocean's choppy surface, confounded.

*What the fuck?*

The only thing Johnson saw was Escobar's unmanned rescue buoy floating on the ocean's surface. The red buoy's yellow nylon lanyard hung straight down beneath the surface, the end of its six-foot length revealing only an open and empty waist belt.

Escobar was nowhere in sight.

Neither was Harden.

Johnson looked toward the beach to find Henderson, who was signaling for him to set the buoy right where he was. Johnson unrolled the line and allowed the anchor to touch bottom before releasing the buoy. He then secured his diving mask and snorkel, inhaled deeply a few times, and dove to the bottom of the ocean.

**66**

Wednesday, December 5, 2001
Mission Beach

M artin Arias did exactly what he was trained *not* to do—he kept his eyes fixed on Escobar as she struggled to find the victim. What he should have done was continue to scan the water to make sure that all other areas were clear.

He snapped out of his trance quickly, though, and scanned the entire beach, turning his head farther to the south, then 180 degrees back to the north. Nobody was in the water, except for the two pier jumpers that were still frolicking way outside the surf line.

Arias then began to consider the peculiarity of the situation, just as Shields had.

*These two idiots are apparently in no hurry to get out of the water. Why the hell are they out there? What is going on?*

The swimmer's sudden appearance was unexplainable and eerie to both Arias and Davis. Neither could identify the swimmer's face, and both of them failed to observe anything that looked like a swimming stroke. They watched the head bobbing up and down while being pulled away from shore by the strong rip current. Arias scanned the area again, hoping to locate a surfboard or boogie board or some other clue that could help him figure out how this person ended up in that spot in the first place, and who that swimmer was. He saw no towels, blankets, beach chairs, or equipment bags. The entire beach was empty.

After a long period of silence on the landline, Davis said, "Martin? Do you see him? I lost him again, and Escobar is freaking taking forever to get out there."

"Negative. I haven't seen him for about thirty seconds."

"Fuck, dude, she better find him fast and pull him up, or he's dead."

Arias focused toward the kelp beds on the far outside and located the small grey skiff that he had noticed earlier. He was still unable to identify an operator, but he noticed that it looked very much like the skiff that Mike Johnson used frequently for fishing. Martin knew that Johnson kept it at his slip by Headquarters, like most of the Patrol's personnel that owned similar crafts did. Again he sensed something unusual occurring.

*Maybe one of his boys is spearfishing, but I haven't seen anyone surface out there. Something's not right about this. Why would that guy swim all the way in from out there? Did he run out of gas? And how could we both miss that? It still doesn't make any sense.*

Arias gave up searching for clues, though, and refocused on the rescue scene. Unit 21 had arrived, and Arias saw Henderson taking the rescue board off the rack of his truck. Then he watched Henderson pull on his wetsuit top and run across the wet sand toward Johnson. He was barely able make out that the two men were speaking, but he noticed Johnson holding his hand up to signify "stop" when Henderson started into the water with his board. A moment later, Arias scanned back out toward the victim and Escobar. He saw Escobar waving one arm frantically over her head. Both he and Davis continued to watch as Escobar then raised both of her arms over her head and crossed them.

"Holy shit, Davis, she's calling for a *Code X.* There's a swimmer on the bottom. You call dispatch . . . she's your guard. I'm hanging up."

Davis hung up the phone, looked at the blinking LCD clock on the counter that read 4:30, and wrote down that time in the tower log. He keyed the mic on Main Lifeguard Dispatch Channel 1, the frequency that all personnel, including fire and police dispatchers, would have set to scan on their radios.

"Lifeguard Headquarters, and all available lifeguard supervisors from Mission Beach main tower. I'm requesting a full code response for one swimmer just outside the surf line at Santa Clara Court. Break. I repeat, submerged swimmer outside Tower 18. Requesting all available resources for *Code X*. Stand by for further."

**67**

Wednesday, December 5, 2001
Mission Beach

As Escobar reached the desolate ocean floor, she felt something grasping her forearm. Realizing quickly that it was her colleague joining her in tandem dive formation, she glanced toward Harden. Through the murky ocean water, she noticed what looked like a small oxygen bottle in Cynthia's mouth.

*Thank God*, Escobar thought.

The bailout bottle was an unexpected and reassuring surprise for the cold and unnerved female lifeguard who was way outside her comfort zone. Marisol gestured toward the bottle with her left hand, expecting to share the much-appreciated oxygen tank, but Cynthia blocked her arm and grabbed her by the elbow. Harden twisted Escobar's arm backward and pushed her down, face-first onto the ocean's floor. Then she quickly climbed on top of and straddled Marisol's body, holding both of Escobar's arms firmly in place, while wrapping her legs around Escobar's hips.

Marisol squirmed violently and rolled her body to one side, but attempting to release herself from Harden's grip seemed impossible. She looked over her shoulder and could see Cynthia's calm and determined eyes through water that was becoming more clouded as the two women scuffled on the ocean's silt-covered floor. Marisol attempted to kick Cynthia away, but her feet moved awkwardly with fins on, and she was unable to gain leverage against the heavier and stronger woman. She summoned all of her strength and desperately attempted to free her arms from Cynthia's grip. She rotated her shoulders, twisted her arms, and rolled her body in both directions until she finally broke free.

Marisol immediately reached for the bailout bottle and pulled it away from Cynthia's mouth, but Cynthia reached out with both hands and regained control of the bottle. Now free from Cynthia's grip, Marisol released the bottle and pushed against Cynthia's chest with both of her arms. As Marisol attempted to move away, Cynthia dropped the bottle and glanced at it as it tumbled onto the cloudy bottom.

Marisol wiggled out of Cynthia's leg grip and placed her feet on the ocean floor. She pulled against the ocean water with both arms, extended her legs upward, and kicked with her fins. She moved rapidly toward the surface and began to pull away from Harden. But just as Escobar was a foot from the surface, ready to break through and gasp for much-needed air, Cynthia grasped her left ankle and pulled Marisol back toward her. She wrapped both of her arms around Escobar's waist. She spun Escobar around and drove her shoulder into Marisol's stomach, much like a linebacker executing a fundamentally perfect open field tackle. Escobar's body folded like a beach chair, and the remaining oxygen was squeezed from her body.

Cynthia drove Escobar to the bottom and climbed onto her chest. She wrapped her legs around Marisol's thighs as her arms continued to bear hug her torso.

Marisol felt Cynthia's neoprene wetsuit rubbing against her cold skin and realized what was happening.

*You slut. It was you the entire time. There's no victim out here.*

Escobar searched for the bailout bottle, her only hope to survive. She strained to focus her eyes through the silty water and spotted it just beyond the reach of her right arm. She used all of her remaining strength to roll Cynthia's body toward the bottle, but was unsuccessful, as Harden adjusted quickly. Escobar again gave it everything she had, which wasn't much, but she managed to tip Harden just enough to free her right arm, and reached for the bottle. She grasped it and immediately placed the mouthpiece between her teeth and inhaled.

Nothing happened.

She tried again, a little more aggressively.

Still nothing.

It was like pulling the trigger on a gun that had just been wrestled away from a burglar, only to find that there was a safety mechanism engaged. No matter how many times the trigger was pulled, the gun would not fire. Fortunately for Escobar, her numb fingers found the right spot and she applied just enough pressure to the small button. The bottle immediately discharged the much-needed oxygen.

Instantly Escobar felt stronger. Again she attempted to roll out of Cynthia's grasp, but Cynthia held on tightly.

*C'mon you bitch, die already,* Harden thought.

Cynthia hadn't noticed that Marisol had gained possession of the bottle. Her head was still tucked into Marisol's breasts and only now, after feeling Marisol's diaphragm expanding and contracting several times as she breathed liberally from the bottle, did Harden lift her head to look at Marisol's face.

Cynthia immediately adjusted her leg hold around Marisol's hips, released her arms from the bear hug, and reached for the bottle with both hands. Marisol attempted to take advantage of a second opportunity to escape, but Cynthia compensated quickly with her strong legs. Escobar could not break free from her grip. Using a forearm, Harden applied leverage against Marisol's cheek, then violently pulled the bottle away from her mouth with her other hand.

Cynthia cleared Marisol's flailing arms with her left arm, squeezed the circumference of the bottle as tightly as she could and thrust it downward like a hammer, squarely striking Escobar's head. The impact caused Cynthia to lose her grip on the bottle and again it fell to the ocean floor.

The blow stunned Marisol. Instantly her vision faded to black. Her will to survive, which had been strong and determined, was now gone.

She suddenly felt warmer and sensed a glowing light coming from above the surface of the dark ocean water. In that light, Marisol saw her father.

Victor Trujillo-Escobar had feared this day from the beginning. Marisol heard the words he had spoken to her years ago in an attempt to dissuade his only daughter from accepting the dangerous permanent ocean lifeguarding position in the first place.

*"Marisol . . . Mija. You don't need this job. That's just your mother talking. She hasn't rested a day in her life, Marisol. Why must you try so hard to be just like her? You are a beautiful, lovely young woman. What man wouldn't want to love and take care of you? Mija, don't go to work on those beaches; it is too dangerous. Just stay at the pool where you will be safe, and happy. We can get you what you want another way."*

Marisol's last thought was of her father grieving for his lost daughter.

*Lo siento Papi . . . I just wanted to make a difference . . . Lo siento.*

When Marisol's lungs were finally emptied of oxygen, she could no longer control them, and as a reflex she gasped. Her lungs then filled with murky seawater and a few seconds later, Marisol Escobar's heart stopped beating.

When Marisol's body went limp, Cynthia retrieved the oxygen bottle and finally drew in a gulp of air. Then she took another and another, thinking, *Whew . . . Holy shit . . . Escobar battled.*

Cynthia looked into the lifeless, open eyes of her victim and stayed next to Marisol long enough to be sure that she was dead. As she began to move away, she noticed a cloud of red water building around Marisol's head.

*Dammit. That's an open wound. They're going to want to know how that got there.*

Cynthia quickly turned her attention to the next phase of her plan. She took another deep breath from the bailout bottle and began kicking due west. After just a few yards, she stopped when a thought occurred to her.

*Improvise.*

She turned back toward the body, hesitated briefly to tap the nozzle again, and took several long, slow breaths before holding the deepest one. She dropped the small stainless steel tank, watched it come to rest just a few feet from Marisol's body, and then kicked rapidly away from the scene.

About a minute later, Cynthia gasped for air when she reached the surface. She scanned the area, looking for any lifeguards. She saw Johnson searching from his rescue board and noticed that Henderson was paddling out through the surf. Slightly relieved, she exhaled slowly, breathed in deeply, and concentrated on lowering her respiration rate.

Solemnly, she reflected for a moment on what she had just done.

*That bitch turned out to be a fighter after all.*

That fighter's mouth and eyes, however, remained wide open, as if they were still gasping for air and searching for help. Her body drifted in and out with the surge, approximately 100 yards offshore, directly outside Tower 18, on the bottom of the Pacific Ocean, where Mike Johnson and a host of SDLP watermen would begin searching for two missing bodies.

*Just don't let anyone find her, Johnson . . . not for at least twenty minutes,* Cynthia thought while stealthily moving away from the body of her adversary.

Sunset
Wednesday, December 5, 2001
Mission Beach

At the surface, about 200 yards outside of the search, Cynthia reached beneath the water, unzipped a fanny pack that was wrapped around her waist, and retrieved a diving mask. She applied the mask, then slid it upward onto her forehead. She couldn't get the image of Marisol's open eyes and mouth out of her head.

*Get a grip, Cyn . . . You can do this. This was the only solution and you know it. You'll be much better off with her gone. Now FOCUS!*

She looked toward the beach and noticed that four lifeguard vehicles were now parked in front of Tower 18, each one with lights flashing. She knew that, before it was all over, the beach would be filled with emergency vehicles. Despite the efficiency of her colleagues, she reminded herself that the timeline of her plan was still on point.

*By the time they find her I'll be on the freeway. Nobody is ever going to know it was me except for Johnson . . . but he won't say a word. I just cannot be seen.*

Cynthia watched as Johnson and Henderson dove in tandem, then surfaced together about a minute later. Moving swiftly away from the scene, she secured the mouthpiece of a second bailout bottle, then turned and spotted a small gray lobster buoy that she had deployed on her way in. It was barely visible on the tops of the choppy wind swells, another 100 yards outside of her position. Her normal breathing pattern had returned, and her heart rate had lowered to a more comfortable pace. She breathed deeply, secured the mask around her eyes and nose, and dove just beneath the surface where she began kicking. She arrived at the buoy quickly. There, she surfaced again briefly to check the status of any additional emergency vessels that she knew would be arriving soon. She heard the screws on *Ocean 1* and watched it bouncing over the swells as it rapidly approached the area. *Rescue 11*, with two crewmen aboard, was not far behind, having just exited the Mission Bay channel. Randy Shields had joined Johnson and Henderson, and all three of the men were now executing search and recovery dives.

Cynthia turned away from the rescue, then pulled herself down to the ocean floor, using a line that attached to the buoy. The line was linked by chain to a thick iron ring set into the top of a huge concrete anchor resting on the ocean floor. Her scuba gear was also clipped to the iron ring. She unclipped the carabiner, opened the master valve on the top of her scuba tank, slightly inflated the buoyancy compensator to lighten the rig, and flipped the vest and tank over her head and shoulders. She clipped the vest across her chest, placed the regulator into her mouth, calmly breathed in and out, and prepared to set out on the final leg of her underwater ops. She retrieved the gray lobster buoy, and neatly coiled the line. She removed the small and versatile Vipor surfing fins from her feet and replaced them with longer diving fins. She placed all of the items into a mesh drawstring bag, mentally inventoried her gear, scanned the area around the concrete block to be sure, then looked up, kicked, and began a gradual ascent toward the kelp beds.

With the longer propulsion fins on her feet, Cynthia moved at a rapid pace. Her visibility was poor—the light in the water had diminished as the sun began to set—so Cynthia used a small diving light to help monitor her course and direction. She maintained a heading of 260 degrees directly toward the pontoon boat that was still somewhat camouflaged by the far western edge of the kelp beds. She easily spotted the fluorescent nylon anchor line, popped her head up out of the water, and was pleased to see the small skiff within her grasp.

Cynthia gained confidence that everything would work out just as she planned. As she completed her underwater flight, however, something began gnawing at her mind. She could not dismiss the tingling sense that she had been seen and that somebody else besides Escobar and Johnson knew that she was out there in the water.

And Escobar's eyes and mouth were freaking her out.

Cynthia reviewed the short list of personnel who might have seen her. In her mind she began a roll call.

*Johnson, Zampese, Shields, Arias, Davis, Escobar, Henderson, and Mercer. Arias or Davis would be most likely to have seen something, Henderson might have seen something from the beach, or maybe Charlie Mercer up in the South Mission tower if he's still watching the channel for some reason . . . but he should be out of the tower long before I head in. I have to find out what they all know before I get back on Monday. Latrelle will know everything by then . . . I just got to get the hell out of here now.*

She cautiously slithered over the inflated pontoon, and secured her gear. She headed south at full throttle until she was directly outside the mouth of the channel, then headed east toward the Bay without crossing paths or being noticed by any of the rescue vessels that were responding to the emergency. Once inside the channel, she hugged the north jetty wall and trawled invisibly under the dark cover of nightfall past the only open bend between her and the floating slip buoy that Johnson had set for her earlier that morning.

Cynthia left Johnson's gear in the skiff, covered the entire craft, and snapped a tarp in place. She gathered the rest of her gear and swam the short distance to shore, still unseen through the flat, calm Bay water. She cautiously hauled her gear across the sandy beach, over a grassy park area to the parking lot, and quickly loaded her gear inside of her uncle's old Blazer.

As she fired up the K5's huge engine, she double-checked the gas gauges on the dashboard that indicated that both tanks were full. She pulled the column-mounted drive lever into gear and placed her foot on the gas pedal. The vehicle purred, growled, and accelerated across the pavement toward Mission Beach Drive.

Still wearing a wetsuit and booties, Cynthia glanced at her diving watch as she gripped the Blazer's steering wheel through rubber gloves.

*Five o'clock . . . nice work, Cyn.*

She had just executed her plan perfectly, and as far as she knew, regardless of her fears to the contrary, nobody had seen her. Johnson was now operating without an explanation, and Cynthia would not answer his calls looking for one. His questions would not be answered anytime soon, if ever, but the answers he gave to any questions that were asked of him, she believed, would certainly provide doubt as to his innocence. Cynthia was counting on Johnson's combative temperament to be his undoing, and she was confident that his inevitable accusations against her would be perceived, by everyone, as desperate bullshit.

Martin Arias was still unsure about what he had observed way out in the kelp beds.

He remained quiet.

Randy Shields did not verbalize his concerns about the timing of the pier jumpers just after the stingray victim was treated and released. Both watermen were watching Mike Johnson closely as he stared at the floor, appearing nervous.

Lt. Morgan appeared to notice Johnson's apprehension, but he offered only his support and his condolences about the incident to the group of watermen assembled in the garage.

"You men go home and get some well-deserved rest tonight. Henderson, Johnson, Shields, and Zampese will go first, at 0900 hours. Everybody else, ten a.m."

The men quietly gathered their gear and, one by one, filed out of the garage. A few minutes later, Morgan turned out the lights and secured the tower.

Earlier, when Shields exited the water, he had concealed the bailout bottle that he found. He wrapped it in a towel and placed the bundle behind the driver's seat in Unit 23's crew cab. He was certain that Johnson was somehow involved, and the two distracting incidents earlier in the evening began to make sense to him now.

*The stingray was bullshit. That was Pence and the jumpers were obviously George and Pablo. The entire thing was a setup. The timing was too perfect.*

He stopped and shook his head, questioning himself and his quick judgment against his longtime nemesis, Mike Johnson.

*But attempted murder? He's a lot of things, but not a killer.*

Shields drove through the dark and Arias sat quietly in the wet seat all the way back to the PB tower. When they arrived, Arias exited the vehicle and reached behind the seat to retrieve a backpack that contained a pair of running shoes, a wetsuit, a diving mask and snorkel, a sharp and sturdy combat knife, and a few other useful items. The towel Shields had placed there earlier lay partially on top of Arias' backpack. When Arias moved the towel, he saw the bottle wrapped inside, but said nothing.

Shields moved to the rear door, retrieved the bundle and his other gear, and locked the vehicle. No conversation took place until after the tower was secure and both men began walking toward the parking lot.

As the two men approached their vehicles, Arias said, "That's not your bailout bottle is it?"

Shields had no choice but to trust Arias now.

"Did you see the inscription on the bottom?"

"No. But I'm guessing you're going to tell me that it's Johnson's."

Shields removed the small bottle and showed Arias two engraved initials on the bottom—*MJ*.

"Yep. I found it out there right next to Escobar's body. This is what caused the bleeding. She got hit in the head with this. I don't plan on telling anybody anything until I know more about what happened out there. Can I trust you to work with me, or do you want me to turn this evidence over to the lieutenant? I will call him right now."

Arias squinted at Shields, slightly confused, but shook his head and said, "No, don't do that. Not yet. Not until we piece this thing together. Once the lieutenant gets involved, we're out. Due process, confidentiality, you know the drill. Tell me what you're thinking . . . I may have seen something, too."

Shields felt a sense of relief.

"I think Johnson somehow planned this. The stingray victim and the pier jumpers were obviously his guys. That entire deal was a setup and a distraction to keep your eyes and my response away from that rip at eighteen. Somebody wanted Escobar to go out there alone. He must have had somebody else out there, but I still can't figure out what happened to Escobar."

Shields frowned.

"Whatever it was, it sure happened fast. Maybe he took the bottle with him and used it underwater where nobody could see him . . . I don't know."

Arias shook his head quickly.

"No. Johnson didn't take that bottle out with him. I watched through the new Zeiss."

"Yeah, those things are awesome."

"I know that's a long distance, but you know how powerful those lenses are, and my eyes are legit. I've scored twenty-ten on eye exams since I was a little kid and I got a twenty-oh-five rating when I tested for POL. If there's one thing I can count on in this world, it's my own two eyes. I got that from my old man."

"No shit?"

"No shit. I watched Johnson drag his board out there with one hand and nothing but his mask and snorkel in the other, fins on his feet. He was fast, man . . . Henderson tossed him the pelican buoy, and he paddled out and set the datum immediately. He was out there in a minute . . . but I never saw a bailout bottle. Somebody else brought that bottle into the water. It wasn't Marisol, though; I can tell you that much for sure. Henderson is the only other possibility besides you, unless like you said, Johnson knew that swimmer out in the rip and that's how the bottle got there."

"What else did you see?"

"I saw a skiff way outside in the kelp beds. It looked just like Johnson's

*Arancia*. You've seen it, right?"

Randy nodded.

Arias continued.

"I saw it out there during the rescue, but it was gone afterward. Maybe whoever was operating the skiff was the one who was using that bottle. That had to be the swimmer out there."

Shields shook his head in disbelief.

"But why, Martin? Do you really think Johnson would try to kill Escobar?"

"She wanted him fired. Everybody knows that. If she made sergeant, it would have only been a matter of time."

Arias paused.

"Like you said, maybe he had one of those assholes he hangs out with do it for him. Those scumbags will do almost anything."

Shields shook his head again.

"There's no point in looking for another body. It isn't out there. The less Johnson knows about what we know, the better. We've all seen him run from the truth before. He won't get away with it this time though."

**70**

2035 Hours
Wednesday, December 5, 2002
Chevron Mini-Mart, Ventura, California

Cynthia exited the freeway in San Clemente and parked the Blazer behind a pair of semis, completely out of view, at the very back of a Carl's Junior parking lot. She stripped out of her wetsuit and rinsed her hair and body with a gallon bottle of water that she had left on the floorboard in the warm air flow of the truck's heater for nearly two hours. She toweled dry, put on sweat pants, a long-sleeve t-shirt, thick socks, Ugg boots, a hooded sweatshirt, and a beanie cap, then pulled up to the drive thru. She ordered chicken stars, barbecue sauce, a bottled water, and a large coffee, then pulled back on to the 5 North.

She stopped again just north of Ventura. She walked inside a convenience store with her phone pressed to her ear, silently handed cash to the attendant, held up four fingers to indicate the number of the pump she would be using to fill the Blazer's tanks, and headed to the restroom when she began speaking into the phone.

Latrelle did not recognize the incoming number, so he didn't answer the call, but the voicemail indicator beeped soon afterward, and right away he retrieved the message that Cynthia had just left.

*"I'm sorry, Stallion. I meant to call you and wish you good luck this morning, but I couldn't get back to sleep, so I just got an early start instead. My crappy phone is jacked up again, so I gave up trying to call you and just drove. I bought this burner at some Radio Shack in Santa Cruz. I'll try you again in a little bit, 'Trelle. I miss you already."*

When his phone rang again, he answered it immediately.

"Cynthia?"

"Yeah, it's me. How was the river testing? You kill it?"

"Fine. All three of us got our certs."

Latrelle's reply was uncharacteristically brief and his voice was flat.

"How's your mother? Are you there now?"

"Yeah, we're just walking into a restaurant for dinner. Do you want to say hello?"

Cynthia expected him to reject her invitation, which he politely did.

"Uh, that's okay."

She giggled.

"My mother is in the ladies' room anyhow. I'm just messing with ya."

When Latrelle didn't laugh and gave no reply, Cynthia realized, *He knows what happened. They didn't find her in time. She's dead.*

Latrelle continued, somber.

"Something really weird happened today at Mission Beach. Coach Escobar is in the hospital. She went out on a rescue at the end of the day. The victim went under and Marisol went down to get her . . . but neither one of them came back up on their own. Marisol was on the bottom. Johnson, Henderson, and Shields pulled her up. It doesn't look good. She's on life support in ICU. They shocked her heart a bunch a times; finally, they got a beat."

Cynthia gasped.

*Oh shit. She survived. They got there too soon.*

"No fucking way," she muttered.

"What?"

"I was just saying I can't believe that all happened."

"Yeah, me neither."

Cynthia said nothing.

"There's still no brain activity. She's totally unresponsive to any stimuli. She can't breathe on her own. She's on a respirator. They don't think she's going to make it."

Cynthia said nothing.

*Shut up. Let him tell you.*

"Henderson said Marisol's head was bleeding when they retrieved her body. He, Johnson, and Shields found her. She was underwater for like, at least twenty minutes. They never found the swimmer."

"Wait. There's a dead swimmer?"

"Nobody knows about that yet . . . but everybody is sure that there was at least one other swimmer out there . . . in a wetsuit with a hood. No missing person's reports have been received."

"Holy crap, Latrelle . . . That's insane."

"We were monitoring the radio on our way back from the river, *Code 3* all the way, but it was pretty much over by the time we got there. Marisol was already in the helicopter when we pulled into the garage. We could hear it taking off from Quivira. We all watched it fly away."

Latrelle sounded sad as he said, "Everybody is totally confused about what happened."

"I'm so sorry, Latrelle."

"I still can't believe it."

Latrelle paused.

Cynthia held her breath and allowed the silence.

Latrelle then continued, a sharper tone in his voice.

"Johnson left the tower tonight without saying a word to anyone. It was really obvious that he was freaking out though. He was a mess."

Latrelle paused for several beats.

"I wouldn't be surprised to find out that he had something to do with this. Everybody knows Marisol was never going to stop coming after him. Whatever happened, I'm pretty sure he's not crying about it."

*Perfect. Well, not perfect, but a step in the right direction.*

"I can't believe it. Nobody saw anything? That sounds totally sketchy to me."

"Seriously Cynthia, Johnson was as dark and gloomy as I've ever seen him. He's never that way after any kind of incident. He's usually like the most unaffected guy there. He knows something . . . I guarantee it. I never trusted that guy."

"I wouldn't be surprised at all to find out that he knows something. If he does, Morgan will figure it out."

She continued, sympathy in her voice.

"We'll just have to wait and see, Latrelle. Let Morgan and Moreland and those other guys take care of it. They'll know what to do."

"Yeah, I guess."

"I'm sorry, Latrelle. I know how close you two were."

*Past tense. Not yet. Shut up, you dumbass.*

Cynthia said good night and hung up the phone. A little dazed, frightened by what she now knew, she walked outside, topped off both tanks, then headed north on Highway 101, just under the speed limit in the far right lane. No longer calm, she ran her fingers through her hair, and shouted loud enough to drown out the Blazer's huge, howling tires, "FUCK! FUCK! FUCK!" She pounded on the steering wheel with her fist and repeated again, and again, "Fuck, fuck, fuck, fuck, fuck..."

The first round of the drowning review was over. Shields, Henderson, Johnson, and Zampese had completed their private interviews with Lt. Morgan, Sgt. Mendenhall, and Sgt. McIntyre. POLs Davis, Mercer, and Arias came down the stairs after completing their interviews and joined the other men that were assembled in the garage, waiting to be dismissed to go on duty, or home for the day.

Johnson stood alone and did not speak.

Shields leaned against the aluminum rollup garage door, his arms folded confidently across his chest, glaring at Johnson.

Arias then broke the silence, and his word to Shields to keep things hush-hush.

"Hey, Johnson. Was that your skiff I saw out there in the kelp beds last night?"

"What?"

"Yeah, your skiff . . . I'm pretty sure I saw it out there in the kelp beds, right at the time Escobar called for the *Code X.*"

Johnson scowled at Arias.

"So what? A friend of mine used it to go spearfishing last night. My skiff is out there all the time. Everybody knows that."

Shields joined in, prepared now to share with the Lieutenant since Arias had just opened the jar.

"You mark all your gear with your initials, don't you, Johnson? You know, in case something gets misplaced or stolen."

"Oh, here we go. Now the fucking altar boy is gonna chime in, too."

"Just your initials, right? On all your gear?"

"First of all, dick-wad, I never misplace my gear, and nobody in their right mind would steal from me. What's *your* fucking point?"

"Never? You never misplace your gear? Really?"

Johnson scowled.

"Yeah, that's what I said. I never misplace my gear."

Shields nodded several times, pushed away from the garage door, and stepped into the room toward Johnson.

"What about a small bailout bottle? Did you misplace one of those, Mike?"

"What bailout bottle? What the fuck are you talking about, Shields?"

Johnson couldn't tell if Shields was bluffing. Cynthia hadn't answered any of his phone calls, and he was still uncertain about what had actually happened in the water. He had no idea what Cynthia was up to, or what else she had done to set him up. Johnson could see, though, that Shields and Arias knew that he had something to do with what had happened.

*I'm fucked . . . Fuck you, Harden . . . You used me . . . I should have known better . . . all you bitches are the same.*

"Like I said, I don't know what you're talking about, Shields. I loaned the only bailout bottles I own to Cynthia Harden a long time ago. She's been using them to dive deeper when she fishes or some goddamn thing . . . at least that's what she told me. You'll have to ask her about that."

Arias cut in.

"Harden? She's in San Francisco. She wasn't even here yesterday. What the hell are you talking about, Mike? Besides, fishing with a bottle is illegal. Everybody knows that. Harden would never use one. She doesn't even need one. She can stay under forever already."

"Like I said . . . ask Harden. I told you, Harden's got both of my bailout bottles and she's had them for weeks. I didn't *mis-place* anything, you fucking jerk-off."

Johnson shook his head.

"I'm not doing this. I'm not saying another word to you two assholes. I gave my statement to the lieutenant. Who do you guys think you are, fucking San Diego vice? Fuck you both, you don't know shit! I'm going back on duty in North PB now. You ass-wipes have a nice fucking day."

Shields replied calmly, "Don't go too far. You've got some answers to come up with. Nobody had more to gain from Escobar being dead than you did, Mike."

Johnson stood up and approached Shields, his arm pumping and his index finger pointing. He stopped a full arm's length away.

"Like I said, Shields . . . FUCK OFF! I've given my answers. You can take your questions and shove 'em up your ass."

He turned and pointed his right arm at both of his interrogators.

"Both you assholes can go fuck yourselves. Let's go, Z."

Combative. Just as Cynthia depended on.

Johnson and a confused Zampese left the garage and headed through the tower's front doors. The duo quickly made their way across the boardwalk, over the wall, and onto the sand, where they hopped into Unit 24. Without speaking, they drove back to North PB to resume their daily routine. Zampese volunteered to take the first tower watch. Johnson drove Unit 24 directly to the Tourmaline parking lot and began making calls on his cell.

Shields left Arias in the garage and climbed into his Ford F-250. He also began making his calls. His first was to Sgt. Moreland, who was on a workout, so the call went directly to voice mail. Shields left a brief message about Johnson's suspected role in the drowning. His second call was to Lt. Morgan, who he knew was unavailable as he was interviewing the Mission and South Mission guards. Again, the call went right to voice mail. He left another message.

While Shields was leaving voice mails, Johnson, now feeling desperate, unsure, and panicked, was on the phone with his boys, explaining exactly what he needed them to do. Big George knew where the hide-a-key to Johnson's Bay Park condo was, and he had instructions to retrieve a twelve-gauge pump, two handguns, and the ammunition boxes that Johnson kept in his master closet. He was told to take them and meet Pence at Johnson's bigger boat at the Shelter Island Marina.

**72**

Thursday, December 6, 2001
North Pacific Beach

Mike Johnson and his longtime friends had talked for years about the day when one or all of them might—for whatever reason—need to take flight quickly and seek refuge in Mexico or somewhere farther south.

Johnson explained to Pence just how desperate he was.

"No, dude, you're not listening to me. She's dead, or she will be soon. It's the other one that set me up . . . that big white chick, Cynthia Harden."

Johnson listened through his cell phone's earpiece for a few moments.

"Yeah, her. The one we all liked so much. SHE tried to kill Escobar last night. She fucking drowned her."

He paused again.

"Yeah, the hot Mexican bitch . . . she's brain dead."

Another pause.

"Yeah, in a fucking coma. I had no idea she was going to do that, but these fuckers here think I had something to do with it. Harden left my bailout bottle out there next to Escobar's fucking body. Shields found it. He convinced all of those fuckers that I tried to kill Escobar. Shields probably thinks you were out in the water, too. But it was Harden. She did it all by herself."

Another pause.

"Yeah, that's the one . . . He's the dick-head that I got into that fight with when RC and that Mormon kid drowned back in '87. He tried to pin that shit on me then, too. I'm fucked, dude. He's been out to get me ever since."

While sitting in the idling lifeguard truck parked behind the tall sandy berm at Tourmaline, Johnson paused again and realized that he'd been played by the female waterman whom he had respected and trusted.

"Fucking Navy diver, man. I knew I shouldn't have trusted her. She totally ate my lunch, bro. I'm completely fucked now. I'm not taking my chances with an attorney and offering up some bullshit plea. I'll end up spending all my money and going to jail anyway. Don't forget, I planned this whole thing; it just didn't end up the way it was supposed to. I'm fucked, man. No matter what happens next, I am fucked."

He paused and briefly listened to Pence.

"No . . . no way. I'm not like you, bro, I can't just go in for a few years and wait like you did. I won't be able to take care of my kids from in there, and, besides, who knows how long I'll be in. Probably a federal location, maximum security . . . no . . . I'm not going to prison, I'm going to Mex. That's my only way out."

Johnson listened intently for a moment before answering his best friend's question.

"Yep . . . and you're coming with me. It's the only way I'll make it. I'll figure out what to do about my kids later, but we're leaving right after I hang up this phone, and I ain't coming back. Now listen to me carefully, Pence; here's what I need you to do."

**73**

Thursday, December 6, 2001
San Diego Bay

Mike Johnson caught a break on the first leg of his departure from San Diego. The drowning review schedule created the need for several relief guards to be called into work that day. Not all of those were POLs, and Sgt. McIntyre had to settle for two veteran seasonal guards with main tower qualifications to fill the Mission strand's duty roster.

When Johnson began a routine PWC patrol on Pacific Beach's Jet 33, those two SOLs were sitting up top in the main towers—one at Mission Beach, the other at South Mission Beach. Neither one of them thought it was unusual for the PWC to be traveling south in front of their towers on the far outside at full throttle. Neither of the inexperienced MT guards thought twice as Jet 33 cleared the open channel on its way toward Ocean Beach.

Senior POL Ryan Lawton, however, noticed as soon as the Waverunner crossed the channel. He attempted to gain a better view through the Ocean Beach main tower's powerful binoculars and he immediately recognized Johnson's large frame beneath a yellow lifeguard vest and a tight-fitting, black wetsuit. As he sat alone in the observation deck, Lawton thought, *What the hell are you doing, Johnson?* He then switched his radio to the mission strand's radio frequency and inquired, "Ocean Beach to Jet 33 on channel two . . . Jet 33? What's your status, Jet 33?"

Lawton repeated the call sign three times, hoping Johnson would hear his voice over the wind and the whining engine noise. Johnson wore a headset beneath his crash helmet, though, and could hear every word Lawton said, but he did not answer verbally. Instead, he extended his left arm upward and made a circle by touching the top of his helmet with his fingertips. He was hoping Lawton would acknowledge the signal for *needing no assistance* and would ask no further questions. Lawton was not convinced, though, and repeated his inquiry.

Johnson still did not reply, but now he knew that his flight had become public knowledge.

*Fucking Lawton . . . You're such a goddam boy scout. At least I made it this far already . . . I may still have a chance,* he thought.

Johnson signaled again with his left hand, this time toward his mouthpiece first, and then made a slashing movement across his throat, hoping to convey the idea that his transmitter's mouthpiece was out of service. He gave the signal several more times before disregarding the OB main tower guard. Lawton did not disregard Johnson, though. He picked up the landline and reported the unusual activity immediately to lifeguard headquarters.

Meanwhile, in the North PB tower, Gary Zampese heard Lawton's transmissions and Johnson's failure to respond. After a short pause, Zampese picked up his landline. His call went to Sgt. Moreland, who had just completed a jog to Sea World and back, and was now taking a long, hot shower in the locker room at headquarters. He heard the phone ring while it lay on the bench next to his Sabre radio. He quickly turned off the water and stepped across the tile floor to retrieve his phone before it rang a third time.

"Moreland."

"Sergeant, it's GZ at North PB. Listen . . . I think Johnson's up to something. Shields and Arias seem to think he had a role in Escobar's drowning last night. Something about Johnson's skiff and a bailout bottle with his initials on it. I have no idea what they're talking about, but there's obviously something going down. Mike said he was going on patrol, but he is way out of district on Jet 33. I'm pretty sure he's on his way to his boat at Shelter Island."

Moreland wiped his head with a soft towel, clearing water and soapsuds from his ears and face. He spoke into a wet mouthpiece.

"What? Repeat that."

"Johnson's on the run. He's going to his boat right now. He had something to do with Escobar's drowning."

"Holy crap. Son of a bitch! He tried to kill her, didn't he?"

"I don't know about that, but I do know that he's on Jet 33 at full speed, heading south toward Cabrillo Point right now."

Moreland was on the move, and began dressing hastily.

"Thanks for the heads-up, Gary. I'm on it."

Moreland immediately checked his voicemail and heard the message from Shields that confirmed GZ's theory. He ran into the lobby to find his crewman, POL Brandon Jenkins, seated at a computer terminal reading his emails. Moreland pointed to the docks just outside the lobby doors and shouted, "BJ! Let's go."

Both men ran to the docks. Moreland hopped up to the wheelhouse as Jenkins released the bow and stern lines. Moreland then signaled to his crewman, pointing with three extended fingers, and pushed the throttle forward.

"*Code 3* all the way. Hang on."

Sgt. Bobby Moreland knew just about every rescue boat operator in San Diego. If he or she worked for an agency that served in San Diego County, it was likely that the native sergeant had worked with, trained with, fished with, surfed with, or drank with each of them at least once. He could have called any of them, but he called his close friend, Coast Guard Captain Rey Vasquez. Vasquez commanded an Immigration and Drug Enforcement strike team that was extremely talented and operated the swiftest, most heavily armed and durable boat Moreland had ever dreamed of commanding.

Vasquez answered his cell on the first ring. Thirty seconds later, he had all the information he needed about Mike Johnson, Jet 33, and Johnson's Bayliner. In less than two minutes, his crew assembled onboard the rigid-hull, twin-engine Interceptor that was now at full speed on its way to the entrance of San Diego Bay.

74

December 6, 2001
San Diego Bay

Johnson moved rapidly at well over 50 miles per hour, heading south along the Sunset Cliffs. As he passed by a beautiful baseball field with a dark green outfield fence, one that sat high above the coastline on the equally beautiful campus of a private Nazarene college, he sped past a group of surfers who were catching tall, peaking waves at one of San Diego's favorite breaks.

He gained a sense of confidence as he put distance between himself and Ocean Beach, the Patrol's southernmost station. If his boys, Pence and George, could work their way through late morning Mission Beach and Point Loma traffic quickly, they might arrive at Shelter Island in time to facilitate his escape into Mexican waters. Johnson knew that Pence would have to slowly guide his boat through the Bay without drawing the attention of the Coast Guard, Navy, or Harbor Patrol. He feared that any delays might require him to throttle his boat up too fast, creating an illegal wake that would blow his cover.

*C'mon you guys . . . get my boat out of there.*

George was way ahead of schedule and arrived at the marina five minutes before Pence. Pence's piece-of-crap pickup truck had fired on all cylinders all the way to the docks, and he had no problem with the late morning traffic. Pence screeched to a stop and jumped out of the battered Dodge Ram, the keys still in the ignition, and left it parked along the curb in a red zone. He sprinted across the parking lot toward the entrance to the private marina, stopped briefly at the security gate, and quickly punched in a four-digit code.

The gate buzzed and popped open.

He passed through the gate, bounded loudly across the flexible wooden deck, and leapt aboard the large vessel Mike had christened *Debbie's Big Johnson,* in honor of his ex-wife, years before their divorce.

George completed securing Johnson's weapons and ammo as Pence moved quickly to the bridge and hit the ignition switch. The powerful, well-tuned inboard engine growled as it came to life. George jumped onto the dock, moved to the forward cleat, unwound the overlapping, figure-eight configuration of the bowline, and tossed it on board. He then detached both spring lines and the stern line, tossed them into the boat, unlinked the various utility cables, and nodded "farewell" to his friend.

Pence throttled up and moved swiftly through the calm, flat water, just enough to create an inconspicuous wake. With the precise timing that Johnson depended on, he pulled Jet 33 alongside his Bayliner and jumped on board. The Waverunner's powerful engine died as soon as Johnson leapt off, sending the versatile rescue pod drifting toward the shoreline. As soon as Johnson was securely on board, Pence throttled up and headed southwest, directly toward the Coronado Islands off the coast of Mexico.

Johnson moved with purpose and shouted, "Where are my guns?"

"Galley!"

Johnson retrieved a Smith and Wesson .45 that held 12-round clips and a Glock 9mm with 15-round clips. He had a spare clip for each and began loading them as Pence continued at full throttle toward Mexico.

Johnson's concentration was interrupted by the sound of Pence's panicked voice from above. Johnson looked up, but continued loading the ammo.

Moreland's boat, *Ocean 1*, was rounding the bend of Cabrillo Point and was heading straight toward them with its lights and sirens fully engaged.

"Shit!"

He turned back toward the harbor and noticed the fully lit up Interceptor pursuing them at full throttle.

"FUCK!!!"

He used the few moments he had left to fill the backup clips with ammunition. Johnson already knew that his Bayliner could outrun *Ocean 1*, the Patrol's fastest vessel, but the Interceptor was built specifically for situations like this.

Johnson yelled to Pence in the wheelhouse, "Don't FUCKING slow down and don't FUCKING stop for anything. Do you hear me!?"

Pence nodded "affirmative" and adjusted his course south, directly toward Tijuana.

Moreland matched Pence's course by completing a 150-degree turn, and piloted his vessel just behind, and alongside, the cruiser at a decreasing angle. The Interceptor was quickly closing the distance, now only 200 yards behind Johnson's fleeing vessel. Johnson used the 9mm and fired three quick rounds across Moreland's bow. Moreland received the message and moved away quickly, out of the range of the handgun.

Vasquez and his crew observed the threat, and the Coast Guard captain responded. He calmly gave orders through his mouthpiece.

"Gunner One. Prepare to fire."

Moreland watched closely, more like a spectator than a participant, as Johnson unloaded the 9mm at the closing Interceptor, missed every time, and tossed the weapon aside. He grabbed the .45 and began rapidly firing the much louder and more powerful rounds. One of the bullets struck the rigid inflatable boat's polyurethane hull just beneath the cabin's windshield. Bullet fragments and shards of hard plastic shattered and ricocheted off the impenetrable glass, striking one of the forward crewmen. Blood splattered onto the bow deck and across the windshield.

"Gunner one, fire."

Half of Johnson's wheelhouse disappeared within seconds, and half of the vessel's pilot disappeared along with it. Pence's legs and part of his bloody torso remained on the deck of the wheelhouse, while other parts of his body were strewn in various directions onto the surface of the Pacific Ocean.

The cruiser immediately stopped accelerating and began to drift. Johnson took aim on the Interceptor again and fired a few stray rounds, then ducked, hoping to take cover. The gunner quickly fired a short burst from the cannon's large, smoking barrel.

Johnson was too slow.

The only round that struck him amputated his left arm just beneath the shoulder, his brachial artery open like an irrigation gate set at full.

The gunner ceased firing and watched, slightly confused, as Johnson remained upright. His heart was still beating, and while spurting onto the deck, blood also continued to supply his brain with just enough oxygen to command his synapses to continue firing. Still alive, breathing, and agonizingly aware of what was happening, he staggered across the deck of his boat, which was shredded by the high-velocity rounds and now covered with his own blood. He spun, reaching across his body with one arm, searching for the other. He staggered, then stumbled, lost his balance, toppled overboard, and crashed into the ocean.

Vasquez and his crew watched as Johnson's disfigured corpse—still wrapped in black neoprene, a yellow lifeguard issue floatation vest, and a red crash helmet—bled out while floating face down on the undulating, choppy surface of the ocean.

Dead.

The scene was still. Nobody said a word.

Moreland was uncertain about what to do next. He looked across the water at Commander Vasquez, who was standing on the Interceptor's bow watching his corpsman treat a superficial wound on his second gunner's forearm.

Vasquez looked across the water, shrugged, and spoke just loud enough for everyone to hear.

"Not a very good ending for those guys, huh? I sure hope they weren't friends of yours."

His crewmen briefly laughed.

The comment helped relieve tension and whatever feelings of remorse the crew may have had after such a brutally violent incident.

The task of recovering and bagging Pence's body parts was too much for one of the Coast Guard crewmen, who excused himself and went to the stern of the Interceptor, where he retched his breakfast onto the ocean's surface.

Johnson's thick and heavy left arm, wrapped in black neoprene, was retrieved with a long gaffe and placed into a heavy plastic bag, still dripping blood as it was lifted out of the water by a crewman wearing thick rubber gloves.

The .50 caliber projectiles had blasted enormous cavities into the hull and the cruiser quickly took on water. Vasquez's crew swept the vessel and secured weapons, fuel, other usable gear, and a briefcase filled with tightly-bound bundles of cash, valuable precious metal coins, and another loaded handgun. They zipped what was left of Pence's corpse into a black body bag and laid it next to the bag containing Johnson's body and severed arm.

A moment of silence took place as the men watched *Debbie's Big Johnson* sink beneath the surface of the ocean.

Moreland turned to his crewman, POL Jenkins, and broke the silence.

"You think that was the guy out in front of eighteen . . . the victim pretending to drown yesterday? You think he drowned Marisol? That Pence character?"

Jenkins shook his head.

"I don't know . . . This one is hard to swallow . . . Escobar didn't deserve this."

"No, she didn't, but those two pricks may have."

# PART 9

Alibi:
The plea or fact that an accused person was elsewhere
than at the scene of the crime

**75**

The Next Evening
Friday, December 7, 2001
The Stanford Inn, Menlo Park, California

Cynthia's plan, although failing to achieve its highest order, had, in some ways, worked even better than she had expected it to. She had spoken with Latrelle on the phone again, and he informed her about Johnson's death. She now realized that the only people who had reason to believe that she was not in northern California at the time of Marisol Escobar's drowning were either dead, dying, or seated across the table from her in the comfortable private dining room of a swanky Menlo Park restaurant.

*Maybe the gas station attendant or the Carl's Junior chick, but there's no way...*

Meckenzie Genaro, Cynthia's mother, sat quietly and listened to her daughter.

"I have no choice but to trust you to do this for me, Mother. You are my only option . . . and my only salvation. What I have done I cannot undo, and I *will* be judged by God for this. I accept that. I only have this one life though, Mother."

She paused and swallowed hard.

"I had another life. It lasted about three months before you walked out of it, and then I started this life without you. That's how I see it."

Meckenzie glared at her daughter but said nothing.

"I never really forgave you for abandoning me. And Daddy."

Cynthia paused and took the last sip from a glass of red wine. After the waiter refilled her glass, she took another sip.

"I appreciate what you did for me when the Navy chose to support that *redneck*, but this is different. I'm actually guilty this time."

She tilted her head and shrugged.

"I could clearly see that this woman was going to continue being a threat to me . . . to the life I earned . . . to the man I love."

Cynthia paused and sipped again. She tipped the long-stemmed glass slightly to one side, visually inspecting its contents. She then rotated her wrist gently, causing the wine to swirl around the inside of the glass. She brought the glass toward her face, placed it just beneath her nose and inhaled.

"Mmmm."

She set the glass down and smiled, then glanced across the linen-covered table that was adorned with two tall crystal candlestick holders, each holding a thin, cream-colored candle, a burning flame atop each one with thin, wispy smoke rising.

Cynthia leaned across the table and locked onto her mother's eyes. She covered her mouth with a silk napkin and said softly, "It was me that tried to kill that lifeguard in San Diego . . . It was me; I did that. I took her to the bottom of the ocean and held her there until she stopped breathing. I stayed with her body until I was absolutely certain that she was dead—at least I thought I had—then I swam away underwater, shuttled back to shore in a little skiff, and drove straight here . . . but they found her body before the golden hour was up. Damn mammalian reflex. The water at the bottom is under fifty degrees, just cold enough."

She shook her head. She breathed in deeply and held it. Closing her eyes as she exhaled, she bowed her head.

"She's still alive. She's in a coma. Totally unresponsive, unable to breathe on her own, but her heart is beating."

She shook her head again.

"If she survives, well, my life as we know it is over."

She leaned forward.

"But Mother . . . if that never happens—which appears the most likely outcome—I am absolutely certain that with your help, nobody will ever know that it was me."

Meckenzie snorted, "Most likely outcome? Now that's reassuring."

Cynthia continued.

"Consider this your penance, Mother. None of this would have ever happened if you had stayed that day and never left. I would never have needed you to do this for me. But now I do"

"That's a little manipulative, wouldn't you say?"

"Yes. It is. No question . . . but you owe me a life . . . you took mine away from me, and I'm calling in that debt. This will be your only payment. You can pay me forward, so maybe I can have something like the life I should have had all along."

Cynthia looked at her mother, intense, committed, and said, "I made a choice to no longer allow an outside influence to determine the outcome of my life . . . somebody with rank over me, or somebody more well-connected, like this woman was. I couldn't let that happen to me again . . . and believe me, Mother . . . it would have. I would have lost to this woman."

Cynthia took a deep breath.

"I was already losing. I would have been beneath her my entire career, she would have done everything in her power to destroy me, and she would have tried to destroy Latrelle, too . . . I know it, Mother. I know it like nothing I've ever known."

After a few long, silent moments, Cynthia took in a deep breath.

"Mother, I have finally created the life that I have always deserved. I know a lot of trustworthy people in San Diego. And, I'm in love with an amazing man who loves me back. My lifestyle couldn't be more perfect. I'm going to keep it *all* this time."

Mother and daughter held each other's gaze.

"And all you have to do is grant me one simple request."

Cynthia felt better after her confession. She set the wine glass down and took a bite of spinach gorgonzola salad, delicately sprinkled with fresh walnut pieces, apple slivers, and balsamic vinegar dressing. She chewed patiently and moaned with pleasure, then stabbed her fork into the dish and consumed another bite. She sipped her wine and washed down the salad as her mother sat quietly, watching her daughter enjoying her meal.

Cynthia pointed her empty fork in Meckenzie's direction.

"Mother, I'm going to need you to confirm that I walked through your front door at five o'clock in the evening on Wednesday, December the fifth. We then went to dinner right here at The Stanford Inn, at around seven . . . just like we're doing tonight. I placed a call to my boyfriend; you excused yourself to go to the ladies' room; and, when you returned, I shared with you the news that I heard from Latrelle Jackson about Marisol Escobar's drowning."

Cynthia stopped, tilted her head, and closed one eye while looking toward the ceiling.

"We came home right after dinner and I went directly to bed. I didn't speak about it again the entire time I was here. That's what happened."

Cynthia's mother remained calm as she sipped her own glass of the dark, cherry-toned Caymus Vineyards 1993 Cabernet Sauvignon. She set her wine glass on the table, reached into a small handbag, and withdrew a long, thin cigarette. The waiter appeared with a clean ashtray and a glimmering crystal lighter that made a gentle click. Meckenzie leaned into the flame, drew the smoke deeply into her lungs, and held it in, enjoying the sensation for several moments before exhaling a long, thin line of bluish smoke upward and away from Cynthia. She tilted her head slightly to the side, squinting at Cynthia as she took in a second, deeper pull. Again, she held it for several moments before exhaling. A small residual cloud of smoke escaped from her nose when she spoke.

"Cynthia, honey, how can you be absolutely sure that there were no eyewitnesses to your presence in San Diego on Wednesday?"

Cynthia leaned forward, looking confident.

"Mother, the entire thing happened underwater. I am absolutely *positive* that there are no eyewitnesses. Nobody will *ever* be able to prove that I did this . . . as long as Escobar never uses her brain again, that is."

Meckenzie drew in another long pull, and before exhaling, she crushed the lit end of the cigarette and broke it in half. She glanced quickly over her shoulder at the waiter, who glided to their table and removed the ashtray. Meckenzie dismissed him with a glance at the doorway. After he left, she looked into Cynthia's eyes.

"What you're telling me is that you planned this entire thing, right up to this dinner, the confession that you just gave me, and the alibi that you are asking me to provide for you."

"Yes ma'am, that's exactly what I'm doing."

"So, your intention was to assassinate that young lady with extreme prejudice . . . in cold blood."

Cynthia breathed in deeply and held it in before she exhaled slowly through tight lips.

"Well . . . I guess you *could* say that."

"That's what the district attorney that prosecutes you will say."

"There won't be any trial . . . at least not one where I'm the defendant . . . not if you do what I just asked you to do."

Meckenzie raised her eyebrows.

"And this was the only solution that you could come up with? Premeditated, first-degree murder?"

"Let's hope so," Cynthia muttered. "She ain't dead yet."

Cynthia paused, reached for her glass of wine, tipped it toward her mother, and drank.

Meckenzie shook her head and reached for her glass. She lifted it, subtly tipped it at Cynthia, and drained its contents. She set the glass down, folded her hands, rested her chin on her thumbs, and extended her fingertips across her lips, barely touching her nose. She ever so slightly tipped her head to one side and squinted at Cynthia, but said nothing.

Cynthia remained silent, knowing that her mother was thinking about what to say.

Meckenzie then shook her head and said, "What happened to you, honey? Did the Navy do this to you? Did you kill someone while you were serving?"

Cynthia paused and considered the classified mission that she was a part of years ago. She figured that since she had already confessed to attempted murder, it probably wouldn't matter much if she revealed top secret military intel.

She shrugged, then began her story.

"They were black market terrorists from Russia, mercenaries. They boarded one of our contracted civilian freighters that ran into some very dense ice off the northern coast of Alaska . . . a place called Point Hope. The hull was breached, the ship was taking on water quickly, and the captain apparently disregarded the classified cargo he was carrying. He sent out a distress signal on an open frequency."

She shook her head and rolled her eyes.

"Somehow these Russians had intel on the cargo and they knew that this freighter was shipping something extremely critical to national security. A Russian sub had been tracking the freighter, about forty miles behind it the entire time, all the way from Northern England. My unit was training in Anchorage, so we were the closest naval response team. None of the SEAL teams were inside of eight hours away. It was us or no one. We made it there under two hours, but the Russians beat us."

Meckenzie's eyes opened a little wider than normal, and the hair on her neck and forearms stood up.

"We flew in a private jet to a small airstrip in a place called Hooper Bay, and then a Coast Guard Sikorsky dropped us in the ocean off the shore of Point Hope. We deployed two of their IRBs and made it close to the site undetected. It was three o'clock in the morning in February, and the weather was brutal. They had no idea that we were coming."

Cynthia paused, sipped her wine, placed the glass on the table, and leaned back into her chair. She continued in a matter-of-fact tone of voice.

"These Russians had already killed two civilians in a brief firefight on the bridge, and they took command of the vessel pretty quickly. But the ship was listing, so they finally realized that there was no way they could off-load the freight onto their sub with a crane through angled bulkheads and hatches. So they tried sinking the ship, hoping for shallow water so they could recover it later—or just to be sure that we wouldn't take delivery of the payload. They had a dive team setting C4 ordnance on the hull. The only way we could prevent them from sinking the vessel was to dive and intercept them before they could blow the vessel out of the water . . . and that's what we did. We intercepted them."

Meckenzie squinted, slack-jawed.

"You dove beneath a sinking ship . . . in freezing water . . . at three o'clock in the morning in stormy seas . . . and engaged Russian mercenaries?"

"That was the mission, yes."

"My God . . ."

Cynthia chuckled.

"Yeah, it was intense. The visibility was zero, and using lighting would have given away our position. We got lucky though, because those assholes were all lit up like Christmas trees."

She smirked and shook her head.

"Me, Captain Reed, and another team member, a guy we called Roadie, dove, while the rest of the team boarded the freighter and retook the bridge. Their divers never saw us coming until it was too late. We engaged all four of them. Reed and Roadie took out the first two without a fight, but the other two weren't so easy. One of them slashed through my wetsuit and into my thigh before I was able to neutralize him with my own knife. I got him in the neck. He kicked toward the surface, but never made it."

Meckenzie gasped, leaned back, and instinctively attempted to look beneath the table at Cynthia's leg.

"The last guy tried choking me, but I was able to get to his regulator first. He tried to surface but Reed held him down and Roadie gutted him. With all their gear on, they just sank to the bottom."

She snorted slightly, narrowed her eyes, and frowned.

"Fuckers tried to kill us."

She nodded, looking proud.

"Our team killed one more and captured the other two."

Meckenzie shook her head, looking frightened.

"You must have been scared to death."

Cynthia chuckled.

"Actually, I was pretty anxious during the flight there, and the dive on approach scared the crap out of me, but once we saw them lit up and knew they couldn't see us, it was all instinct and reaction. I didn't hesitate . . . none of us did."

She rubbed her thigh, tracing the path of the thick, long, raised scar that she could feel through her knee-length dress.

"Captain Reed had prepared us very well for that moment. *You ticked like a Rolex . . . meticulous and precise.* That's what Reed told us. A Navy anti-sub frigate arrived about an hour later, but the Russian sub had long before disappeared from the sonar. We prevented the ship from sinking and secured all the cargo crates."

She sipped the wine.

"I still have no idea what was in those boxes. But we killed five of the CIA's most wanted mercs, and we captured two others. We all received a Navy commendation and three of us were given Purple Hearts."

Meckenzie shook her head.

"That's not the life I imagined you would have."

"Yeah, well, me neither—at least not until dad died. It just kind of worked out that way, you know?"

Meckenzie sat still, looking into her daughter's eyes, but said nothing. Neither did Cynthia.

The waiter discreetly glanced into the room and noticed that both wine glasses were empty. He gained Meckenzie's attention and she nodded. He appeared quickly, presented another bottle of red wine, waited for Counselor Genaro to nod her approval, then uncorked it. Meckenzie examined the cork while he allowed the wine to breathe. She set the cork on the table, looked up and smiled at the handsome, middle-aged waiter, and watched him fill new glasses. He smiled and nodded at both of the well-dressed women, picked the cork up from the table, turned away, and left the room with the uncorked bottle in hand.

Meckenzie picked up her glass, tipped it across the table, and drank.

Cynthia did the same.

Meckenzie then looked down at the table. She did not look up before she said, "Your father shared with me a few things before he passed away, right after I called him when I saw you on the television playing water polo."

"Shared what things?"

"He asked me to never tell you."

"Are you going to tell me now?"

Meckenzie looked up.

"I am, and I need some answers before we agree on an alibi."

Cynthia snorted.

"Now *you're* going to manipulate me, huh?"

Meckenzie shrugged.

"Like mother, like daughter, right?"

"Touché," Cynthia replied.

Meckenzie picked up her glass and sipped. No tipping this time.

While still holding her glass, Meckenzie said, "I just want to know what happened that made you want to join an elite military unit, an assignment that you knew would likely require you to kill people. Where did that conviction come from?"

Cynthia swallowed, then looked away.

"Cynthia, your father told me about the abortion, but he would not share with me who it was that got you pregnant. He said it was too disturbing, and that he wanted to spare me from the truth. I've not stopped thinking about it since. He made me promise to never ask you about it. I hope he will forgive me for breaking my promise, but, honey, who was this boy?"

Cynthia swallowed again, but did not answer.

"Honey, you just confessed murder; what could be worse than that?"

"She ain't dead yet."

"I'm sorry, Cynthia, but I refuse to believe that murder was in your heart when I gave birth to you. You were the sweetest, most innocent thing I have ever seen. You have no idea how difficult it was for me to leave your father after you were born."

She looked away, then said softly, "I was young. I just wasn't ready to be a mother, but your father begged me, prayed with me, implored me, not to abort the pregnancy . . . and now, here you are, my gift of life."

Cynthia bowed her head.

"Cynthia, I say this not to hurt you, or to compare our lives or the choices that we each have made. I say this because I know that something more terrible than me leaving you must have happened to you. You were an innocent, fragile, trusting child of God. Honey, tell me, please, who was it? Did he rape you?"

Cynthia inhaled deeply and exhaled slowly.

"It was Brady. Dad's little brother. My uncle . . . I thought I loved him. He never raped me, but he made it hard for me to say no a couple of times toward the end. I took care of that though."

"Your father never mentioned his brother to me."

"I suppose he wouldn't have. The whole thing happened when dad was deployed. There's not a whole lot more to say. At the time, it felt right. He was a lot older, so I looked up to him. I grew up with him . . . I trusted him. He protected me. I didn't know any better. I allowed it to happen."

Meckenzie scowled and shook her head.

"What happened to him?"

Cynthia snorted through her nostrils, almost a chuckle, a chagrined look appearing on her face.

"Dad killed him. He did it just before he died. He was laying there in bed telling me everything on the night that he died in his sleep. He said that he never wanted that 'bastard' to interfere with my life again. He said that the only way that he could be sure to prevent that was to kill him."

Meckenzie's eye opened wide. She remained silent.

"He said that Brady was obsessed with me, that he would never stop feeling that way, and that he would continue to attempt to reconcile with me for the rest of our lives."

Meckenzie froze, her face showing horror.

"So he killed him."

Cynthia drank.

Meckenzie drank more.

Cynthia continued.

"You know what else he told me?"

"What?"

Cynthia glared into her mother's eyes, her tone sincere but cold.

"He told me that someday I might have to do the same thing to protect somebody that I love. He was right . . . and this is what I have done. Or what I'm trying to do . . . dammit."

"Good lord, honey. Oh . . . the things that must be running around inside your head. And, in your heart."

Cynthia snort-chuckled.

"Ya think? Look, don't you worry about me; my mind is clear, and my heart is strong. But I will not let somebody get in my way. I'll sneak into that hospital and pull the plug myself if I have to. Mother . . . I mean it."

Meckenzie reached into her purse and took out another cigarette. The waiter immediately appeared with the lighter. She leaned into the gentle flame and inhaled deeply. She blew the smoke upward, took another quick hit, broke the cigarette in the ashtray, and exhaled. She looked at Cynthia, and said, "Okay, I think maybe I do owe you that much. You're right, if I'd been there, none of this would have happened."

She shook her head and paused. The two women sat quietly, looked away from each other, and sipped at their wine.

Meckenzie looked back at Cynthia and said, "But this matter of her still living, makes me an accessory. She opens her eyes and her mouth again, we're both done. This is conspiracy."

Cynthia remained silent.

Several long moments passed while mother and daughter looked into each other's eyes, wondering what the other was thinking—and feeling.

Cynthia's mother then reached into her purse for another cigarette and nodded at the waiter.

"Now, start from the very beginning and tell me everything that you did to set this up."

"Okay. Let me think."

"And most importantly, before we can agree to any of that, you're going to have to ensure me that this woman will never be able to identify you."

76

Three Days Later
Monday, December 10, 2001
Mission Beach Main Tower

She heard the first ring as she arrived at the back door, quickly pressed the numbered keys on a security panel, and moved through the doorway. She set her gear bag on a large, padded bench along the wall of the first aid room and walked briskly through the large lobby to the front counter.

Cynthia picked up the ringing phone.

"Mission Beach, POL Harden speaking."

"Good morning, Ms. Harden. Welcome back."

"Oh, good morning, sir. Whew. I just hurried in through the door to catch the phone. Can you give me a second to set my things down? I'll be right with you."

"Go ahead, Cynthia . . . I'll be right here."

"Okay, I'll be right back."

She pressed "hold," set the receiver down, and stepped away from the counter. She stood motionless, and stared at the phone as if it were ticking and she needed to disarm it. She retreated to the first aid room and placed her purse and backpack next to her other gear on the bench.

She then walked into the locker room, and looked at the reflection of her eyes in a full-length mirror that hung on the wall. She breathed in deeply and nodded.

*This is a good thing. Let the show begin.*

She walked back to the phone and pressed the flashing button that reconnected the call.

In a calm tone of voice, Cynthia said, "Yes, sir. I'm sorry to make you wait. How can I help you?"

"Cynthia, I'm sure by now you know what happened while you were away."

"Yes, sir. Latrelle Jackson and I spoke on the phone that night while I was having dinner with my mother up in Menlo Park. He's very upset. I don't know what to say."

"It is very upsetting and tragic. I don't think anybody knows what to say. We still have very much to learn about what happened. One dead lifeguard, one lifeguard in a coma, and one dead civilian have left us with many unanswered questions."

Cynthia did not reply.

"Listen, Ms. Harden . . . whatever happened, as an agency we still need to move forward. A relief guard is on his way to Mission Beach now. He should be there any minute. I'm here with Lt. Morgan in his office now. We want to meet with you immediately."

"Yes, sir. I'll leave as soon as the relief guard arrives."

"Don't bother waiting."

Mayor Eddie Peete hung up the phone without saying goodbye.

*Breathe, Harden. You can do this.*

She laughed nervously as the image of Nico Cianfraco appeared in her head. She remembered the words of wisdom he offered her on that late, glowing night in the parking lot of his strip club. His words rang clear as a bell, and resounded in her head as if he had spoken them to her only yesterday.

*Be nice to these men, Cynthia . . . and sweet. Use sugar and honey, not piss and vinegar.*

Cynthia used Lt. Morgan's office phone to make the call to the woman who had delivered her into this world. Meckenzie was seated at her office desk, waiting for the call.

"Hello, this is Meckenzie Genaro."

"Mother, it's me. I'm here with my lieutenant. His name is Richard Morgan. He'd like to speak with you briefly. Do you have time to speak with him now?"

"Of course, dear."

Cynthia handed the phone to Morgan, who cleared his throat nervously before he began speaking.

"Good morning, Mrs. Genaro. Thank you for taking my call. I apologize for interrupting your morning."

"No need to apologize, Lieutenant. Cynthia mentioned your name this weekend. She is quite impressed with you and has expressed to me that she is very happy working for your Patrol. What can I do for you?"

"Thank you, ma'am. We are very pleased to have her working for us as well. Ma'am . . . the reason for my call, as Cynthia may have mentioned, is . . . well, our agency, and our city, really, experienced some misfortune here in San Diego while she was visiting you in Northern California."

"Yes, Lieutenant, I understand. We watched a report on the television. Cynthia was very quiet most of the weekend, however. She spoke very little about it. She was very upset, though; I could tell that much. However, Lieutenant, I had no desire to invade my daughter's private thoughts and feelings about what happened in San Diego while she was away. I'm sure you can appreciate that. I really don't know much about what happened."

"Yes, ma'am, of course . . . but with the heaviest of hearts and sincerest intentions, I need to ask you a couple of questions. The Coast Guard's involvement in the incident has created some very sensitive circumstances. Their investigation and the police department's investigation will be very thorough, and our own internal investigation is underway as well. I am sure that you understand the value of us knowing all of the facts, so we can offer support to whoever needs it. That includes Cynthia, obviously, and it includes the victims' families as well."

Meckenzie glanced at a sheet of paper containing the lieutenant's biographical information, then looked at her computer's monitor that showed a professional head shot of a handsome man, the photo cropped just beneath the highly adorned breast of his Class A uniform.

"Yes, Lieutenant, I understand how important it is to offer support after such a tragic event . . . but I'm still unclear about why you wish to speak with me. What do Cynthia or I have to do with your, or anybody else's, investigation of these tragic events?"

"It's actually quite simple, Mrs. Genaro. I just need to ask you about Cynthia's whereabouts. When did you first see your daughter last week, ma'am?"

"Lieutenant, I'm sure that you already know this about my daughter, but allow me to indulge myself, if you don't mind. I learned very quickly that Cynthia makes plans and remains focused on accomplishing her goals like very few people I have ever known."

Meckenzie paused and reached for a lit cigarette in an ashtray that rested alongside a tall open window. She inhaled, then exhaled a thin line of smoke.

"She keeps her word when she offers it, Lieutenant. I admire that about her more than you can imagine. The lack of good character that I consistently deal with in my profession had turned me into a somewhat resigned and cynical person before Cynthia reached out to me unexpectedly, right after her father passed. Since that day, she has continued to inspire me by keeping her word so well."

"Yes, she does do that."

She took another hit from her cigarette, exhaled, gently rolled the lit end of the cigarette against the top edge of the ashtray, then took another pull.

"Her willingness and the discipline required to do things exactly as she says she will, well, I'm sure that you and your agency value that highly."

"Oh, yes, ma'am, we most certainly do."

Meckenzie got the sense that the lieutenant was open to suggestion, and his support for Cynthia was probably unconditional. She used caution and expertise as she continued.

"Cynthia told me only that she would arrive in time for us to make our dinner reservations at seven p.m. last Wednesday night. That is exactly what she did. She actually arrived early, so she took her time unpacking. She showered, dressed, and we left for the restaurant at around six-forty-five."

"Cynthia was in Menlo Park at six-forty-five, last Wednesday night?"

"She arrived well before that, Lieutenant. Five p.m. at the very latest."

Morgan was silent.

"Lieutenant? Is that all that you wanted to ask me?"

"Yes, ma'am. That is all I needed to know. Thank you for your cooperation."

"You're welcome, Lieutenant. It was a pleasure speaking with you. Perhaps next time we will have something more uplifting to discuss, like Cynthia's future."

"Yes ma'am. That would be nice."

"Good luck with your investigation, and please extend my condolences to those who experienced such a great loss."

"Thank you, ma'am, we appreciate that. Good day, Mrs. Genaro."

The mayor had avoided eye contact and remained silent since saying "Hello" to Cynthia when she entered Morgan's office. During the call, Cynthia had experienced more apprehension and anxiety than she had expected to. As she watched Morgan nod and shift his glance between her and the mayor, she struggled to control her rampant thoughts and swirling emotions. Now that the call had ended, she remained anxious, but sat silently, watching and waiting for the lieutenant to act.

Morgan hung up the phone, and stood next to a tall chair behind his desk. Eddie Peete leaned against the office's closed door and gazed out at Mission Bay through the glass wall behind the lieutenant.

Morgan stared at Cynthia, expressionless.

Cynthia did the same.

The air in the room was still and heavy. Cynthia felt claustrophobic, similar to the way she had felt during her Navy dive training, just before she participated in a drill that required each of those who were attempting to attain a spot on the team to remain underwater until they lost consciousness, trusting their squad mates to revive them.

Morgan exhaled, then nodded at Cynthia.

"Thank you for your patience, Cynthia. We needed to confirm that you were not in San Diego when any of this happened. Your name being mentioned caused us to become concerned about your safety."

The lieutenant sighed and scowled.

"And it obviously raised some questions about your possible involvement."

He paused and all three of them shook their heads before Morgan continued.

"It doesn't surprise me at all, however, that Johnson attempted to pin something he did on somebody else. He's done that before. He was the only one that had any real motive. But, we still don't know for sure what happened to Marisol."

Cynthia began to relax, and was now calmer than she had been since just before the mayor's early phone call startled her. She was relieved that, apparently, and hopefully, the worst was behind her. She was uncertain, however, about what would happen next, and remained silent. She simply followed the chain of command and would not move or speak until she was ordered to do so. The lieutenant looked at the mayor, who nodded his agreement before turning to look directly at Cynthia. Harden returned the mayor's glance.

The mayor was suspicious, but said nothing. His face was void of expression as he looked into Cynthia's eyes.

*You had something to do with this, didn't you?*

Morgan unknowingly interrupted their thought transference.

"We're confident that an accomplice met Johnson out in the water that evening, and they acted together. The individual who was shot along with Johnson on his boat seems to be the most likely suspect that was pretending to be the swimmer in distress that day."

The mayor nodded after Morgan looked over at him.

Morgan continued.

"Our investigation's records, once complete, will be turned over to SDPD, and the Coast Guard. I expect Dr. Villareal to turn over every stone though . . . so you may have to answer some questions again. I don't mean to sound as though I lack sympathy, because I do mourn for their family. I also fear that her mother may eventually try to hold the city and me, personally, responsible for what happened to Marisol because I chose not to terminate Johnson a long time ago."

The mayor stepped forward and nodded.

"That would be a reasonable assumption and we wish to be as prepared as we possibly can to avoid that outcome, of course."

Morgan continued.

"It could get very ugly, but you should be cleared of any involvement in that investigation, Cynthia. Before we can proceed, though, I do have to ask you a couple more questions that will likely be asked of you, and most of our crews later."

Cynthia still hadn't moved. Her confidence had grown, though, and she felt certain that she could come up with a few more answers.

Morgan began.

"Cynthia, did you ever have any kind of conversation with Mike

Johnson about a plan to undermine, or hurt, Marisol Escobar?"

Harden and Morgan looked into each other's eyes, just as they had at the coffee shop years ago. Without blinking, and without hesitation, Cynthia subtly shook her head and replied calmly, "No, sir, none whatsoever."

"During any vehicle patrol or at any time while on duty or off duty, did Mike Johnson ever say anything to you about a plan to undermine, or hurt, Marisol Escobar?"

"Negative. No, sir."

"Do you have any knowledge at all about anything related to Mike Johnson's intentions to undermine, or hurt, Marisol Escobar?"

"No, sir. I never heard a thing about any plan to undermine, or hurt her—not from Johnson or from anybody else."

Peete interrupted.

"That's enough, Lieutenant. This was all Mike Johnson and his civilian cohort. We need to proceed."

The mayor looked at Cynthia and offered a smile.

Morgan continued.

"Please understand the responsibility I have to be thorough. I need to cover all angles, Cynthia, and I believe that I have. I know that you had nothing to do with any of this."

The mayor verbalized his agreement

"Absolutely not. There's no way. Please accept my apology as well, Cynthia."

Cynthia replied with a tone of humility.

"Neither of you should ever apologize to me. This is your agency, not mine."

The mayor and Morgan both smiled.

Morgan moved from behind his desk into the center of the room.

"Well then, Cynthia . . . despite the tragic circumstances, this is still a day that we can celebrate. Congratulations, Sergeant Harden. Welcome to the team."

The mayor stepped forward and stood next to his Lieutenant.

"I second that. And, like I told you it most likely would, Miss

Harden, the universe has a way of balancing itself."

Cynthia stood, then Peete embraced her with a warm bear hug and held it for several moments before releasing her to Morgan, who did the same thing. Both men had no fear that their gestures would be considered uninvited or inappropriate, and they each knew that their first ranking female officer would never perceive their behaviors as sexual in nature. Cynthia held on to Morgan tightly and maintained a firm grip on his bicep as she stepped back and looked him in the eyes, tears forming in her own.

"Thank you, Lieutenant. You've been a man of your word since we first met. You've been so supportive, and if you don't mind me saying so, you've become a father figure to me."

She turned to Mayor Peete.

"You, too, Mister Mayor. I appreciate the words of wisdom that you offered me the night we met at your office, and I won't forget them. I'm looking forward to more of that from each of you, and I will never let either one of you down. Whatever you need, whenever you need it, just let me know, and I'll be there."

Three weeks later,
Monday, December 31, 2001
Scripps Hospital ICU
San Diego, California

Early each morning, Cynthia was awakened by nightmare images of Marisol Escobar's face gasping and searching for help, her body on the ocean floor in murky, surging water—dead, but not dead. The images were beginning to eat away at her brain like maggots infesting carrion, stressing her out, creeping her out, and definitely freaking her out. Cynthia got out of bed before 2 a.m. each day. Each dark, damp, cold morning since she was promoted to sergeant, she woke abruptly, stressed, and uncertain; afraid . . . all new feelings for her.

Once the dreams hit, she'd roll out of her bunk wide awake, use the head, make coffee, gather what she needed, and drive toward the Scripps Hospital at Torrey Pines. She would park her Uncle Brady's Blazer along a curb in a residential area a mile away. She would set out at a moderate pace, and jog on tree-covered sidewalks, creep quietly through dark alleys and easements, and move unseen until she reached the hospital campus. Each of those mornings she wore a black beanie cap, a black hoodie, black cotton sweatpants, black socks, and black Converse; appropriate attire for an athlete obviously committed to early morning training.

This early morning, however, she was dressed differently, prepared to take on a different role; this time a specific mission was at hand.

After visiting the Scripp's Hospital ICU with Latrelle and Vanessa three times already, and while in uniform, on duty, as countless SDLP personnel had done as well, Cynthia learned that the lobbies and elevators had sweeping security cameras monitoring every activity. She also noticed that many of the stairwells, and the loading dock along the rear of the building that backed into wooded cliffs, did not.

In addition to transitioning to sergeant, the past three weeks Cynthia had become focused on not much other than getting familiar with the layout of the hospital, and the timing and urgency of her current mission. She had taken other visits during various times of the day and night, and now, after 20 days of observation, she knew where her points of ingress and egress were located.

She monitored the spot from 50 yards away, across a small service road, behind a row of thick bushes that wound through a forest of tall pines. During the previous eight early, early mornings, she had been closely observing personnel entering and exiting the facility through double glass doors that only slid open and closed after a code was pressed into a keypad located on an adjacent wall. As she watched more closely, she could see that these hospital employees were dressed almost exclusively in uniforms. Those wearing white tops and pants went to the kitchen, and those wearing dark coveralls went to various floors to do various types of cleaning and maintenance. There were others dressed in street clothes, but the primary function of this doorway was to provide the kitchen and janitorial staff quick access and close proximity to their department's offices, locker rooms, and storage areas.

She learned early that the medical staff all used an entirely different entry. That entryway was highly visible, adjacent to a well-lit parking lot, and had several security and administrative personnel on site 24 hours a day. She had avoided that side of the complex for days now.

The kitchen and janitorial staff encountered no security desk or personnel, unless a solo security guard was on a golf cart patrol, which took place only once an hour between the hours of midnight and 6 a.m., after which time the frequency of the patrols increased to two per hour. On those early mornings, the security guards would normally glide by the area without showing much interest, and occasionally they would park on the walkway, enter the facility, and return to the cart in less than three minutes.

*Restroom break.*

There was much less lighting along the back of the building, and no one was there to sign the employees in or out. Although entrance seemed easy enough, it was still way too visible. Plus, cameras scanned the small lobby just inside the doorway.

*Can't use it.*

Cynthia had also noticed two men entering and exiting the facility by way of a heavy steel door, painted white and located about 25 yards to the right of the double glass doors.

**DELIVERY** was stenciled neatly on the door in forest green letters.

The two men used the door at different times. They each used a single key to unlock a sturdy doorknob and a thick deadbolt set high on the door. Both men immediately locked and dead-bolted the door behind them each time they passed through it.

*Maybe the chef, maybe the baker, who knows? Not important.*

Further to the right were two tall rollup freight doors that were used to load or unload clean and dirty laundry, wooden crates, shrink-wrapped pallets of cardboard boxes, buckets, barrels, drums, and large sacks of food, sundries, cleaning supplies, and tools. The rollup doors were used only during normal daytime business hours, as deliveries and pick-ups were made by vendors who worked normal daytime business hours.

Three days a week, however, very early in the morning, Enrique De La Cruz delivered fresh fruit and vegetables to the hospital where Marisol Escobar was being kept alive. He also had a key to the heavy door, and he worked alone.

His hands being full almost the entire time he worked, he obviously didn't have an extra one to open and close the door each time he passed through, so he swung the door all the way open and pushed it up against the wall. He used a half-sized, broken cinder block to prop the door open for about 15 minutes every delivery.

Cynthia looked at her watch.

*3:07 a.m. On time again.*

He arrived in a white Freightliner refrigerator box truck, backed it in, parked, turned the engine off, hopped out, and skipped up six concrete stairs leading to the loading dock. Standing on a rubber-coated deck, the rear of his truck setting perfectly against the padded dock, he unlocked the truck's rear rolling, insulated door, slid it smoothly upward, entered the large, cool, well-organized space, and retrieved a sturdy hand cart with inflatable tires.

Cynthia watched Enrique, who whistled softly—a happy man—as he began his work. She stood 10 feet away from the rear of the truck, just around the corner, secluded behind a rolling baker's rack. The large, box-shaped rack was at least five and a half feet tall, provided excellent cover, and could be moved if necessary.

Cynthia watched as Enrique wheeled the hand cart to the heavy door, unlocked the door, propped it open, pushed the dolly inside, then returned with a full load of empty cardboard boxes stacked on the tilting cart. Enrique wheeled his load to the back of the cold box, toward the front of the truck. Cynthia knew he would be unstacking and re-stacking the re-usable cardboard boxes for at least 45 seconds. She crept around the rack, moved without a sound, and was invisibly through the cinder-blocked doorway in less than five.

She glanced down a long hallway to her left, saw nothing out of the ordinary, then turned to her right and scanned a staging area large enough to fit two of Enrique's trucks. A second heavy door was located in a wall directly across from her, just inside the hallway. It was propped open with a large potted plant that normally sat clear of the door's arc. She ducked through the doorway, into a second long, bright, clean hallway— the kitchen to her right, a stairwell to her left—and never broke stride until she reached a white door with a diamond-shaped glass window set at head height.

She leaned slowly and checked through the glass.

Clear.

She opened the door without a sound, stepped through, and silently closed the door. The stairway in front of her was made of heavy steel and painted white. Each stair had black, gritty strips arranged diagonally across them, a yellow stripe of granular paint, centered. The grey aluminum railing was sturdy, with five parallel rails reaching up to an eight-by-eight platform. From the platform, rising upward over her shoulder, the next set of stairs led to the second floor doorway. Cynthia ducked as she passed that door and arrived at the third floor doorway quickly, silently, and invisibly.

She peaked through the window, crouched down, cracked the door open an inch, and surveyed the hallway for two minutes, listening closely, watching for any motion. She had made it this far into the hospital unnoticed twice before. Both times she had seen Leon—a thin, healthy-looking, middle-aged black man dressed in a forest green jumpsuit, who wore a dark baseball cap pulled low, the way a baseball cap is supposed to be worn.

*Must have been a ball player.*

Leon made $21 an hour, worked 40 hours a week, and had his name embroidered in cursive on the breast of his coveralls. He swept, mopped, buffed floors, cleaned windows and bathrooms, emptied trash, and made sure the ICU sparkled. Cynthia had seen him using the same door and stairwell where she now stood, carrying full trash bags. She had watched him exit through the propped open doors, then walk across the loading dock, down the six concrete stairs, and across a black asphalt parking lot. She knew that he would turn the first corner to his left and arrive at a fenced-in area that secured five white and two green dumpsters. The wiry, athletic janitor would set the bags down, pull a key from his hip, and unlock the chain link gate. He would then lift a black plastic lid upward and begin chucking bags into the bin. He always closed the lid gently, locked the gate, and walked over to a small garden-like sitting area located along the sidewalk leading to the employee entrance. He sat and smoked about a half a cigarette, Cynthia imagining that he didn't think about much other than the air and sky, probably listening to sounds of crashing surf when a swell attacked Black's Beach.

This morning, Cynthia was dressed in a dark green jumpsuit, the same color as the smoking janitor's jumpsuit. She wore a matching green cap, pulled low, her hair tucked all the way up inside the hat.

She looked like a man, and a ball player, just like Leon.

As she peered through the cracked doorway, she heard Leon approaching. She heard his soft sneakers drumming lightly across the smooth surface of the shiny, white tile floor, and, before he turned the corner to approach the door, three full trash bags in each hand, Cynthia climbed to the fourth floor platform above and hid. Leon stepped through the door and lightly climbed down to the loading dock level, as Cynthia moved through the third floor doorway and stepped into the ICU.

The stairwell doorway was located in a back corner, next to a locker room and an unlocked storage closet. She entered the closet, grabbed a push broom, left the room, and cautiously closed the door. Escobar's room was located around two corners, the first of which was located about 50 feet down the same hallway that Leon had just walked through.

Cynthia moved, keeping her head low, swift, unnoticed as she swept the floor. She reached the corner, and paused. She peeked and saw the nurse's station, just 15 feet in front of her. She heard the sound of fingers on a keyboard, and Hall and Oates' *Maneater* playing softly through a single speaker on a clock radio that sat on the nurse's enormous desk. The entire nurses station was filled with desktops and free-standing equipment. Real-time monitors tracked Marisol's and one other patient's vitals and indicated that neither patient was responsive. Both had a pulse, but breathed only with the assistance of a respirator. Cynthia heard steady humming from various sophisticated machines, and rhythmic blips and chimes coming from others.

The nurse's station was located to her right. The typing nurse sat at a computer behind a tall, gray metal filing cabinet blocked from view. Her back was to Cynthia. The highly-trained ICU specialist worked her shift with just one other nurse and, of course, Leon, who kept the place neat, shiny, and sanitized. The second nurse was on a lunch break, seated at a table in the cafeteria enjoying a packaged Caesar salad, Cheetos, and a small carton of chocolate milk.

Cynthia looked to her left at the second corner, around which Marisol's was the first, unmonitored doorway. She scampered across the hall, pushing the broom—not making a sound, still unseen.

She heard no voices.

Amanda Villareal was not there.

Victor Trujillo-Escobar was not there.

Victor's body guard, Vuna, who had been spending nights dozing on a couch on Marisol's floor, was not there. They were each at their homes, asleep, but not at all restfully. One of them would be in Marisol's room, right next to her, before 6 a.m.

**79**

Monday, December 31, 2001
Scripps Hospital ICU

Each day Marisol survived drove Cynthia farther from sanity. She was agitated, couldn't sleep, and found she needed red wine to calm her nerves. This week, however, she kept her word to her mother, and had remained completely sober. Their agreement, and plan, depended on Cynthia's highest level of competence. She would not drink again until well after her current mission's outcome was achieved.

Definitely sober now, on her fullest alert, Cynthia leaned the broom handle against the wall, crept around the final corner, and slipped quickly into Marisol's room. She slid behind a thin curtain and stood motionless, breathing as softly, as lightly, as possible.

With her eyes closed, Cynthia breathed in deeply. She opened her eyes, then silently exhaled through her mouth only. She did not move for 30 seconds.

Nothing in her external environment changed.

Still clear.

She located the respirator and its power source. She already knew where everything was located, what it was, and how it contributed to Marisol's survival; she knew the respirator was the lifeline.

Escobar's heart rate showed a steady 53 beats per minute, blood pressure normal at 118/78, respirations held in cadence at 12 breaths per minute. The most important monitoring device, though, was an electroencephalograph, which measured electrical activity in the brain. That monitor showed a flat line, her brain exhibiting zero activity since just before Marisol's body was pulled out of the ocean by Johnson, Henderson, and Shields. Although very few held much hope that there would ever again be activity shown on this screen, Cynthia and Meckenzie both knew that there was only one way to be sure.

Cynthia took one step. She stopped.

She then stepped again. She was no longer concealed behind the curtain.

She looked at her watch.

*3:10. You got about one minute to get out of here before Leon gets back.*

She pulled a pair of sturdy pliers from a pocket.

Wire cutters for the respirator's power cord.

Cynthia took another step, her eyes on Marisol's body. It was connected to strands of tubes, wires, and conduits linked to her mouth, nose, head, chest, arms, and long compression socks. The socks covered her legs all the way to her kneecaps, and a bladder valve pumped air in and out of the socks to assist circulation and prevent blood from pooling in her lower legs.

Cynthia took another step toward the respirator.

She now stood just in front of the EKG machine that had been blipping at a rate of just over once per second.

The machine's blipping cadence suddenly increased.

Cynthia froze.

*Whoa. What's going on?*

She took one more step, now almost within reach of the respirator's power cord.

Marisol's heart rate jumped again, up to a rate of 90 bpm and rising.

*What the hell?*

Cynthia reached for the power cord.

Marisol's heart rate leapt to 150 beats per minutes.

Blip, blip, blip, blip, blip, blip. Like an alarm.

The nurse stood from her chair; a pager buzzed on the cafeteria table next to the male nurse.

*No. Too much attention. What the hell is happening? Get out. Now.*

Cynthia froze, then turned 180 degrees. She stepped behind the curtain. She leaned, attempting to see the nurse's station, but it was around the corner, and out of sight. She pulled the curtain aside gently, reached the doorway, scurried to the corner, crept quickly around it, and arrived at the bulky filing cabinet that separated the hallway from the nurse's station.

*Shit. The broom.*

She heard the nurse speaking on a phone, "Cardiac alert, ICU 1. *Code Red*."

Cynthia heard the phone's handset being replaced, and stood taller to gain a view. The nurse had already trotted down the hall, and was now standing at Escobar's side. Cynthia heard the blipping slow—to 90 again, then quickly to 75. Within 15 seconds, Escobar's heart rate returned to 53 beats per minute.

Like nothing had ever happened.

No activity had appeared on the electroencephalograph.

*WTF was that?*

Cynthia turned to retrieve the broom, but two unfamiliar voices from the hallway grew louder, footsteps approaching, pounding the floor with a cadence much faster than a walking pace.

*Dammit.*

She stopped, left the broom where it stood, crept away, headed down to the back corner of the ICU, passed the storage room, and arrived at the exit door quickly, quietly. She stood and cautiously peeked through the window into the stairwell.

Pressed up against the window glass, an inch away from her face, eye-to-eye, Cynthia looked into Marisol's decaying, bluish, bloated, and blood-streaked face. Marisol's eyes were wide open, but now alive, moving—her mouth not gasping, but screaming.

She heard Marisol's loud voice in her ears; a shrieking, bone-chilling scream, "Harden!"

She gasped out loud, uncertain if what she had heard was real, uncertain if her owns gasps had been heard. She turned her back to the door, slid down to the floor, and curled into a ball for a moment, wincing, startled, her own heart rate spiking. She tightly closed her eyes, shook her head, rocked her body back and forth, and cleared the familiar image that woke her up early in the morning. She almost wept, but stopped herself.

*She's not here. She's not here. She's not here.*

After a long, deep breath, she stood and checked the window again. Clear.

*She's not here.*

She moved through the door, glided down the stairs, and stopped at the first propped-open door. She glanced across the open hallway, saw nothing, and hopped to the outer doorway.

Still inside the outer door, she crouched, listened, and remained still. She heard Enrique, still whistling happily, pushing his dolly and heading toward her from the walk-in refrigerator.

*Crap.*

She had about 10 seconds to act.

She listened for Leon out on the docks.

She squatted, crouched low, then peeked outside. One of Leon's white sneakers came directly toward her rapidly, less than a foot away. He almost tripped, but stopped in time, just before kicking her in the face.

Leon stumbled, but caught himself.

"What in the hell are you doing down there?"

Cynthia froze, but thought quickly. In a deep, low voice, she said, "I dropped my key. Here it is. I'm sorry, bro. My bad."

She moved quickly away from the doorway, without looking up. She walked casually across the loading dock, then skipped down and away from the stairs.

Leon shouted, "Hey, wait, where are you going? Who are you? What floor are you coming from?"

Cynthia never turned back, but raised her arm, two fingers extended as if holding a cigarette, brought her hand close to her mouth, and pulled it away. She walked to the garden area, paused, and reached into her pocket, acting like she was digging for a pack of cigarettes. With her hand raised to the brim of her hat, shielding her face, she glanced up quickly at Leon, who still stood in the doorway.

Leon tilted his head to one side, confused, not recognizing the janitor with the strange voice, uncertain as to why a crewman from another floor would exit the building on a smoke break without bringing along a few bags of trash.

He snorted, shrugged his shoulders, and returned to the third floor, which was suddenly ablaze with activity and crowded with personnel. He saw two security guards standing at the nurse's station, and a police officer questioning the nurse, taking notes.

Leon paused. He turned his head back toward the stairway. He stepped through the door and onto the landing, and looked down the stairwell. He paused again, but then quickly ran back down the stairs, out the doorway, and onto the docks. He moved quickly to the smoking area, but saw no one.

Cynthia was gone.

Back on the third floor, in the background, just barely over all of the commotion, Darryl Hall's voice could be heard coming through the speaker on the radio, *"Oh-oh here she comes . . . Watch out boy, she'll chew you uh-up. Oh-oh here she comes . . . She's a man eater."*

The end.

Book 2:

# RETRIBUTION
## COMING SOON

# ACKNOWLEDGMENTS

I will heed the advice of my editors and avoid the awkward rambling of an overstated acceptance speech given during the Academy Awards. There are far too many individuals in my life to acknowledge on this page, and out of respect, I will not name the professionals, colleagues, and friends that I served with in coastal safety. However, many of those men and women that I worked with were indeed cornerstones that helped me create this story.

I must start, however, by acknowledging my wife, Liane. Her encouragement was unyielding, and her devotion to the success of my first novel inspired me, even during my darkest moments of resignation when I wanted to delete the entire manuscript. There is absolutely no way I could have completed this project without her unconditional support and love, and there is no way that a wretch like me has actually earned the privilege of enjoying the great life that I now have with her. You are a gift that has changed my life, Liane. Thank you.

To my amazing sister, Janet, thank you for snapping me out of a trance. The theft of my laptop, all of my backup discs, my printer, speakers, reams of paper, pens, pencils, and a tall stack of notepads and journals that contained every unsaved word of all of my previous writing projects, left me numb, and empty. Attempting to retrieve those words physically, by memory, or re-creation, was obviously an exercise in futility. Your message of "let it go" woke me up. The birth of *Tower 18* occurred the very next day. Perhaps, someday, I will again attempt to write *The*

*Wanderlust Crew.*

And finally, to the men and women who provide public safety on every guarded beach on planet Earth, know that you are respected, admired, and trusted. What you do requires a certain temperament, and a quality of character that is unique to emergency response. Not every individual that has accepted the responsibility of making ocean rescues experiences the humility that comes with actually *preventing the death of another human being,* just moments before that human's life, most certainly, would have ended. Those of you who really, really know what that feels like, please consider that the God of your understanding blessed not just your rescued victim, but you as well. You made a difference, and your actions influenced the timeline of human history, for nothing would have remained the same regarding that being's family, friends, and so many others.

Always remember to embrace that moment of divine intervention that so many others will never know, or feel. There is a reason that your God chose you.

I hope you enjoyed my story.

TB

# ABOUT TONY BATHEY

Born on a -20 degree December day in a U.S. Army hospital, Tony Bathey spent the first year of his life in Fairbanks, AK. For the next seven years he lived on an Army base in Huntsville, Alabama before his Dad, an Airborne Master Sergeant, retired after 26 years of service. Tony's family then moved to the east side of Tucson, AZ in the early 1970s.

The desert became home, and soon competing in sports, and cheering for any team that represented the University of Arizona became Tony's passion. After his high school graduation, Tony supported himself by working various construction jobs, bartending in numerous western states, commercial fishing in Alaska, and eventually coaching baseball back in Tucson. All the while he kept a journal, from which developed his interest in writing.

Without organized athletics in his life, however, he found that he missed the unique comradery that developed only between teammates and coaches. He then chose to pursue a degree in education so he could teach at the high school level, coach team sports, and again experience what he considers the greatest elixir in life; victory and the pursuit of a championship.

While enjoying 15 years of teaching secondary PE, serving as an athletic director, and coaching various varsity team sports to a number of championship seasons, he spent most of his summers vacationing on the beaches in San Diego, watching and wondering if he had what it took to become an ocean lifeguard. Upon returning to Tucson each fall, his heart eventually remained behind, missing the ocean, so Tony left Arizona, and chose to pursue ocean lifeguarding as a new career. He was pleased to learn that he did have what it takes, and spent the next 10 years making rescues and instructing junior lifeguards, on various southern California beaches. While working on one of those beaches, he met his current wife, Liane, with whom he now lives and works, in La Jolla, CA.

Tony wrote several unpublished short stories and toiled with two unfinished novels, before completing *Tower 18*.

# elevate
## publishing

**DELIVERING TRANSFORMATIVE MESSAGES**
**TO THE WORLD**

Visit www.elevatepub.com for our latest offerings.

# NO TREES WERE HARMED IN THE MAKING OF THIS BOOK.

OK, so a few did make the ultimate sacrifice.

In order to steward our environment, we are partnered with *Plant With Purpose,* to plant a tree for every tree that paid the price for the printing of this book.

To learn more, visit www.elevatepub.com/about

PLANT W TH PURPOSE | WWW.PLANTWITHPURPOSE.ORG

CPSIA information can be obtained
at www.ICGtesting.com
Printed in the USA
BVOW11s0502070417
480612BV00002B/4/P